ABOUT THE AUTHOR

Frank Herbert, who died in 1986, was best-known for his immensely popular and successful science-fiction novels, but his books included non-fiction works on ecology and home computers, as well as contemporary fiction. His classic novel *Dune* and its sequels have all been world-wide bestsellers, and *Dune* itself was made into a major film.

Before turning to writing full-time, Herbert was for many years a journalist, holding a senior position on a San Francisco newspaper. His colourful and varied career also included stints as a radio news commentator, oyster diver and jungle survival instructor.

Also by Frank Herbert in Gollancz

Dune
Children of Dune
God Emperor of Dune
Heretics of Dune
The Dosadi Experiment
The Jesus Incident

CHAPTER HOUSE
DUNE

Frank Herbert

www.orionbooks.co.uk

The right of Frank Herbert to be identified as the
author of this work has been asserted by him in accordance
with the Copyright, Designs and Patents Act 1988.

First published in Great Britain in 1985 by
Victor Gollancz Ltd

This edition published in Great Britain in 2003 by Gollancz
An imprint of the Orion Publishing Group
Orion House, 5 Upper St Martin's Lane, London WC2H 9EA
An Hachette Livre UK Company

10

A CIP catalogue record for this book is
available from the British Library

ISBN 978-0-575-07518-4

Printed in Great Britain by
Clays Ltd, St Ives plc

The Orion Publishing Group's policy is to use papers that
are natural, renewable and recyclable products and
made from wood grown in sustainable forests. The logging
and manufacturing processes are expected to conform to
the environmental regulations of the country of origin.

Those who would repeat the past must control the teaching of history.

— **Bene Gesserit Coda**

When the ghola-baby was delivered from the first Bene Gesserit axolotl tank, Mother Superior Darwi Odrade ordered a quiet celebration in her private dining room atop Central. It was barely dawn, and the two other members of her Council—Tamalane and Bellonda—showed impatience at the summons, even though Odrade had ordered breakfast served by her personal chef.

"It isn't every woman who can preside at the birth of her own father," Odrade quipped when the others complained they had too many demands on their time to permit of "time-wasting nonsense".

Only aged Tamalane showed sly amusement.

Bellonda held her over-fleshed features expressionless, often her equivalent of a scowl.

Was it possible, Odrade wondered, that Bell had not exorcized resentment of the relative opulence in Mother Superior's surroundings? Odrade's quarters were a distinct mark of her position but the distinction represented her duties more than any elevation over her sisters. The small dining room allowed her to consult aides during meals.

She had her own private kitchen with chef on standby though most of her meals came up from communal facilities. You never knew when an extra guest might sit at her table or when she and aides might need to restore depleted energies.

Major assistance stood near. Someone from Bell's Archives could be here in minutes or, by projection to the worktable, within seconds.

Bellonda glanced this way and that around Odrade's dining room, obviously impatient to be gone. Much effort had been

1

expended without success in attempts to break through Bellonda's coldly remote shell.

"It felt very odd to hold that baby in my arms and think: This is my father," Odrade said.

"I heard you the first time!" Bellonda spoke from the belly, almost a baritone rumbling as though each word caused her vague indigestion.

She understood Odrade's jest, though. The old Bashar Miles Teg had, indeed, been the Mother Superior's father. And Odrade herself had collected cells (as fingernail scrapings) to grow this new ghola, part of a long-time "possibility plan" should they ever succeed in duplicating Tleilaxu tanks. But Bellonda would be drummed out of the Bene Gesserit rather than smile at Odrade's witticism.

"I find this frivolous at such a time," Bellonda said. "Those madwomen hunting us to exterminate us and you want a celebration!"

Odrade held herself to a mild tone with some effort. "If the Honoured Matres find us before we are ready perhaps it will be because we failed to keep up our morale."

Bellonda's silent stare directly into Odrade's eyes carried frustrating accusation: *Those terrible women already have exterminated sixteen of our planets!"*

As she frequently did, Bellonda without even speaking the words managed to focus the Mother Superior's attention on the hunters who stalked them with such savage persistence. It spoiled the mood of quiet success Odrade had hoped to achieve this morning.

She forced herself to think of the new ghola. *Teg!* If his original memories could be restored, the Sisterhood once more would have the finest Bashar ever to serve them. A Mentat Bashar! A military genius whose prowess already was the stuff of myths in the Old Empire.

But would even Teg be of use against these women returned from the Scattering?

By whatever gods may be, the Honoured Matres must not find us! Not yet!

Teg represented too many disturbing unknowns and possibilities. Mystery surrounded the period before his death in the destruction of Dune. *He did something on Gammu to ignite the unbridled fury of the Honoured Matres. His suicidal stand on Dune should not have been enough to bring this berserk response.* There were rumours, bits and pieces from his days on Gammu before the Dune disaster. *He could move too fast for the human eye to see!* Had he done that? Another outcropping of wild abilities in the Atreides genes? Mutation? Or just more of the Teg myth? The Sisterhood had to learn as soon as possible.

An acolyte brought in the three breakfasts and the sisters ate quickly, as though this interruption must be put behind them without delay because time wasted was dangerous.

Those damnable hunters! Always somewhere in our thoughts!

Even after the others had gone, Odrade was left with the aftershock of Bellonda's unspoken fears.

And my fears.

She arose and went to the wide window that looked across lower rooftops to part of the ring of orchards and pastures around Central. Late spring and already fruit beginning to form out there. *Rebirth. A new Teg was born today!* No feeling of elation accompanied the thought. Usually she found the view restorative but not this morning.

What are my real strengths? What are my facts?

The resources at a Mother Superior's command were formidable: profound loyalty in those who served her, a military arm under a Teg-trained Bashar (far away now with a large portion of their troops guarding the school planet, Lampadas), artisans and technicians, spies and agents throughout the Old Empire, countless workers who looked to the Sisterhood for survival, and all the Reverend Mothers with Other Memories reaching into the dawn of life.

Odrade knew without false pride that she represented the peak of what was strongest in a Reverend Mother. If her personal memories did not provide needed information, she had others around her to fill the gaps. Machine-stored data as well, although she admitted to a native distrust of such things. *Didn't it all come through human hands? Then let the humans judge and present it!*

Odrade found herself tempted to go digging in those other lives she carried as secondary memory—a spectrum of subterranean layers deep in awareness. Perhaps she could find brilliant solutions to their predicament in experiences of Others. Dangerous! You could lose yourself for hours in there, fascinated by the multiplicity of human variations. Better to leave Other Memories balanced in there, ready on demand or intruding out of necessity. Consciousness, that was the fulcrum and her grip on identity.

Duncan Idaho's odd Mentat metaphor helped.

Self awareness: facing mirrors that pass through the universe, gathering new images on the way—endlessly reflexive. The infinite seen as finite, the analogue of consciousness carrying the sensed bits of infinity.

She had never heard words come closer to her wordless awareness. "Specialized complexity," Idaho called it. "We gather, assemble and reflect our systems of order."

Indeed, it was the Bene Gesserit view that humans were life designed by evolution to create order.

And how does that help us against these disorderly women who hunt us? What branch of evolution are they? Is evolution just another name for God?

Her sisters would sneer at such "bootless speculation".

Still, there *might* be answers in Other Memory.

Ahhhh, how seductive!

How desperately she wanted to project her beleaguered self into past identities and feel what it had been to live then. The immediate peril of this enticement chilled her. She felt Other Memory crowding the edges of awareness. *"It was like this!" "No! It was more like this!"* How greedy they were. You had to pick and choose, discretely animating the past. And was that not the purpose of consciousness, the very essence of being alive?

Select from the past and match it against the present: learn consequences.

That was the Bene Gesserit view of history, ancient Santayana's words resonating in their lives: *"Those who cannot remember the past are condemned to repeat it."*

The buildings of Central itself, this most powerful of

4

all Bene Gesserit establishments, reflected that attitude wherever Odrade turned. Usiform, that was the commanding concept. Little about any Bene Gesserit working centre was allowed to become non-functional, preserved out of nostalgia. The Sisterhood had no need for archaeologists. Reverend Mothers embodied history.

We have no attic storerooms. Recycle everything!

Slowly (much slower than usual) the view out her high window had its calming effect. What her eyes reported, that was Bene Gesserit order.

But the Honoured Matres could end that order in the next instant. The Sisterhood's situation was far worse than what they had suffered under the Tyrant. Odrade felt many of the decisions she was forced to make were odious. Some of that feeling bled off into her surroundings. The workroom where she went now was less agreeable because of actions taken here.

Write off our Bene Gesserit Keep on Palma?

That suggestion was in Bellonda's morning report waiting on the worktable. Odrade fixed an affirmative notation to it. *"Yes."*

Write it off because Honoured Matre attack is imminent and we cannot defend them or evacuate them.

Eleven hundred Reverend Mothers and the Fates alone knew how many acolytes, postulants and others dead or worse because of that one word.

No rescue operation possible. No. No. Retreat once more. Yes. Yes.

No and yes became equally offensive.

The strain of such decisions produced a new kind of weariness in Odrade. Was it a weariness of the soul? Did such a thing as a soul exist? She felt a deep fatigue where consciousness could not probe. Weary, weary, weary.

Even Bellonda showed the strain and Bell feasted on violence. Tamalane alone appeared above it but that did not fool Odrade. Tam had entered the age of superior observation that lay ahead of all sisters if they survived into it. Nothing mattered then except observations and judgments. Most of this was never uttered except in fleeting expressions on wrinkled features. Tamalane spoke few words these days, her comments so sparse as to be almost ludicrous.

"Buy more no-ships."

"Brief Sheeana."

"Review Idaho records."

"Ask Murbella."

Sometimes, only grunts issued from her, as though words might betray her.

And always the hunters roamed out there, sweeping space for any clue to the location of Chapter House.

In her most private thoughts, Odrade saw the no-ships of the Honoured Matres as corsairs on those infinite seas between the stars. They flew no black flags with skull and crossbones, but that flag was there nonetheless. Nothing whatsoever romantic about them. *Kill and pillage! Amass your wealth in the blood of others. Drain that energy and build your killer no-ships on ways lubricated with blood.*

And they did not see that they would drown in the red lubricant if they kept on this course.

There must be furious people out there in that human Scattering where the Honoured Matres originated, people who live out their lives with a single fixed idea: Get them!

It was a very dangerous universe where such ideas were allowed to float around freely. Good civilizations took care that such ideas did not gain energy, did not even get the chance for birth. When they did occur, by chance or accident, they were to be diverted quickly because they tended to gather mass.

Odrade was astonished that the Honoured Matres did not see this or, seeing it, ignored it.

"Full-blown hysterics," Tamalane called them.

"Xenophobia," Bellonda disagreed, always correcting, as though control of Archives gave her a better hold on reality.

Both were right, Odrade thought. The Honoured Matres behaved hysterically. All *outsiders* were the enemy. The only people they appeared to trust were the men they sexually enslaved, and those only to a limited degree. Constantly testing, according to Murbella (*our only captive Honoured Matre*), to see if their hold was firm.

6

"Sometimes out of mere pique they may eliminate someone just as an example to others." Murbella's words and they forced the question: *Are they making an example of us?* "See! *This is what happens to those who dare oppose us!*"

Xenophobia was not a new experience to the Bene Gesserit. *Our response*, Odrade thought, *is the response of balanced intelligence that dampens the wide oscillations we find.* And wasn't there too much pride in such a thought?

"We have our own personal xenophobia," she had cautioned her Council. "We have fallen into defensive paranoia focused on the Honoured Matres."

And what did captive Honoured Matre Murbella say to all of this?

"You've aroused them. By all accounts, once aroused, they will not desist until they have destroyed you."

Get the outsiders!

Singularly direct. "A weakness in them if we play it right," Odrade said.

Xenophobia carried to a ridiculous extreme?

Quite possibly.

Odrade pounded a fist on her worktable, aware that the action would be seen and recorded by sisters who kept a constant watch on Mother Superior's behaviour. She spoke aloud then for the omnipresent comeyes and the watchdog sisters behind them.

"We will not sit and wait in defensive enclaves! We've become as fat as Bellonda (*and let her fret over that!*) thinking we've created an untouchable society and enduring structures."

Odrade swept her gaze around the familiar room.

"This place is one of our weaknesses!"

She took her seat behind the worktable thinking (of all things!) about architecture and community planning. Well, that was a Mother Superior's right!

Sisterhood communities seldom grew at random. Even when they took over existing structures (as they had with the old Harkonnen Keep on Gammu) they did so with rebuilding plans. They wanted pneumotubes to shunt small packages and messages. Lightlines and hardray projectors to transmit

7

encrypted words. They considered themselves masters at safeguarding communications. Acolyte and Reverend Mother couriers (committed to self-destruction rather than betray their superiors) carried the more important messages.

She could visualize it out there beyond her window and beyond this planet—her web, superbly organized and manned, each Bene Gesserit an extension of the others. Where Sisterhood survival was concerned, there was an untouchable core of loyalty. Backsliders there might be, some spectacular (as the Lady Jessica, grandmother of the Tyrant) but they slid only so far. Most upsets were temporary. "I know better than you!" vanished when threats to the order were recognized.

And all of that was Bene Gesserit pattern. A weakness.

Odrade admitted a deep agreement with Bellonda's fears. *But I'll be damned if I allow such things to depress all joy of living!* That would be giving in to the very thing those rampaging Honoured Matres wanted.

"It's our strengths the hunters want," Odrade said, looking up at the ceiling comeyes. *Like ancient savages eating the hearts of enemies. Well . . . we will give them something to eat all right! And they will not know until too late that they cannot digest it!*

Except for preliminary teachings tailored to acolytes and postulants, the Sisterhood did not go in much for admonitory sayings, but Odrade had her own private watchwords: *"Someone has to do the ploughing."* She smiled to herself as she bent to her work much refreshed. This room, this Sisterhood, these were her garden and there were weeds to be removed, seeds to plant. *And fertilizer. Mustn't forget the fertilizer.*

> When I set out to lead humanity along my Golden Path I promised a lesson their bones would remember. I know a profound pattern humans deny with words even while their actions affirm it. They say they seek security and quiet, conditions they call peace. Even as they speak, they create seeds of turmoil and violence.
>
> —Leto II, the God Emperor

8

So she calls me Spider Queen!

Great Honoured Matre leaned back in a heavy chair set high on a dais. Her withered breast shook with silent chuckles. *She knows what will happen when I get her in my web! Suck her dry, that's what I'll do.*

A small woman with unremarkable features and muscles that twitched nervously, she looked down on the skylighted yellow-tile floor of her audience room. A Bene Gesserit Reverend Mother sprawled there in shigawire bindings. The captive made no attempt to struggle. Shigawire was excellent for this purpose. *Cut her arms off, it would!*

The chamber where she sat suited Great Honoured Matre as much for its dimensions as for the fact that it had been taken from others. Three hundred metres square, it had been designed for convocations of Guild Navigators here on Junction, each Navigator in a monstrous tank. The captive on that yellow floor was a mote in immensity.

This weakling took too much joy in revealing what her so-called Superior named me! She's loaded with shere, too!

But it still was a lovely morning, Great Honoured Matre thought. Except that no tortures or mental probes worked on these witches. How could you torture someone who might choose to die at any moment. And did! They had ways of suppressing pain, too. Very wily, these primitives.

Great Honoured Matre relished the fact that thumb screws, iron boots and the blessed auto-da-fé of Thomas Torquemada's day had given way to the trappings of science for extracting desired responses from captives. T-probes and their various improvements from the Scattering could remove data even from newly dead brains. Pain induction did not require that you destroy flesh, only (occasionally) nerves. A major improvement, Great Honoured Matre thought. The brain within the flesh knew it would survive for more and even greater agonies.

Of course, a science that produced one powerful tool always seemed to give rise to a countervailing force—a science to obstruct pain-makers and T-probes. *Shere!* A body infused with that damnable drug deteriorated beyond the reach of probes before it could be examined adequately.

Great Honoured Matre signalled an aide. That one nudged the sprawled Reverend Mother with a foot and, at a further signal, eased the shigawire bindings to allow minimal movement.

"What is your name, Child?" Great Honoured Matre asked. Her voice rasped hoarsely with age and false bonhomie.

"I am called Sabanda." Clear young voice, still untouched by the pain of probings.

"Would you like to watch us capture a weak male and enslave him?" Great Honoured Matre asked.

Sabanda knew the proper response to this. They had been warned. "I will die first." She said it calmly, staring up at that ancient face the colour of a dried root left too long in the sun. Those odd orange flecks in the crone's eyes. A sign of anger, Proctors had told her.

A loosely-hung red-gold robe with black dragon figures down its open face and red leotards beneath it only emphasized the scrawny figure they covered.

Great Honoured Matre did not change expression even with a recurrent thought about these witches: *Damn them!* "What was your task on that dirty little planet where we took you?"

"A teacher of the young."

"I'm afraid we didn't leave any of your young alive." *Now why does she smile? To offend me! That's why!*

Great Honoured Matre lifted the little finger of her right hand. A waiting aide approached the captive with an injection. Perhaps this new drug would free a witch's tongue, perhaps not. No matter.

Sabanda grimaced when the injector touched her neck. In seconds she was dead. Servants carried the body away. It would be fed to captive Futars. Not that Futars were much use. Wouldn't breed in captivity, wouldn't obey the most ordinary commands. Sullen, waiting.

"Where Handlers?" one might ask. Or other useless words would spill from their humanoid mouths. Still, Futars provided some pleasures. Captivity also demonstrated they were vulnerable. Just as these primitive witches were. *We'll find the witches' hiding place. It's only a matter of time.*

10

The person who takes the banal and ordinary and illuminates it in a new way can terrify. We do not want our ideas changed. We feel threatened by such demands. "I already know the important things!" we say. Then Changer comes and throws our old ideas away.

—**The Zensunni Master**

Miles Teg enjoyed playing in the orchards around Central. Odrade had first taken him here when he could just toddle. One of his earliest active memories: hardly more than two years old and already aware he was a ghola, though he did not understand the word's full meaning.

"You are a special child," Odrade said. "We made you from cells taken from a very old man."

Although he was a precocious child and her words had a vaguely disturbing sound, he was more interested then in running through tall summer grass beneath the trees.

Later, he added other orchard days to that first one, accumulating as well impressions about Odrade and the others who taught him. He recognized quite early that Odrade enjoyed the excursions as much as he did.

One afternoon in his fourth year, he told her: "Spring is my favourite time."

"Mine, too."

When he was seven and already showing the mental brilliance coupled to holographic memory that had caused the Sisterhood to place such heavy responsibilities on his previous incarnation, he suddenly saw the orchards as a place touching something deep inside him.

This was his first real awareness that he carried memories he could not recall. Deeply disturbed, he turned to Odrade who stood outlined in light against the afternoon sun, and said: "There are things I can't remember!"

"One day you will remember," she said.

He could not see her face against the bright light and her words came from a great shadow place, as much within him as from Odrade.

That year he began studying the life of the Bashar Miles Teg whose cells had started his new life. Odrade had explained

11

some of this to him, holding up her fingernails. "I took tiny scrapings from his neck—cells of his skin and they held all we needed to bring you to life."

There was something intense about the orchards that year, fruit larger and heavier, bees almost frenetic.

"It's because of the desert growing larger down there in the south," Odrade said. She held his hand as they walked through a dew-fresh morning beneath burgeoning apple trees.

Teg stared southward through the trees, momentarily mesmerized by leaf-dappled sunlight. He had studied about the desert, and he thought he could feel the weight of it on this place.

"Trees can sense their end approaching," Odrade said. "Life breeds more intensely when threatened."

"The air is very dry," he said. "That must be the desert."

"Notice how some of the leaves have gone brown and curled at the edges? We've had to irrigate heavily this year."

He liked it that she seldom talked down to him. It was mostly one person to another. He saw curled brown on leaves. The desert did that.

Before leaving Central with Odrade that morning, he had listened silently while a farm overseer uttered questions full of tensions. *Couldn't Weather Control be more generous? What was the use of all those satellites and reflectors in orbit up there if they could not put a bit more water where it was so desperately needed?*

Deep in the orchard, they listened quietly for a time to birds and insects. Bees working the clover of a nearby pasture came to investigate but he was pheromone-marked as were all who walked freely on Chapter House. Bees buzzed past him, sensed identifiers and went away about their business with blossoms.

"He's one of us."

Odrade, caught by the linear persistence of human association with fruit trees, spoke of this as they stood there.

Apples. She pointed westward. *Peaches.* His attention went where she directed. And yes, there were the cherries east of them beyond the pasture. He saw resin ribbing on the limbs.

Seeds and young shoots had been brought here on the

original no-ships some fifteen hundred years ago, she said, and had been planted with loving care.

Teg visualized hands grubbing in dirt, gently patting earth around young shoots, careful irrigation, the fencing to confine the cattle to wild pastures around the first Chapter House plantations and buildings.

By this time he already had begun learning about the giant sandworm the Sisterhood had spirited from Rakis. Death of that worm had produced creatures called sandtrout. Sandtrout were why the desert grew. Some of this history touched accounts of his previous incarnation—a man they called "The Bashar". A great soldier who had died when terrible women called Honoured Matres destroyed Rakis.

Teg found such studies both fascinating and troubling. He sensed gaps in himself, places where memories ought to be. The gaps called out to him in dreams. And, sometimes when he fell into reverie, faces appeared before him. He could almost hear words. Then there were times he knew the names of things before anyone told him. Especially names of weapons.

Momentous things grew in his awareness. This entire planet would become desert, a change started because Honoured Matres wanted to kill these Bene Gesserits who raised him.

Reverend Mothers who controlled his life often awed him— black-robed, austere, those blue-in-blue eyes with absolutely no white. The spice did that, they said.

Only Odrade showed him anything he took for real affection and Odrade was someone *very* important. Everyone called her Mother Superior and that was what she told him to call her except when they were alone in the orchards. Then he could call her Mother.

On a morning walk near harvest time in his ninth year, just over the third rise in the apple orchards north of Central, they came on a shallow depression free of trees and lush with many different plants. Odrade put a hand on his shoulder and held him where they could admire black stepping stones in a meander track through massed greenery and tiny flowers. She was in an odd mood. He heard it in her voice.

13

"Ownership is an interesting question," she said. "Do we own this planet or does it own us?"

"I like the smells here," he said.

She released him and urged him gently ahead of her. "We planted for the nose here, Miles. Aromatic herbs. Study them carefully and look them up when you get back to the library. Oh, do step on them!" when he started to avoid a plant runner in his path.

He placed his right foot firmly on green tendrils and inhaled pungent odours.

"They were made to be walked on and give up their savour," Odrade said. "Proctors have been teaching you how to deal with nostalgia. Have they told you nostalgia often is driven by the sense of smell?"

"Yes, Mother." Turning to look back at where he had stepped, he said: "That's rosemary."

"How do you know?" Very intense.

He shrugged. "I just know."

"That may be an original memory." She sounded pleased.

As they continued their walk in the aromatic hollow, Odrade's voice once more became pensive. "Each planet has its own character where we draw patterns of Old Earth. Sometimes, it's only a faint sketch, but here we have succeeded."

She knelt and pulled a twig from an acid green plant. Crushing it in her fingers, she held it to his nose. "Sage."

She was right but he could not say how he knew.

"I've smelled that in food. Is that like melange?"

"It improves flavour but won't change consciousness." She stood and looked down at him from her full height. "Mark this place well, Miles. Our ancestral worlds are gone, but here we have recaptured part of our origins."

He sensed she was teaching him something important. She had spoken of ownership several times today, a word he had investigated because a Proctor commanded it. He knew why. It was because of Yorgi, a boy from the plantations who had come almost every day for two years to share playtime. Yorgi, a year or so younger, tagged along with obvious worship of his older playmate, trying to do everything the

14

way Teg did it. But Yorgi had not appeared at playtime for almost three weeks and this had angered Teg when no one explained.

"I want my friend!"

"*Your* friend?" the Proctor asked in that deceptively mild way they had. "You think you *own* Yorgi?"

For almost an hour they explored the meanings of ownership.

Remembering, he asked Odrade: "Why did you wonder if this planet owned us?"

"My Sisterhood believes we are stewards of the land. Do you know about stewards?"

"Like Roitiro, Yorgi's father. Yorgi says his oldest sister will be steward of their plantation someday."

"Correct. We have a longer residence on some planets than any other people we know of but we are only stewards."

"If you don't own Chapter House, who does?"

"Perhaps nobody. My question is: How have we marked each other, my Sisterhood and this planet?"

He looked up at her face then down at his hands. Was Chapter House marking him right now?

"Most of the marks are deep inside us." She took his hand. "Come along." They left the aromatic dell and climbed into Roitiro's domain, Odrade speaking as they went.

He listened with only occasional questions, enjoying these moments, learning things about Bene Gesserits, especially about this moody woman he called Mother.

The Sisterhood seldom created botanical gardens, she said. "Gardens must support far more than eyes and nose."

"Food?"

"Yes, supportive first of our lives. Gardens produce food. That dell back there is harvested for our kitchens."

He felt her words flow into him, lodging there among the gaps. Some things were planted for descendants, she said. "Not necessarily blood relations." He sensed planning for centuries ahead: trees to replace building beams, to hold watersheds, plants to keep lake and river banks from crumbling, to hold topsoil safe from rain and wind, to maintain seashores and even in the waters to make places for fish to breed. The Bene Gesserits also thought of trees for shade and shelter, or to cast interesting shadows on lawns.

"Trees and other plants for all of our symbiotic relationships," she said.

"Symbiotic?" It was a new word.

She explained with something she knew he already had encountered—going out with others to harvest mushrooms.

"Fungi won't grow except in the company of friendly roots. Each has a *symbiotic* relationship with a special plant. Each growing thing takes something it needs from the other."

She went on at length and, bored with learning, he kicked a clump of grass, then saw how she stared at him in that disturbing way. He had done something offensive. Why was it right to step on one growing thing and not on another?

"Miles! Grass keeps the wind from carrying topsoil into difficult places such as the bottoms of rivers."

He knew that tone. Reprimanding. He stared down at the grass he had offended.

"These grasses feed our cattle. Some have seeds we eat in bread and other foods. Some cane grasses are windbreaks."

He knew *that!* Trying to divert her, he said: "Windbrakes?" spelling it.

She did not smile and he knew he had been wrong to think he could fool her. Resigned to it, he listened as she went on with the lesson.

There were deeply penetrating rootcrops, she said, to bring up sustenance from far under the surface of the land.

"Farmers once said their grapevines and some berry bushes have roots that 'go to hell' for their water, stealing it from damned souls."

"Did they really believe that?" The Missionaria's Proctors said souls were an illusion.

"Perhaps, but they taught us never to irrigate if a plant will support itself without it. Sweeter fruits, richer in things our bodies need, grow when you don't irrigate."

Irrigation again. Circling him back to the desert. She stopped him beneath an apple tree heavy with fruit and Teg listened with care, seeking to restore himself to her favour.

When the desert came, she told him, grapes, their taproots down several hundred metres, probably would be the last to go. Orchards would die first.

"Why do they have to die?"

"To make room for more important life."

"Sandworms and melange."

He saw he had pleased her by knowing the relationship between sandworms and the spice Bene Gesserits needed for their existence. He was not sure how that need worked but he imagined a circle: *Sandworms to sandtrout to melange and back again.* And Bene Gesserits took what they needed from the circle.

He was still tired of all this teaching, and asked: "If all these things are going to die anyway, why do I have to go back to the library and learn their names?"

"Because you're human and humans have this deep desire to classify, to be Linnaeus applying labels, Latin or otherwise, to everything."

He knew there was an ancient language called Latin but she had to spell Linnaeus for him, reminding: "Look it up."

"Why do we have to name things like that?"

"Because that way we lay claim to what we name. We assume an ownership that can be misleading and dangerous."

So she was back on *ownership.*

"My street, my lake, my planet, my friend," she said, a sneer in her voice. "My label forever."

He winced when she said "my friend" but she was not through with him. "A label you give to a place or thing may not even last out your lifetime except as a polite sop granted by conquerors . . . or as a sound to remember in fear."

"Dune," he said.

"You are quick!"

"Honoured Matres burned Dune."

"They'll do the same to us if they find us."

"Not if I'm your Bashar!" The words were out of him without thought but, once spoken, he felt they might have some truth. Library accounts said the Bashar had made enemies tremble just by appearing on a battlefield.

As though she knew what he was thinking, Odrade said:

"The Bashar Teg was just as famous for creating situations where no battle was necessary."

"But he fought your enemies."

"Never forget Dune, Miles. He died there."

"I know."

"Do the Proctors have you studying Caladan yet?"

"Yes. It's called Dan in my histories."

"Labels, Miles. Names are interesting reminders but most people don't make other connections. Boring history, eh? Names—convenient pointers, useful mostly with your own kind?"

"Are you my kind?" It was a question that plagued him but not in those words until this instant.

"We are Atreides, you and I. Remember that when you return to your study of Caladan."

When they went back through the orchards and across a pasture to the vantage knoll with its limb-framed view of Central, Teg saw the administrative complex and its barrier plantations with new sensitivity. He held this close as they went down the fenced lane to the arch into First Street.

"A living jewel," Odrade called Central.

As they passed under it, he looked up at the street name burned into the entrance arch. Galach in an elegant script with flowing lines, Bene Gesserit decorative. All streets and buildings were labelled in that same cursive.

"There's no reason communication should be ugly," Odrade told him when he asked why they did that.

"Where did you learn to write names that way?"

"Thousands upon thousands of years ago. We learned it from artists whose names only we remember."

She was referring to Other Memory, he realized. An awesome thing about which these women seemed so casual.

Looking around him at Central, the dancing fountain in the square ahead of them, the elegant details, he sensed a depth of human experience. Bene Gesserits had made this place supportive in ways he did not quite fathom. Things picked up in studies and orchard excursions, simple things and complex, came to new focus. It was a latent Mentat response but he did not know this, only sensing that his unfailing memory had

18

shifted some relationships and reorganized them. He stopped suddenly and looked back the way they had come—the orchard out there framed in the arch of the covered street. It was all related. Central's effluent produced methane and fertilizer. (He had toured the plant with a Proctor.) Methane ran pumps and powered some of the refrigeration.

"What are you looking at, Miles?"

He did not know how to answer. But he remembered an autumn afternoon when Odrade had taken him over Central in a 'thopter to tell him about these relationships and give him "the overview". Only words then (another of her *lessons!*) but now the words had meaning.

"As near to a closed ecological circle as we can create," Odrade had said in the 'thopter. "Weather Control's orbiters monitor it and order the flow lines."

"Why are you standing there looking at the orchard, Miles?" Her voice was full of imperatives against which he had no defences.

"In the ornithopter, you said it was beautiful but dangerous."

They had taken only one 'thopter trip together. She caught the reference immediately. *"The ecological circle."*

He turned and looked up at her, waiting.

"Enclosed," she said. "How tempting it is to raise high walls and keep out change. Rot here in our own self satisfied comfort."

Her words filled him with disquiet. He felt he had heard them before . . . some other place with a different woman holding his hand.

"Enclosures of any kind are a fertile breeding ground for hatred of outsiders," she said. "That produces a bitter harvest."

Not exactly the same words but the same lesson.

He walked slowly beside Odrade, his hand sweaty in hers.

Once more, his mind made that odd shift, reorganizing data, posing new relationships. Mentat force held him dumb while internal changes occurred. Autumn: regulated and set in a cycle of seasons. Soon it would be harvest time—circles turning out there and in his mind. All ordered according to

19

needs of gardens and orchards first, other comforts second.

"Why are you so silent, Miles?"

"You're farmers," he said. "That's really what you Bene Gesserits do."

She saw immediately what had happened, Mentat training coming out in him without his knowing. Best not explore that yet. "We are concerned about everything that grows, Miles. It was perceptive of you to see this."

As they parted, she to return to her tower, he to his quarters in the school section, Odrade said: "I will tell your Proctors to place more emphasis on subtle uses of power."

He misunderstood. "I'm already training with lasguns. They say I'm very good."

"So I've heard. But there are weapons you cannot hold in your hands. You can only hold them in your mind."

Rules build up fortifications behind which small minds create satrapies. A perilous state of affairs in the best of times, disastrous during crises.

—Bene Gesserit Coda

Stygian blackness in Great Honoured Matre's sleeping chamber. Logno, a Grand Dame and Senior aide to the High One, entered from the unlighted hallway as she had been summoned to do and, seeing darkness, shuddered. These consultations with no illumination terrified her and she knew Great Honoured Matre took pleasure from that. It could not be the only reason for darkness, though. Was Great Honoured Matre fearful of attack? Several High Ones had been deposed in bed. No . . . not just that, although it might bear on the choice of setting.

Grunts and moans in the darkness.

Some Honoured Matres snickered and said Great Honoured Matre dared bed a Futar. Logno thought it possible. This Great Honoured Matre dared many things. Had she not salvaged some of The Weapons from the disaster of the Scattering? Futars, though? The sisters knew Futars could not be bonded by sex. At least not by sex with humans. That might be the way the Enemies of Many Faces did it, though. Who knew?

There was a furry smell in the bed chamber. Logno closed the door behind her and waited. Great Honoured Matre did not like to be interrupted in whatever she did there within shielding blackness. *But she permits me to call her Dama.*

Another moan, then: "Sit on the floor, Logno. Yes, there by the door."

Does she really see me or only guess?

Logno did not have the courage to test it. *Poison. I'll get her that way someday. She's cautious but she can be distracted.* Although her sisters might sneer at it, poison was an accepted tool of succession . . . provided the successor possessed other ways to maintain ascendancy.

"Logno, those Ixians you spoke with today. What do they say of The Weapon?"

"They do not understand its function, Dama. I did not tell them what it was."

"Of course not."

"Will you suggest again that Weapon and Charge be united?"

"Are you sneering at me, Logno?"

"Dama! I would never do such a thing."

"I hope not."

Silence. Logno understood that they both considered the same problem. Only three hundred units of The Weapon survived the disaster. Each could be used only once, provided the Council (which held the Charge) agreed to arm them. Great Honoured Matre, controlling The Weapon itself, had only half of that awful power. Weapon without Charge was merely a small black tube that could be held in the hand. With its Charge, it cut a brief swath of bloodless death across the arc of its limited range.

"The Ones of Many Faces," Great Honoured Matre muttered.

Logno nodded to the darkness where that muttering originated.

Perhaps she can see me. I do not know what else she salvaged or what the Ixians may have provided her.

And the Ones of Many Faces, curse them through eternity, had caused the disaster. Them and their Futars! The ease with which all but that handful of The Weapon had been confiscated! Awesome powers. *We must arm ourselves well before we return to that battle. Dama is right.*

"That planet—Buzzell," Great Honoured Matre said. "Are you sure it's not defended?"

"We detect no defences. Smugglers say it is not defended."

"But it is rich in Soostones!"

"Here in the Old Empire, people seldom dare attack the witches."

"I do not believe there are only a handful of them on that planet! It's a trap of some kind."

"That is always possible, Dama."

"I do not trust smugglers, Logno. Bond a few more of them and test this thing of Buzzell again. The witches may be weak but I do not think they are stupid."

"Yes, Dama."

"Tell the Ixians they will displease us if they cannot duplicate The Weapon."

"But without the Charge, Dama . . ."

"We will deal with that when we must. Now, leave."

Logno heard a hissing "Yessssss!" as she let herself out. Even the darkness of the hallway was welcome after the bedchamber and she hurried toward the light.

We tend to become like the worst in those we oppose.

—Bene Gesserit Coda

The water images again!

We're turning this whole damned planet into a desert and I get water images!

Odrade sat in her workroom, the usual morning clutter around her, and sensed Sea Child floating in the waves,

22

washed by them, carried by them. The waves were the colour of blood. Her Sea Child self anticipated bloody times.

She knew where these images originated: the time before Reverend Mothers ruled her life; childhood in the beautiful home on the Gammu seacoast. Despite immediate worries, she could not prevent a smile. Oysters prepared by Papa. The stew she still preferred.

What she remembered best of childhood was the sea excursions. Something about being afloat spoke to her most basic self. The lift and fall of waves, the sense of unbounded horizons with strange new places just beyond the curved limits of the watery world, that thrilling edge of danger implicit in the very substance that supported her. All of it combined to assure her she was Sea Child.

Papa was calmer there, too. And Mama Sibia happier, face turned into the wind, dark hair blowing. A sense of balance radiated from those times, a reassuring message spoken in a language older than Odrade's oldest Other Memory. *"This is my place, my medium. I am Sea Child."*

Her personal concept of sanity came from those times. *The ability to balance on strange seas. The ability to maintain your deepest self despite unexpected waves.*

Mama Sibia had given Odrade that ability long before the Reverend Mothers came and took away their "hidden Atreides scion". Mama Sibia, *only* a foster mother, had taught Odrade to love herself.

In a Bene Gesserit society where any form of love was suspect, this remained Odrade's ultimate secret.

At root, I am happy with myself. I do not mind being alone. Not that any Reverend Mother was ever truly alone after the Spice Agony flooded her with Other Memories.

But Mama Sibia and, yes, Papa, too, acting *in loco parentis* for the Bene Gesserit, had impressed a profound strength upon their charge during those hidden years. The Reverend Mothers had been reduced to amplifying that strength.

Proctors had tried to root out Odrade's "deep desire for personal affinities", but failed at last, not quite sure they had failed but always suspicious. They had sent her to Al Dhanab finally, a place deliberately maintained as a mimic of the worst in Salusa Secundus, there to be conditioned on a planet of constant testing. A place worse than Dune in some respects: high cliffs and dry gorges, hot winds and frigid winds, too little moisture and too much. The Sisterhood had thought of it as a proving ground for those destined to survive on Dune. But none of this had touched that secret core within Odrade. Sea Child remained intact.

And it is Sea Child warning me now.

Was it a prescient warning?

She had always possessed this *bit of talent*, this little twitching that told of immediate peril to the Sisterhood. Atreides genes reminding her of their presence. Was it a threat to Chapter House? No . . . the ache she could not touch said it was others in danger. Important, though.

Lampadas? Her bit of talent could not say.

The Breeding Mistresses had tried to erase this dangerous prescience from their Atreides Line but with limited success. "We dare not risk another kwisatz haderach!" They knew of this quirk in their Mother Superior, but Odrade's late predecessor, Taraza, had advised "cautious use of her talent". It had been Taraza's view that Odrade's prescience worked only to warn of dangers to the Bene Gesserit.

Odrade agreed. She experienced unwanted moments when she glimpsed threats. Glimpses. And lately she dreamed.

It was a vividly recurring dream, every sense attuned to the immediacy of this thing occurring in her mind. She walked across a chasm on a tightrope and someone (she dared not turn to see who) was coming from behind with an axe to cut the rope. She could feel the rough twists of fibre beneath bare feet. She felt a cold wind blowing, a smell of burning on that wind. And she *knew* the one with the axe approached!

Each perilous step required all of her energy. Step! Step! The rope swayed and she stretched her arms out straight on each side, struggling for balance.

If I fall, the Sisterhood falls!

The Bene Gesserit would end in the chasm beneath the rope. As with any living thing, the Sisterhood must end sometime. A Reverend Mother dared not deny it.

But not here. Not falling, the rope severed. We must not let

24

the rope be cut! I must get across the chasm before the axe-wielder comes. "I must! I must!"

The dream always ended there, her own voice ringing in her ears as she awoke in her sleeping chamber. Chilled. No perspiration. Even in the throes of nightmare, Bene Gesserit restraints did not permit unnecessary excesses.

Body does not need perspiration? Body does not get perspiration.

She could feel the room's temperature. Not cold at all. Subjective reaction to the wind across the dream chasm. Chilled bodies do not sweat.

As she sat in her workroom remembering the dream, Odrade felt the depth of reality behind that metaphor of a slender rope: *The delicate strand on which I carry the fate of my Sisterhood.* Sea Child sensed the approaching nightmare and intruded with images of bloody waters. This was no trivial warning. Ominous. She wanted to stand and shout: "Scatter into the weeds, my chicks! Run! Run!"

And wouldn't that shock the watchdogs!

The duties of a Mother Superior required her to put a good face on her tremors and act as though nothing mattered except the formal decisions in front of her. Panic must be avoided! Not that any of her immediate decisions were truly trivial in these times. But calm demeanour was required.

Calm, calm, calm!

Some of her chicks already were running, gone off into the unknown. Shared lives in Other Memory. The rest of her chicks here on Chapter House would know when to run. *When we are discovered.* Their behaviour would be governed then by the necessities of the moment. All that really mattered was their superb training. That was their most reliable preparation.

She could take reasonable precautions, send their *eggs* into that infinite Scattering where the Honoured Matres originated, but the *egg* of true importance remained here on Chapter House. Archives could be reproduced (and had been). Other Memory persisted.

Each new Bene Gesserit cell, wherever it finally went, was prepared as was Chapter House: total destruction rather than submission. The screaming fire would engorge itself on precious flesh and records. All a captor would find would be useless wreckage: twisted shards peppered with ashes.

Some Chapter House sisters might escape. But flight at the moment of attack—how futile!

Key people Shared Other Memory anyway. Preparation. Mother Superior avoided it. *Reasons of morale!*

Where to run? That was the real question. If the Honoured Matres captured ghola-Idaho or the new ghola-Teg, there might never again be a hiding place for any of them.

Angry frustration said: "Should've killed Idaho the minute we got him! We should never have grown ghola-Teg."

Only her Council members, immediate advisers and some among the watchdogs shared her suspicion. They sat on it with reservations. None of them felt really secure about those two gholas, not even after mining the no-ship, making it vulnerable to the screaming fire.

In those last hours before his heroic sacrifice, had Teg been able to *see* the unseeable (including no-ships)? *How did he know where to meet us on that desert of Dune?*

And if Teg could do it, the dangerously talented Duncan Idaho with his uncounted generations of accumulated Atreides (and unknown) genes might also stumble upon the ability.

I might do it myself!

With sudden shocking insight, Odrade realized for the first time that Tamalane and Bellonda watched their Mother Superior with the same fears that Odrade felt in watching the two gholas.

Merely knowing it could be done—that a human could be sensitized to detect no-ships and the other forms of that shielding—would have an unbalancing effect on their universe. It would certainly set the Honoured Matres on a runaway track. There were uncounted Idaho offspring loose in the universe. He had always complained he was "no damned stud for the Sisterhood", but he had performed for them many times.

Always thought he was doing it for himself. And maybe he was.

26

Any mainline Atreides offspring might have this talent the Council suspected had come to flower in Teg.

The chasm beneath her slender rope contained sharp spikes. Other Memory added warnings to the clamour. *Dream-reality is time-reality.* She could hear the Lady Jessica's long-ago words to her son, Paul Muad'Dib: "Is this the way you were taught?" The remembered words returned her awareness to the workroom.

Where did the months and years go? And the days? Another harvest season and the Sisterhood remained in its terrible limbo. Midmorning already, Odrade realized. The sounds and smells of Central made themselves known to her. People out there in the corridor. Chicken and cabbage cooking in the communal kitchen. Everything normal.

What was normal to someone who dwelt in water images even during these working moments? Sea Child could not forget Gammu, the smells, the breeze-blown substance of ocean weeds, the ozone that made every breath oxygen-rich, and the splendid freedom in those around her so apparent in the way they walked and spoke. Conversation on the sea went deeper in a way she had never plumbed. Even smalltalk had its subterranean elements there, an oceanic elocution that flowed with the currents beneath them.

Odrade felt compelled to remember her own body afloat in that childhood sea. She needed to recapture the forces she had known there, take in the strengthening qualities she had learned in more innocent times.

Face down in salty water, holding her breath as long as she could, she floated in a sea-washed *now* that cleansed away woes. This was stress management reduced to its essence. A great calmness flooded her.

I float, therefore I am.

Sea Child warned and Sea Child restored. Without ever admitting it, she had needed restoration desperately.

Odrade had looked at her own face mirrored in a workroom window the previous night, shocked by the way age and responsibilities combined with fatigue to suck in her cheeks and turn down the corners of her mouth: the sensual lips thinner, the gentle curves of her face elongated. Only the

27

all-blue eyes blazed with their accustomed intensity and she still was tall and muscular.

On impulse, Odrade punched up the call symbols and stared at a projection above the table: the no-ship sitting on the ground at the Chapter House spacefield—visible to the eyes in this quiescent mode but invisible to any prescient searcher and to instruments that simulated this talent.

There it sat on the ground, a giant bump of mysterious machinery, separated from Time. Lumpy and grotesque. *You would expect such a thing to be as smooth as an egg, but it isn't.* Her projection displayed a wild conglomeration of exotic alloys, protrusions and juttings with no apparent purpose.

Over the years of its semi-dormancy, it had depressed a great sunken area into the landing flat, becoming almost wedged there. It was a great lump, its engines ticking away only enough to keep it hidden from prescient searchers (especially from Guild Navigators who would take a special joy in selling out the Bene Gesserit). The no-ship's standby mode was not enough to blend it into the visual background—imitating dirt, rocks and stones. *More like imitating a mountain.*

Why had she called up this image just now?

Because of the three people confined there—Scytale, the last surviving Tleilaxu Master; Murbella and Duncan Idaho: the sexually-bonded pair, held as much by their mutual entrapment as they were by the no-ship.

Not simple, any of it.

There seldom were simple explanations for any major Bene Gesserit undertaking. The no-ship and its mortal contents could only be classified as a major effort. Costly. Very costly in energy even in this mode.

The appearance of parsimonious metering to all of that expenditure spoke of energy crisis. One of Bell's concerns. You could hear it in her voice even when she was being her most objective: "Down to the bone and nowhere else to cut!" Every Bene Gesserit knew the watchful eyes of Accounting were on them these days, critical of the Sisterhood's outflowing vitality.

Bellonda strode into the workroom unannounced with a roll of ridulian crystal records under her left arm. She walked as though she hated the floor, stamping on it as if to say: "There! Take that! And that!" Beating the floor because it was guilty of being underfoot.

Odrade felt her chest tighten as she saw the look in Bell's eyes. The ridulian records went "Slap!" as Bellonda threw them on to the table.

"Lampadas!" Bellonda said and there was agony in her voice.

Odrade had no need to open the roll. *Sea Child's bloody water has become reality.*

"Survivors?" Her voice sounded strained.

"None." Bellonda slumped into the chairdog she kept on her side of Odrade's table.

Tamalane entered then and sat beside Bellonda. Both looked stricken.

No survivors.

Odrade permitted herself a slow shudder that went from her breast to the soles of her feet. She did not care that the others saw such a revealing reaction. This workroom had seen worse behaviour from sisters.

"Who reported?" Odrade asked.

Bellonda said, "It came through our CHOAM spies and had the special mark on it. The Rabbi supplied the information, no doubt of it."

Odrade did not know how to respond. She glanced at the wide bow window behind her companions, seeing a soft flutter of snowflakes. Yes, this news deservedly went with winter marshalling its forces out there.

The sisters of Chapter House were unhappy about the sudden plunge into winter. Necessities had forced Weather Control to let the temperature drop precipitately. No gradual decline into winter, no kindness to growing things that now must pass through the freezing dormancy. This was three and four degrees colder every night. Get the whole thing over in a week or so and plunge them all into the seemingly interminable chill.

Cold to match the news about Lampadas.

29

One result of this weather shift was fog. She could see it dissipating as the brief snow flurry ended. Very confusing weather. They got the dewpoint next to the air temperature and the fog rolled into the remaining wet spots. It lifted from the ground in tulle mists that wandered through leafless orchards like a poisonous gas.

The sisters all went about their tasks with a tender edge on their sensitivities, covering it fairly well for non-initiates but the sense of misery was there for any Reverend Mother to detect. It made everybody cross, short tempered in Council and not giving an inch of passageway in the corridors. All very childish and they laughed at it eventually, clearing the air somewhat, but the chill of an abrupt winter and the constant threat from Honoured Matres remained.

No survivors at all?

Bellonda shook her head from side to side in answer to Odrade's questioning look.

Lampadas—a jewel in the Sisterhood's network of planets, home of their most prized school, another lifeless ball of ashes and hardened melt. And the Bashar Alef Burzmali with all of his hand-picked defence force. *All dead?*

"All dead," Bellonda said.

Burzmali, favourite student of the old Bashar Teg, gone and nothing gained by it. Lampadas—the marvellous library, the brilliant teachers, the premier students . . . all gone.

"Even Lucilla?" Odrade asked. The Reverend Mother Lucilla, vice chancellor of Lampadas, had been instructed to flee at the first sign of trouble, taking with her as many of the doomed as she could store in Other Memory.

"The spies said all dead," Bellonda insisted.

It was a chilling signal to surviving Bene Gesserits: "You may be next!"

How could any human society be anaesthetized to such brutality? Odrade wondered. She visualized the news with breakfast at some Honoured Matre base: "They've destroyed another Bene Gesserit planet. Ten billion dead, they say. That makes six planets this month, doesn't it? Pass the cream, will you, dear?"

Almost glassy-eyed with horror, Odrade picked up the

report and glanced through it. *From the Rabbi, no doubt of that.* She put it down gently and looked at her Councillors.

Bellonda—old, fat and florid, Mentat-Archivist, wearing lenses to read now, uncaring what that revealed about her. Bellonda showed her blunt teeth in a wide grimace that said more than words. She had seen Odrade's reaction to the report. Bell might argue once more for retaliation in kind. That could be expected from someone valued for her natural viciousness. She needed to be thrown back into Mentat mode where she would be more analytical.

In her own way, Bell is right, Odrade thought. *But she won't like what I have in mind. I must be cautious in what I say now. Too soon to reveal my plan.*

"There are circumstances where viciousness can blunt viciousness," Odrade said. "We must consider it carefully."

There! That would forestall Bell's outburst.

Tamalane shifted slightly in her chair. Odrade looked at the older woman. Tam, composed there behind her mask of critical patience. Snowy hair above that narrow face: the appearance of aged wisdom.

Odrade saw through the mask to Tam's extreme severity, the pose that said she disliked everything she saw and heard.

In contrast to the surface softness of Bell's flesh, there was a bony solidity to Tamalane. She still kept herself in trim, her muscles as well-toned as possible. In her eyes, though, was the thing that belied this: *a sense of withdrawing there, pulling back from life.* Oh, she observed yet, but something had begun the final retreat. Tamalane's famed intelligence had become a kind of shrewdness, relying mostly on past observations and past decisions rather than on what she saw in the immediate present.

We must begin readying a replacement. It will be Sheeana, I think. Sheeana is young and shows great promise. And Sheeana was blooded on Dune.

Odrade focused on Tamalane's shaggy eyebrows. They tended to hang over her lids in a concealing disarray. *Yes. Sheeana to replace Tamalane.*

Knowing the complicated problems they must solve, Tam would accept the decision. At the moment of announcement,

Odrade knew she would only have to turn Tam's attention to the enormity of their predicament.

I will miss her, dammit!

> You cannot know history unless you know how leaders move with its currents. Every leader requires outsiders to perpetuate his leadership. Examine my career: I was leader and outsider. Do not assume I merely created a Church-State. That was my function as leader and I copied historical models. Barbaric arts of my time reveal me as outsider. Favourite poetry: Epics. Popular dramatic ideal: heroism. Dances: wildly abandoned. Stimulants to make people sense what I took from them. What did I take? The right to choose a role in history.
>
> ——Leto II (The Tyrant)
> Vether Bebe Translation

I am going to die! Lucilla thought.

Please, dear sisters, don't let it come before I pass along the precious burden I carry in my mind!

Sisters!

The idea of family seldom was expressed among the Bene Gesserit but it was there. In a genetic sense, they *were* related. And because of Other Memory, they often knew where. They had no need for special terms such as "second cousin" or "great aunt". They saw the relationships as a weaver sees his cloth. They knew how the warp and weft created the fabric. A better word than Family, it was the *fabric* of the Bene Gesserit that formed the Sisterhood but it was the ancient instinct of Family that provided the warp.

Lucilla thought of her sisters only as Family now. The Family needed what she carried.

I was a fool to seek refuge on Gammu!

But her damaged no-ship would limp no further. How diabolically extravagant the Honoured Matres had been! The hatred this implied terrified her.

Strewing the escape lanes around Lampadas with death-traps, the Foldspace perimeter seeded with small no-globes,

32

each containing a field projector and a lasgun to fire on contact. When the laser hit the Holzmann generator in the no-globe, a chain reaction released the nuclear energy. Bzzz into the trap field and a devastating explosion spread silently across you. Costly but efficient! Enough such explosions and even a giant Guildship would become a crippled derelict in the void. Her ship's system of defensive analyses had penetrated the nature of the trap only when it was too late, but she had been lucky, she supposed.

She did not feel lucky as she looked out the second storey window of this isolated Gammu farmhouse. The window was open and an afternoon breeze carried the inevitable smell of oil, something dirty in the smoke of a fire out there. The Harkonnens had left their oily mark on this planet so deep it might never be removed.

Her contact here was supposedly a Suk doctor but she knew him as much more, something so secret that only a limited number in the Bene Gesserit shared it. The knowledge lay in a special classification: *The secrets of which we do not speak, even among ourselves for that would harm us. The secrets we do not pass from sister to sister in the Sharing of lives for there is no open path. The secrets we dare not know until a need arises.* Lucilla had stumbled into it after veiled remarks by Odrade.

"You know an interesting thing about Gammu? Mmmmm, there's a whole society there that bands itself on the basis that they all eat consecrated foods. A custom brought in by immigrants who have never been assimilated. Keep to themselves, frown on outbreeding, that sort of thing. They ignite the usual mythic detritus, of course: whispers, rumours. Serves to isolate them even more. Precisely what they want."

Lucilla knew of an ancient society that fitted itself neatly into this description. She was curious. The society she had in mind supposedly had died out shortly after the Second Interspace Migrations. Judicious browsing in Archives whetted her curiosity even more. Living styles, rumour-fogged descriptions of religious rituals—especially the candelabra—and the keeping of special holy days with a proscription against any work on those days. And they were not just on Gammu!

33

Odrade's casual remarks took on the colour of something profoundly secret.

One morning, taking advantage of an uncommon lull, Lucilla entered the workroom to test her "projective surmise", something not as reliable as a Mentat's equivalent but more than theory.

"You have a new assignment for me, I suspect."

"I see you've been spending time in Archives."

"It seemed a profitable thing to do just now."

"Making connections?"

"A surmise." *That secret society on Gammu—they're Jews, aren't they?*

"You may have need of special information because of where we are about to post you." Extremely casual.

Lucilla sank into Bellonda's chairdog without invitation.

Odrade picked up a stylus, scribbled on a sheet of disposable and passed it to Lucilla in a way that hid it from the comeyes.

Lucilla took the hint and bent over the message, holding it close beneath the shield of her head.

"Your surmise is correct. You must die before revealing it. That is the price of their cooperation, a mark of great trust." Lucilla shredded the message.

Odrade used eye and palm identification to unseal a panel on the wall behind her. She removed a small ridulian crystal and handed it to Lucilla. It was warm but Lucilla felt a chill. What could be so secret? Odrade swung the security hood from beneath her worktable and pivoted it into position.

Lucilla dropped the crystal into its receptacle with a trembling hand and pulled the hood over her head. Immediately, words formed in her mind, an oral sense of extremely old accents clipped for recognition: "The people to whom your attention has been called are the Jews. They made a defensive decision eons ago. The solution to recurrent pogroms was to vanish from public view. Space travel made this not only possible but attractive. They hid on countless planets—their own Scattering—and they probably have planets where only their people live. This does not mean they have abandoned age-old practices in which they excelled out of survival necessity. The old religion is sure to persist even though somewhat

34

altered. It is probable that a rabbi from ancient times would not find himself out of place behind the Sabbath minora of a Jewish household in your age. But their secrecy is such that you could work a lifetime beside a Jew and never suspect. They call it 'Complete Cover', although they know its dangers."

Lucilla accepted this without question. That which is so secret would be perceived as dangerous by anyone who even suspected its presence. *"Else why do they keep it secret, eh? Answer me that!"*

The crystal continued to pour its secrets into her awareness: "At the threat of discovery, they have a standard reaction, 'We seek the religion of our roots. It is a revival, bringing back what is best from our past.'"

Lucilla knew this pattern. There were always "nutty revivalists". It was guaranteed to blunt most curiosity. "Them? Oh, they're another bunch of revivalists."

"The masking system (the crystal continued) did not succeed with us. We have our own well-recorded Jewish heritage and a fund of Other Memory to tell us reasons for secrecy. We did not disturb the situation until I, Mother Superior during and after the battle of Corrin (*Very old, indeed!*), saw that our Sisterhood had need of a secret society, a group responsive to our requests for assistance."

Lucilla felt a surge of scepticism. *"Requests?"*

The long-ago Mother Superior had anticipated scepticism. "On occasion, we make demands they cannot avoid. But they make demands on us, as well."

Lucilla felt immersed in the mystique of this underground society. It was more than ultrasecret. Her clumsy questions in Archives had elicited mostly rejections. "Jews? What's that? Oh, yes—an ancient sect. Look it up for yourself. We don't have time for idle religious research."

The crystal had more to impart: "Jews are amused and sometimes dismayed at what they interpret as our copying them. Our breeding records dominated by the female line to control the mating pattern are seen as Jewish. You are only a Jew if your mother was a Jew."

It's a wise child who knows his own father, Lucilla thought. It

35

was amusing. Reverend Mothers often did not know their parents even after the Agony. Memory had to be brought forward and organized, breaking through barriers at times. Selective Memory was a reality else all was chaos in a new Reverend Mother. "The title carries great meaning but it is not a licence for omnipotence," Proctors had warned her.

The crystal came to its conclusion: "The diaspora will be remembered. Keeping this secret involves our deepest honour."

Lucilla lifted the hood from her head. She felt that she had spent a lifetime under it, coming out a person profoundly changed.

"You are a very good choice for an extremely touchy assignment on Lampadas," Odrade had said, restoring the crystal to its hiding place.

That is the past and likely dead. Look where Odrade's "touchy assignment" has brought me!

From her vantage in the Gammu farmhouse, Lucilla noted that a large produce carrier had entered the grounds. There was a bustle of activity below her. Workers came from all sides to meet the big carrier with towbins of vegetables. She smelled the pungent juices from the cut stems of marrows.

Lucilla did not move from the window. Her host had supplied her with local garments—a long gown of drab grey everwear and a bright blue headscarf to confine her sandy hair. It was important to do nothing calling undue attention to herself. She had seen other women pause to watch the farm work. Her presence here could be taken as curiosity.

It was a large carrier, its suspensors labouring under the load of produce already piled in its articulated sections. The operator stood in a transparent house at the front, hands on the steering lever, eyes straight ahead. His legs were spread wide and he leaned into the web of sloping supports, touching the power bar with his left hip. He was a large man, face dark and deeply-wrinkled, hair laced with grey. His body was an extension of the machinery—guiding ponderous movement. He flicked his gaze up to Lucilla as he passed, then back to the track into the wide loading area defined by buildings below her.

Built into his machine, she thought. That said something about the way humans were fitted to the things they did. Lucilla sensed a weakening force in this thought. If you fitted yourself too tightly to one thing, other abilities atrophied. *We become what we do.*

She pictured herself suddenly as another operator in some great machine, no different from that man in the carrier.

We move ahead with stately determination, each bent on a secret course. Bent is the proper word. As the operator is bent, so goes the course. Everything that happens can be blamed on Fate. A most useful function for Fate or God. If things go wrong you have someone other than yourself to blame. Sacrificial goats, the mortal shape of ancient gods. And how am I better than a chauffeur to vegetables?

Self-pity! How easy to fall into that trap.

The big carrier trundled past her out of the yard, its operator not sparing her another glance. He had seen her once. Why look twice?

Her hosts had made a wise choice in this hiding place, she thought. A sparsely populated area with trustworthy workers in the immediate vicinity and little curiosity among the people who passed. Hard work dulled curiosity. She had noted the character of the area when she was brought here. Evening then and people already trudging toward their homes. You could measure the urban density of an area by when work stopped. Early to bed and you were in a loosely-packed region. Night activity said people remained restless, twitchy with inner awareness of others active and vibrating too near.

What has brought me to this introspective state?

Early in the Sisterhood's first retreat, before the worst onslaughts of the Honoured Matres, Lucilla had experienced difficulty coming to grips with belief that "someone out there is hunting us with intent to kill".

Pogrom! That was what the Rabbi had called it before going off that morning "to see what I can do for you".

She knew the Rabbi had chosen his word from long and bitter memory, but not since her first experience of Gammu before this *pogrom* had Lucilla felt such confinement to circumstances she could not control.

I was a fugitive then, too.

The Sisterhood's present situation bore similarities to what they had suffered under the Tyrant, except that the *God Emperor* obviously (in retrospect) never intended to exterminate the Bene Gesserit, only to rule them. And he certainly ruled!

Where is that damned Rabbi?

He was a large, intense man with old fashioned spectacles. A broad face browned by much sunlight. Few wrinkles despite the age she could read in his voice and movements. The spectacles focused attention on deeply set brown eyes that watched her with peculiar intensity. *Couldn't he unbend from his damned religion enough to use the common medical adjustments for eyesight problems? In extreme cases, there are always wearever contacts. Or is this a small gesture on his part, something to say: "I don't go for all of this technological nonsense."*

But he said he had been a Suk doctor. Retired now, but still . . .

"Honoured Matres," he had said (right here in this barewalled upper room) when she explained her predicament. "Oh, my! That is difficult."

Lucilla had expected that response and, what was more, she could see he knew it.

"There is a Guild Navigator on Gammu helping the search for you," he said. "It is one of the Edrics, very powerful, I am told."

"I have Siona blood. He cannot *see* me."

"Nor me nor any of my people and for the same reason. We Jews adjust to many necessities, you know."

"This Edric is a gesture," she said. "He can do little."

"But they have brought him. I'm afraid there is no way we can get you safely off the planet."

"Then what can we do?"

"We will see. My people are not entirely helpless, you understand?"

She recognized sincerity and concern for her. He spoke quietly of resisting the sexual blandishments of Honoured Matres, "doing it unobtrusively so as not to arouse them."

38

"I will go whisper in a few ears," he said.

She felt oddly restored by this. There often was something coldly remote and cruel about falling into the hands of the medical professions. She reassured herself with the knowledge that Suks were conditioned to be alert to your needs, compassionate and supportive (*all of those things that can fall by the wayside in emergencies*). She had noted this lapse even among Sisters who became Suks: an objective posture that dulled their clinical sensitivity.

That was why Proctors often said their charges should welcome quick (even violent) ends, "provided, of course, you can Share your memories."

My present predicament exactly.

She bent her efforts then to restoring calm, focusing on the personal mantra she had gained in *solo death education*.

If I am to die, I must pass along a transcendental lesson. I must leave with serenity.

That helped but still she felt a trembling. The Rabbi had been gone too long. Something was wrong.

Was I right to trust him?

He spoke so much of understanding and knowing. *Comprehension*. It was an attitude Bene Gesserits were taught to distrust. "Comprehension strews tacks in your path." Ready comprehension was the most dangerous and could be the most painful. But there was always the lure of *understanding*. It raised opaque screens against learning. "Understand nothing. All comprehension is temporary."

Despite a growing sense of doom, Lucilla forced herself to practise Bene Gesserit naivete as she reviewed her encounter with the Rabbi. Her Proctors had called this "the innocence that goes naturally with inexperience, a condition often confused with ignorance". Into this naivete all things flowed. It was close to Mentat performance. Information entered without prejudgment. "You are a mirror upon which the universe is reflected. That reflection is all you experience. Images bounce from your senses. Hypotheses arise. Important even when wrong. Here is the exceptional case where more than one wrong can produce dependable decisions."

"We are your willing servants," the Rabbi had said.

That was guaranteed to alert a Reverend Mother.

We look for the profit.

The explanations of Odrade's crystal felt suddenly inadequate. *It's almost always profit.* She accepted this as cynical but from vast experience. Attempts to weed it out of human behaviour always broke up on the rocks of application. Socializing and communistic systems only changed the counters that measured profits. Enormous managerial bureaucracies—the counter was power.

Lucilla warned herself that the manifestations were always the same. Look at this Rabbi's extensive farm! Retirement retreat for a Suk? She had seen something of what lay behind the establishment: servants, richer quarters. And there must be more. No matter the system it was always the same: the best foods, beautiful lovers, unrestricted travel, magnificent holiday accommodations.

It gets very tiresome when you've seen it as often as we have.

She knew her mind was jittering but felt powerless to prevent it. *Money and other counters in an endless game. Trade goods. Melange could dominate that again. On Dune, it was water. Survival. The very bottom of the demand system is always survival.*

And I threaten the survival of the Rabbi and his people.

He had fawned upon her. *Always beware of those who fawn upon us, nuzzling up to all of that power we're supposed to have. How flattering to find great mobs of servants waiting and anxious to do our bidding! How utterly debilitating.*

The mistake of the Honoured Matres.

What is delaying the Rabbi?

Was he seeing how much he could get for the Reverend Mother Lucilla? *Always those economic considerations that devolved to questions of energy. A great deal of visible energy in this farm. How many people? How many man-hours? Atrocious concept. Reduce humans to the level of beasts. On a par with horsepower. Manpower, horsepower—what was the difference except in applied energy?*

Lucilla reined in her thoughts. The difference lay in what the Bene Gesserit did, the constant struggle to perfect human society. Wild beasts engaged in murder and cannibalism without thought. *Consciousness*. That was the name of constant challenge. *Of what am I aware?* There lay her leverage: Even if you lumped in all of the "worst times", humans committed fewer acts of violence than did wild animals.

We're a different sort of beast. It's conscious cruelty that most offends us. The aware bestiality. Gloating cruelty that indulges in creating pain for the enjoyment of watching it. Sadism. The mindless beast in the depths.

The worm that guarded the pearl of great price was only a metaphor to describe the beast in every human. And she had seen no gloating cruelty in the Rabbi. This reassured her.

A door slammed below her, shaking the floor under her feet. She heard hurried footsteps on a stairway. How primitive these people were. Stairways! Lucilla turned as the door opened. The Rabbi entered bringing a rich smell of melange. He stood by the door assessing her mood.

"Forgive my tardiness, dear lady. I was summoned for questioning by Edric, the Guild Navigator."

That explained the smell of spice. Navigators were forever bathed in the orange gas of melange, their features often fogged by the vapours. Lucilla could visualize the Navigator's tiny "V" of a mouth and the ugly flap of nose. Mouth and nose appeared so small on a Navigator's gigantic face with its pulsing temples. She knew how threatened the Rabbi must have felt listening to the singsong ululations of the Navigator's voice with its simultaneous mechtranslation into impersonal Galach.

"What did he want?"

"You."

"Does he . . ."

"He does not know for sure but I am certain he suspects us. However, he suspects everybody."

"Did they follow . . ."

"Not necessary. They can find me any time they want."

"What shall we do?" She knew she spoke too fast, much too loud.

"Dear lady . . ." He came three steps closer and she saw the perspiration on his forehead and nose. Fear. She could smell it.

41

"Well, what is it?"

"The economic view behind the activities of the Honoured Matres—we find them quite interesting."

His words crystallized her fears. *I knew it! He's selling me out!*

"As you Reverend Mothers know very well, there are always gaps in economic systems."

"Yes?" Profoundly wary.

"Incomplete suppression of trade in any commodity always increases the profits of the tradesmen, especially the profits of the senior distributors." His voice was warningly hesitant. "That is the fallacy of thinking you can control unwanted narcotics by stopping them at your borders."

What was he trying to tell her? His words described elementary facts known even to acolytes. Increased profits were always used to buy safe paths past border guards, often by buying the guards themselves.

Has he bought servants of the Honoured Matres? Surely, he doesn't believe he can do that safely.

She waited while he composed his thoughts, obviously forming a presentation he believed most likely to gain her acceptance.

Why did he point her attention toward border guards? That certainly was what he had done. Guards always had a ready rationalization for betraying their superiors, of course. "If I don't, someone else will." There was the further inescapable fact that guards soon became cynical with knowledge of how their superiors chose which commodities to keep out. It was based mostly on taxation.

"Pass only those things you can safely tax without alienating those who support you."

(Meaning those things upon which it was possible to collect the duty.) Smugglers were only gadflies in this. The real aim was to keep unwanted imports to a manageable minimum.

"There are always power brokers," the Rabbi said.

She thought he was going to say more but again, he hesitated.

Power brokers? The people at the top knew very well they could not provide perfect barriers at their borders.

42

Furthermore, they knew they made their whole operation important for their own employment by promising perfect barriers. Another grand illusion. Guards know there would be fewer of them if the unwanted items were allowed past the borders without any interference except a minimal duty.

Am I such an unwanted item?

She dared to hope.

The Rabbi cleared his throat. It was apparent he had found the words he wanted and had placed them in order.

"I do not believe there is any way to get you off Gammu alive."

She had not expected such a blunt condemnation. "But the . . ."

"The information you carry, that is a different matter," he said.

So that was behind all of the focusing on borders and guards!

"You don't see it, Rabbi. My information is not just a few words and some warnings." She tapped a finger against her forehead. "In here are many precious lives, all of those irreplaceable experiences, learning so vital that . . ."

"Ahhh, but I do understand, dear lady. Our problem is that *you* do not understand."

Always these references to understanding!

"It is your honour upon which I depend at this moment," he said.

Ahhh, the legendary honesty and trustworthiness of the Bene Gesserit when we have given our word!

"You know I will die rather than betray you," she said.

He spread his hands wide in a rather helpless gesture. "I am fully confident of that, dear lady. The question is not one of betrayal but of something we have never before revealed to your Sisterhood."

"What are you trying to tell me?" Quite peremptory, almost with Voice (which she had been warned not to try on these Jews).

"I must exact a promise from you. I must have your word that you will not turn against us because of what I am about to reveal. You must promise to accept my solution to our dilemma."

43

"Sight unseen?"

"Only because I ask it of you and assure you that we honour our commitment to your Sisterhood."

She glared at him, trying to see through this barrier he had erected between them. His surface reactions could be read but not the mysterious thing beneath his unexpected behaviour.

The Rabbi waited for this fearsome woman to reach her decision. Reverend Mothers always made him uneasy. He knew what her decision must be and pitied her. He saw that she could read the pity in his expression. They knew so much and so little. Their powers were manifest. And their knowledge of Secret Israel so perilous!

We owe them this debt, though. She is not of the Chosen, but a debt is a debt. Honour is honour. Truth is truth.

The Bene Gesserit had preserved Secret Israel in many hours of need. And a pogrom was something his people knew without lengthy explanations. Pogrom was imbedded in the psyche of Secret Israel. And thanks to the *Unspeakable*, the chosen people would never forget. No more than they could forgive.

Memory kept fresh in daily ritual (with periodic emphasis in communal sharings) cast a glowing halo on what the Rabbi knew he must do. And this poor woman! She, too, was trapped by memories and circumstances.

Into the cauldron! Both of us!

"You have my word," Lucilla said.

The Rabbi returned to the room's only door and opened it. An older woman in a long brown gown stood there. She stepped in at the Rabbi's beckoning gesture. Hair the colour of old driftwood neatly bound in a bun at the back of her head. Face pinched in and wrinkled, dark as a dried almond. The eyes, though! Total blue! and that steely hardness within them . . .

"This is Rebecca, one of our people," the Rabbi said. "As I am sure you can see, she has done a dangerous thing."

"The Agony," Lucilla whispered.

"She did it long ago and she serves us well. Now, she will serve you."

Lucilla had to be certain. "Can you Share?"

"I have never done it, lady, but I know it." As Rebecca spoke, she approached Lucilla and stopped when they were almost touching.

They leaned toward each other until their foreheads made contact. Their hands went out and gripped the offered shoulders.

As their minds locked, Lucilla forced a projective thought: "This must get to my sisters!"

"I promise, dear lady."

There could be no deception in this total mixing of minds, this ultimate candour powered by imminent and certain death or the poisonous melange essence that ancient Fremen had rightly called "the little death". Lucilla accepted Rebecca's promise. This wild Reverend Mother of the Jews committed her life to the assurance. Something else! Lucilla gasped as she saw it. The Rabbi intended to sell her to the Honoured Matres. The driver of the produce carrier had been one of their agents come to confirm that there was indeed a woman of Lucilla's description at the farm house. *Nothing more bent than that!*

Rebecca's candour gave Lucilla no escape: "It is the only way we can save ourselves and maintain our credibility."

So that was why the Rabbi had made her think of guards and power brokers! *Clever, clever. And I accept it as he knew I would.*

> *Confine yourself to observing and you always miss the point of your own life. The object can be stated this way: live the best life you can. Life is a game whose rules you learn if you leap into it and play it to the hilt. Otherwise, you are caught off balance, continually surprised by the shifting play. Non-players often whine and complain that luck always passes them by. They refuse to see that they can create some of their own luck.*
>
> —Darwi Odrade

"Have you studied the latest comeye record of Idaho?" Bellonda asked.

"Later! Later!" Odrade knew she was feeling peckish and it had come out in this response to Bell's pertinent question.

Pressures confined the Mother Superior more and more these days. She had always tried to face her duties with an attitude of broad interest. The more things to interest her, the wider her scan and that was sure to bring more usable data. Using the senses improved them. Substance, that was what her questing interests desired. Substance. It was like hunting for food to assuage a deep hunger.

But her days were becoming duplicates of this morning. Her liking for personal inspections was well known but these workroom walls held her. She must be where she could be reached. Not only reached, but able to dispatch communications and people on the instant.

Damn! I will make the time. I must!

It was time pressure as much as anything.

Sheeana said: "We trundle along on borrowed days."

Very poetic! Not much help in the face of pragmatic demands. They had to get as many Bene Gesserit cells as possible Scattered before the axe fell. Nothing else had that priority. The Bene Gesserit fabric was being torn apart, sent to destinations no one on Chapter House could know. Sometimes, Odrade saw this flow as rags and remnants. They went flapping away in their no-ships, a stock of sandtrout in their holds, Bene Gesserit traditions, learning and memories as guide. But the Sisterhood had done this long ago in the first Scattering and none came back or sent a message. Not one. Only Honoured Matres returned. If they had ever been Bene Gesserit, they now were a terrible distortion, blindly suicidal.

Will we ever be whole again?

Odrade looked down at the work waiting on her table: more selection charts. Who shall go and who shall remain? There was little time to pause and take a deep breath. Other Memory from her late predecessor, Taraza, took on an "I told you so!" character. "See what I had to go through?"

And I once wondered if there was room at the top.

There might be room at the top (as she was fond of telling acolytes) but there was seldom enough time.

When she thought of the largely passive non-Bene Gesserit populace "out there", Odrade sometimes envied them. They were permitted their illusions. What a comfort. You could pretend your life was forever, that tomorrow would be better, that the gods in their heavens watched you with care.

She recoiled from this lapse with disgust at herself. The unclouded eye was better, no matter what it saw.

"I've studied the latest Idaho records," she said, looking across the table at the patient Bellonda.

"He has interesting instincts," Bellonda said.

Odrade thought about that. Comeyes throughout the no-ship missed little. The Council's theory about ghola Idaho became daily less a theory and more a conviction. How many memories from the serial Idaho lifetimes did this ghola contain?

"Tam is raising doubts about their children," Bellonda said.

That was to be expected. The three children Murbella had borne Idaho in the no-ship had been removed at birth. All were being observed with care as they developed. Did they have that uncanny reactive speed Honoured Matres displayed? Too early to say. It was a thing that developed in puberty, according to Murbella.

Their captive Honoured Matre accepted the removal of her children with angry resignation. Idaho, however, showed little reaction. Odd. Did something give him a broader view of procreation? Almost a Bene Gesserit view?

"Another Bene Gesserit breeding programme," he sneered.

Odrade let her thoughts flow. Was it really the Bene Gesserit attitude they saw in Idaho? The Sisterhood said emotional attachments were ancient detritus—important for human survival in their day but not required in the Bene Gesserit plan.

Instincts.

Things that came with egg and sperm. Often vital and loud: "This is the species talking to you, dolt!"

Loves . . . offspring . . . hungers . . . All of those unconscious motives to compel specific behaviour. It was dangerous

47

to meddle in such matters. The Breeding Mistresses knew this even while they did it. The Council debated it periodically and ordered a careful watch on consequences.

"You've studied the records. Is that all the answer I get?" Quite plaintive for Bellonda.

Bell knows what I'm doing! Odrade thought. *Composing my response with care. I cannot say anything without it being interpreted through the universal Bene Gesserit filter, everything suspect and always that unspoken question: "What did she really mean?"*

The comeye record of such interest to Bell: Idaho questioning Murbella about Honoured Matre sexual-addiction techniques. *Why?* His parallel abilities came from Tleilaxu conditioning impressed on his cells in the axolotl tank. Idaho's abilities originated as an unconscious pattern akin to instincts but the result was indistinguishable from the Honoured Matre effect: Ecstasy amplified until it drove out all reason and bound its victims to the source of such rewards.

Murbella went only so far in a verbal exploration of her abilities. Obvious residual fury that Idaho had addicted her with the same techniques she had been taught to use. She knew he had done this in response to the Tleilaxu triggers. That had redirected part of her suppressed anger toward the Bene Tleilax. Bell thought that might be useful when they turned Murbella's attention toward Scytale.

"Murbella blocks up when Idaho questions motives," Bellonda said.

Yes, I've seen that.

"I could kill you and you know it!" Murbella had said.

The comeye record showed them in bed in Murbella's no-ship quarters, having just satiated their mutual addiction. Sweat glistened on bare flesh. Murbella lay with a blue towel across her forehead, green eyes staring up at the comeyes. She appeared to be looking directly at the observers. Little orange flecks in her eyes. Anger flecks from her body's residual store of the spice substitute Honoured Matres employed. She was on melange now—and no adverse symptoms.

Idaho lay beside her, black hair in disarray around his face, a sharp contrast to the white pillow beneath his head. His eyes were closed but the lids flickered. Thin. He wasn't eating enough despite tempting dishes sent by Odrade's own chef. His high cheekbones were strongly defined. The face had become craggy in the years of his confinement.

Murbella's threat was backed by physical ability, Odrade knew, but it was psychologically false. *Kill her lover? Not likely!*

Bellonda was thinking along these same lines. "What was she doing when she demonstrated her physical speed? We've seen that before."

"She knows we watch."

The comeyes showed Murbella defying post-coital fatigue to leap from bed. Moving with blurred speed (so much faster than anything the Bene Gesserit had ever achieved), she kicked out with her right foot, stopping the blow only a hair's breadth from Idaho's head.

At her first movement, Idaho opened his eyes. He watched without fear, without flinching.

That blow! Fatal if it struck. You had only to see such a thing once to fear it. Murbella moved with no resort to her central cortex. Insect-like, an attack triggered by nerves at the point of muscle ignition.

"You see!" Murbella lowered her foot and glared down at him.

Idaho smiled.

Watching it, Odrade reminded herself that the Sisterhood had three of Murbella's children, all female. The Breeding Mistresses were excited. In time, Reverend Mothers born of this line might match that Honoured Matre ability.

In time we probably don't have.

That was a necessary, if constant, reminder of the hunter's axe.

But Odrade shared the excitement of the Breeding Mistresses. That speed! Add that to the nerve-muscle training, the great prana-bindu resources of the Sisterhood! What that might create lay wordlessly within her.

"She did that for us, not for him," Bellonda said.

Odrade was not sure. Murbella resented the constant watch over her but she had come to an accommodation with it. Many of her actions obviously ignored the people behind the com-eyes. This record showed her returning to her place in the bed beside Idaho.

"I have restricted access to that record," Bellonda said. "Some acolytes are becoming troubled."

Odrade nodded. *Sexual addiction*. That aspect of Honoured Matre abilities created disturbing ripples in the Bene Gesserit, especially among acolytes. Very suggestive. And most of the sisters on Chapter House knew that the Reverend Mother Sheeana, alone among them, practised some of these techni-ques in defiance of a general fear that this could weaken them.

"We must not become Honoured Matres!" Bell was always saying that. *But Sheeana represents a significant control factor. She teaches us something about Murbella.*

One afternoon, catching Murbella alone in her no-ship quarters and obviously relaxed, Odrade had tried a direct question. "Before Idaho, were none of you ever tempted to, let us say, 'join in the fun'?"

Murbella had recoiled with angry pride. "He caught me by accident!"

The same kind of anger she showed to Idaho's questions. Remembering this, Odrade leaned over her worktable in Central and called up the original record.

"Look at how angry she gets," Bellonda said. "A hypno-trance injunction against answering such questions. I'd stake my reputation on it."

"That'll come out in the Spice Agony," Odrade said.

"If she ever gets to it!"

"Hypnotrance is supposed to be our secret."

Bellonda chewed on the obvious inference: *No sister we sent out in the original Scattering ever returned.*

It was written large in their minds: "Did renegade Bene Gesserits create the Honoured Matres?" Much suggested it. Then why did they resort to sexual enslavement of males? Murbella's historical prattlings did not satisfy. Everything about this went against Bene Gesserit teaching.

"We have to learn," Bellonda insisted. "What little we know is very disturbing."

Odrade recognized the concern. How much of a lure was

this ability? Very big, she thought. Acolytes complained that they dreamed about becoming Honoured Matres. Bellonda was rightly worried.

Create and/or arouse such unbridled forces and you built carnal fantasies of enormous complexity. You could lead whole populations around by their desires, by their fantasy projections.

There was the terrible power the Honoured Matres dared use. Let it be known that they had the key to blinding ecstasy and they had won half the battle. The simple clue that such a thing existed, that was the beginning of surrender. People at Murbella's level in that other sisterhood might not understand this but the ones at the top . . . Was it possible they merely used this power without caring or even suspecting its deeper force? *If that were the case, how were our first Scattered Ones lured into this dead end?*

Earlier, Bellonda had offered her hypothesis:

Honoured Matre with captive Reverend Mother taken prisoner in that first Scattering. "Welcome, Reverend Mother. We would like you to witness a small demonstration of our powers." Interlude of sexual demonstration followed by a display of Honoured Matre physical speed. Then—withdrawal of melange and injection of the adrenalin-based substitute laced with a hypnodrug. In that hypothetical trance, the Reverend Mother was sexually imprinted.

That coupled to the selective agony of melange withdrawal (Bell suggested) might make the victim deny her origins.

Fates help us! Were the original Honoured Matres all Reverend Mothers? Do we dare test this hypothesis on ourselves? What can we learn of this from that pair in the no-ship?

Two sources of information lay there under the Sisterhood's watchful eyes but the key had yet to be found.

Woman and man no longer just breeding partners, no longer a comfort and support to each other. Something new has been added. The stakes have been escalated.

In the comeye record playing at the worktable, Murbella said something that caught the Mother Superior's full attention.

51

"We Honoured Matres did this to ourselves! Can't blame anyone else."

"You hear that?" Bellonda demanded.

Odrade shook her head sharply, wanting all of her attention on this exchange.

"You can't say the same about me," Idaho objected.

"That's an empty excuse," Murbella accused. "So you were conditioned by the Tleilaxu to snare the first Imprinter you encountered!"

"And to kill her," Idaho corrected. "That's what they intended."

"But you didn't even try to kill me. Not that you could have."

"That's when . . ." Idaho broke off with an involuntary glance at the recording comeyes.

"What was he about to say there?" Bellonda pounced. "We must find out!"

But Odrade continued her silent observation of the captive pair. Murbella demonstrated a surprising insight. "You think you caught me through some accident in which you were not involved?"

"Exactly."

"But I see something in you that accepted all of it! You didn't just go along with your conditioning. You performed to your limits."

An inward look filmed Idaho's eyes. He tipped his head back, stretching his chest muscles.

"That's a Mentat expression!" Bellonda accused.

All of Odrade's analysts suggested this but they had yet to wrest an admission from Idaho. If he was a Mentat, why withhold that information?

Because of the other things implied by such abilities. He fears us and rightly so.

Murbella spoke with a sneer. "You improvised and improved on what the Tleilaxu did to you. There was something in you that made no complaint whatsoever!"

"That's how she deals with her own guilt feelings," Bellonda said. "She has to believe it's true or Idaho would not have been able to trap her."

52

Odrade pursed her lips. The projection showed Idaho amused. "Perhaps it was the same for both of us."

"You can't blame the Tleilaxu and I can't blame the Honoured Matres."

Tamalane entered the workroom and sank into her chairdog beside Bellonda. "I see it has your interest, too." She gestured at the projected figures.

Odrade shut down the projector.

"I've been inspecting our axolotl tanks," Tamalane said. "That damned Scytale has withheld vital information."

"There's no flaw in our first ghola, is there?" Bellonda demanded.

"Nothing our Suks can find."

Odrade spoke in a mild tone: "Scytale has to keep some bargaining chips."

"It's a dirty business," Tamalane complained.

Odrade could only agree. Information poured from their captive Tleilaxu. *We ask and Scytale reveals . . . up to his bargaining limits.*

Both sides shared a fantasy: Scytale was paying the Bene Gesserit for rescue from the Honoured Matres and sanctuary on Chapter House. But every Reverend Mother who studied him knew something else drove the last Tleilaxu Master.

Clever, clever, the Bene Tleilax. Far more clever than we suspected. And they have dirtied us with their axolotl tanks. The very word "tank"—another of their deceptions. We pictured containers of warmed amniotic fluid, each "tank" the focus of complex machinery to duplicate (in a subtle, discreet and controllable way) the workings of the womb. The "tank" is there all right! But look at what it contains.

The Tleilaxu solution was direct: Use the original. Nature already had worked it out over the eons. All the Bene Tleilax need do was add their own control system, their own way of replicating information stored in the cell.

"The Language of God," Scytale called it. *Language of Shaitan was more appropriate.*

Feedback. The cell directed its own womb. That was more or less what a fertilized ovum did anyway. The Tleilaxu merely refined it.

53

"Is not the original birth already in the cell?"

Scytale always asked it in a coy and devilish way.

A sigh escaped Odrade bringing sharp glances from her companions. *Does Mother Superior have new troubles?*

Scytale's revelations trouble me. And what those revelations have done to us. Oh, how we recoiled from the "debasement". Then, rationalizations. And we knew they were rationalizations! "If there is no other way. If this produces the gholas we need so desperately. Volunteers probably can be found." Were found! Volunteers!

Bellonda intruded. "How much and what kind of planning goes into the creation of an Honoured Matre? That's what we must learn."

Bell knows what troubles me and she doesn't care to think about it any more than I do.

Odrade's glance flickered over Bellonda's face and then went searching across the workroom's walls. *What am I looking for? How cold this morning's light.*

That had been Bellonda-the-Breeding-Mistress. She wanted to know how like the Bene Gesserit were Honoured Matres in the powerful shaping of human potential.

Odrade felt cynical about the question.

What planning went into my occurrence?

She often liked to think of herself as an occurrence in the sexual cycle of humankind. A Reverend Mother had been sent to seduce and breed with the late Bashar Miles Teg. Result: One Darwi Odrade, another branching in the long Atreides line whose records Bell guarded so carefully. Bell thought of this as an essential part of a tightly-controlled breeding plan.

But accidentals always intrude, Bell.

The *occurrence* named Darwi Odrade possessed a secret randomity that pleased Odrade. *Uniqueness is never to be sneered at even when it takes the form of a Muad'Dib or his son, the Tyrant.*

Darwi Odrade, unique occurrence. And what do I do with my uniqueness? How does the careful plan progress?

It was that ages-old argument about Free Will. Mentats sharpened their abilities on it or were blunted by it and discarded. *We tend to ignore it.*

"You're woolgathering!" Tamalane grumbled. She glanced at Bellonda, started to say something and thought better of it.

Bellonda's face went soft-bland, a frequent accompaniment to her darker moods (and she had such moods despite her training and despite denials). Her voice came out little more than a guttural whisper. "I strongly urge that we eliminate Idaho. And as for that Tleilaxu monster . . ."

"Why do you make such a suggestion with a euphemism?" Tamalane demanded.

"Kill him then! And the Tleilaxu should be subjected to every persuasion we . . ."

"Stop it, both of you!" Odrade ordered.

She pressed both palms briefly against her forehead and, staring at the bow window, saw icy rain out there. Weather Control was making more mistakes. Couldn't blame them. Try to tune for rain across a wide area and you get sleet in some places. Attempt a regional temperature between twenty and twenty-two and the bottom dropped out of the system. You got frost and rime ice on puddles where the sleet had slushed. Nothing humans hated more than the unpredictable. *"We want it natural!" Whatever that means.*

When such thoughts came over her, Odrade longed for an existence confined to the order that pleased her: an occasional walk in the orchards. She enjoyed them in all seasons. A quiet evening with friends, the give and take of probing conversations that only the Sisterhood's initiates had carried to such high subtlety. *Jesuits magnified.* She liked to dredge up ancient Jesuitical arguments and parade them in newly-refined garb to please those for whom she felt warmth. *Affection? Yes.* The Mother Superior dared much—even love of companions. And good meals with drinks chosen for their enhancement of flavours. She wanted that, too. How fine it was to play upon the palate. And later . . . yes, later—a warm bed with a gentle companion sensitive to her needs as she was sensitive to his.

Most of this could not be, of course.

Responsibilities! What an enormous word. How it burned.

"I'm getting hungry," Odrade said. "Shall I order lunch served here?"

Bellonda and Tamalane stared at her. "It's only half past eleven," Tamalane complained.

"Yes or no?" Odrade insisted.

Bellonda and Tamalane exchanged a private look. "As you wish," Bellonda said.

There was a saying in the Bene Gesserit (Odrade knew) that the Sisterhood ran smoother when Mother Superior's stomach was satisfied. That had just tipped the scales.

Odrade keyed the intercom to her private kitchen. "Lunch for three, Duana. Something special. You choose."

Smiling her warmest, Odrade said: "It pleases me that you two can share Duana's artistry."

Tamalane did not change expression. Bellonda shrugged.

But she is an artist and they know it, Odrade thought. Her chef was a failed Reverend Mother, one who had been denied the Agony because of a genetically-determined metabolic flaw—something simple for a Suk to adjust but it would have come completely unstrung in the Agony. Duana compensated by being the best at what she enjoyed—cooking.

Lunch, when it came, featured a dish Odrade especially enjoyed, a veal casserole. Duana displayed a delicate touch with herbs, a bit of rosemary in the veal, the vegetables not overcooked. Superb.

Odrade savoured every bite. The other two plodded through the meal, spoon-to-mouth, spoon-to-mouth.

Is this one of the reasons I am Mother Superior and they are not?

While an acolyte cleared away the remains of lunch, Odrade turned to one of her favourite questions: "What is the gossip in the common rooms and among the acolytes?"

She remembered in her own acolyte days how she had hung on the words of the older women, expecting great truths and getting mostly small talk about Sister So-and-so or the latest problems of Proctor X. Occasionally, though, the barriers came down and important data flowed.

"Too many acolytes talk of wanting to go out in our Scattering," Tamalane rasped. "Sinking ships and rats, I say."

"There's a great interest in Archives lately," Bellonda said. "Sisters who know better come looking for confirmation—

whether such and so acolyte has a heavy Siona gene-mark."

Odrade found this interesting. Their common Atreides ancestor from the Tyrant's eons, Siona Ibn Fuad al-Seyefa Atreides, had imparted to her descendants this ability that hid them from prescient searchers. Every person walking openly on Chapter House shared that ancestral protection.

"A heavy mark?" Odrade asked. "Do they doubt that the ones in question are protected?"

"They want reassurance," Bellonda growled. "And now may I return to Idaho? He has the genetic mark and he does not. It worries me. Why do some of his cells not have the Siona marker? What were the Tleilaxu doing?"

"Duncan knows the danger and he's not suicidal," Odrade said.

"We don't know what he is," Bellonda complained.

"Probably a Mentat and we all know what that could mean," Tamalane said.

"I understand why we keep Murbella," Bellonda said. "Valuable information. But Idaho and Scytale . . ."

"That's enough!" Odrade snapped. "Watchdogs can bark too long!"

Bellonda accepted this grudgingly. *Watchdogs*. Their Bene Gesserit term for constant monitoring by sisters to see that you did not fall into shallow ways. Very trying to acolytes but just another part of life to Reverend Mothers.

Odrade had explained it one afternoon to Murbella, the two of them alone in a grey-walled interview chamber of the no-ship. Standing close together facing each other. Eyes at a level. Quite informal and intimate. Except for the knowledge of those comeyes all around them.

"Watchdogs," Odrade said, responding to a question from Murbella. "It means we are mutual gadflies. Don't make that more than it is. We seldom nag. A simple word can be enough."

Murbella, her oval face drawn into a look of distaste, the wide-set green eyes intent, obviously thought Odrade referred to some common signal, a word or saying the sisters used in such situations.

"What word?"

57

"Any word, dammit! Whatever's appropriate. It's like a mutual reflex. We share a common 'tic' that comes not to annoy us. We welcome it because it keeps us on our toes."

"And you'll watchdog *me* if I become a Reverend Mother?"

"We want our watchdogs. We'd be weaker without them."

"It sounds oppressive."

"We don't find it so."

"I think it's repellent." She looked at the glittering lenses in the ceiling. "Like those damned comeyes."

"We take care of our own, Murbella. Once you're a Bene Gesserit, you're assured of lifelong maintenance."

"A comfortable niche." Sneering.

Odrade spoke softly. "Something quite different. You are challenged throughout your life. You repay the Sisterhood right up to the limits of your abilities."

"Watchdogs!"

"We're always mindful of each other. Some of us in positions of power can be authoritarian at times, familiar even, but only to a point carefully measured for the requirements of the moment."

"Never really warm or tender, eh?"

"That's the rule."

"Affection, maybe, but no love?"

"I've told you the rule." And Odrade could see the reaction clearly on Murbella's face: *There it is! They will demand that I give up Duncan!*

"So there's no love among the Bene Gesserit." How sad her tone. There was hope for Murbella yet.

"Loves occur," Odrade said, "but my sisters treat them as aberrations."

"So what I feel for Duncan is aberration?"

"And sisters will try to treat it."

"Treat! Apply correctional therapy to the afflicted!"

"Love is considered a sign of rot in sisters."

"I see signs of rot in you!"

As though she followed Odrade's thoughts, Bellonda dragged Odrade out of reverie. "That Honoured Matre will never commit herself to us!" Bellonda wiped a bit of luncheon gravy from the corner of her mouth. "We're wasting our time trying to teach her our ways."

At least Bell was no longer calling Murbella "whore", Odrade thought. *That was an improvement.*

> All governments suffer a recurring problem: Power attracts pathological personalities. It is not that power corrupts but that power is a magnet to the corruptible. Such people have a tendency to become drunk on violence, a condition to which they are quickly addicted.

> —Missionaria Protectiva, Text QIV (decto)

Rebecca knelt on the yellow tile floor as she had been ordered to do, not daring to look up at the Great Honoured Matre seated so remotely high, so dangerous. Two hours Rebecca had waited here almost in the centre of the giant room while the Great Honoured Matre and her companions ate a lunch served by obsequious attendants. Rebecca marked the manners of the attendants with care and emulated them.

Her eye sockets still ached from the transplants the Rabbi had given her less than a month ago. These eyes showed a blue iris and white sclera, no clue to the Spice Agony in her past. It was a temporary defence. In less than a year, the new eyes would betray her with total blue.

She judged the ache in her eyes to be the least of her problems. An organic implant fed her metered doses of melange, concealing her dependence. The supply was gauged to last about sixty days. If these Honoured Matres held her longer than that, withdrawal would plunge her into an agony that would make the original appear mild by comparison. The most immediately dangerous thing was the shere being metered to her with the spice. If these women detected it, they certainly would be suspicious.

You are doing well. Be patient. That was Other Memory from the horde of Lampadas. The voice rang softly in her head. It had the sound of Lucilla but Rebecca could not be sure.

It had become a familiar voice in the months since the

Sharing when it had announced itself as "Speaker of your Mohalata." *These whores cannot match our knowledge. Remember that and let it give you courage.*

The presence of Others Within who subtracted none of her attention from what went on around her had filled her with awe. *We call it Simulflow*, Speaker had said. *Simulflow multiplies your awareness.* When she had tried to explain this to the Rabbi, he had reacted in anger.

"You have been tainted by unclean thoughts!"

They had been in the Rabbi's study late at night. "Stealing time from the days allotted us," he called it. The study was an underground room, it's walls lined with old books, ridulian crystals, scrolls. The room was protected from probes by the best Ixian devices and they had been modified by his own people to improve them.

She was allowed to sit beside his desk at such times while he leaned back in an old chair. A glowglobe placed low beside him cast an antique yellow light on his bearded face, glinting off the spectacles he wore almost as a badge of office.

Rebecca pretended confusion. "But you said it was required of us to save this treasure from Lampadas. Have the Bene Gesserit not been honourable with us?"

She saw the worry in his eyes. "You heard Levi talking yesterday of the questions being asked here. Why did the Bene Gesserit witch come to us? That is what they ask."

"Our story is consistent and believable," Rebecca protested. "The sisters have taught us ways that even Truthsay cannot penetrate."

"I don't know . . . I don't know." The Rabbi shook his head sadly. "What is a lie? What is truth? Do we condemn ourselves with our own mouths?"

"It is pogrom that we resist, Rabbi!" That usually stiffened his resolve.

"Cossacks! Yes, you are right, daughter. There have been cossacks in every age and we are not the only ones who have felt their knouts and swords as they rode into the village with murder in their hearts."

It was odd, Rebecca thought, how he managed to give the impression that these events were of recent occurrence and that his eyes had seen them. Never to forgive, never to forget. Lidice was yesterday. What a powerful thing that was in the memory of Secret Israel. Pogrom! Almost as powerful in its continuity as these Bene Gesserit presences she carried in her awareness. Almost. That was the thing the Rabbi resisted, she told herself.

"I fear that you have been taken from us," the Rabbi said. "What have I done to you? What have I done? And all in the name of honour."

He looked at the instruments on his study wall that reported the nightly power accumulations from the vertical-axis windmills placed around the farmstead. The instruments said the machines were humming away up there, storing energy for the morrow. That was a gift of the Bene Gesserit: freedom from Ix. Independence. What a peculiar word.

Without looking at Rebecca, he said: "I find this thing of Other Memory very difficult and always have. Memory should bring wisdom but it does not. It is how we order the memory and where we apply our knowledge."

He turned and looked at her, his face falling into shadows. "What is it this one inside you says? This one you think of as Lucilla?"

Rebecca could see it pleased him to say Lucilla's name. If Lucilla could speak through a daughter of Secret Israel, then she still lived and had not been betrayed.

Rebecca lowered her gaze as she spoke. "She says we have these inner images, sounds and sensations that come at command or intrude under necessity."

"Necessity, yes! And what is that except reports of senses from flesh that may have been where you should not have been and done things offensive to God?"

Other bodies, other memories, Rebecca thought. Having experienced this she knew she could never willingly abandon it. *Perhaps I have indeed become Bene Gesserit. That is what he fears, of course.*

"I will tell you a thing," the Rabbi said. "This 'crucial intersection of living awareness', as they call it, that is nothing unless you know how your own decisions go out from you like threads into the lives of others."

"To see our own actions in the reactions of others, yes, that is how the sisters view it."

"That is wisdom. What is it the lady says they seek?"

"Influence on the maturing of humankind."

"Mmmmmm. And she finds that events are not beyond her influence, merely beyond her senses. That is almost wise. But maturity . . . ahhh, Rebecca. Do we interfere with God's plan? Is it the right of humans to set limits on the nature of God? I think Leto II understood that. This lady in you denies it."

"She says he was a damnable tyrant."

"He was but there have been wise tyrants before him and doubtless will be more after us."

"They call him Shaitan."

"He had Satan's own powers. I share their fear of that. He was not so much prescient as he was a cement. He fixed the shape of what he saw."

"That is what the lady says. But she says it is their grail that he preserved."

"Again, they are almost wise."

A great sigh shook the Rabbi and once more he looked to the instruments on his wall. *Energy for the morrow*.

He returned his attention to Rebecca. She was changed. He could not avoid awareness of it. She had become very like the Bene Gesserits. It was understandable. Her mind was filled with all of those *people* from Lampadas. But they were not Gadarene swine to be driven into the sea and their diabolism with them. *And I am not another Jesus*.

"This thing they tell you about the Mother Superior Odrade—that she often damns her own Archivists and the Archives with them. What a thing! Are not Archives like the books in which we preserve our wisdom?"

"Then am I an Archivist, Rabbi?"

Her question confounded him but it also illuminated the problem. He smiled. "I tell you something, daughter. I admit to a little sympathy with this Odrade. There is always something grumbling about Archivists."

"Is that wisdom, Rabbi?" How slyly she asked it!

"Believe me, daughter, it is. How carefully the Archivist

62

suppresses even the smallest hint of judgment. One word after another. Such arrogance!"

"How do they judge which words to use, Rabbi?"

"Ahhh, a bit of wisdom comes to you, daughter. But these Bene Gesserits have not achieved wisdom and it is their grail that prevents it."

She could see it on his face. *He tries to arm me with doubts about these lives I carry.*

"Let me tell you a thing about the Bene Gesserits," he said. Nothing came into his mind then. No words, no sage advice. This had not happened to him for years. There was only one course open to him: speak from the heart.

"Perhaps they have been too long on the road to Damascus without a blinding flash of illumination, Rebecca. I hear them say they act for the benefit of humankind. Somehow, I cannot see this in them, nor do I believe the Tyrant saw it."

When Rebecca started to reply, he stopped her with an upraised hand. "Mature humanity? That is their grail? Is it not the mature fruit that is plucked and eaten?"

On the floor of Junction's Great Hall, Rebecca remembered these words, seeing the personification of them not in the lives she preserved but in the actions of her captors.

Great Honoured Matre had finished eating. She wiped her hands on the gown of an attendant.

"Let her approach," Great Honoured Matre said.

Pain lanced Rebecca's left shoulder and she lurched forward on her knees. The one called Logno had come up behind with the stealth of a hunter and had jabbed a shuntgoad into the captive's flesh.

Laughter echoed through the room.

Rebecca staggered to her feet and, staying just ahead of the goad, arrived at the foot of the steps leading up to the Great Honoured Matre where the goad stopped her.

"Down!" Logno emphasized the command with another jab.

Rebecca sank to her knees and stared straight ahead at the risers of the steps. The yellow tiles displayed tiny scratches. Somehow, these flaws reassured her.

Great Honoured Matre said: "Let her be, Logno. I wish

answers, not screams." Then to Rebecca: "Look at me, woman!"

Rebecca raised her eyes and stared up at the face of death. What an unremarkable face it was to have that threat in it. So . . . so evenly featured. Almost plain. Such a small figure. This amplified the peril Rebecca sensed. What powers the small woman must have to rule these terrible people.

"Do you know why you are here?" Great Honoured Matre demanded.

In her most obsequious tones, Rebecca said: "I was told, O Great Honoured Matre, that you wished me to recount the lore of Truthsay and other matters of Gammu."

"You were mated to a Truthsayer!" It was accusation.

"He is dead, Great Honoured Matre."

"No, Logno!" This was directed at the aide who lunged forward with the goad. "This wretch does not know our ways. Now, go stand at the side, Logno, where I will not be annoyed by your impetuosity."

"You will speak to me only in response to questions or when I command it, wretch!" Great Honoured Matre shouted.

Rebecca cringed.

Speaker whispered in Rebecca's head: *That was almost Voice. Be warned.*

Voice! This ability to control another merely by vocal intonations matched to observed weaknesses was a Bene Gesserit accomplishment that dismayed Rebecca. It demeaned the person you manipulated.

"Have you ever known any of the ones who call themselves Bene Gesserit?" Great Honoured Matre asked.

Really now! "Everyone has encountered the witches, Great Honoured Matre."

"What do you know of them?"

"Only what I have heard, Great Honoured Matre."

"Are they brave?"

"It is said they always try to avoid risks, Great Honoured Matre."

You are worthy of us, Rebecca. That is the pattern of these whores. The marble rolls down the incline in its proper channel. They think you dislike us.

"Are these Bene Gesserits rich?" Great Honoured Matre asked.

The Rabbi had warned her they would ask this question. "Everything that measures power—they desire it all. That is why they have their eyes on us."

There was no single bourse any more. A species of subterranean webworks could be defined, he said. But it was knit extremely loose, based on old compromises and temporary agreements.

"It resembles an old garment with frayed edges and patched holes."

Lampadas agreed. It no longer was the tightly-bound trading network of the Old Empire. So people wore the old garment, treating it with the contempt of familiarity, longing always for something new. But not the new that these Honoured Matres brought. Not that.

"I think the witches are poor beside you, Honoured Matre," Rebecca said.

"Why do you say that? Do not speak just to please me!"

"But Honoured Matre, could the witches send a great ship from Gammu to here just to carry me? And where are the witches now? They hide from you."

"Yes, where are they?" Honoured Matre demanded.

Rebecca shrugged.

"Were you on Gammu when the one they called Bashar fled us?" Honoured Matre asked.

She knows you were. "I was there, Great Honoured Matre, and heard the stories. I do not believe them."

"Believe what we tell you to believe, wretch! What are the stories you heard?"

"That he moved with a speed the eye could not see. That he killed many . . . people with only his hands. That he stole a no-ship and fled into the Scattering."

"Believe that he fled, wretch." *See how she fears! She cannot hide the trembling.*

"Speak of the Truthsay," Great Honoured Matre commanded.

"Great Honoured Matre, I do not understand the Truthsay.

65

I know only the words of my Sholem. I can repeat his words if you wish."

Great Honoured Matre considered this, glancing from side to side at her aides and councillors who were beginning to show signs of boredom. *Why doesn't she just kill this wretch?*

Rebecca, seeing the violence in eyes that glared orange at her, shrank into herself. Sholem's words comforted. He had shown the "proper talent" while still a child. Some called it an instinct but Shoel had never used that word. "Trust your gut feelings. That's what my teachers always said."

It was such a down-to-earth expression that he said it usually threw off the ones who came seeking "the esoteric mystery".

"There is no secret. It's training and hard work like anything else. You exercise what they call 'petit perception', the ability to detect very small variations in human reactions."

Rebecca could see such small reactions in those who stared down at her. *They want me dead. Why?*

Speaker had advice. *The great one likes to show off her power over the others. She does not do what others want but what she thinks they do not want.*

"Great Honoured Matre," Rebecca ventured, "you are so rich and powerful. Surely you must have a place of menial employment where I may be of service to you."

"You wish to enter my service?" *What a feral grin!*

"It would make me happy, Great Honoured Matre."

"I am not here to make you happy."

Logno took a step forward on to the floor. "Then make us happy, Dama. Let us have some sport with . . ."

"Silence!" *Ahhh, that was a mistake, calling her by the intimate name here among the others.*

Logno drew back and almost dropped the goad.

Great Honoured Matre stared down at Rebecca with an orange glare. "You will go back to your miserable existence on Gammu, wretch. I will not kill you. That would be a mercy. Having seen what we could give you, live your life without it."

"Great Honoured Matre!" Logno protested. "We have suspicions about . . ."

"I have suspicions about you, Logno. Send her back and alive! Hear me? Do you think us incapable of finding her if we ever have need of her?"

"No, Great Honoured Matre."

"We are watching you, wretch," Great Honoured Matre said.

Bait! She thinks of you as something to capture larger game. How interesting. This one has a head and uses it in spite of her violent nature. So that's how she came to power.

All the way back to Gammu, confined to stinking quarters in a ship that had once served the Guild, Rebecca considered her predicament. Surely, those whores had not expected her to mistake their intent. But . . . perhaps they did. Subservience, cringing. *They revel in such things.*

She knew this came from a bit of her Shoel's Truthsay as much as from the Lampadas advisers.

"You accumulate a lot of small observations, sensed but never brought to consciousness. Cumulatively, they say things to you but not in a language anyone speaks. Language isn't necessary."

She had thought that one of the oddest things she had ever heard. But that was before her own Agony. In bed at night, comforted by darkness and the touch of loving flesh, they had acted wordlessly but had shared words, too.

"Language obstructs you," Sholem had said. "What you do is learn to read your own reactions. Sometimes, you can find words to describe this . . . sometimes . . . not."

"No words? Not even for the questions?"

"Words you want, is it? How are these? Trust. Belief. Truth. Honesty."

"Those are good words, Shoel."

"But they miss the mark. Don't depend on them."

"Then what do you depend on?"

"My own internal reactions. I read myself, not the person in front of me. I always know a lie because I want to turn my back on the liar."

"So that's how you do it!" Pounding his bare arm.

"Others do it differently. One person I heard say she knew a lie because she wanted to put her arm through the liar's arm and walk a way, comforting the liar. You may think that's nonsense, but it works."

"I think it's very wise, Shoel." Love speaking. She did not really know what he meant.

"My precious love," he said, cradling her head on his arm, "Trúthsayers have a Truthsense that, once awakened, works all the time. Please don't tell me I'm wise when it's your love speaking."

"I'm sorry, Shoel." She liked the smell of his arm and buried her head in the crook of it, tickling him. "but I want to know everything you know."

He pushed her head into a more comfortable position. "You know what my Third Stage instructor said? 'Know nothing! Learn to be totally naive.'"

She was astonished. "Nothing at all?"

"You approach it with a clean slate, nothing on you or in you. Whatever comes is written there by itself."

She began to see it. "Nothing to interfere."

"Correct. You are the original ignorant savage, completely unsophisticated to the point where you back right into ultimate sophistication. You find it without looking for it, you might say."

"Now, that is wise, Shoel. I'll bet you were the best student they ever had, the quickest and the . . . ."

"I thought it was interminable nonsense."

"You didn't!"

"Until, one day I read a little twitch in me. It wasn't the movement of a muscle or something someone else might detect. Just a . . . a twitch."

"Where was it?"

"Nowhere I could describe. But my Fourth Stage instructor had prepared me for it. 'Grab that thing with gentle hands. Delicately.' One of the students thought he meant your real hands. Oh, how we laughed."

"That was cruel." She touched his cheek and felt the beginning of his dark stubble. It was late but she did not feel sleepy.

"I suppose it was cruel. But when the twitch came, I knew it. I had never felt such a thing before. I was surprised by it, too, because knowing it then, I knew it had been there all along. It was familiar. It was my Truthsense twitching."

She thought she could feel Truthsense stirring within herself. The feeling of wonder in his voice aroused something.

"It was mine then," he said. "It belonged to me and I belonged to it. No separation ever again."

"How wonderful that must be." Awe and envy in her voice.

"No! Some of it I hate. Seeing some people this way is like seeing them eviscerated, their guts hanging out."

"That's disgusting!"

"Yes, but there are compensations, love. There are people you meet, people who are like beautiful flowers extended to you by an innocent child. Innocence. My own innocence responds and my Truthsense is strengthened. That is what you do for me, my love."

The no-ship of the Honoured Matres arrived at Gammu and they sent her down to the Landing Flat in the garbage lighter. It disgorged her beside the ship's discards and excrement but she did not mind. *Home! I'm home and Lampadas survives.*

The Rabbi, however, did not share her enthusiasm.

Once more, they sat in his study, but now she felt more familiar with Other Memory, much more confident. He could see this.

"You are even more like them than ever! It's unclean."

"Rabbi, we all have unclean ancestors. I am fortunate in that I know some of mine."

"What is this? What are you saying?"

"All of us are descendants of people who did nasty things, Rabbi. We don't like to think of barbarians in our ancestry but they're there."

"Such talk!"

"Reverend Mothers can recall them all, Rabbi. Remember, it is the victors who breed. You understand?"

"I've never heard you talk so boldly. What has happened to you, daughter?"

"I survived, knowing that victory sometimes is achieved at a moral price."

"What is this? These are evil words."

"Evil? Barbarism is not even the proper word for some of

the evil things our ancestors did. The ancestors of all of us, Rabbi."

She saw that she had hurt him and felt the cruelty of her own words but could not stop. How could he escape the truth of what she said? He was an honourable man.

She spoke more softly but her words cut him even deeper. "Rabbi, if you shared witness to some of the things Other Memory has forced me to know, you would come back seeking new words for evil. Some things our ancestors have done debase the worst label you could imagine."

"Rebecca . . . Rebecca . . . I know that necessities of . . ."

"Don't make excuses about 'necessities of the times'! You, a Rabbi, know better. When are we without a moral sense? It's just that sometimes we don't listen."

He put his hands over his face, rocking back and forth in the old chair. It creaked mournfully.

"Rabbi, you I have always loved and respected. I went through the Agony for you. I shared Lampadas for you. Do not deny what I have learned from this."

He lowered his hands. "I do not deny, daughter. But permit me my pain."

"Out of all these realizations, Rabbi, the thing I must deal with most immediately and without respite is that there are no innocents."

"Rebecca!"

"Guilty may not be the right word, Rabbi, but our ancestors did things for which payment must be made."

"That I understand, Rebecca. It is a balance that . . ."

"Don't tell me you understand when I know you don't." She stood and glared down at him. "It's not a balance book that you set aright. How far back would you go?"

"Rebecca, I am your Rabbi. You must not talk this way, especially to me."

"The farther back you go, Rabbi, the worse the evil atrocities and higher the price. You cannot go back that far but I am forced to it."

Turning, she left him, ignoring the pleading in his voice, the painful way he said her name. As she closed the door, she heard him say: "What have we done? Israel, help her."

The writing of history is largely a process of diversion. Most historical accounts distract attention from the secret influences behind great events.

—The Bashar Teg

When left to his own devices, Idaho often explored his no-ship prison. So much to see and learn about this Ixian artifact. It was a cave of wonders.

He paused on this afternoon's restless walk through his quarters and looked at the tiny comeyes built into the glittering surface of a doorway. They were watching him. He had the odd sensation of seeing himself through those prying eyes. What did the sisters think when they looked at him? The blocky ghola child from Gammu's long dead Keep had become a lanky man: dark skin and hair. The hair was longer than when he had entered this no-ship on the last day of Dune.

Bene Gesserit eyes peered below the skin. He was sure they suspected he was a Mentat and he feared how they might interpret that. How could a Mentat expect to hide the fact from Reverend Mothers indefinitely? Foolishness! He knew they already suspected him of Truthsay.

He waved at the comeyes and said: "I'm restless. I think I'll explore."

Bellonda hated it when he took that jocular attitude toward surveillance. She did not like him to roam the ship. She did not try to hide it from him. He could see the unspoken question in her glowering features whenever she came to confront him: *"Is he looking for a way to escape?"*

Exactly what I'm doing, Bell, but not in the way you suspect.

The no-ship presented him with fixed limits: the exterior forcefield he could not penetrate, certain machinery areas where the drive (so he was told) had been temporarily disabled, guard quarters (he could see into some of them but not enter), the armoury, the section reserved to the captive Tleilaxu, Scytale. He occasionally met Scytale at one of the barriers and they peered at each other across the silencing field that held them apart. Then there was the information barrier—sections of Shiprecords that would not respond to his questions, answers his warders would not give.

Within these limits lay a lifetime of things to see and learn, even the lifetime of some three hundred Standard Years he could reasonably expect.

If Honoured Matres do not find us.

Idaho saw himself as the game they sought, wanting him even more than they wanted the women of Chapter House. He had no illusions about what the hunters would do to him. They knew he was here. The men he trained in sexual bonding and sent out to plague the Honoured Matres—those men taunted the hunters.

Honoured Matres would not be seeking Murbella. They did not yet know she lived. To them, she had died on Gammu in those last desperate days when the Sisterhood became fugitives.

What fury it would arouse when they learned of Murbella. An Honoured Matre being instructed in the ways of the Bene Gesserit? A clear intention to win her over, make her into a Reverend Mother and learn *all* Honoured Matre secrets.

As usual, a war of both minds and flesh.

Murbella took it with surprising calm. "We're in a special school, Duncan. Most schools are a kind of prison."

She thinks becoming a Reverend Mother is her key to freedom. Ahhh, my love, what a shock is in store for you.

He dared not discuss this with her. Too revealing to the watchers. When the Sisters learned of his Mentat ability they would know immediately that his mind carried the memories of more than one ghola lifetime. *The original did not have that talent.* They would suspect he was a latent kwisatz haderach. Look how they rationed his melange. They were clearly terrified of repeating the mistake they had made with Paul Atreides and his Tyrant son. *Thirty-five hundred years of bondage!*

But dealing with Murbella required Mentat awareness. He entered every encounter with her not expecting to achieve answers then or later. It was a typical Mentat approach: concentrate on the questions. Mentats accumulated questions the way others accumulated answers. Questions created their own patterns and systems. This produced the most important *shapes*. You looked at your universe through self-created

72

patterns—all composed of images, words and labels (everything temporary) all mingled in sensory impulses that reflected off his internal constructs the way light bounced from bright surfaces.

Idaho's original Mentat instructor had formed the temporary words for that first tentative construct: "Watch for consistent movements against your internal screen."

From that first hesitant dip into Mentat powers, Idaho could trace the growth of a sensitivity to changes in his own observations, always *becoming* Mentat. *The old idea of "changing your mind" brought to new sophistication.*

Bellonda was his most severe trial. He dreaded her penetrating gaze and slashing questions. Mentat probing Mentat. He met her forays delicately, with reserve and patience. *Now, what are you after?*

As if he didn't know.

He wore patience as a mask. But fear came naturally and there was no harm in showing it. Bellonda did not hide her wish to see him dead. Their meetings were a deadly fencing match. Skill clashed with skill.

Idaho accepted the fact that soon the watchers would see only one source for the skills he was forced to use.

He is not just a Truthsayer!

A Mentat's real skills lay in that mental *construct* they called "the great synthesis". It required a patience that non-Mentats did not even imagine possible. Mentat schools defined it as perseverance. You were a primitive tracker, able to read minuscule signs, tiny disturbances in the environment, and follow where these led. At the same time, you remained open to broad motions all around and within. This produced naivete, the basic Mentat posture akin to that of Truthsayers but far more sweeping.

"You are open to whatever the universe may do," his first instructor had said. "Your mind is not a computer; it is a response-tool keyed to whatever your senses display."

Idaho always recognized when Bellonda's senses were open. She stood there, gaze slightly withdrawn, and he knew few preconceptions cluttered her mind. His defence lay in her basic flaw: opening the senses required an idealism that was foreign to Bellonda. She did not ask the best questions and he wondered at this. Would Odrade use a flawed Mentat? It went against her other performances.

I seek the questions that form the best images.

Doing this, you never thought of yourself as clever, that you had *the* formula to provide *the* solution. You remained as responsive to new questions as you did to new patterns. Testing, re-testing, shaping and re-shaping. A constant process, never stopping, never satisfied. It was your own private pavane, similar to that of other Mentats but it carried always your own unique posture and steps.

"You are never truly a Mentat. That is why we call it 'The Endless Goal'." The words of his teachers were burned into his awareness.

As he accumulated observations of Bellonda, he came to appreciate a viewpoint of those great Mentat Masters who had taught him. "Reverend Mothers do not make the best Mentats."

No Bene Gesserit appeared capable of completely removing herself from that binding absolute she achieved in the Spice Agony: loyalty to her Sisterhood.

His teachers had warned against absolutes. They created a serious flaw in a Mentat.

"Everything you do, everything you sense and say is experiment. No deduction final. Nothing stops until dead and perhaps not even then because each life creates endless ripples. Induction bounces within and you sensitize yourself to it. Deduction conveys illusions of absolutes. Kick the truth and shatter it!"

Bellonda's questions about Murbella told him the Sisterhood thought her a cornucopia of information about Honoured Matres. When Bellonda touched on the relationship between himself and Murbella, he saw vague emotional responses. *Amusement? Jealousy?* He could accept amusement (and even jealousy) about the compelling sexual demands of this mutual addiction. (*Is the ecstasy truly that great?*)

They watched everything. And he could imagine their comments. *"See how they resist but cannot avoid the sexual contact?"*

Bellonda appeared oddly susceptible to mental fidgeting. He recognized it in her because he could see the same susceptibility in himself. *The mirror sees the mirror.*

He wandered through his quarters this afternoon feeling displaced, as though newly here and not yet accepting these rooms as home. *That is emotion talking to me.*

Over the years of his confinement, these quarters had taken on a lived-in appearance. This was his cave, the former supercargo suite: large rooms with slightly curved walls—bedroom, library-workroom, sitting room, a green-tiled bath with dry and wet cleansing systems, and a long practice hall he shared with Murbella for exercise.

The rooms bore a unique collection of artifacts and marks of his presence: that sling chair placed at just the right angle to the console and projector linking him to Shipsystems, those ridulian records on that low side table. And there were stains of occupancy—that dark brown blot on the worktable. Spilled food had left its indelible mark.

There were few noises here that he could not identify at some level of consciousness. That ticking was his console over there reminding him that he had left it activated. The projector's fibrous tips glowed green.

He moved restlessly into his sleeping quarters. The light was dimmer. His ability to identify the familiar held true for odours. There was a saliva-like smell to the bed—the residue of last night's sexual collision.

That is the proper word: Collision.

The no-ship's air—filtered, recycled and sweetened—often bored him. No break in the no-ship maze to the exterior world ever remained open long. He sometimes sat silently sniffing, hoping for a faint trace of air that had not been adjusted to this prison's demands.

There is a way to escape!

He wandered out of his quarters and down the corridor, took the dropchute at the end of the passage and emerged in the ship's lowest level.

What is really happening out there in that world open to the sky?

The bits Odrade told him about events filled him with dread

75

and a trapped feeling. *No place to run! Am I wise to share my fears with Sheeana? Murbella merely laughed at him. "I will protect you, love. Honoured Matres won't hurt me." Another false dream.*

But Sheeana . . . how quickly she had picked up the hand language and entered the spirit of his conspiracy. Conspiracy? No . . . I doubt that any Reverend Mother will act against her sisters. Even the Lady Jessica went back to them in the end. But I don't ask Sheeana to act against the Sisterhood, only that she protect us from Murbella's folly.

The enormous powers of the hunters made only the destruction predictable. A Mentat had only to look at their disruptive violence. They brought something else as well, something hinting at matters out there in the Scattering. What were these *Futars* Odrade mentioned with such casualness? *Part human, part beast?* That had been Lucilla's guess. *And where is Lucilla?*

He found himself presently in the Great Hold, the kilometre-long cargo space where they had carried the last giant sandworm of Dune, bringing it to Chapter House. The area still smelled of spice and sand, filling his mind with long-ago and the dead far-away. He knew why he came so often to the Great Hold, doing it sometimes without even thinking, as he had just done. It both attracted and repelled. The illusion of unlimited space with traces of dust, sand and spice carried the nostalgia of lost freedoms. But there was another side. This is where it always happened to him.

Will it happen today?

Without warning, the sense of being in the Great Hold would vanish. Then . . . the net shimmering in a molten sky. He was aware when the vision came that he was not really *seeing* a net. His mind translated what the senses could not define.

A shimmering net undulating like an infinite borealis.

Then the net would part and he would see the two people— man and woman. How ordinary they appeared and yet extraordinary. A grandmother and grandfather in antique clothing: bib coveralls for the man and a long dress with headscarf for the woman. Working in a flower garden! He thought it

76

must be more of the illusion. *I am seeing this but it is not really what I see.*

They always noticed him eventually. He heard their voices. "There he is again, Marty," the man would say, calling the woman's attention to Idaho.

"I wonder how it is he can look through?" Marty asked once. "Doesn't seem possible."

"He's spread pretty thin, I think. Wonder if he knows the danger?"

Danger. That was the word that always jerked him out of the vision.

"Not at your console today?"

For just an instant, Idaho thought it was the vision, the voice of that odd woman, then he realized it was Odrade. Her voice came from close behind. He whirled and saw that he had failed to close the hatch. She had followed him into the Hold, stalking him quietly, avoiding the scattered patches of sand that might have grated underfoot and betrayed her approach.

She looked tired and impatient. *Why did she think I would be at my console?*

As though answering his unspoken question, she said: "I find you at your console so often lately. For what do you search, Duncan?"

He shook his head without speaking. *Why do I suddenly feel in peril?*

It was a rare feeling in Odrade's company. He could remember other occasions, though. Once when she had stared suspiciously at his hands in the field of his console. *Fear associated with my console. Do I reveal my Mentat hungers for data? Do they guess that I have hidden my private self there?*

"Do I get no privacy at all?" Anger and attack.

She shook her head slowly from side to side as much as to say, "You can do better than that."

"This is your second visit today," he accused.

"I must say you're looking well, Duncan." More circumlocution.

"Is that what your watchers say?"

"Don't be petty. I came for a chat with Murbella. She said you'd be down here."

"As if you needed her to tell you!"

"Much that you do is boring, Duncan." Definite anger and from a Reverend Mother!

"I suppose you know Murbella's pregnant again." Was that trying to placate her?

"For which we are grateful. I came to tell you that Sheeana wants to visit you again."

Why would Odrade announce that?

Her words filled him with images of the Dune waif who had become a full Reverend Mother (the youngest ever, so they said). Sheeana, his confidante, out there watching over that last great sandworm. Had it finally perpetuated itself? Why should Odrade interest herself in Sheeana's visit?

"Sheeana wants to discuss the Tyrant with you."

She saw the surprise this produced.

Damn! Odrade always used such a well-planned approach to him. She had something specific in mind, another Bene Gesserit scheme. Did they want his *male viewpoint* as she had said so many times? But what in the name of all the Missionaria's false gods was a male viewpoint?

The Mother Superior was being extremely cautious with him. That much was clear.

Sheeana?

They needed him for something. He could feel it. But he was dealing with ultimate professionals in human motivation. *What are they doing? Keeping the Bene Gesserit alive, of course. Manipulating the non-Bene Gesserit around them where they can. Power brokers. Arbiters. Long-time conservators of data. Never overlook Other Memory.*

"What could I possibly add to Sheeana's knowledge of Leto II?" he demanded. "She's a Reverend Mother."

"You knew the Atreides intimately."

Ahhhhh. She's hunting for the Mentat.

"But you said she wanted to discuss Leto and it's not safe to think of him as Atreides."

"Oh, but he was. Refined into something more elemental than anyone before him, but one of us, nonetheless."

One of us! She reminded him that she, too, was Atreides. Calling in his never-ending debt to the Family!

78

"So you say."

"Shouldn't we stop playing this foolish game?"

Caution gripped him. He knew she saw it. Reverend Mothers were damnably sensitive. He stared at her, not daring to speak, knowing that even this told her too much.

"We believe you remember more than one ghola lifetime." And when he still did not respond, "Come, come, Duncan! Are you a Mentat?"

The way she spoke, as much accusation as question, he knew concealment had ended. It was almost a relief.

"And if I am?"

"The Tleilaxu mixed the cells from more than one Idaho ghola when they grew you."

Idaho ghola! He refused to think of himself in that abstraction. "Why is Leto suddenly so important to you?" No escaping the admission in that response.

"Our worm has become sandtrout."

"Are they growing and propagating?"

"Apparently."

"Unless you contain them or eliminate them, Chapter House may become another Dune."

"You figured that out, did you?"

"Leto and I together."

"So you remember many lives. Fascinating. It makes you somewhat like us." How unswerving her stare!

"Very different, I think." *Have to get her off that track!*

"You acquired the memories during your first encounter with Murbella?"

Who guessed it? Lucilla? She was there and might have guessed, confiding her suspicions to her sisters. He had to bring the deadly issue into the open. "I'm not another kwisatz haderach!"

"You're not?" Studied objectivity. She allowed this to reveal itself, a cruelty, he thought.

"You know I'm not!" He was fighting for his life and knew it. Not so much with Odrade as with those others who watched and reviewed the comeye records.

"Tell me about your serial memories." That was a command from the Mother Superior. No escaping it.

"I know those . . . lives. It's like one lifetime."

"That accumulation could be very valuable to us, Duncan. Do you also remember the axolotl tanks?"

Her question sent his thoughts into the misty probings that caused him to imagine strange things about the Tleilaxu—great mounds of human flesh softly visible to the imperfect newborn eyes, blurred and unfocused images, almost-memories of emerging from birth canals. How could that accord with *tanks*?

"Scytale has provided us with the knowledge to make our own axolotl system," Odrade said.

System? Interesting word. "Does that mean you also duplicate Tleilaxu spice production?"

"Scytale bargains for more than we will give. But spice will come in time, one way or another."

Odrade heard herself speak firmly and wondered if he detected uncertainty. *We might not have the time to do it.*

"The sisters you Scatter are hobbled," he said, giving her a small taste of Mentat awareness. "You're drawing on your spice stockpiles to supply them and those must be finite."

"They have our axolotl knowledge and sandtrout."

He was shocked to silence by the possibility of countless Dunes being reproduced in an infinite universe.

"They will solve the problem of melange supply with tanks or worms or both," she said. This she could say sincerely. It came from statistical expectation. One among those Scattered bands of Reverend Mothers should accomplish it.

"The tanks," he said. "I have strange . . . dreams." He had almost said "musings".

"And well you should." Briefly, she told him how female flesh was incorporated.

"For making the spice, too?"

"We think so."

"Disgusting!"

"That's juvenile," she chided.

In such moments, he disliked her intensely. Once, he had reproached her for the way Reverend Mothers removed themselves from "the common stream of human emotions", and she had given him that identical answer.

Juvenile!

"For which there probably is no remedy," he said. "A disgraceful flaw in my character."

"Were you thinking to debate morality with me?"

He thought he heard anger. "Not even ethics. We work by different rules."

"Rules are often an excuse to ignore compassion."

"Do I hear a faint echo of conscience in a Reverend Mother?"

"Deplorable. My sisters would exile me if they thought conscience ruled me."

"You can be prodded, but not controlled."

"Very good, Duncan! I like you much better when you're openly Mentat."

"I distrust your liking."

She laughed aloud. "How like Bell!"

He stared at her dumbly, plunged by her laughter into the unexpected knowledge of a way to escape his warders . . . how to remove himself from the constant Bene Gesserit manipulations and live his own life. The way out lay not in machinery but in the Sisterhood's flaws. The absolutes by which they thought they surrounded and held him—there was the way out!

And Sheeana knows! That's the bait she dangles in front of me.

When Idaho did not speak, Odrade said: "Tell me about those other lives."

"Wrong. I think of them as one continuous life."

"No deaths?"

He let a response form silently. Serial memories: the deaths were as informative as the lives. Killed so many times by Leto himself!

"The deaths do not interrupt my memories."

"An odd kind of immortality," she said. "You know, don't you, that Tleilaxu Masters recreated themselves? But you—what did they hope to achieve, mixing different gholas in one flesh?"

"Ask Scytale."

"Bell felt sure you were a Mentat. She will be delighted."

81

"I think not."

"I will see to it that she is delighted. My! I have so many questions I'm not sure where to begin." She studied him, left hand to her chin.

Questions? Mentat demands flowed through Idaho's mind. He let the questions he had asked himself so many times move of themselves, forming their patterns. *What did the Tleilaxu seek in me?* They could not have included cells from all of his ghola selves for this incarnation. Yet . . . he had all of the memories. What cosmic linkage accumulated all of those lives in this one self? Was that the clue to the visions that beset him in the Great Hold? Half-memories formed in his mind: his body in warm fluid, fed by tubes, massaged by machines, probed and questioned by Tleilaxu observers. He sensed murmurous responses from semi-dormant selves. The words had no meaning. It was as though he listened to a foreign language coming from his own lips but he knew it was ordinary Galach.

The scope of what he sensed in Tleilaxu actions awed him. They investigated a cosmos no one but the Bene Gesserit had ever dared touch. That the Bene Tleilax did this for selfish reasons did not subtract from it. The endless rebirths of Tleilaxu Masters were a reward worthy of daring.

Face Dancer servants to copy any life, any mind. The scope of the Tleilaxu dream was as awesome as Bene Gesserit achievements.

"Scytale admits to memories of Muad'Dib's times," Odrade said. "You might compare notes with him someday."

"That kind of immortality is a bargaining chip," he said. "Could he sell it to the Honoured Matres?"

"He might. Come. Let's go back to your quarters."

In his workroom, she gestured him to the chair at his console and he wondered if she was still hunting for his secrets. She bent over him to manipulate the controls. The overhead projector produced a scene of desert to a horizon of rolling dunes.

"Chapter House," she said. "A wide band along our equator."

"Why do you reveal this to me now?"

82

"Our days of tricking each other are past."

Excitement gripped him. "Sandtrout, you said. But are there any new worms?"

"Sheeana expects them soon."

"They require a large amount of spice as catalyst."

"We've gambled a great deal of melange out there. Leto told you about the catalyst, didn't he? What else do you remember of him?"

"He killed me so many times it's an ache when I think about it."

She had the records for Dar-es-Balat on Dune to confirm this. "Killed you himself, I know. Did he just throw you away when you were used up?"

"I sometimes performed up to expectations and was allowed a natural death."

"Was his Golden Path worth it?"

We don't understand his Golden Path nor the fermentations that produced it. He said this.

"Interesting choice of word. A Mentat thinks of the Tyrant's eons as fermentation."

"That erupted in the Scattering."

"Driven also by the Famine Times."

"You think he didn't anticipate famines?"

She did not reply, held to silence by his Mentat view. *Golden Path: humankind "erupting" into the universe . . . never again confined to any single planet and susceptible to a singular fate. All of our eggs no longer in one basket.*

"Leto thought of all humankind as a single organism," he said.

"But he enlisted us in his dream against our will."

"You Atreides always do that."

You Atreides! "Then you've paid your debt to us?"

"I didn't say that."

"Do you appreciate my present dilemma, Mentat?"

"How long have the sandtrout been at work?"

"More than eight Standard Years."

"How fast is our desert growing?"

Our Desert! She gestured at the projection. "That's more than three times larger than it was before the sandtrout."

83

"So fast!"

"Sheeana expects to see small worms any day."

"They tend not to surface until they reach about two metres."

"So she says."

He spoke in a musing tone. "Each with a pearl of Leto's awareness in his 'endless dream'."

"So *he* said and he never lied about such things."

"His lies were more subtle. Like a Reverend Mother's."

"You accuse us of lying?"

"Why does Sheeana want to see me?"

"Mentats! You think your questions are answers." Odrade shook her head in mock dismay. "She must learn as much as possible about the Tyrant as the centre of religious adoration."

"Gods below! Why?"

"The cult of Sheeana has spread. It's all over the Old Empire and beyond, carried by surviving priests from Rakis."

"From Dune," he corrected her. "Don't think of it as Arrakis or Rakis. It fogs your mind."

She accepted his correction. He was fully Mentat now and she waited patiently.

"Sheeana talked to the sandworms on Dune," he said. "They responded." He met her questioning stare. "Up to your old tricks with your Missionaria Protectiva, eh?"

"The Tyrant is known as Dur and Guldur in the Scattering," she said, feeding his Mentat naivete.

"You have a dangerous assignment for her. Does she know?"

"She knows and you could make it less dangerous."

"Then open your data systems to me."

"No limits?" She knew what Bell would say to that!

He nodded, unable to allow himself the hope that she might agree. *Does she suspect how desperately I want this?* It was an ache where he held his knowledge of how he might escape. *Unimpeded access to information! She will think I want the illusion of freedom.*

"Will you be my Mentat, Duncan?"

"What choice do I have?"

"I will discuss your request in Council and give you our answer."

Is the escape door opening?

"I must think like an Honoured Matre," he said, arguing for the comeyes and the watchdogs who would review his request.

"Who could do it better than the one who lives with Murbella?" she asked.

> *Corruption wears infinite disguises.*
>
> —Tleilaxu Thu-zen

They do not know what I think nor what I can do, Scytale thought. *Their Truthsayers cannot read me.* That, at least, he had salvaged from disaster—the art of deception learned from his perfected Face Dancers.

He moved softly through his area of the no-ship, observing, cataloguing, measuring. Every look weighed people or place in a mind trained to seek flaws.

Each Tleilaxu Master had known that someday God might set him a task to test his commitment.

Very well! This was such a task. The Bene Gesserits who claimed they shared his Great Belief swore it falsely. They were unclean. He no longer had companions to cleanse him on his return from alien places. He had been cast into the powindah universe, made prisoner by servants of Shaitan, was hunted by whores from the Scattering. But none of those evil ones knew his resources. None suspected how God would help him in this extremity.

I cleanse myself, God!

When the women of Shaitan had plucked him from the hands of the whores, promising sanctuary and "every assistance", he had known them false.

The greater the test, the greater my faith.

Only a few minutes ago, he had watched through a shimmering barrier as Duncan Idaho took a morning walk down the long corridor. The forcefield that kept them apart prevented the passage of sound, but Scytale saw Idaho's lips move and read the curse. *Curse me, ghola, but we made you and still may use you.*

God had introduced a *Holy Accident* into the Tleilaxu plan for this ghola, but God always had larger designs. It was the task of the faithful to fit themselves into God's plans and not demand that God follow the designs of humans.

Scytale set himself to this test, renewing his holy pledge. It was done without words in the ancient Bene Tleilax way of *s'tori*. "To achieve s'tori no understanding is needed. S'tori exists without words, without even a name."

The magic of his God was his only bridge. Scytale felt this deeply. The youngest Master in the highest kehl, he had known from the beginning he would be chosen for this ultimate task. That knowledge was one of his strengths and he saw it every time he looked in a mirror. *God formed me to deceive the powindah!* His slight, childlike appearance was formed in a grey skin whose metallic pigments blocked scanning probes. His diminutive shape distracted those who saw him and hid the powers he had accumulated in serial ghola incarnations. Only the Bene Gesserit carried older memories, but he knew that evil guided them.

Scytale rubbed his breast, reminding himself of what was hidden there with such skill that not even a scar marked the place. Each Master had carried this resource—a nullentropy capsule preserving the seed cells of a multitude: fellow Masters of the central kehl, Face Dancers, technical specialists and *others* he knew would be attractive to the women of Shaitan . . . and to many weakling powindah! Paul Atreides and his beloved Chani were there. (Oh what that had cost in searching garments of the dead for random cells!) The original Duncan Idaho was there, with other Atreides minions—the Mentat Thufir Hawat, Gurney Halleck, the Fremen Naib Stilgar . . . enough potential servants and slaves to people a Tleilaxu universe.

The prize of prizes in the nullentropy tube, the ones he longed to bring into existence, made him catch his breath when he thought of them. Perfect Face Dancers! Perfect mimics. Perfect recorders of a victim's persona. Capable of deceiving even the witches of the Bene Gesserit. Not even shere could prevent them from capturing the mind of another.

The tube he thought of as his ultimate bargaining power. No one must know of it. For now, he catalogued flaws.

There were enough gaps in the no-ship's defences to gratify him. In his serial lifetimes, he had collected skills the way his fellow Masters collected pleasing baubles. They had always considered him too serious but now he had found the place and time for vindication.

Study of the Bene Gesserit had always attracted him. Over the eons, he had acquired a body of knowledge about them. He knew it held myths and misinformation, but faith in the purposes of God assured him the view he held would serve the Great Belief, no matter the rigours of Holy Testing.

Did God not send his prophet to Rakis, there to test us and teach us?

There were many things to evaluate about the women of Shaitan and he saw himself in a position to broaden his knowledge, refining it for God's purposes.

Part of his Bene Gesserit catalogue, he called "Typicals," from the frequent remark: "That's typical of them!"

The *typicals* fascinated him.

It was *typical* for them to tolerate gross but non-threatening behaviour in others they would not accept in themselves. "Bene Gesserit standards are higher." Scytale had heard that even from some of his late companions.

"We have the gift of seeing ourselves as others see us," Odrade said.

Scytale included this among *typicals*, but her words did not accord with the Great Belief. Only God saw your ultimate self! Odrade's boast had the sound of hubris.

"They tell no casual lies. Truth serves them better."

He often wondered about that. Mother Superior herself quoted it as a rule of the Bene Gesserit. There remained the fact that witches appeared to hold a cynical view about truth. She dared claim it was Zensunni. *"Whose truth? Modified in what way? In what context?"*

They had been seated the previous afternoon in his no-ship quarters. *A prison with bars God can sunder!*

He had asked for "a consultation on mutual problems", his euphemism for bargaining. They were alone except for comeyes and the comings and goings of watchful sisters.

. His quarters were comfortable enough: three plaz-walled rooms in restful green, a soft bed, chairs reduced to fit his diminutive body.

This was an Ixian no-ship and he felt certain his warders did not suspect how much he knew of them. *As much as the Ixians.* Ixian machines all around but never an Ixian to be seen. He doubted there was a single Ixian on Chapter House. The witches were notorious for doing their own maintenance.

Odrade moved and spoke slowly, watching him with care. *"They are not impulsive."* You heard that often.

She asked after his comfort and appeared concerned for him. *"Petty behaviour demeans you."* Scytale had seen this in a copy of the Bene Gesserit Coda. It accorded with Folk Wisdom about the witches.

Then what of their much-feared punishments? More than once, the Tleilaxu had suffered under the Bene Gesserit lash.

Odrade responded to his questions with a lecture: "Punishments are administered only to teach a valuable lesson. What good is punishment if it only causes pain?"

"Testing to extinction?" Scytale probed.

"Come, come," she chided him. "Have we not preserved you from extinction?"

He sighed deeply. "So it appears." He glanced around his sitting room. "I see no Ixians."

She pursed her lips with displeasure. "Is this why you asked for consultation?"

Of course not, witch! I merely practise my arts of distraction. You would not expect me to mention things I wished to conceal. Then why would I call your attention to Ixians when I know it is unlikely there are any dangerous intruders walking freely on your accursed planet? Ahhh, the much vaunted Ixian connection we Tleilaxu maintained so long. You know of that! You punished Ix memorably more than once.

The women of Shaitan closed the obvious security gaps but were blind to the obvious!

The technocrats of Ix might hesitate to irritate the Bene

Gesserit, he thought, but they would be extremely careful not to arouse the ire of Honoured Matres. Secret trading was indicated by the presence of this no-ship but the price must have been ruinous and the circumlocutions exceptional. Very nasty, those whores from the Scattering. They might need Ix themselves, he guessed. And Ix might secretly defy the whores to make an arrangement with the Bene Gesserit. But the limits were tight and chances of betrayal many.

These thoughts comforted him as he bargained. Odrade, in a brittle mood, unsettled him several times with silences during which she stared at him in that disturbing Bene Gesserit way.

He could see that she found him repulsive—the way her gaze fixed sequentially on each of his features. He knew what she was thinking. *An elfin figure with narrow face and puckish eyes. Widows peak.* Her gaze moved down: *tiny mouth with sharp teeth and pointed canines.*

Scytale knew himself to be a figure out of humankind's most dangerously disturbing mythologies. Odrade would ask herself: *Why did the Bene Tleilax choose this particular physical appearance when their control of genetics could have given them something more impressive?*

For the very reason that it disturbs you, powindah dirt!

"The ones who cannot learn will fall by the wayside," she said. "Brought down by things they cannot face within themselves. A weeding process on all that lives."

Oh, how very true, witch.

"No allowance for accidents?" He asked it slyly. Holy Accidents were an integral part of the Great Belief.

"Accidents occur. But what do accidents teach?" And she answered her own question: "Be resilient. Be strong. Be ready for changes, for the new. Gather many experiences."

"Is that what you do in Other Memory?" Very bland, realizing she would interpret this as his ordinary slyness. *How little you powindah know of what I have gathered.*

Her answer reassured him. "We don't let ourselves be tangled in our pasts. We only interpret."

That had the sound of Mentat thinking but she refused to expand when he posed more questions.

They were trying to confuse him.

He thought of another *typical*: "The Bene Gesserit seldom scatter dirt."

Scytale had seen the dirty aftermath of many Bene Gesserit actions. *Look at what happened to Dune! Burnt to cinders because you women of Shaitan chose that holy ground to challenge the whores. Even the revenants of our Prophet gone to their reward. Everyone dead!*

And he hardly dared contemplate his own losses. No Tleilaxu planet had escaped the fate of Dune. *The Bene Gesserit caused that!* And he must suffer their tolerance—a refugee with only God to support him.

He asked Odrade about *scattered dirt* on Dune.

"You find that only when we are in extremis."

"Is that why you attracted the violence of those whores?"

She refused to discuss it.

One of Scytale's late companions had said: "Bene Gesserits leave straight tracks. You might think them complex, but when you look closely their way smooths."

That companion and all the others had been butchered by the whores. His only survival lay in cells of a nullentropy capsule. So much for a dead Master's wisdom!

Odrade wanted more technical information about axolotl tanks. Ohhhh, how cleverly she worded her questions!

Was it wrong to supply them even with limited knowledge? He realized now he had told them far more than the bare biotechnical details to which he had confined himself. They definitely deduced how Masters had created a limited immortality—always a ghola-replacement growing in the tanks. That, too, was lost! He wanted to scream this at her in his frustrated rage.

Questions . . . obvious questions.

He parried her questions with wordy arguments about "my need for Face Dancer servants and my own Shipsystem console."

She was slyly adamant, probing for more knowledge of the tanks. "The information to produce melange from our tanks might induce us to be more liberal with our guest."

Our tanks! Our guest!

These women were like a plasteel wall. No tanks for his personal use. *All of that Tleilaxu power gone.* It was a thought full of mournful self pity. He restored himself with a reminder: God obviously tested his resourcefulness. *They think they hold me in a trap.* But their restrictions hurt. No Face Dancer servants? Very well. He would seek other servants. Not Face Dancers.

Scytale felt the deepest anguish of his many lives when he thought of his lost Face Dancers—his mutable slaves. *Damn these women and their pretence that they shared the Great Belief! Omnipresent acolytes and Reverend Mothers always snooping around. Spies! And comeyes everywhere. Oppressive.*

He did not believe the witches were simple to understand. Complexity, that was their hallmark. It was said (They said it of themselves!) that they employed complexity "on occasion" because of barriers in their path. More deception!

"Often we use the Gordian-knot solution," Odrade boasted. "You don't even see the knife but the strands of complexity are all around and you know we have cut."

They were never that simple.

On first coming to Chapter House, he had sensed a shyness about his gaolers, a privacy that became intense when he probed into the workings of their order. Later, he came to see this as a circling up, all facing outward at any threat. *What is ours is ours. You may not enter!*

Scytale recognized a parental posturing in this, a maternal view of humankind: "Behave or we will punish you!" And Bene Gesserit punishments certainly were to be avoided.

As Odrade continued to demand more than he would give, Scytale fastened his attention on a *typical* he felt sure was true: *They cannot love.* But he was forced to agree. Neither love nor hate were purely rational. He thought of such emotions as a dark fountain shadowing the air all around, a primitive gusher that sprayed unsuspecting humans.

How this woman does chatter! He watched her, not really listening. What were their flaws? Was it a weakness that they avoided music? Did they fear the secret play on emotions? The aversion appeared to be heavily conditioned.

"It elicits useless memories," Odrade said.

The conditioning did not always succeed. In his many lives he had seen witches appear to enjoy music. When he questioned Odrade, she became quite heated, and he suspected a deliberate display to mislead him.

"We cannot let ourselves be distracted!"

"Don't you ever replay great musical performances in memory? I'm told that in ancient times . . ."

"Of what use is music played on instruments no longer known to most people?"

"Oh? What instruments are those?"

"Where would you find a piano?" *Still in that false anger.* "Terrible instruments to tune and even more difficult to play."

How prettily she protests. "I've never heard of this . . . this . . . piano, did you say? Is it like the baliset?"

"Distant cousins. But it could only be tuned to an approximate key. An idiosyncrasy of the instrument."

"Why do you single out this . . . this piano?"

"Because I sometimes think it too bad we no longer have it. Producing perfection from imperfection is, after all, the highest of art forms."

Scytale felt a deep wariness. Her words fitted themselves so neatly into her claim that the Bene Gesserit sought only to perfect human society. So she thought she could teach him! Another *typical*: "They see themselves as teachers."

When he expressed doubt of her intentions, she said, "Naturally we build up pressures in societies we influence. We do it that we may direct those pressures."

"I find this discordant," he complained.

"Why Master Scytale! It's a very common pattern. Governments often do this to produce violence against chosen targets. You did it yourselves! And see where it got you."

So she dares claim the Tleilaxu brought this calamity on themselves!

"We follow the lesson of The Great Messenger," she said, using the Islamiyat for the Prophet Leto II. The words sounded alien on her lips, but he was taken aback. She knew how all Tleilaxu revered the Prophet.

But I have heard these women call Him Tyrant!

Still speaking Islamiyat, she demanded, "Was it not His goal to divert violence, producing a lesson of value to all?"

Does she joke about the Great Belief?

"That is why we accepted him," she said. "He did not play by our rules but he played for our goal."

She dared say that *she* accepted the Prophet!

He did not challenge her, although the provocation was great. A delicate thing, a Reverend Mother's view of herself and her behaviour. He suspected they constantly readjusted this view, never bouncing far in any direction. No self-hate, no self-love. Confidence, yes. Maddening self-confidence. But that did not require hate or love. Only a cool head, every judgment ready for correction, just as she claimed. It would seldom require praise. *A job well done? Well, what else did you expect?*

"Bene Gesserit training strengthens the character." That was Folk Wisdom's most popular *typical*.

He tried to start an argument with her on this. "Don't Honoured Matres do the same thing? Look at Murbella!"

"Is it generalities you want, Scytale?" *Was that amusement in her tone?*

"A collision between two conditioning systems, isn't that a good way to view this confrontation?" he ventured.

"And the more powerful will emerge victorious, of course." *Definitely sneering!*

"Isn't that how it always works?" His anger not well bridled.

"Must a Bene Gesserit remind a Tleilaxu that subtleties are another kind of weapon? Have you not practised deception? A feigned weakness to deflect your enemies and lead them into traps? Vulnerabilities can be created."

Of course! She knows about the eons of Tleilaxu deception, creating an image of inept stupidities.

"So that's how you expect to deal with our foes?"

"We intend to punish them, Scytale."

Such implacable determination!

New things he learned about the Bene Gesserit filled him with misgivings.

Odrade, taking him for a well-guarded afternoon stroll in the cold winter outside the ship (burly Proctors just a pace behind), stopped to watch a small procession coming from Central. Five Bene Gesserit women, two of them acolytes by their white-trimmed robes, but the other three in an unrelieved grey not known to him. They wheeled a cart into one of the orchards. A frigid wind blew across them. A few old leaves whipped from the dark branches. The cart bore a long bundle shrouded in white. A body? It was the right shape.

When he asked, Odrade regaled him with an account of Bene Gesserit burial practices.

If there was a body to bury, it was done with the casual dispatch he now witnessed. No Reverend Mother ever had an obituary or wanted time-wasting rituals. Did her memory not live on in her Sisters?

He started to argue that this was irreverent but she cut him off.

"Given the phenomenon of death, all attachments in life are temporary! We modify that somewhat in Other Memory. You did a similar thing, Scytale. And now we incorporate some of your abilities in our bag of tricks. Oh, yes! That's the way we think of such knowledge. It merely modifies the pattern."

"An irreverent practice!"

"Nothing irreverent about it. Into the dirt they go where, at least, they can become fertilizer." And she continued to describe the scene without giving him a chance for further protests.

They had this regular routine he now observed, she said. A large mechanical auger was wheeled into the orchard where it drilled a suitable hole in the earth. The corpse, bound in that cheap cloth, was buried vertically and an orchard tree planted over it. Orchards were laid out in grid patterns, a cenotaph at one corner where the locations of burials were recorded. He saw the cenotaph when she pointed it out, a square green thing about three metres high.

"I think that body's being buried at about C-21," she said, watching the auger at work while the burial team waited, leaning against the cart. "That one will fertilize an apple tree." She sounded ungodly happy about it!

As they watched the auger withdraw and the cart being tipped, the body sliding into the hole, Odrade began to hum.

Scytale was surprised. "You said the Bene Gesserit avoided music."

"Just an appropriate old ditty." She sang it for him slowly, explaining the ancient references: "Ashes to ashes, dust to dust, if the Camels don't get you, the Fatimas must."

"Our ancestors inhaled smoke from these Fatima things you describe? A narcotic, of course."

"A deadly narcotic: nicotine. There was such widespread addiction and bureaucratic dependence on taxing them that it continued for centuries." She grinned. "That was a war song. Laughter in the face of death. Our way exactly."

The Bene Gesserit remained a puzzle and, more than ever, he saw the weakness of *typicals*. There was, for instance, the claim that they did without most bureaucratic systems and record keeping. Except for Bellonda's Archives, of course, and every time he mentioned those, Odrade said "Heaven guard us!" or something equivalent.

"But how do you maintain yourselves without officials and records?" He was deeply puzzled.

"A thing needs doing, we do it. Bury a sister?" She pointed to the scene in the orchard where shovels had been brought into play and dirt was being tamped on the grave.

"That's how it's done and there's always someone around who's responsible. They know who they are."

Why did she continue holding his attention on the burial? Was it a threat? He tried to divert her but she would not be moved.

"Down the hole she goes! Earth on top. A new orchard tree on that spot by this time tomorrow." Odrade faced him, staring down in that hard-eyed Bene Gesserit way. "Healthy trees, abundant fruit: Death in the service of life!"

"Who . . . who takes care of this unwholesome . . . ?"

"It's not unwholesome! It's part of our education. Failed sisters usually supervise. Acolytes do the work."

"Don't they . . . I mean, isn't this distasteful to them? Failed sisters, you say. And acolytes. It would seem to be more of a punishment than . . ."

"Punishment! Come, come, Scytale. Have you only one song to sing?" She pointed at the burial party. "After their

95

apprenticeship, all of our people willingly accept their jobs."

"But no . . . ahhh, bureaucratic . . ."

"We're not stupid!"

Again, he did not understand, but she responded to his silent puzzlement.

"Surely you know that bureaucracies always become voracious aristocracies after they attain commanding power."

He had difficulty seeing the relevance. Where was she leading him?

When he remained silent, she said: "Honoured Matres have all the marks of bureaucracy. Ministers of this, Great Honoured Matres of that, a powerful few at the top and many functionaries below."

She obviously saw this as a weakness, but he failed to see how it was a weakness and, if so, how she could exploit it.

"They already are full of adolescent hungers," she said, as though that explained everything. And when he failed to respond: "Voracious predators never consider how they exterminate their prey. A tight relationship: reduce the numbers of those upon whom you feed and you bring your own structure crashing down."

He found it difficult to believe the witches really saw Honoured Matres this way and said so.

"If you survive, Scytale, you will see my words made real. Great cries of rage by those unthinking women at the necessity to retrench. Much new effort to wring the most out of their prey. Capture more of them! Squeeze them harder! It will just mean quicker extermination. Idaho says they're already in the die-back stage."

"The ghola says this?" *So she was using him as a Mentat!* "Where do you get such ideas? Surely this does not originate with your ghola." *Continue to believe he's yours!*

"He merely confirmed our assessment. An example in Other Memory alerted us."

"Ohh?" This thing of Other Memory bothered him. Could their claim be true? Memories from his own multiple lives were of enormous value. He asked for confirmation.

"We remembered the relationship between a food animal called a snowshoe rabbit and a predatory cat called a lynx. The

96

cat population always grew to follow the population of the rabbits and then, overfeeding dumped the predators into famine times and severe die-back."

"An interesting term. Die-back?"

"Descriptive of what we intend for the Honoured Matres."

When their meeting ended (without anything gained to ease his restrictions), Scytale found himself more confused than ever. Was that truly their intent? The damnable woman! He could not be sure of anything she said.

When she returned him to his quarters in the ship, Scytale stood for a long time looking through the barrier field at the long corridor where Idaho and Murbella sometimes came on their way to their practice floor. He knew that must be where they went through a wide doorway down there. They always emerged sweating and breathing deeply.

Neither of his fellow prisoners appeared, although he loitered there for more than an hour.

She uses the ghola as a Mentat! That must mean he has access to a Shipsystems console. Surely, she would not deprive her Mentat of his data. Somehow, I must contrive it that Idaho and I meet intimately. There's always the whistling language we impress on every ghola. I must not appear too anxious. A small concession in the bargaining, perhaps. A complaint that my quarters are confining. They see how I chafe at imprisonment.

> *Education is no substitute for intelligence. That elusive quality is defined only in part by puzzle-solving ability. It is in the creation of new puzzles reflecting what your senses report that you round out the definition.*
>
> —Mentat Text One (decto)

They wheeled Lucilla into Great Honoured Matre's presence in a tubular cage—a cage within a cage. Shigawire netting confined her to the centre of the thing.

"I am Great Honoured Matre," the woman in the heavy black chair greeted her. *Small woman, red-gold leotards.* "The cage is for your protection should you try to use Voice. We are immune. Our immunity takes the form of a reflex. We kill. A

97

number of you have died that way. We know Voice and use it. Remember it when I release you from your cage." She waved away the servants who had brought the cage. "Go! Go!"

Lucilla looked around at the room. Windowless. Almost square. Lighted by a few silvery glowglobes. Acid green walls. Typical interrogation setting. It was somewhere high. They had brought her cage in a nulltube shortly after dawn.

A panel behind Great Honoured Matre snapped aside and a smaller cage came sliding into the room on a hidden mechanism. This cage was square and in it stood what she thought at first was a naked man until he turned and looked at her.

Futar! It had a wide face and she saw the canines.

"Want back rub," the Futar said.

"Yes, darling. I'll rub your back later."

"Want eat," the Futar said. It glared at Lucilla.

"Later, darling."

The Futar continued to study Lucilla. "You Handler?" it asked.

"Of course she's not a Handler!"

"Want eat," the Futar insisted.

"Later, I said! For now, you just sit there and purr for me."

The Futar squatted in its cage and a rumbling sound issued from its throat.

"Aren't they sweet when they purr?" Great Honoured Matre obviously did not expect an answer.

The presence of the caged Futar puzzled Lucilla. Those things were supposed to hunt and kill Honoured Matres. It was caged, though.

"Where did you capture it?" Lucilla asked.

"On Gammu." She did not see what she had revealed.

And this is Junction, Lucilla thought. She had recognized it from the lighter the evening before.

The Futar stopped purring. "Eat," it grumbled.

Lucilla would have liked something to eat. They had not fed her in three days and she was forced to suppress hunger pangs. Small sips of water from a literjon left in the cage helped but that was almost empty. The servants who had brought her had laughed at her request for food. "Futars like lean meat!"

It was the absence of melange that plagued her most. She

had begun to feel the first withdrawal pains that morning.

I shall have to kill myself soon.

The Lampadas horde pleaded for her to endure. *Be brave. What if that wild Reverend Mother fails us?*

Spider Queen. That is what Odrade calls this woman.

Great Honoured Matre continued to study her, hand to chin. It was a weak chin. In a face without positive features, the negative attracted the gaze.

"You will lose in the end, you know," Great Honoured Matre said.

"Whistling past the graveyard," Lucilla said and then had to explain the expression.

There was a polite show of interest on Great Honoured Matre's face. *How interesting.*

"Any of my aides would have killed you immediately for saying that. This is one of the reasons we are alone. I am curious why you would say such a thing?"

Lucilla glanced at the squatting Futar. "Futars did not occur overnight. They were genetically created from wild animal stock for one purpose."

"Careful!" Orange flamed in Great Honoured Matre's eyes.

"Generations of development went into the creation of the Futars," Lucilla said.

"We hunt them for our pleasure!"

"And the hunter becomes the hunted."

Great Honoured Matre leaped to her feet, eyes completely orange. The Futar became agitated and began whining. This calmed the woman. Slowly, she sank back into her chair. One hand gestured at the caged Futar. "It's all right, darling. You'll eat soon and then I'll rub your back."

The Futar resumed its purring.

"So you think we came back here as refugees," Great Honoured Matre said. "Yes! Don't try to deny it."

"Worms often turn," Lucilla said.

"Worms? You mean like those monstrosities we destroyed on Rakis?"

It was tempting to prod this Honoured Matre and evoke the dramatic response. Alarm her enough and she would certainly kill.

Please, sister! the Lampadas horde begged. *Endure.*

You think I can escape from this place? That silenced them, except for one faint protest. *Remember! We are the ancient doll: seven times down, eight times up.* It came with a rocking image of a small red doll, grinning Buddha face and hands clasped over its fat belly.

"You're obviously referring to the revenants of the God Emperor," Lucilla said. "I had something else in mind."

Great Honoured Matre took her time considering this. The orange faded from her eyes.

She's playing with me, Lucilla thought. *She intends to kill me and feed me to her pet.*

But think of the tactical information you could provide if we did escape!

We! But there was no avoiding the accuracy of that protest. They had brought her cage from the lighter while it was still daylight. Approaches to the Spider Queen's lair were well planned for difficult access but the planning amused Lucilla. Very ancient, out-of-date planning. Narrow places in the approach lanes with observation turrets projecting from the ground like dull grey mushrooms appearing at the proper places on their mycelium. Sharp turns at critical points. No ordinary ground vehicle could negotiate such turns at speed.

There was mention of this in Teg's critique of Junction, she recalled. Nonsense defences. One had only to bring in heavy equipment or go over such crude installations another way and the things were isolated. Linked underground, naturally, but that could be disrupted by explosives. Ligate them, cut them off from their source, and they would fall piecemeal. *No more precious energy coming down your tube, idiots!* Visible sense of security and Honoured Matres kept it. For reassurance! Their defenders must spend a great deal of energy on useless displays to give these women a false sense of security.

The hallways! Remember the hallways.

Yes, the hallways in this gigantic building were enormous, the better to accommodate giant tanks in which Guild Navigators were forced to live groundside. Ventilation systems low along the halls to take out and reclaim spilled melange gas. She could imagine hatches thumping open and closed with disturbing reverberations. Guildsmen never seemed to mind loud noises. Energy transmission lines for mobile suspensors were thick black snakes winding across passages and into every room she had glimpsed. Wouldn't do to keep a Navigator from snooping any place he desired.

Many of the people she had seen wore guide pulsers. Even Honoured Matres. So they got lost here. Everything under the one giant mound of a roof with its phallic towers. The new residents found this attractive? Heavily insulated from the crude outdoors (where none of the important people go anyway except to kill things or watch the slaves at their amusing work and play). Through much of it, she had seen a shabbiness that said minimal expenditure on maintenance. *They are not changing much. Teg's groundplan is still accurate.*

See how valuable your observations could be?

Great Honoured Matre stirred from her reverie. "It is just possible that I could permit you to live, provided you satisfy some of my curiosity."

"How do you know I won't respond to your curiosity with a flow of pure shit?"

Vulgarity amused Great Honoured Matre. She almost laughed. Apparently no one had ever warned her to beware of Bene Gesserits when they resorted to vulgarity. The motivation for it was sure to be something distressing. *No Voice, eh? She thinks that's my only resource?* Great Honoured Matre had said enough and reacted enough to give any Reverend Mother a sure handle on her. Body and speech signals always carried more information than was necessary for comprehension. There was inevitable extra information to be sampled.

"Do you find us attractive?" Great Honoured Matre asked.

Odd question. "People from the Scattering all possess a certain attraction." *Let her think I've seen many of them, including her enemies.* "You're exotic, meaning strange and new."

"And our sexual prowess?"

I said "exotic", Madame Spider, not "erotic". "There's an aura to that, naturally. Exciting and magnetic to some."

101

"But not to you."

Go for the chin! It was a suggestion from the horde. *Why not?*

"I've been studying your chin, Great Honoured Matre."

"You have?" Surprised.

"It's obviously your childhood chin and you should be proud of that youthful remembrance."

Not pleased at all but unable to show it. Hit the chin again.

"I'll bet your lovers often kiss your chin," Lucilla said.

Angry now and still unable to vent it. Threaten me, will you! Warn me not to use Voice!

"Kiss chin," the Futar said.

"I said later, darling. Now will you shut up!"

Taking it out on her poor pet.

"But you have questions you want to ask me," Lucilla said. Sweetness itself. Another warning signal to the knowledgeable. *I'm one of those who pours sugar syrup over everything. "How nice! Such a pleasant time when we're with you. Isn't that beautiful! Weren't you clever to get it so cheaply! Easily. Quickly." Supply your own adverb.*

Great Honoured Matre was a moment composing herself. She sensed that she had been placed at a disadvantage but could not say how. She covered the moment with an enigmatic smile, then: "But I said I would release you." She pressed something on the side of her chair and a section of the tubular cage swung aside, taking the shigawire netting with it. In the same instant, a low chair lifted from a panel in the floor directly in front of her and not a pace away.

Lucilla seated herself in the chair, knees almost touching her inquisitor. *Feet. Remember they kill with their feet.* She flexed her fingers, realizing then that she had been gripping her hands into fists. Damn the tensions!

"You should have some food and drink," Great Honoured Matre said. She pushed something else on the side of her chair. A tray came up beside Lucilla—plate, spoon, a glass brimming with red liquid. *Showing off her toys.*

Lucilla picked up the glass.

Poison? Smell it first.

She sampled the drink. Stimtea and melange! *I'm hungry.*

Lucilla returned an empty glass to the tray. The stim on her tongue smelled sharply of melange. *What is she doing? Wooing me?* Lucilla felt a flow of relief at the spice. The plate proved to hold beans in a piquant sauce. She ate it all after sampling the first bite for unwanted additives. Garlic in the sauce. She was hung up for the barest fraction of a second on Memory of this ingredient—adjunct to fine cooking, specific against werewolves, potent treatment for flatulence.

"You find our food pleasant?"

Lucilla wiped her chin. "Very good. You are to be complimented on your chef." *Never compliment the chef in a private establishment. Chefs can be replaced. Hostess is irreplaceable.* "A nice touch with garlic." *No more distractions. This is not the moment to recount the past of garlic users.*

"We've been studying some of the library salvaged from Lampadas." Gloating: *See what you lost?* "So little of interest buried in all of that prattle."

Does she want you to be her librarian? Lucilla waited silently.

"Some of my aides think there may be clues to your witches' nest there or, at least, a way to eliminate you quickly. So many languages!"

Does she need a translator? Be blunt!

"What interests you?"

"Very little. Who could possibly need accounts of the Butlerian Jihad?"

"They destroyed libraries, too."

"And that ancient . . . What was his name? Oh, yes: Karl Marx. What possible pertinence could his writings have in our day?"

She's circling around whatever it is that interests her. Give her a small discourse.

"Karl Marx made the mistake most jealous humans make: thinking everything he hated was evil and that he had the best correctives. He never faced the fact that jealousy and hatred themselves are the problem. The first correction has to be within you."

"Another one of your witches' illusions!"

"No one is immune from illusion, Great Honoured Matre.

You can, however, fortify yourself against disillusion."

"Don't patronize me!"

She's sharper than we thought. Keep it blunt.

"I thought I was the object of patronage."

"Listen to me, witch! You think you can be ruthless in defence of your nest but you do not understand what it is to be ruthless."

"I don't think you have yet told me how I can satisfy your curiosity."

"It's your science we want, witch!" She pitched her voice lower. "Let us be reasonable. With your help we could achieve utopia."

And conquer all of your enemies and achieve orgasm every time.

"You think science holds the keys to utopia?"

"And better organization for our affairs."

Remember: Bureaucracy elevates conformity . . . make that "fatal stupidity" . . . to the status of religion.

"Paradox, Great Honoured Matre. Science must be innovative. It brings change. That's why science and bureaucracy fight a constant war."

Does she know her roots?

"But think of the power! Think of what you could control!"

She doesn't know.

Honoured Matre assumptions about control fascinated Lucilla. You controlled your universe; you did not balance with it. You looked outward, never inward. You did not train yourself to sense your own subtle responses, you produced muscles (forces, powers) to overcome everything you defined as an obstacle. Were these women blind?

When Lucilla did not speak, Honoured Matre said: "We found much in the library about the Bene Tleilax."

Even the Tleilaxu saw the fallacy of "control".

"You joined the Bene Tleilax for many projects, witch. Multiple projects: how to nullify a no-ship's invisibility, how to penetrate the secrets of the living cell, your Missionaria Protectiva and something called 'The Language of God'."

There it is! That interests her!

Lucilla produced a tight smile. Did they fear there might be

104

a real god out there somewhere? *Give her a little taste! Be candid.*

"We joined the Tleilaxu in nothing. Your people misinterpret what they found. You worry about being patronized? How do you think God would feel about it? We plant protective religions to help us. That is the Missionaria's function. The Tleilaxu have only one religion."

"You organize religions?"

"Not quite. The organizational approach to religion is always apologetic. We do not apologize."

"You are beginning to bore me. Why did we find so little about the God Emperor?" Pouncing!

She's heating up again!

"Perhaps your people destroyed it."

"Ahhhh, then you do have an interest in him."

And so do you, Madame Spider!

"I would have presumed, Great Honoured Matre, that Leto II and his Golden Path were subjects of study at many of your academic centres."

That was cruel!

"We have no academic centres!"

See?

"I find your interest in him surprising."

"Casual interest, no more."

And that Futar sprang from an oak tree struck by lightning!

"We call his Golden Path 'the paper chase'. He blew it into the infinite winds and said: 'See? There is where it goes.' That's the Scattering."

"Some prefer to call it The Seeking."

And you call it the empire you lost.

"Could he really predict our future? Is that what interests you?"

Bullseye!

Great Honoured Matre coughed into her hand.

"We say Muad'Dib created a future. Leto II un-created it."

"But if I could know . . ."

"Please! Great Honoured Matre! People who demand that the oracle predict their lives, really want to know where the treasure is hidden."

105

"But of course!"

"Know your entire future and nothing will ever surprise you? Is that it?"

"In so many words."

"You don't want the future, you want now extended forever."

"I could not have said it better."

"And you said I bored you!"

"What?"

Orange in her eyes. Careful.

"Never another surprise? What could be more boring?"

"Ahhhh . . . Oh! But that's not what I mean."

"Then I'm afraid I do not understand your question, Great Honoured Matre."

"No matter. We'll return to it tomorrow."

Reprieve!

Great Honoured Matre stood. "Back into your cage."

"Eat?" The Futar sounded plaintive.

"I have some wonderful food for you downstairs, darling. Then I'll rub your back."

Lucilla entered her cage. Great Honoured Matre threw a chair cushion in after her. "Use that against the shigawire. See how kind I can be?"

The cage door sealed with a click.

The Futar in its cage slid back into the wall. The panel snapped closed over it.

"They get so restless when they're hungry." Great Honoured Matre said. She opened the door to the room and turned to contemplate Lucilla for a moment. "You will not be disturbed here. I am refusing permission for anyone else to enter this room."

Many things we do naturally become difficult only when we try to make them intellectual subjects. It is possible to know so much about a subject that you become totally ignorant.

—Mentat Text Two (dicto)

Periodically, Odrade went for dinner with the acolytes and their Proctor-Watchers, the most immediate warders in this *mind-prison* from which many would never be released.

What the acolytes thought and did really informed the depths of Mother Superior's consciousness on how well Chapter House functioned. Acolytes responded from their moods and forebodings more directly than Reverend Mothers. Full sisters got very good at not being seen at their worst. They did not try to conceal essentials, but anyone could walk in an orchard or close a door and be out of the view of watchdogs.

Not so the acolytes.

There was little slack time in Central these days. Even the dining halls had their constant streams of occupants no matter the hour. Workshifts were staggered and it was easy for a Reverend Mother to adjust her circadian rhythms to off-beat time. Odrade could not waste energy on such adjustments. At the evening meal, she paused at the door to the Acolyte Hall and heard the sudden hush.

Even the way they conveyed food to their mouths said something. Where did the eyes go as the chopsticks progressed mouthward? Was it a quick stab and a rapid chew before a convulsive swallow? That was a one to watch. She was brewing upsets. And that thoughtful one over there who looked at each mouthful as though wondering how they hid the poison in such slop? A creative mind behind those eyes. Test her for a more sensitive position.

Odrade entered the Hall.

The floor had a large chequerboard pattern, black and white plaz, virtually unscratchable. Acolytes said the pattern was for Reverend Mothers to use as a game board: "Place one of us here and another over there and some along that central line. Move them thus—winner take all."

Odrade took a seat near the corner of a table beside the western windows. The acolytes made room for her, their movements quietly unobtrusive.

This hall was part of the oldest construction on Chapter House. Built of wood with clear-span beams overhead, enormously thick and heavy things finished in dull black. They were some twenty-five metres long without a joint. Somewhere on Chapter House there was a grove of genetically-tailored oaks reaching up to sunlight in their carefully-tended plantations. Trees going up thirty metres at least without a limb, and more than two metres through the boles. They had been planted when this hall was built, replacements for these beams when age weakened them. Nineteen hundred SY the beams were supposed to endure.

Odrade did not know precisely where the replacements had been planted—somewhere in the northern hemisphere. She merely knew of their existence and general location. An administrative detail that need not trouble Mother Superior. She wondered, though, how the trees were doing in the climate changes. How close were they to the advancing desert?

Such exquisite attention to details, a hallmark of Bene Gesserit intrusions on any planet, reassured Odrade. A valuable thing about a closely-monitored and interlinked eco-system was that it kept down pollution. One creature's poison could be another's food. Many niches: mutual support.

How carefully the acolytes around her watched Mother Superior without ever appearing to look directly at her.

Odrade turned her head to peer out the western windows at the sunset. *Dust again.* The spreading intrusion from the desert inflamed the setting sun and set it glowing like a distant ember that might explode into uncontrollable fire at any instant.

Odrade suppressed a sigh. Thoughts such as these recreated her nightmare: *The chasm . . . the tightrope.* She knew if she closed her eyes she would feel herself swaying on the rope. The hunter with the axe was nearer!

Acolytes eating close by stirred nervously as though they sensed her disquiet. Perhaps they did. Odrade heard the movement of fabrics and this dragged her out of her nightmare. She had become sensitized to a new note in the sounds of Central. There was a grating noise behind the most commonplace movements—that chair being shifted behind her . . . and the opening of that kitchen door. Rasping grit. Cleaning crews complained of sand and "the damnable dust".

Odrade stared out the window at the source of that

irritation: wind from the south. A dull haze, something between tan and earth brown, drew a curtain across the horizon. After the wind, dustings of its deposits would be found in building corners and on lee sides of hills. There was a flinty aroma to it, something alkaline that irritated the nostrils.

She looked down at the table as a serving acolyte placed her meal in front of her.

Odrade found herself enjoying this change from quick meals in her workroom and private dining room. When she ate alone up there, acolytes brought food so quietly and cleared away with such silent efficiency that sometimes she was surprised to find everything gone. Here, dining was bustle and conversation. In her quarters, Chef Duana might come in clucking, "You are not eating enough." Odrade generally heeded such admonitions. Watchdogs had their uses.

Tonight's meal was sligpork in a sauce of soy and molasses, minimal melange, a touch of basil and lemon. Fresh green beans cooked al dente with peppers. Dark red grape juice to drink. She took a bite of sligpork with anticipation and found it passable, a bit overcooked for her taste. Acolyte chefs had not missed it by much.

Then why this feeling of too many such meals?

She swallowed and hypersensitivity identified additives. This food was not here just to replenish Mother Superior's energy. Someone in the kitchen had asked for her day's nutrition list and adjusted this plate accordingly.

Food is a trap, she thought. *More addictions.* She did not like the cunning ways Chapter House chefs concealed things they put in the food "for the good of the diners". They knew, of course, that a Reverend Mother could identify ingredients and adjust metabolism within her limits. They were watching her right now, wondering how Mother Superior would judge tonight's menu.

Somewhere, purity of taste should triumph, Odrade thought. Even at the expense of what chefs called "alimentation".

As she ate, she listened to the other diners. None intruded on her—not physically or vocally. Sounds returned almost to what they had been before her entrance. Waggling tongues

109

always changed their tone slightly when she entered and resumed at lower volume.

Edited for Mother Superior.

An unspoken question lay in all of those busy minds around her: *Why is she here tonight?*

Odrade sensed quiet awe in some nearby diners, a reaction Mother Superior sometimes employed to her advantage. Awe with an edge on it. Acolytes whispered among themselves (so the Proctors reported) "She has Taraza." They meant Odrade possessed her late predecessor as Primary. The two of them were an historical pair, required study for postulants.

Dar and Tar, already a legend.

Even Bellonda (dear old vicious Bell) came at Odrade obliquely because of this. Few frontal attacks, very little blaring in her accusatory arguments. Taraza was credited with saving the Sisterhood. That silenced much opposition. Taraza had said Honoured Matres were essentially barbarians and their violence, although not totally deflectable, could be guided into bloody displays. Events had more or less verified this.

Correct up to a point, Tar. None of us anticipated the extent of their violence.

Taraza's classical veronica (how apt the bullring image) had aimed the Honoured Matres into such episodes of carnage that the universe was mordant with potential supporters of their brutalized victims.

We have moved the nature of individual decision into a new arena.

The importance of words to describe the necessities faded farther into the background every day. Not only words, but the languages that ruled the tuning of thoughts. Language could not move itself, nor could it be removed from the people who flowed with it and changed it. Only the individual could step aside and become wordless.

Is it there I would influence our destiny?

Human destiny had never been completely manageable. And in a Scattered universe, that fact became dangerous reality.

110

How do I defend us?

It was not so much that their defensive plans were inadequate. They could become irrelevant.

That, of course, is what I seek. We must be purified and made ready for a supreme effort.

Bellonda had sneered at that idea. "For our demise? Is that why we must be purified?"

Bellonda would be ambivalent when she discovered what Mother Superior planned. Bellonda-vicious would applaud. Bellonda-Mentat would argue for delay "until a more propitious moment".

But I will seek my own peculiar way despite what my sisters think.

And many sisters thought Odrade quite the strangest Mother Superior they had ever accepted. Elevated more with the left hand than with the right. *Taraza Primary. I was there when you died, Tar. No one else to gather your persona. Elevation by accident?*

Many disapproved of Odrade. But when opposition arose, back they went to "Taraza Primary—the best Mother Superior in our history".

Amusing! Taraza Within was the quickest to laugh and ask: *"Why don't you tell them about my mistakes, Dar? Especially about how I misjudged you."*

Odrade chewed reflectively on a bite of sligpork. *I'm overdue for a visit to Sheeana. South into the desert and that soon. Sheeana must be made ready to replace Tam.*

The changing landscape loomed large in Odrade's thoughts. More than fifteen hundred years of Bene Gesserit occupancy on Chapter House. *Signs of us everywhere.* Not just in special groves or vineyards and orchards. What it must be doing to the collective psyche, seeing such changes come over their familiar land.

The acolyte seated beside Odrade made a soft throat-clearing sound. Was she about to address Mother Superior? A rare occurrence. The young woman continued to eat without speaking.

Odrade's thoughts returned to the prospective journey into the desert. Sheeana must have no forewarning. *I must be sure she is the one we need*. There were questions for Sheeana to answer.

Odrade knew what she would find on inspection stops en route. In sisters, in plant and animal life, in the very foundations of Chapter House, she would see changes gross and changes subtle, things to wrench at Mother Superior's vaunted serenity. Even Murbella, seldom out of the no-ship (and never without guards), sensed these changes.

Only that morning, seated with her back to her console, Murbella had listened with new attentiveness to Odrade standing over her. Edgy alertness in the captive Honoured Matre. Her voice betrayed doubts and unbalanced judgments.

"*All* is transient, Mother Superior?"

"That is knowledge impressed on you by Other Memory. No planet, no land or sea, no part of any land or sea is here forever."

"A morbid thought!" Rejection.

"Wherever we stand, we are only stewards."

"A useless viewpoint." Hesitant, questioning why Mother Superior chose this moment to say such things.

"I hear Honoured Matres talking through you. They gave you greedy dreams, Murbella."

"So you say!" Deeply resentful.

"Honoured Matres think they can buy infinite security: a small planet, you know, with plenty of subservient population."

Murbella produced a grimace.

"More planets!" Odrade snapped. "Always more and more and more! That's why they come swarming back."

"Poor pickings in this Old Empire."

"Excellent, Murbella! You're beginning to think like one of us."

"And that makes me a *nothing*!"

"Neither fish nor fowl, but your own true self? Even there, you're only a steward. Beware, Murbella! If you think you own something, that's like walking on quicksand."

This got a puzzled frown. Something would have to be done about the way Murbella allowed her emotions to play so openly on her face. It was permissible here, but someday . . .

"So nothing is safely owned. So what!" Bitter, bitter.

112

"You speak some of the right words but I don't think you've yet found a place in yourself where you can endure for your lifetime."

"Until an enemy finds me and slaughters me?"

Honoured Matre training clings like glue! But she spoke to Duncan the other night in a way that tells me she is ready. The Van Gogh painting, I do believe, has sensitized her. I heard it in her voice. I must review that record.

"Who would slaughter you, Murbella?"

"You'll never withstand an Honoured Matre attack!"

"I've already stated the basic fact that concerns us: No place is eternally safe."

"Another of your useless damned lessons!"

In the Acolyte Hall, Odrade recalled she had not found time to review that comeye record of Duncan and Murbella. A sigh almost escaped her. She covered it with a cough. Never do to let the young women see disturbance in Mother Superior.

To the desert and Sheeana! Inspection tour as soon as I can make time for it. Time!

Again, the acolyte seated beside Odrade made that throat noise. Odrade watched peripherally—blonde, short black dress trimmed in white—Intermediate Third Stage. No movement of the head toward Odrade, no sidelong glances.

This is what I will find on my inspection tour: Fears. And in the landscape, those things we always see when we run out of time: trees left uncut because woodcutters have gone—dragooned into our Scattering, gone to their graves, gone to unknown places, perhaps even to peonage. Will I see architectural Fancies becoming attractive because they are incomplete, builders departed? No. We don't go in much for Fancies.

Other Memory held examples she wished she might find: old buildings more beautiful because they are unfinished. The builder bankrupt, an owner angered at his mistress . . . Some things were more interesting because of that: old walls, old ruins. Time sculpture.

What would Bell say if I ordered a Fancy in my favourite orchard?

The acolyte beside Odrade said: "Mother Superior?"

Excellent! They so seldom find the courage.

"Yes?" Faint questioning. *This had better be important.* Would she hear?

She heard. "I intrude, Mother Superior, because of the urgency and because I know your interest in the orchards."

Superb! This acolyte had thick legs but that did not extend to her mind. Odrade stared at her silently.

"I am the one making the map for your bedchamber, Mother Superior."

So this was a reliable adept, a person trusted with work for Mother Superior. Even better.

"Will I have my map soon?"

"Two days, Mother Superior. I am adjusting projection overlays where I will mark the desert's daily growth."

A brief nod. That had been in the original order: an acolyte to keep the map current. Odrade wanted to awaken each morning, her imagination ignited by that changing view, the first thing impressed on awareness at arising.

"I put a report in your workroom this morning, Mother Superior. 'Orchard Management'. Perhaps you did not see it."

Odrade had seen only the label. She had been late coming from exercises, anxious to visit Murbella. So much depended on Murbella!

"The plantations around Central must either be abandoned or action taken to sustain them," the acolyte said. "That's the gist of the report."

Odrade pursed her lips. *This one has access to Weather's data. Of course! That's necessary for her to mark my map.* And they all knew how Mother Superior felt about the precious orchards. Save them? It was a decision only Odrade could make and the acolyte had rightly called attention to it.

"Repeat the report verbatim." *An Intermediate Third Stage acolyte should be able to do that.*

Night fell and the room lights brightened as Odrade listened. Concise. Terse even. The report carried a note of admonishment Odrade recognized as originating with Bellonda. No Archival signature but Weather's warnings went through Archives and this acolyte had lifted some of the original words.

The acolyte fell silent, report concluded.

How do I respond? Orchards, pastures and vineyards were not merely a buffer against alien intrusions, pleasant decorations on the landscape. They supported Chapter House morale and tables.

They support my morale.

How quietly this acolyte waited. Curly blonde hair and round face. Pleasing countenance, though the mouth was wide. Food remained on her plate but she was not eating. Hands folded in her lap. *I am here to serve you, Mother Superior.*

No need for more speech. This one would not prod unless necessity required it. Wrong to ignore that report. Best thing a government could do was to set a good example. Bad examples produced a bad populace. A fact as old as the Sisterhood's oldest memories. Basic: *The best teaching is by example.* "Hands-on," as the awful old expression had it, was better. *Do it yourself.*

How arch such expressions were. This moment required no arch expressions. That would create fantasies.

While Odrade composed her response, memory intruded—an old incident simulflowing over immediate observations. She remembered her ornithopter training course. *Two acolyte students with instructor at mid-day high over the wetlands of Lampadas.* She had been paired with as inept an acolyte as could have been accepted by the Sisterhood. Obviously a gene-choice. The Breeding Mistresses wanted her for a characteristic to be passed along to offspring. *It certainly wasn't emotional balance or intelligence!* Odrade remembered the name: Linchine.

Linchine had shouted at their instructor: "I am going to fly this damned 'thopter!"

And all the while a whirling sky and landscape of trees and marshy lakeshore dizzied them. *That was how it seemed: us stationary and the world moving.* Linchine doing the wrong thing every time. Each movement created worse gyrations.

The instructor cut her out of the system by pulling the disconnect only he could reach. He did not speak until they were flying straight and level.

"No way are you ever going to fly this, lady. Not ever! You

115

don't have the right reactions. You have to begin training those into someone like you before puberty."

"I am! I am! I'll fly this damned thing." Hands jerking at the useless controls.

"You're washed out, lady. Grounded!"

Odrade breathed easier, realizing she had known all along that Linchine might kill them.

Whirling toward Odrade in the rear, Linchine screamed: "Tell him! Tell him he must obey a Bene Gesserit!"

Addressing the fact that Odrade, several years ahead of Linchine, already displayed a commanding presence.

Odrade sat in silence, features immobile.

Silence is often the best thing to say, some Bene Gesserit humorist had scrawled on a washroom mirror. Odrade found that good advice then and later.

Recalling herself to the needs of the acolyte in the dining hall, Odrade wondered why that old memory had come of itself. Such things seldom happened without purpose. *Not silence now, certainly. Humour?* Yes! That was the message. Odrade's humour (applied later) had taught Linchine something about herself. *Humour under stress.*

Odrade smiled at the acolyte beside her in the dining hall. "How would you like to be a horse?"

"What?" The word was startled out of her but she responded to Mother Superior's smile. Nothing alarming in that. Warm even. Everyone said Mother Superior permitted affections.

"You don't understand, of course," Odrade said.

"No, Mother Superior." Still smiling and patient.

Odrade allowed her gaze to quest over the young face. Clear blue eyes not yet touched by the engulfing blue of Spice Agony. A mouth almost like Bell's but without the viciousness. Dependable muscles and dependable intelligence. She would be good at anticipating Mother Superior's needs. Witness her map assignment and that report. Sensitive. Went with her superior intelligence. Not likely to rise to the very top but always in key positions where you needed her qualities.

Why did I sit beside this one?

Odrade frequently selected a particular companion at

116

mealtime visits. Acolytes mostly. They could be so revealing. Reports often found their way to Mother Superior's workroom: personal observations from Proctors about one acolyte or another. But sometimes, Odrade chose a seat for no reason she could explain. *As I did tonight. Why this one?*

Conversation rarely occurred unless Mother Superior initiated it. Gentle initiation usually, easing into more intimate matters. Others around them listened avidly.

At such moments, Odrade often produced a manner of almost religious serenity. It soothed nervous ones. Acolytes were . . . well, acolytes, but Mother Superior was the supreme witch of them all. Nervousness was natural.

Someone behind Odrade whispered: "She has Streggi on the coals tonight."

On the coals. Odrade knew the expression. It had been used in her acolyte days. So this one was named Streggi. *Let it be unspoken for now. Names carry magic.*

"Do you enjoy tonight's dinner?" Odrade asked.

"It's acceptable, Mother Superior." One tried not to give false opinions, but Streggi was confused by the shift in conversation.

"They've overcooked it," Odrade said.

"Serving so many, they cannot please everyone, Mother Superior." *So she defends her companions on tonight's kitchen detail.*

"And they please no one," Odrade said.

"Serving so many, how can they please everyone, Mother Superior?"

She speaks her mind and speaks it well.

"Your left hand is trembling," Odrade said.

"I'm nervous with you, Mother Superior. And I've just come from the practice floor. Very tiring today."

Odrade analysed the tremors. "They have you doing the long-arm lift."

"Was it painful in your day, Mother Superior?" (In those ancient times?)

"Just as painful as today. Pain teaches, they told me."

That softened things. Shared experiences, the patter of the Proctors.

117

"I don't understand about horses, Mother Superior." Streggi looked at her plate. "This cannot be horse meat. I'm sure I . . ."

Odrade laughed loudly, attracting startled looks. She put a hand on Streggi's arm and subsided to a gentle smile. "Thank you, my dear. No one has made me laugh that much in years. I hope this is the beginning of a long and joyous association."

"Thank you, Mother Superior, but I . . ."

"I will explain about the horse, my own little joke and no intent to demean you. I want you to carry a young child on your shoulders, to move him more rapidly than his short legs will carry him."

"As you wish, Mother Superior." No objections, no more questions. Questions were there, but the answers would come in their own time and Streggi knew it.

Magic time.

Withdrawing her hand, Odrade said: "Your name?"

"Streggi, Mother Superior. Aloana Streggi."

"Rest easy, Streggi. I will see to the orchards. We need them for morale as much as for food. You report to Reassignment tonight. Tell them I want you in my workroom at six tomorrow morning."

"I will be there, Mother Superior."

She would be, too. Dependable. A fortunate discovery. Odrade did not believe in omens but, like Taraza before her, felt the strong hand of coincidence.

"Will I continue to mark your map, Mother Superior?" As Odrade was rising to leave.

"For now, Streggi. But ask Reassignment for a new acolyte and begin training her. Soon, you will be much too busy for the map."

"Thank you, Mother Superior. The desert is growing very fast."

Streggi's words gave Odrade a certain satisfaction, dispelling gloom that had hampered her most of the day.

The cycle was getting another chance, turning once more as it was impelled to do by those subterranean forces called "life" and "love" and other unnecessary labels.

Thus it turns. Thus it renews. Magic. What witchery could take your attention from this miracle?

In her workroom, she issued an order to Weather, then silenced the tools of her office and went to the bow window. Chapter House glowed pale red in the night from reflections of groundlights against low clouds. It gave a romantic appearance to rooftops and walls that Odrade quickly rejected.

Romance? There was nothing romantic about what she had done in the Acolyte Dining Hall.

I have finally done it. I have committed myself. Now, Duncan must restore our Bashar's memories. A delicate assignment.

She continued to stare into the night, suppressing knots in her stomach.

I not only commit myself but I commit what remains of my Sisterhood. So this is how it feels, Tar.

This is how it feels and your plan is tricky.

It was going to rain. Odrade sensed it in the air coming through the ventilators around the window. No need to read a Weather Dispatch. She seldom did that these days, anyway. Why bother? But Streggi's report carried a potent warning.

Rains were becoming rarer here and rather to be welcomed. Sisters would emerge to walk in it despite the cold. There was a touch of sadness in the thought. Each rain she saw brought the same question: *Is this the last one?*

The people of Weather did heroic things to keep an expanding desert dry and the growing areas irrigated. Odrade did not know how they had managed this rain to comply with her order. Before long, they would not be able to obey such commands, even from Mother Superior. *The desert will triumph because that is what we have set in motion.*

She opened the central panes of her window. The wind at this level had stopped. Just the clouds moving overhead. Wind at higher elevations harrying things along. A sense of urgency in the weather. The air was chilly. So they had made temperature adjustments to bring this bit of rain. She closed the window, feeling no desire to go outside. Mother Superior had no time to play the game of *last rain*. One rain at a time. And always out there the desert moving inexorably toward them.

That, we can map and watch. But what of the hunter behind

me—the nightmare figure with the axe? What map tells me where she is tonight?

> *Religion (emulation of adults by the child) encysts past mythologies: guesses, hidden assumptions of trust in the universe, pronouncements people made in search of personal power, all mingled with shreds of enlightenment. And always an unspoken commandment: Thou shalt not question! We break that commandment daily. Our work is the harnessing of human imagination to our deepest creativity.*
>
> —Bene Gesserit Credo

Murbella sat cross-legged on the practice floor, alone, shivering after her exertions. Mother Superior had been here less than an hour this afternoon. And, as often happened, Murbella felt she had been abandoned in a fever dream.

Odrade's parting words reverberated in the dream: "The hardest lesson for an acolyte to learn is that she must always go to the limit. Your abilities will take you farther than you imagine. Don't imagine, then. Extend yourself!

What is my response? That I was taught to cheat?

Odrade had done something to call up the patterns of childhood and Honoured Matre education. *I learned cheating as an infant. How to simulate a need and gain attention.* Many "how-to's" in the cheating pattern. The older she got, the easier the cheating. She had learned what the *big people* around her were demanding. *I regurgitated on demand. That was called "education".* Why were the Bene Gesserit so remarkably different in their teaching?

"I don't ask you to be honest with me," Odrade had said. "Be honest with yourself."

Murbella despaired of ever rooting out all of the cheating in her past. *Why should I?* More cheating!

"Damn you, Odrade!"

Only after the words were out did she realize she had spoken them aloud. She started to put a hand to her mouth and aborted the movement. Fever said: "What's the difference?"

120

"Educational bureaucracies dull a child's questing sensitivity." *Odrade explaining.* "The young must be dampened down. Never let them know how good they can be. That brings change. Spend lots of committee time talking about how to deal with exceptional students. Don't spend any time dealing with how the conventional teacher feels threatened by emerging talents and squelches them because of a deep-seated desire to feel superior and safe in a safe environment."

She was talking about Honoured Matres.

Conventional teachers?

There it was: behind that facade of wisdom, the Bene Gesserit were unconventional. They often did not think about teaching; they just did it.

Gods! I want to be like them!

The thought shocked her and she leaped to her feet, launching herself into a training routine for wrists and arms.

Realization bit deeper than ever. She did not want to disappoint these teachers. *Candour and honesty.* Every acolyte heard that. "Basic tools of learning," Odrade said.

Distracted by her thoughts, Murbella tumbled hard and stood up, rubbing a bruised shoulder.

She had thought at first that the Bene Gesserit protestation must be a lie. *I am being so candid with you that I must tell you about my unswerving honesty.*

But actions confirmed their claim. Odrade's voice persisted in the fever dream: "That is how you judge."

They had something in the mind, in memory and a balance of intellect no Honoured Matre had ever possessed. This thought made her feel small. *Enter corruption.* It was like liver spots in her feverish thoughts.

But I have talent! It required talent to become an Honoured Matre.

Do I still think of myself as an Honoured Matre?

The Bene Gesserit knew she had not fully committed herself to them. *What skills do I have that they could possibly want? Not the skills of deception.*

"*Do actions agree with words? There's your measure of reliability. Never confine yourself to the words.*"

Murbella put her hands over her ears. *Shut up, Odrade!*

121

"How does a Truthsayer separate sincerity from a more fundamental judgment?"

Murbella dropped her hands to her sides. *Maybe I'm really sick.* She swept her gaze around the long room. No one there to utter these words. Anyway, it was Odrade's voice.

"If you convince yourself, sincerely, you can speak utter balderdash (marvellous old word; look it up), absolute poppy-larky in every word and you will be believed. But not by one of our Truthsayers."

Murbella's shoulders sagged. She began to wander aimlessly around the practice floor. Was there no place to escape?

"Look for the consequences, Murbella. That's how you ferret out things that work. That's what our much-vaunted truths are all about."

Pragmatism?

Idaho found her then and responded to the wild look in her eyes. "What's wrong?"

"I think I'm sick. Really sick. I thought it was something Odrade did to me but . . ."

He caught her as she fell.

"Help us!"

For once, he was glad of the comeyes. A Suk was with them in less than a minute. She bent over Murbella where Idaho cradled her on the floor.

The examination was brief. The Suk, a greying older Reverend Mother with the traditional diamond brand on her forehead, straightened and said: "Overstressed. She's not trying to find her limits, she's going beyond them. We'll put her back into the sensitizing class before we let her continue. I'll send the Proctor."

Odrade found Murbella in the Proctor's Ward that evening, propped up in a bed, two Proctors taking turns testing her muscle responses. A small gesture and they left Odrade alone with Murbella.

"I tried to avoid complicating things," Murbella said. *Candour and honesty.*

"Trying to avoid complications often creates them." Odrade sank into a chair beside the bed and put a hand on Murbella's arm. Muscles quivered under the hand. "We say

122

'words are slow, feeling's faster'." Odrade withdrew. "What decisions have you been making?"

"You let me make decisions?"

"Don't sneer." She lifted a hand to prevent interruption. "I didn't take your previous conditioning into sufficient account. The Honoured Matres left you practically incapable of making decisions."

"Is that right?" Still touchy about criticism of her *former sisters*.

"Typical of power-hungry societies. Teach their people to diddle around forever. 'Decisions bring bad results!' That's the routine. You teach avoidance."

"What's that have to do with me collapsing?" Resentful.

"Murbella! The worst products of what I'm describing are almost basket cases—can't make decisions about anything, or leave them until the last possible second and then leap at them like desperate animals."

"You told me to go to the limit!" Almost wailing.

"Your limits, Murbella. Not mine. Not Bell's or those of anyone else. Yours."

"I've decided I want to be like you." Very faint.

"Marvellous! I don't believe I've ever tried to kill myself. Especially when I was pregnant."

In spite of herself, Murbella grinned.

Odrade stood. "Sleep. You're going into a special class tomorrow where we'll work on your ability to mesh your decisions with sensitivity to your limits. Remember what I told you. We take care of our own."

"Am I yours?" Almost whispered.

"Since you repeated the oath before the Proctors." Odrade turned out the lights as she left. Murbella heard her speak to someone before the door closed. "Stop fussing with her. She needs rest."

Murbella closed her eyes. The fever dream was gone but in its place was her own memory. "I am a Bene Gesserit. I exist only to serve."

She heard herself saying those words to the Proctors but memory gave them an emphasis not in the original.

They knew I was being cynical.

What could you hide from such women?

She felt the remembered hand of the Proctor on her forehead and heard the words that had possessed no meaning until this moment.

"I stand in the sacred human presence. As I do now, so should you stand some day. I pray to your presence that this be so. Let the future remain uncertain for that is the canvas to receive our desires. Thus the human condition faces its perpetual tabula rasa. We possess no more than this moment where we dedicated ourselves continuously to the sacred presence we share and create."

Conventional but unconventional. She realized that she had not been physically or emotionally prepared for this moment. Tears flowed down her cheeks.

> *Laws to suppress tend to strengthen what they would prohibit. This is the fine point on which all the legal professions of history have based their job security.*
>
> **—Bene Gesserit Coda**

On her restless prowlings through Central (infrequent these days but more intense because of that), Odrade looked for signs of slackness and especially for areas of responsibility that were running too smoothly.

The *Senior Watchdog* had her own watch*words*: "Show me a completely smooth operation and I'll show you someone who's covering mistakes. Real boats rock."

She said this often and it became an identifying phrase the sisters (and even some acolytes) employed to comment on Mother Superior.

"Real boats rock." Soft chuckles.

Bellonda accompanied Odrade on today's early morning inspection, not mentioning that "once a month" had been stretched to "once every two months"—if that. This inspection was a week past the mark. She wanted to use this time for warnings about Idaho. And she had dragged Tamalane along although Tam was supposed to be reviewing Proctor performance at this hour.

Two against one? Odrade wondered. She did not think Bell or Tam suspected what Mother Superior intended. Well, it would come out, as had Taraza's plan. *In its own time, eh, Tar?*

Bellonda had not yet mentioned Idaho. Waiting for "the right moment". It was coming. Bell had been out in the no-ship yesterday, a long session with Idaho and Murbella.

Down the corridors they stalked, black robes swishing with urgency, eyes missing little. It was all familiar and yet they looked for things that were new. Odrade carried her Ear-C over her left shoulder like a misplaced diving weight. *Never be out of communication range these days.*

Behind the scenes in any Bene Gesserit centre were the support facilities: clinic-hospital, kitchen, morgue, garbage control, reclamation systems (attached to sewage and garbage), transport and communications, kitchen provisioning, training and physical maintenance halls, schools for acolytes and postulants, quarters for all of the denominations, meeting centres, testing facilities and much more. Personnel often changed because of the Scattering and movement of people into new responsibilities, all according to subtle Bene Gesserit awareness. But tasks and places for them remained.

As they strode swiftly from one area to another, Odrade spoke of the Sisterhood Scattering, not trying to hide her dismay at "the atomic family" they had become.

"Lebensraum! No limits on it any more. Move your furniture into this wide open space, humanity! Arrange it as you please."

"Then why do Honoured Matres come looking for our places?" Tam wanted to know.

Tam begged the question. *How would it please you to furnish your universe if you were an Honoured Matre?* Honoured Matres carried an unknown "furnishing" in their minds.

"I find it difficult to contemplate humankind spreading into an unlimited universe," Tam said. "The possibilities . . ."

"Infinite numbers game." Odrade stepped across a broken curb. "That should be repaired. We've been playing the infinity game since we learned to jump Foldspace."

There was no joy in Bellonda. "It's not a game!"

125

Odrade could appreciate Bellonda's feelings. *We have never seen empty space. Always more galaxies. Tam's right. It's daunting when you focus on that Golden Path.*

Memories of explorations gave the Sisterhood a statistical handle on it but little else. So many habitable planets in a given assemblage and, among those, an expected additional number that could be terraformed.

"Infinity Paradox." Odrade spoke to Tamalane as they passed a storeroom being emptied of large transparent cubes. *Preserved peaches.*

"What's evolving out there?" Tamalane demanded.

A question they could not answer. Ask what Infinity might produce and the only answer possible was, "Anything."

Any good, any evil; any god, any devil.

"What if Honoured Matres are fleeing something?" Odrade asked. "Interesting possibility?"

"These speculations are useless," Bellonda muttered. "We don't even know if Foldspace introduces us to one universe or many . . . or even an infinite number of expanding and collapsing bubbles."

"Did the Tyrant understand this any better than we do?" Tamalane asked.

They paused while Odrade looked into a room where five Advanced Acolytes and a Proctor studied a projection of regional melange stores. The crystal holding the information performed an intricate dance in the projector, bouncing on its beam like a ball on a fountain. Odrade saw the summation and turned away before scowling. Tam and Bell did not see Odrade's expression. *We will have to start limiting access to melange data. Too depressing to morale.*

Administration! It all came back to Mother Superior. Delegate heavily to only the same people and you fell into bureaucracy.

Odrade knew she depended too much on her inner sense of administration. A system frequently tested and revised, using automation only where essential. "The machinery" they called it. By the time they became Reverend Mothers, all of them had some sensitivity to "the machinery" and tended to use it without question thereafter. There lay the danger.

Odrade pressed for constant improvements (even tiny ones) to introduce change into their activities. Randomity! No absolute patterns that others could find and use against them. One person might not see such shifts in a lifetime but differences over longer periods were sure to be measurable.

Odrade's party came down to ground level and on to the major thoroughfare of Central. "The Way," Sisters called it. An in-joke, referring to the training regimen popularly known as "The Bene Gesserit Way."

The Way reached from the square beside Odrade's tower to the southern outskirts of the urban area—straight as a lasgun beam, almost twelve klicks of tall buildings and low ones. The low ones all had something in common: they had been built strong enough to expand upward.

Odrade flagged an open transporter with empty seats and the three of them crowded into a space where they could continue to talk. Frontage on The Way carried an old-fashioned appeal, Odrade thought. Buildings such as these with their tall rectangular windows of insulating plaz had framed Bene Gesserit "Ways" through much of the Sisterhood's history. Down the centre ran a line of elms genetically tailored for height and narrow profile. Birds nested in them and the morning was bright with flitting spots of red and orange—orioles, tanagers.

Is it dangerously patterned for us to prefer this familiar setting?

Odrade led them off the transporter at Tipsy Trail, thinking how Bene Gesserit humour came out in curious names. Waggish in the streets. Tipsy Trail because the foundation of one building had subsided slightly, giving that structure a curiously drunken appearance. The one member of the group stepping out of line.

Like Mother Superior. Only they don't know it yet.

They came to Tower Lane and turned to the south. Tower Lane: all one-storey buildings. A busy street this morning— two troops of advanced acolytes coming from some sweaty exertion, a contingent of senior Proctors looking worried. Odrade was tempted to stop them and inquire where they were going but they were in a hurry.

127

Her Ear-C buzzed as she was considering whether to follow the Proctors. "Mother Superior?" It was Streggi. Without stopping, Odrade signalled that she was on-line "You asked for a report on Murbella? Suk Central says she is fit for assigned classes."

"Then assign her." They continued down Tower Lane.

Odrade spared a brief glance for the low buildings on both sides of the street. A two-storey addition was being added to one of them. Might be a real Tower Lane here someday and the joke (such as it was) abandoned.

It was argued that naming was just a convenience anyway and they might as well enjoy this venture into what was a delicate subject for the Sisterhood.

One seldom laughed with a Reverend Mother and never at her. You might smile a bit if asked to meet Reverend Mother so and so at an address on Giggletree Way. The Sisters, though, seldom analysed names their predecessors had given to streets and passages and buildings. These were like another language, bits of a past that continued in use because it would be too disruptive to change (like that tipsy building on Tipsy Trail) and besides those were the names everyone used. Why cause upset by requiring everyone to learn other names?

This is one of our patterns. Perhaps not dangerous as long as we confine it to our own places.

Odrade stopped abruptly on a busy walkway and turned to her companions. "What would you say if I suggested that we name streets and places after departed sisters?"

"You're full of nonsense today!" Bellonda accused.

"They are not departed," Tamalane said.

Odrade resumed her prowling walk. She had expected that. Bell's thoughts could almost be heard. *We carry the "departed" around in Other Memory!*

Odrade wanted no argument here in the open but she thought her idea had merit. Some sisters died without Sharing. Major Memory Lines were duplicated but you lost a thread and its terminated carrier. Schwangyu of the Gammu Keep had gone that way, killed by attacking Honoured Matres. Plenty of memories remained to carry her good qualities . . .

and complexities. One hesitated to say her mistakes taught more than her successes.

Bellonda increased her pace to walk beside Odrade in a relatively empty stretch. "I must speak of Idaho. A Mentat, yes, but those multiple memories. Supremely dangerous!"

They were passing a morgue, the strong smell of antiseptics even in the street. The arched doorway stood open.

"Who died?" Odrade asked, ignoring Bellonda's anxiety.

"A Proctor from Section Four and an orchard maintenance man," Tamalane said. Tam always knew.

Bellonda was furious at being ignored and made no attempt to hide it. "Will you two stick to the point?"

"What is the point?" Odrade asked. Very mild.

They emerged on the south terrace and stopped at the stone rail to look over the plantations—vineyards and orchards. The morning light had a dusty haze in it not at all like the mists created of moisture.

"You know the point!" Bell would not be deflected.

Odrade stared at the vista, pressing herself against the stones. The railing was frigid. That mist out there was a different colour, she thought. Sunlight came through dust with a different reflective spectrum. More bounce and sharpness to the light. Absorbed in a different way. The nimbus was tighter. The blowing dust and sand crept into every crevice the way water did but the grating and rasping betrayed its source. The same with Bell's persistence. No lubrication.

"That's desert light," Odrade said, pointing.

"Stop avoiding me," Bellonda said.

Odrade chose not to answer. The dusty light was a classical thing, but not reassuring in the way of the elder painters and their misty mornings.

Tamalane came up beside Odrade. "Beautiful in its own way." The remote tone said she made Other Memory comparisons similar to Odrade's.

If that's how you were conditioned to look for beauty. But something deep within Odrade said this was not the beauty for which she longed.

In the shallow swales below them, where once there had been greenery, now there was dryness and a sense of the earth being gutted the way ancient Egyptians had prepared their dead—dried to essential matter, preserved for their Eternity. *Desert as death-master, swaddling the dirt in natron, embalming our beautiful planet with all of its jewels concealed.*

Bellonda stood behind them, muttering and shaking her head, refusing to look at what their planet would become.

Odrade almost shuddered in a sudden thrust of simulflow. Memory flooded her: She felt herself searching Sietch Tabr's ruins, finding desert-embalmed bodies of spice pirates left where killers had dropped them.

What is Sietch Tabr now? A molten flow solidified and without anything to mark its proud history. Honoured Matres: killers of history.

"If you won't eliminate Idaho, then I must protest your using him as a Mentat."

Bell was such a fussy woman! Odrade noted that she was showing her age more than ever. Reading lenses on her nose even now. They magnified her eyes until she had the look of a great-orbed fish. Use of lenses and not one of the more subtle prostheses said something about her. She flaunted a reverse vanity that announced: "I am greater than the devices my failing senses require."

Bellonda was definitely irritated by Mother Superior. "Why are you staring at me that way?"

Odrade, caught by abrupt awareness of a weakness in her Council, shifted her attention to Tamalane. Cartilage never stopped growing and this had enlarged Tam's ears, nose and chin. Some Reverend Mothers adjusted this by metabolism control or sought regular surgical correction. Tam would not bow to such vanity. *"Here's what I am. Take it or leave it."*

My advisers are too old. And I . . . I should be younger and stronger to have these problems on my shoulders. Oh, damn this for a lapse into self pity!

Only one supreme danger: action against survival of the Sisterhood.

What we cannot afford is self pity or, for that matter, self indulgence. Now that Honoured Matres have proved a Reverend Mother can die as easily as anyone, there must be better reasons for our actions.

130

"Duncan is a superb Mentat!" Odrade spoke with all the force of her position. "But I use none of you beyond your capabilities."

Bellonda remained silent. She knew a Mentat's weaknesses.

Mentats! Odrade thought. They were like walking Archives but when you most needed answers thèy relapsed into questions.

"I don't need another Mentat," Odrade said. "I need an inventor!"

Let Bell chew on that. Inspiration, that was what the Sisterhood required. Something subterranean whose exact workings had never been subjected to clinical autopsy. Rationality would kill it and they all knew this. *We couldn't even plant a fruit tree over it!*

When Bellonda still did not speak, Odrade said: "I am freeing his mind, not his body."

"I insist on an analysis before you open all data sources to him!"

Considering Bellonda's usual stance, that was mild. But Odrade did not trust it. She detested those sessions—endless rehashing of Archival reports. Bellonda doted on them. Bellonda of Archival minutiae and boring excursions into irrelevant details! Who cared if Reverend Mother "X" preferred skimmed milk on her porridge?

Odrade turned her back on Bellonda and looked at the southern sky. *Dust! We would sift more dust!* Bellonda would be flanked by assistants. Odrade felt boredom just imagining it.

"This is reliable!" the assistants mimed with every gesture. As though they wrote their precious words like some antique clerk seated at his high table, peering at his ledgers through half glasses. Self-satisfied looks of wisdom for all questioners.

"No more analysis." Odrade spoke more sharply than she had intended. But Archives was jammed with inaccessible data. Accurate? Reliable? Who knew? Exhaustively prepared? For sure! Exhausting to contemplate as well. Tiny accumulations of datum after datum after datum.

"I do have a point of view." Bellonda sounded hurt.

131

Point of view? Are we no more than sensory windows on our universe, each with only a point of view?

Instincts and memories of all types . . . even Archives— none of these things spoke for themselves except by compelling intrusions. None carried weight until formulated in a living consciousness. But whoever produced the formulation tipped the scales. *All order is arbitrary!* Why this datum rather than some other? Any Reverend Mother knew events occurred in their own flux, their own relative environment. Why couldn't a Mentat Reverend Mother act from that knowledge?

"Do you refuse council?" That was Tamalane. Was she siding with Bell?

"When have I ever refused council?" Odrade let her outrage show. "I am refusing another of Bell's Archival merry-go-rounds."

Bellonda intruded. "Then, in reality . . ."

"Bell! Don't talk to me about reality!" Let her simmer in that! Reverend Mother *and* Mentat! *There is no reality. Only our own order imposed on everything. A basic Bene Gesserit dictum.*

There were times (and this was one of them) when Odrade wished she had been born in an earlier era—a Roman matron in the long pax of the aristocrats, or a much-pampered Victorian. But she was trapped by time and circumstances.

Trapped forever?

Must face that possibility. The Sisterhood might have only a future confined to secret hideaways, always fearing discovery. The future of the hunted. *And here at Central we may be allowed no more than one mistake.*

"I've had enough of this inspection!" Odrade called for private transport and hurried them back to her workroom.

What will we do if the hunters come upon us here?

Each of them had her own scenario, a little playlet full of planned reactions. But every Reverend Mother was a sufficient realist to know her playlet might be more hindrance than help.

In the workroom, morning light harshly revealing on everything around them, Odrade sank into her chair and waited for Tamalane and Bellonda to take their seats.

No more of those damned analysis sessions. She really needed access to something better than Archives, better than anything they had ever used before. Inspiration. Odrade rubbed her legs, feeling muscles tremble. She had not slept well for days. This inspection left her feeling frustrated.

One mistake could end us and I am about to commit us to a no-return decision.

Am I being too tricky?

Her advisers argued against tricky solutions. They said the Sisterhood must move with steady assurance, the ground ahead known in advance. Everything they did lay counterpoised by the disaster awaiting them at the slightest misstep.

And I am on the tightrope over the chasm.

Did they have room to experiment, to test possible solutions? They all played that game. Bell and Tam screened a constant flow of suggestions but nothing more effective than their atomic Scattering.

"We must be prepared to kill Idaho at the slightest sign he is a kwisatz haderach," Bellonda said.

"Don't you have work to do? Get out of here, both of you!"

As they stood, the workroom around Odrade took on an alien feeling. What was wrong? Bellonda stared down at her with that awful look of censure. Tamalane appeared more wise than she could possibly be.

What is it about this room?

The workroom would have been recognized for its function by humans from pre-space history. What felt so alien? A worktable was a worktable and the chairs were in convenient positions. Bell and Tam preferred chairdogs. Those would have seemed odd to the early human in Other Memory she suspected was colouring her view. The ridulian crystals might glisten strangely, the light pulsing in them and blinking. Messages dancing above the table might be surprising. Instruments of her labours could appear strange to an early human sharing her awareness.

But it felt alien to me.

"Are you all right, Dar?" Tam spoke with concern.

Odrade waved her away but neither woman moved.

Things were happening in her mind that could not be

blamed on the long hours and insufficient rest. This was not the first time she had felt she worked in alien surroundings. The previous night while eating a snack at this table, the surface littered with assignment orders as it was now, she had found herself just sitting and staring at uncompleted work.

Which sisters could be spared from what posts for this terrible Scattering? How could they improve survival chances of the few sandtrout the Scattered sisters took? What was a proper allotment of melange? Should they wait before sending more sisters into the unknown? Wait for the possibility that Scytale could be induced to tell them how axolotl tanks produced the spice.

Odrade recalled that the alien feeling had occurred to her as she chewed on a sandwich. She had looked at it, opening it slightly. *What is this thing I'm eating?* Chicken liver and onions on some of the best Chapter House bread.

Questioning her own routines, that was part of this alien sensation.

"You look ill," Bellonda said.

"Just fatigue," Odrade lied. They knew she was lying but would they challenge her? "You both must be equally tired." Affection in her tone.

Bell was not satisfied. "You set a bad example!"

"What? Me?" The jesting was not lost on Bell.

"You know damned well you do!"

"It's your displays of affection," Tamalane said.

"Even for Bell."

"I don't want your damned affection! It's wrong."

"Only if I let it rule my decisions, Bell. Only then."

Bellonda's voice fell to a husky whisper. "Some think you're a dangerous romantic, Dar. You know what that could do."

"Ally sisters with me for other than our survival. Is that what you mean?"

"Sometimes you give me a headache, Dar!"

"It's my duty and right to give you a headache. When your head fails to ache, you become careless. Affections bother you but hates don't."

"I know my flaw."

You couldn't be a Reverend Mother and not know it.

The workroom once more had become a familiar place but now Odrade knew a source of her alien feelings. She was thinking of this place as part of ancient history, viewing it as she might when it was long gone. As it certainly would be if her plan succeeded. She knew what she had to do now. Time to reveal the first step.

Careful.

Yes, Tar, I'm as cautious as you were.

Tam and Bell might be old but their minds were sharp when necessity required it.

"Bell, do you still insist we not punish the hunters, violence for violence?" Odrade asked.

"We dare not feed that fire. Not yet."

"But we also dare not sit here witlessly waiting for them to find us. Lampadas and our other disasters tell us what will happen when they come. When, not if."

As she spoke, Odrade sensed the chasm beneath her, the nightmare hunter with the axe ever nearer. She wanted to sink into the nightmare, turning there to identify the one who stalked them, but dared not. That had been the mistake of the kwisatz haderach.

You do not see that future, you create it.

Tamalane wanted to know why Odrade asked that question. "Have you changed your mind, Dar?"

"Our ghola Teg is ten years old."

"Much too young for us to attempt restoring his original memories," Bellonda said.

Odrade drew in a deep breath and looked down at her worktable. It had come at last. On that morning when she had removed the baby ghola from his obscene "tank", she had sensed this moment waiting for her. Even then she had known she would put this ghola into the crucible before his time. Ties of blood notwithstanding.

Reaching beneath her table, Odrade touched a call field. Her two councillors stood silently waiting. They knew she was about to say something important. One thing a Mother Superior could be sure of—her sisters listened to her with great care, with an intensity that would have gratified someone more ego-bound than a Reverend Mother.

"Politics," Odrade said.

That snapped them to attention! A loaded word. When you entered Bene Gesserit politics, marshalling your powers for the rise to eminence, you became a prisoner of responsibility. You saddled yourself with duties and decisions that bound you to the lives of those who depended on you. This was what really tied the Sisterhood to their Mother Superior. That one word told councillors and the watchdogs the First-Among-Equals had reached a decision.

They all heard the small scuffling sound of someone arriving outside the workroom door. Odrade touched the white plate in the near right corner of her table. The door behind her opened and Streggi stood there awaiting the Mother Superior's orders.

"Bring him," Odrade said.

"Yes, Mother Superior." Almost emotionless. A very promising acolyte, that Streggi.

She stepped out of sight and returned leading Miles Teg by the hand. The boy's hair was quite blond but streaked with darker lines that said the light colouration would go dark when he matured. His face was narrow, nose just beginning to show that hawkish angularity so characteristic of Atreides males. His blue eyes moved alertly taking in room and occupants with expectant curiosity.

"Wait outside, please, Streggi."

Odrade waited for the door to close.

The boy stood looking at Odrade with no sign of impatience.

"Miles Teg, ghola," Odrade said. "You remember Tamalane and Bellonda, of course."

He favoured the two women with a short glance but remained silent, apparently unmoved by the intensity of their inspection.

Tamalane frowned. She had disagreed from the first calling this child a ghola. Gholas were grown from cells of a cadaver. This was a clone, just as Scytale was a clone.

"I am going to send him into the no-ship with Duncan and Murbella," Odrade said. "Who better than Duncan to restore Miles to his original memories?"

"Poetic justice," Bellonda agreed. She did not speak her

objections although Odrade knew they would come out when the boy had gone. *Too young!*

"What does she mean, poetic justice?" Teg asked. His voice had a piping quality.

"When the Bashar was on Gammu, he restored Duncan's original memories."

"Is it really painful?"

"Duncan found it so."

Some decisions must be ruthless.

Odrade thought that a great barrier to accepting the fact that you could make your own decisions. Something she would not be required to explain to Murbella.

How do I soften the blow?

There were times when you could not soften it; in fact when it was kinder to rip off the bandages in one swift shot of agony.

"Can this . . . this Duncan Idaho really give me back my memories from . . . before?'

"He can and he will."

"Are we not being too precipitous?" Tamalane asked.

"I've been studying accounts of the Bashar," Teg said. "He was a famous military man and a Mentat."

"And you're proud of that, I suppose?" Bell was taking out her objections on the boy.

"Not especially." He returned her gaze without flinching. "I think of him as someone else. Interesting, though."

"Someone else," Bellonda muttered. She looked at Odrade with ill-concealed disagreement. "You're giving him the deep teaching!"

"As his birth mother did."

"Will I remember her?" Teg asked.

Odrade gave him a conspiratorial smile, one they had shared often in their orchard walks. "You will."

"Everything?"

"You'll remember all of it—your wife, your children, the battles. Everything."

"Send him away!" Bellonda said.

The boy smiled but looked to Odrade, awaiting her command.

"Very well, Miles," Odrade said. "Tell Streggi to take you

137

to your new quarters in the no-ship. I'll come along later and introduce you to Duncan."

"May I ride on Streggi's shoulders?"

"Ask her."

Impulsively, Teg dashed up to Odrade, lifted himself on to his toes and kissed her cheek. "I hope my real mother was like you."

Odrade patted his shoulder. "Very much like me. Run along now."

When the door closed behind him, Tamalane said: "You haven't told him you're one of his daughters!"

"Not yet."

"Will Idaho tell him?"

"If it's indicated."

Bellonda was not interested in petty details. "What are you planning, Dar?"

Tamalane answered for her. "A punishment force commanded by our Mentat Bashar. It's obvious."

She took the bait!

"Is that it?" Bellonda demanded.

What has her suspicious?

Odrade favoured them both with a hard stare. "Teg was the best we ever had. If anyone can punish our enemies . . ."

"We'd better start growing another one," Tamalane said.

"I don't like the influence Murbella may have on him," Bellonda said.

"Will Idaho cooperate?" Tamalane asked.

"He will do what an Atreides asks of him."

Odrade spoke with more confidence than she felt but the words opened her mind to another source of the alien feelings.

I'm seeing us as Murbella sees us! I can think like at least one Honoured Matre!

We do not teach history; we recreate the experience. We follow the chain of consequences—the tracks of the beast in its forest. Look behind our words and you see the broad sweep of social behaviour that no historian has ever touched.

—BG Panoplia Propheticus

138

Scytale whistled while he walked down the corridor fronting his quarters, taking his afternoon exercise. Down and back. Whistling.

Get them accustomed to me whistling.

As he whistled, he composed a ditty to go with the sound: "Tleilaxu sperm does not talk." Over and over, the words rolled in his mind. They could not use his cells to bridge the genetic gap and learn his secrets.

They must come to me with gifts.

Odrade had stopped by to see him earlier "on my way to confer with Murbella". She mentioned the captive Honoured Matre to him frequently. There was a purpose but he had no idea what it might be. Threat? Always possible. It would be revealed eventually.

"I hope you are not fearful," Odrade had said.

They had been standing at his food slot while he waited for lunch to appear. The menu was never quite to his liking but acceptable. Today, he had asked for seafood. No telling what form it would take.

"Fearful? Of you? Ahhh, dear Mother Superior, I am priceless to you alive. Why should I fear?"

"My Council reserves judgment on your latest requests."

I expected that.

"It's a mistake to hobble a useful tool," he said. "Limits your choices. Weakens you."

Those words had taken several days of planning for him to compose. He waited for their effect.

"It depends on how one intends to employ the tool, Master Scytale. Some tools break when you don't use them properly."

Damn you, witch!

He smiled, showing his sharp canines. "Testing to extinction, Mother Superior?"

She made one of her rare sallies into humour. "Do you really expect me to strengthen you? For what do you bargain now, Scytale?"

So I'm no longer Master *Scytale. Strike her with the flat of the blade!*

"You Scatter your sisters, hoping some will escape destruc-

139

tion. What are the economic consequences of your hysterical reaction?"

Consequences! They always talk about consequences.

"We trade for time, Scytale." Very solemn.

He gave this a silent moment of reflection. The comeyes were watching them. Never forget it! *Economics, witch! Who and what do we buy and sell?* This alcove by the food slot was a strange place for bargaining, he thought. Bad management of the economy. The management hustle, the planning and strategy session, should occur behind closed doors, in high rooms with views that did not distract the occupants from the business at hand.

The serial memories of his many lives would not accept that. *Necessity. Humans conduct their merchant affairs wherever they can—on the decks of sailing ships, in tawdry streets full of bustling clerks, in the spacious halls of a traditional bourse with information flowing above their heads for all to see.*

Planning and strategy might come from those high rooms but the evidence of it was like the common information of the bourse—there for all to see.

So let the comeyes watch.

"I keep reminding myself that you're not really young," Odrade said.

He was momentarily disconcerted and wondered if he concealed it. *Do they read minds?*

"What are your intentions toward me, Mother Superior?"

"To keep you alive and strong."

Careful, careful.

"But not give me a free hand."

"Scytale! You speak of economics and then want something free?"

"But my strength is important to you?"

"Believe it!"

"I do not trust you."

The food slot took that moment to disgorge his lunch: a white fish sautéed in a delicate sauce. He smelled herbs. Water in a tall glass, faint aroma of melange. A green salad. *One of their better efforts.* He felt himself salivating.

"Enjoy your lunch, Master Scytale. There is nothing in it to harm you. Is that not a measure of trust?"

When he did not respond, she said: "What does trust have to do with our bargaining?"

What game is she playing now?

"You tell me what you intend for Honoured Matres but you do not say what you intend for me." He knew he sounded plaintive. Unavoidable.

"I intend to make the Honoured Matres aware of their mortality."

"As you do with me!"

Was that satisfaction in her eyes?

"Scytale." *How soft her voice.* "People thus made aware truly listen. They hear you." She glanced at his tray. "Would you like something special?"

He drew himself up as best he could. "A small stimulant drink. It helps when I must think."

"Of course. I'll see that it's sent down at once." She turned her attention out of the alcove toward the main room of his quarters. He watched where she paused, her gaze shifting from place to place, item to item.

Everything in its place, witch. I am not an animal in its cave. Things must be convenient, where I can find them without thinking. Yes, those are stimpens beside my chair. So I use 'pens. But I avoid alcohol. You notice?

The stimulant, when it came, tasted of a bitter herb he was a moment identifying. Casmine. A genetically-modified blood strengthener from the Gammu pharmacopoeia.

Did she intend to remind him of Gammu? They were so devious, these witches!

Poking fun at him over the question of economics. He felt the sting of this as he turned at the end of his corridor and continued his exercise in a brisk walk back to his quarters. What glue had actually held the Old Empire together? Many things, some small and some large, but mostly economic. Lines of connection thought of often as conveniences. And what kept them from blasting each other out of existence? The Great Convention. "You blast anyone and we unite to blast you."

141

He stopped outside his door, brought up short by a thought.

Was that it? How could punishment be enough to stop the greedy powindah? Did it come down to a glue composed of intangibles? The censure of your peers? But what if your peers balked at no obscenity? You could do anything. And that said something about Honoured Matres. It certainly did.

He longed for a sagra chamber in which to bare his soul.

The Yaghist is gone! Am I the last Mashiekh?

His chest felt empty. It was an effort to breathe. Perhaps it would be best to bargain more openly with the women of Shaitan.

No! That is Shaitan himself tempting me!

He entered his chambers in a chastened mood.

I must make them pay. Make them pay dearly. Dearly, dearly, dearly. Each *dearly* accompanied a step toward his chair. When he sat, his right hand reached out automatically for a 'pen. Soon, he felt his mind driving at speed, thoughts pouring through in marvellous array.

They do not guess how well I know the Ixian ship. It's here in my head. Here in my head. Here in my head.

He spent the next hour deciding how he would record these moments when it came time to tell his fellows how he had triumphed over the powindah. *With God's help!*

They would be glittering words, filled with drama and the tensions of his testing. History, after all, was always written by the victors.

> They say Mother Superior can disregard nothing—a
> meaningless aphorism until you grasp its other significance:
> I am the servant of all my sisters. They watch their servant
> with critical eyes. I cannot spend too much time on generali-
> ties nor on trivia. Mother Superior must display insightful
> action else a sense of disquiet penetrates to the farthest
> corners of our order.
>
> —Darwi Odrade

Something of what Odrade called "my servant-self" went with her as she walked the halls of Central this morning, making this her exercise rather than take time on a practice floor. *A disgruntled servant!* She did not like what she saw.

We are too tightly bound up in our difficulties, almost incapable of separating petty problems from great ones.

What had happened to their conscience?

Although some denied it, Odrade knew there was a Bene Gesserit conscience. But they had twisted and reshaped it into a form not easily recognized.

She felt loath to meddle with it. Decisions taken in the name of survival, the Missionaria (their interminable Jesuitical arguments!)—all diverged from something far more demanding of human judgment. The Tyrant had known this.

To be human, that was the issue. But before you could be human, you had to feel it in your guts.

No clinical answers! It came down to a deceptive simplicity whose complex nature appeared when you applied it.

Like me.

You looked inward and found who and what you believed you were. Nothing else would serve.

So what am I?

"*Who asks that question?*" It was a skewering thrust from Other Memory.

Odrade laughed aloud and a passing Proctor named Praska stared at her in astonishment. Odrade waved to Praska and said: "It's good to be alive. Remember that."

Praska produced a faint smile before going on about her business.

Odrade paused in the doorway to a postulant training room. They were beginning rigorous postural stances that would fix in their awareness the place and function of every muscle. Agonizing at this stage, Odrade recalled, observing how the young women trembled in their strained positions.

So who asks: What am I?

Dangerous question. Asking it put her in a universe where nothing was quite human. Nothing matched the undefined thing she sought. All around her, clowns, wild animals and puppets reacted to hidden strings. She sensed the strings that jerked *her* into movement.

143

Odrade continued along the corridor toward the tube that would take her up to her quarters.

Strings. What came with the egg? *We speak glibly of "the mind at its beginning". But what was I before the pressures of living shaped me?*

It wasn't enough to seek something "natural". No "Noble Savage". She had seen plenty of those in her lifetime. The strings jerking them were quite visible to a Bene Gesserit.

Odrade triggered the tube door and waited. A buzz told her it was in use. She turned and glanced back toward the room where the postulants were taking their first steps on her pathway. *They are so precious.*

She felt the taskmaster within her. Strong today. It was a force she sometimes disobeyed or avoided. Taskmaster said: "You are fitted for these activities. Do them well. Improve yourself. Strengthen your talents. Do not flow gently in the current. Swim! Use it or lose it."

With a gasping sensation of near panic, she realized she had barely retained her humanity, that she had been on the point of losing it.

I've been trying too hard to think like an Honoured Matre! Manipulating and manoeuvring anyone I could. And all in the name of Bene Gesserit survival!

Bell said there were no limits beyond which the Sisterhood would refuse to go in preserving the Bene Gesserit. A modicum of truth in this boast but it was the truth of all boasting. There were indeed things a Reverend Mother would not do to save the Sisterhood.

We would not block the Tyrant's Golden Path.

Survival of humankind took precedence over survival of the Sisterhood. *Else our Grail of human maturity is meaningless.*

But oh, the perils of leadership in a species so anxious to be told what to do. How little they knew of what they created by their demands. Leaders made mistakes. And those mistakes, amplified by the numbers who followed without questioning, moved inevitably toward great disasters.

Lemming behaviour.

Odrade had only to skim the surface of Other Memory to

gather examples—blind masses following charismatic leaders off precipices.

It was right that her sisters watched her carefully. All governments needed to remain under suspicion during their time of power. *Trust no government! Not even mine!*

They are watching me this very instant. Very little escapes my sisters. They will know my plan in time.

It required constant mental cleansing to face up to the fact of her great power over others. *I did not seek this power. It was thrust upon me.* And she thought: *Power attracts the corruptible. Suspect all who seek it.* She knew the chances were great that such people were susceptible to corruption or already lost.

Odrade made a mental note to scribe and transmit a Coda memo to Archives. (Let Bell sweat this one!) "We should grant power over our affairs only to those who are reluctant to hold it and then only under conditions that increase the reluctance."

Perfect description of the Bene Gesserit!

"Are you well, Dar?" It was Bellonda's voice from the tube door beside Odrade. "You look . . . strange."

"I just thought of something to do. You getting off?"

Bellonda stared at her as they exchanged places. The tubefield caught Odrade and whisked her away from that questioning gaze.

Odrade emerged in the corridor to her workroom. *You do not grasp your humanity fiercely; you watch it with a benevolent eye.*

Many things she had done met Taskmaster Standards but there were forces in her Bene Gesserit experiences pushing her farther and farther from a central lodestone of humanity.

Odrade entered the workroom and saw her table piled with things her aides thought only she could resolve.

Lodestone. Soul calling to her. Taskmaster, Soul, a sense of balance. Something always judged whatever she did.

Politics, she recalled as she sat at her table and prepared to deal with responsibilities. Tam and Bell heard her clearly the other day but they had only the vaguest idea of what they would be asked to support. They were worried and increasingly watchful. *As they should be.*

Almost any subject had political elements, she thought. As emotions were whipped up, political forces came more and more into the foreground. This put *lie!* to that old nonsense about "separation of church and state". Nothing more susceptible to emotional heat than religion.

No wonder we distrust emotions.

Not all emotions, of course. Only the ones you could not escape in moments of necessity: love, hate. Let in a little anger sometimes but keep it on a short leash. That was the Sisterhood's belief. Utter nonsense!

The Tyrant's Golden Path made their mistake no longer tolerable. The Golden Path left the Bene Gesserit in a perpetual backwater. You could not minister to Infinity!

Bell's recurrent question had no answer. "What did he really want us to do?" *Into what actions was he manipulating us? (As we manipulate others!)*

Why look for meaning where there is none? Would you follow a path you knew led nowhere?

Golden Path! A track laid down in one imagination. *Infinity is nowhere!* And the finite mind balked. Here was where Mentats found mutable *projections*, always producing more questions than answers. It was the empty grail of those who, noses close to an endless circle, looked for "the one answer to all things".

Looking for their own kind of god.

She found it hard to censure them. The mind recoiled in the face of infinity. The Void! Alchemists of any age were like rag pickers bent over their bundles, saying: "There must be order in here somewhere. If I keep on, I'm sure to find it."

And all the time, the only order was the order they themselves created.

Ahhh, Tyrant! You droll fellow. You saw it. You said: "I will create order for you to follow. Here is the path. See it? No! Don't look over there. That is the way of the Emperor-Without-Clothes (a nakedness apparent only to children and the insane). Keep your attention where I direct it. This is my Golden Path. Isn't that a pretty name? It's all there is and all there ever will be."

Tyrant, you were another clown. Pointing us into endless

recycling of cells from that lost and lonely ball of dirt in our common past.

You knew the human universe could never be more than communities and weak glue binding us when we Scattered. A common birth tradition so far away in our past that pictures of it carried by descendants are mostly distorted. Reverend Mothers carry the original, but we cannot force it on to unwilling people. You see, Tyrant? We heard you: "Let them come asking for it! Then, and only then . . ."

And that was why you preserved us, you Atreides bastard! That's why I must get to work.

Despite the peril to her sense of humanity, she knew she would continue to insinuate herself into the ways of Honoured Matres. *I must think as they think.*

The hunters' problem: predator and prey shared it. Not quite needle-in-the-haystack. More a question of tracking across a terrain littered with the familiar and the unfamiliar. Bene Gesserit deceptions insured that the familiar would cause Honoured Matres at least as much difficulty as the unfamiliar.

But what have they done for us?

Interplanetary communication worked for the hunted. Limited by economics for millennia. Not much of it except among Important People and Traders. Important meant what it had always meant: rich, powerful; bankers, officials, couriers. Military. "Important" labelled many categories—negotiators, entertainers, medical personnel, skilled technicians, spies and other specialists. It was not much different in kind from the days of the Master Masons on Old Terra. Mainly a difference in numbers, quality and sophistication. Boundaries were transparent to some as they had always been.

She felt it important to review this occasionally, looking for flaws.

The great mass of planet-bound humanity spoke of "the silence of space", meaning they could not afford the cost of such travel or communication. Most people knew the news they received across this barrier was managed for special interests. It had always been that way.

147

On a planet, terrain and avoiding telltale radiation dictated the communications systems used: tubes, messengers, light-lines, nerve riders and many permutations. Secrecy and encryption were important, not only between planets but on them.

Odrade saw it as a system Honoured Matres could tap if they found an entry point. Hunters had to begin by deciphering the system, but then: Where did a trail to Chapter House originate?

Untrackable no-ships, Ixian machines and Guild Navigators—all contributed to the blanket of silence between planets except for the privileged few. Give hunters no starting points!

It came as a surprise then when an ageing Reverend Mother from a Bene Gesserit punishment planet appeared at Mother Superior's workroom shortly before the lunch break. Archives identified her: *Name: Dortujla. Sent to special perdition years ago for an unforgivable infraction.* Memory said it had been a love affair of some kind. Odrade did not ask for details. Some of them were displayed anyway. (Bellonda interfering again!) Emotional upheaval at the time of Dortujla's banishment, Odrade noted. Futile attempts by the lover to prevent separation.

Odrade recalled gossip about Dortujla's disgrace. "The Jessica crime!" Much valuable information arrived via gossip. Where the devil had Dortujla been posted? Never mind. Not important at the moment. More important: *Why is she here? Why did she dare a trip that might lead the hunters to us?*

Odrade asked Streggi when she announced the arrival. Streggi did not know. "She says what she must reveal is for your ears alone, Mother Superior."

"Alone?" Odrade almost chuckled. That was a misnomer considering the constant monitoring (surveillance was a better term), Mother Superior's every action recorded by sisters to whom the word "every" conveyed an intensity few outside the Bene Gesserit even suspected possible. "MetaWatch" was the accepted label. No physical intrusions, though!

"Nothing must hamper Mother Superior in her essential functions. No irritations outside of those employed to keep her alert."

"This Dortujla has not said why she is here?"

"The ones who told me to interrupt you, Mother Superior, said they thought you should see her."

Odrade pursed her lips. The fact that the banished Reverend Mother had penetrated this far aroused Odrade's curiosity. A persistent Reverend Mother could cross ordinary barriers but these barriers were not ordinary. Dortujla's reason for coming already had been told. Others had heard and passed her. It was apparent that Dortujla had not relied on Bene Gesserit wiles to persuade her sisters. That would have brought immediate rejection. No time for such nonsense! So she had observed the chain of command. Her action spoke of careful assessment, a message within whatever message she brought.

"Bring her."

Dortujla had aged smoothly on her backwater planet. She revealed her years mostly in shallow wrinkles around her mouth. The hood of her robe concealed her hair but the eyes peering from beneath it were bright and alert.

"Why are you here?" Odrade's tone said: "This had damned well better be important."

Dortujla's story was straightforward enough. She and three Reverend Mother associates had spoken to a band of Futars from the Scattering. Dortujla's post had been searched out and asked to get a message to Chapter House. Dortujla had filtered the request through Truthsense, she said, reminding Mother Superior that even in backwaters there could be *some* talent. Judging the message truthful, her sisters concurring, Dortujla had acted with speed, not unmindful of caution.

"All due dispatch in our own no-ship," was the way she put it. The ship, she said, was small, a smuggler type.

"One person can operate it."

The heart of the message was fascinating. Futars wished to ally themselves with Reverend Mothers in opposition to Honoured Matres. How much of a force these Futars had to support them was difficult to assess, Dortujla said.

"They refused to say when I asked."

Odrade had assessed many stories about Futars. Killers of Honoured Matres? There were reasons to believe it but Futar

149

performance was confusing, especially in accounts from Gammu.

"How many in this party?"

"Sixteen Futars and four Handlers. That's what they called themselves: Handlers. And they say Honoured Matres have a dangerous weapon they can use only once."

"You only mentioned Futars. Who are these Handlers? And what is this about a secret weapon?"

"I reserved mention of them. They appear to be human within variables noted from the Scattering: three men and a woman. As to the weapon, they would not say more."

"Appear to be human?"

"There you have it, Mother Superior. I had the odd first impression they were Face Dancers. None of the criteria applied. Pheromones negative. Gestures, expressions—everything negative."

"Just that first impression?"

"I cannot explain it."

"What of the Futars?"

"They matched all of descriptions. Human in outward appearance but unmistakable ferocity. Cat family origins, I would judge."

"So others have said."

"They speak but it's an abbreviated Galach. Word bursts, I thought them. 'When eat?' 'You nice lady.' 'Want head scratch.' 'Sit here?' They appeared immediately responsive to the Handlers but not fearful. Between Futars and Handlers I had the impression there was mutual respect and liking."

"Knowing the risks, why did you think this important enough to bring immediately?"

"These are people from the Scattering. Their offer of alliance is an opening into places where Honoured Matres originate."

"You asked about them, of course. And about conditions in the Scattering."

"No answers."

The fact, simply stated. One could not sneer at the banished sister no matter how much of a cloud she carried over her past. More questions were indicated. Odrade asked them, observing closely as answers came, watching the old mouth like a withered fruit opening purple and closing pink.

Something in Dortujla's service, the long years of penitence perhaps, had gentled her but left the core of Bene Gesserit toughness untouched. She spoke with a natural hesitancy. Her gestures were softly fluid. She looked at Odrade with kindness. (*There* was the flaw her sisters condemned: Bene Gesserit cynicism held at bay.)

Dortujla interested Odrade. Sister to Sister, she spoke, a strong and well-composed mind behind her words. A mind toughened by adversity in the years at a punishment post. Doing what she could now to make up for that lapse of her youth. No attempt to appear some time server not up on current affairs. An account pared to essentials. Let it be known that she had as full as possible an awareness of necessities. Bowed to Mother Superior's decisions and caution about the dangerous visit but still felt that "you should have this information".

"I'm convinced it's not a trap."

Dortujla's demeanour was above reproach. Direct gaze, eyes and face held in proper composure but no attempts at concealment. A sister could read through this mask for a proper assessment. Dortujla acted from a sense of urgency. She had been a fool once but she no longer was a fool.

What was the name of her punishment planet?

The worktable's projector produced it: Buzzell.

That name brought an alertness to Odrade. *Buzzell!* Her fingers danced in the console, confirming memories. Buzzell: mostly ocean. Cold. Very cold. Hard scrabble islands, none bigger than a large no-ship. The Bene Gesserit once had considered Buzzell a punishment. Object lesson: "Careful, girl, or you'll be sent to Buzzell." Odrade recalled the other key then: soostones. Buzzell was a place where they had naturalized the monoped sea creature, Cholister, whose abraded carapace produced marvellous tumours, one of the most valued jewels in the universe.

Soostones.

Dortujla was wearing one of the things just visible above the tuck of her neckline. The workroom light turned it an elegant blend of deeply glowing seagreen and mauve. It was larger than a human eyeball, flaunted there like a declaration of wealth. They probably thought little of such decorations on Buzzell. Pick them up on the beaches. All of these soostones were Bene Gesserit property, of course. Mother Superior had only to reach out and say, "Give me that."

Odrade remained silent.

Soostones. That was significant. By Bene Gesserit design, Dortujla had frequent dealings with smugglers. (Witness her possession of that no-ship.) This must be addressed with care. No matter the sister-to-sister discussion, it was still Mother Superior and Reverend Mother from a punishment planet.

Smuggling. A major crime to Honoured Matres and others who had not faced the fact of unenforceable laws. Stupid laws were broken by clever people. Depended, naturally, on what you defined as stupid. Foldspace had not changed it for smuggling, just made small intrusions easier if anything. Tiny no-ships. How small could you make one of them? A gap in Odrade's knowledge. Archives corrected it: "Diameter, metres 140."

Small enough, then. Soostones were a cargo with natural attraction. Foldspace was a critical economic barrier: How valuable a cargo compared to size and mass? You could spend many Solars moving massive stuff. Soostones—magnetic to smugglers. They had special interest to Honoured Matres as well. Simple economics? Always a big market. As attractive to smugglers as melange now that the Guild was being so free with it. The Guild had always stockpiled with generations of spice in scattered storage and (doubtless) many hidden backups.

They think they can buy immunity from Honoured Matres! But that offered something she sensed might be turned to advantage. In their wild anger, Honoured Matres had destroyed Dune, only known *natural* source of melange. Still unthinking of consequences (odd, that) they had eliminated the Tleilaxu whose axolotl tanks had flooded the Old Empire with spice.

And we have creatures capable of recreating Dune. We also may have the only living Tleilaxu Master. Locked in Scytale's mind—the way to turn axolotl tanks into a melange cornucopia. If we can get him to reveal it.

The immediate problem was Dortujla. The woman conveyed her ideas with a conciseness that did her credit. Handlers and their Futars, she said, were disturbed by something they would not reveal. Dortujla had been wise not to attempt Bene Gesserit persuasives. No telling how people from the Scattering might react. But what disturbed them?

"Some threat other than Honoured Matres," Dortujla suggested. She would not venture more but the possibility was there and had to be considered.

"The essential thing is that they say they want an alliance," Odrade said.

"Common cause for a common problem," was the way they had put it. Despite Truthsense, Dortujla advised only "a cautious exploration of the offer".

Why go to Dortujla at all? Because Honoured Matres had missed Buzzell or judged it insignificant in their angry sweeps?

"Not likely," Dortujla said.

Odrade agreed. Dortujla, no matter how grubby her original posting, now commanded a valuable property and, much more important, she was a Reverend Mother with a no-ship to take her to Mother Superior. She knew the location of Chapter House. Useless to the hunters, of course. They knew a Reverend Mother would kill herself before betraying that secret.

Problems compounded problems. But first, some sisterly sharing. Dortujla was sure to make a correct interpretation of Mother Superior's motives. Odrade shifted the conversation into personal matters.

It went well. Dortujla was clearly amused but willing to talk.

Reverend Mothers on lonely posts tended to have what sisters called "other interests". An earlier age had called them hobbies but attention devoted to interests often was extreme. Odrade thought most *interests* boring but found it significant that Dortujla called hers a hobby. *She collected old coins, did she?*

"What kind?"

"I have two early Greek in silver and a perfect gold obol."

"Authentic?"

"They're real." Meaning she had done a self-scan of Other Memory to authenticate them. Fascinating. She exercised her abilities in a strengthening way, even with her hobby. Inner history and exterior coincided.

"This is all very interesting, Mother Superior," Dortujla said finally. "I appreciate your reassurance that we are still sisters and find your interest in ancient paintings a parallel hobby. But we both know why I risked coming here."

"The smugglers."

"Of course. Honoured Matres cannot have overlooked my presence on Buzzell. Smugglers will sell to high bidders. We must assume they have profited from their valuable knowledge about Buzzell, the soostones and a resident Reverend Mother with attendants. And we must not forget that Handlers found me."

Damn! Odrade thought. *Dortujla is the kind of adviser I like to have near me. I wonder how many more such buried treasures are out there, tucked away for mean motives? Why do we so often shunt our talented ones aside? It's an ancient weakness the Sisterhood has not exorcized.*

"I think we have learned something valuable about Honoured Matres," Dortujla said.

There was no need to nod agreement. This was the core of what had brought Dortujla to Chapter House. The ravening hunters had come swarming into the Old Empire, killing and burning wherever they suspected the presence of Bene Gesserit establishments. But the hunters had not touched Buzzell even though its location must be known.

"Why?" Odrade asked, voicing what was in their minds.

"Never damage your own nest," Dortujla said.

"You think they're already on Buzzell?"

"Not yet."

"But you believe Buzzell is a place they want."

"Prime projection."

Odrade merely stared at her. So Dortujla had another *hobby!* She burrowed into Other Memory, revived and perfected talents stored there. Who could blame her? Time must drag on Buzzell.

"A Mentat summation," Odrade accused.

154

"Yes, Mother Superior." Very meek. Reverend Mothers were supposed to dig into Other Memory this way only with Chapter House permission and then only with guidance and support from companion sisters. So Dortujla remained a rebel. She followed her own desires the way she had with her forbidden lover. Good! The Bene Gesserit needed such rebels.

Odrade was amused, thinking of Bellonda's reaction. Bell certainly was monitoring them. Disobedient Sisters—very dangerous. Bell would come storming in here later with warnings and admonishments.

"They want Buzzell undamaged," Dortujla said.

"A water world?"

"It would make a suitable home for amphibian servants. Not the Futars or Handlers. I studied them carefully."

The evidence suggested a plan by Honoured Matres to bring in enslaved servants, amphibians perhaps, to harvest soo-stones. Honoured Matres *could* have amphibian slaves. Knowledge that produced Futars might create many forms of sentient life.

"Slaves, dangerous imbalance," Odrade said.

Dortujla showed her first strong emotion, deep revulsion that drew her mouth into a tight line.

Odrade was pleased. Dortujla had abandoned ordinary reserves. Mutual trust was established. *Repetition of historic stupidities revolts all of us!*

It was a pattern the Sisterhood had long recognized: the inevitable failure of slavery and peonage. You created a reservoir of hate. Implacable enemies. If you had no hope of exterminating all of these enemies, you dared not try. Temper your efforts by the sure awareness that oppression will make your enemies strong. The oppressed *will* have their day and heaven help the oppressor when that day comes. It was a two-edged blade. The oppressed always learned from and copied the oppressor. When the tables were turned, the stage was set for another round of revenge and violence—roles reversed. And reversed and reversed ad nauseam.

"Will they never mature?" Odrade asked.

Dortujla had no answer but she did have an immediate

suggestion. "I must return to Buzzell."

Odrade considered this. Once more, the banished Reverend Mother was ahead of Mother Superior. As disagreeable as the decision was, they both knew it as their best move. Futars and Handlers would return. More important, with a planet Honoured Matres desired, odds were high that visitors from the Scattering had been observed. Honoured Matres would have to make a move and that move could reveal much about them.

"Of course, they think Buzzell is bait for a trap," Odrade said.

"I could let it be known that I was banished by my sisters," Dortujla said. "It can be verified."

"Use yourself as bait?"

"Mother Superior, what if they could be tempted into a parley?"

"With us?" *What a startling idea!*

"I know their history is not one of reasonable negotiations but still . . ."

"It's brilliant! But let us make it even more enticing. Say I am convinced I must come to them with a proposal for submission of the Bene Gesserit."

"Mother Superior!"

"I have no intention of surrendering. But what better way to get them to talk?"

"Buzzell is not a good place for a meeting. Our facilities are very poor."

"They are on Junction in force. If they suggested Junction as a meeting place, could you let yourself be persuaded?"

"It would take careful planning, Mother Superior."

"Oh, *very* careful." Odrade's fingers flickered in her console. "Yes, tonight," she said answering a visible question, and then, speaking to Dortujla across the cluttered worktable: "I want you to meet with my Council and others before you return. We will brief you thoroughly but I give you my personal assurance you will have an open assignment. The important thing is to get them to a meeting on Junction . . . and I hope you know how much I dislike using you as bait."

When Dortujla remained deep in thought and not responding, Odrade said: "They may ignore our overtures and wipe
you out. Still, you're the best bait we have."

Dortujla showed she still had her sense of humour. "I don't
much like the idea of dangling on a hook myself, Mother
Superior. Please keep a firm grip on the line." She stood and
with a worried look at the work on Odrade's table, said: "You
have so much to do and I fear I have kept you far past lunch."

"We will dine here together, Sister. For the moment, you
are more important than anything else."

All states are abstractions.

—**Octun Politicus,**
BG Archives

Lucilla cautioned herself not to assume too familiar a feeling
about this acid-green room and the recurring presence of
Great Honoured Matre. This was Junction, stronghold of the
ones who sought extermination of the Bene Gesserit. This was
the enemy. Day seventeen.

The infallible mental clock that had been set ticking during
the Spice Agony, told her she had adapted to the planet's
circadian rhythms. Awake at dawn. No telling when she would
be fed. Honoured Matre confined her to one meal a day.

Treating me like an animal. Here's your bone!

And always that Futar in its cage. A reminder: *Both of you
in cages. This is how we treat dangerous animals. We may let
them out occasionally to stretch their legs and give us pleasure
but back to the cage afterward.*

Minimal amounts of melange in the food. Not being parsimonious. Not with their wealth. A small show of "what could
be yours if you would only be reasonable".

When will she come today?

Great Honoured Matre arrivals had no set time. Random
appearances to confuse the captive? Probably. There would be
other demands on a commander's time. Fit the dangerous pet
into the regular schedule wherever you could.

I may be dangerous, Spider Lady, but I am not your pet.

Lucilla felt the presence of scanning devices, things that did more than provide stimulus for eyes. These looked *into* flesh, probing for concealed weapons, for the functioning of organs. *Does she have strange implants? What about additional organs surgically added to her body?*

None of those, Madame Spider. We rely on things that come with birth.

Lucilla knew her greatest immediate danger—that she would feel inadequate in such a setting. Her captors had her at a terrible disadvantage but they had not destroyed her Bene Gesserit capabilities. She could will herself to die before the shere in her body was depleted to the point of betrayal. She still had her mind . . . and the horde from Lampadas.

And we read you, Spider Queen. You are a palimpsest displayed before us and we see writing underneath that you have tried to erase.

The Futar panel opened and it came sliding out in its cage. So Spider Queen was on her way. Displaying threat ahead of her as usual. *Early today. Earlier than ever.*

"Good morning, Futar." Lucilla spoke with a merry lilt.

The Futar looked at her but did not speak.

"You must hate it in that cage," Lucilla said.

"Not like cage."

She had already determined that these creatures possessed a degree of language facility but the extent of it still eluded her.

"I suppose she keeps you hungry, too. Would you like to eat me?"

"Eat:" Definite show of interest.

"I wish I were your Handler."

"You Handler?"

"Would you obey me if I were?"

Spider Queen's heavy chair lifted from its concealment under the floor. No sign of her yet but it had to be assumed she listened to these conversations.

The Futar stared at Lucilla with peculiar intensity.

"Do Handlers keep you caged and hungry?"

"Handler?" Clear inflections of a question.

"I want you to kill Great Honoured Matre." That would be no surprise to them.

"Kill Dama!"

"And eat her."

"Dama poison." Dejected.

Ooooh. Isn't that an interesting bit of information!

"She's not poison. Her meat is the same as mine."

The Futar approached her to the cage's limits. The left hand peeled down its lower lip. Angry redness of a scar there, appearance of a burn.

"See poison," it said, dropping its hand.

I wonder how she did that? No smell of poison about her. Human flesh plus adrenalin-based drug to produce orange eyes in response to anger . . . and those other responses Murbella revealed. A sense of absolute superiority. *Assassin effect without hashish, somewhat longer life. How much longer?* Murbella did not know. *A poison to others? Not likely.*

How far did Futar comprehension go? "Was it a bitter poison?"

The Futar grimaced and spat.

Action faster and more powerful than words.

"Do you hate Dama?"

Bared canines.

"Do you fear her?"

Smile.

"Then why don't you kill her?"

"You not Handler."

It requires a kill command from a Handler!

Great Honoured Matre entered and sank into her chair.

Lucilla pitched her voice in the merry lilt: "Good morning, Dama."

"I did not give you permission to call me that." Low and with beginning flecks of orange in the eyes.

"Futar and I have been having a conversation."

"I know." More orange in the eyes. "And if you have spoiled him for me . . ."

"But Dama . . ."

"Don't call me that!" Out of her chair, eyes blazing orange.

"Do sit down," Lucilla said. "This is no way to conduct an interrogation." Sarcasm, a dangerous weapon. "You said yesterday you wanted to continue our discussion of politics."

"How do you know what time it is?" Sinking back in her chair but eyes still flaming.

"All Bene Gesserits have this ability. We can feel the rhythms of any planet after a short time on it."

"A strange talent."

"Anyone can do it. A matter of being sensitized."

"Could I learn this?" Orange fading.

"I said *anyone*. You're still human, aren't you?" *A question not yet fully answered.*

"Why do you say you witches have no government?"

Wants to change the subject. Our abilities worry her. "That's not what I said. We have no *conventional* government."

"Not even a social code?"

"There's no such thing as a social code to meet all necessities. A crime in one society can be a moral requirement in another society."

"People always have government." Orange completely faded. *Why does this interest her so much?*

"People have politics. I told you that yesterday. Politics: the art of appearing candid and completely open while concealing as much as possible."

"So you witches conceal."

"I did not say that. When we say 'politics', that's a warning to our sisters."

"I don't believe you. Humans always create some form of . . ."

"Accord?"

"As good a word as any!" *It angers her.*

"You're inquiring after the system, whatever passes for executives, law-makers, a judiciary—judges, juries, the trappings of human management since time immemorial."

"You have them. I know it!" *You're like us.*

When Lucilla remained silent, Great Honoured Matre leaned forward. "What are you doing right now? You're concealing!"

"Isn't it my right to hide from you things that might help you defeat us?" *There's a juicy morsel of bait!*

"I thought so!" Leaning back with a look of satisfaction.

"However, since I don't think you capable of understanding, why not reveal it?"

Dangled right in front of her!

"I forgive the insult." *Do continue!*

"You think the spheres of authority may vary but the niches are always there for the filling. You don't see what that says about my Sisterhood."

"Oh, please tell me." *Heavy-handed with her sarcasm.*

"You believe all of this conforms to instinctual demands, an association going back to tribal days and beyond. The Chief and his Elders. The Mystery Mother and her Council. And before that, the Strong Man (or Woman) who saw to it that everyone was fed, that all were guarded by fire at the cave's mouth."

"I've never thought of it that way but it makes sense."

Does it really?

"Oh, I agree. Evolution of the forms is quite clearly laid out, a sequential development any Reverend Mother can parade before herself with Other Memory."

She doesn't like it when you talk about our abilities.

"Evolution, witch! One thing piled on another."

Evolution. See how she snaps at key words?

"It's a force that can be brought under control by turning it upon itself."

Control! Look at the interest you've aroused. She loves that word.

"So you make laws just like anyone else!"

"Regulations, perhaps, but isn't everything temporary?"

"What's the difference between a regulation and a law?"

"How do we define them?"

Intensely interested. "Of course."

"The word you choose for yourself is fixed in cement and administered by bureaucrats who know they cannot apply the slightest imagination to what they do."

"That's a difference?" *Really puzzled. Look at her scowl.*

"Your difference, Honoured Matre."

"Great Honoured Matre!" *Isn't she touchy!*

"Why don't you permit me to call you Dama?"

161

"We're not intimates."

"Is Futar an intimate?"

"Stop changing the subject!"

"Want tooth clean," the Futar said.

"You shut up!" Really blazing.

The Futar sank to its haunches but it was not cowed.

Great Honoured Matre turned her orange gaze toward Lucilla. "What about bureaucrats?"

"I was explaining that they have no room to manoeuvre because that restriction is the way their superiors grow fat. Unrocked boats bring the best banquets. If you do not see the difference between regulation and law, both have the force of law."

"I see no difference." *She does not know what she reveals.*

"Laws convey the myth of enforced change. A bright new future will come because of this law or that one. Laws enforce the future. Regulations are believed to enforce the past."

"Believed?" *She doesn't like that word, either.*

"In each instance, action is illusory. Like appointing a committee to study a problem. The more people on the committee, the more preconceptions applied to the problem."

Careful! She's really thinking about this, applying it to herself.

Lucilla pitched her voice in its most reasonable tones. "You ask about differences? But you live by a past-magnified and try to understand some unrecognized future."

"We don't believe in prescience." *Yes, she does! At last. This is why she keeps us alive.*

"Dama, please. There's always something unbalanced about confining yourself to a tight circle of laws."

Be careful! She didn't bridle at your calling her Dama.

Great Honoured Matre's chair creaked as she shifted in it. "But laws are necessary! Otherwise, chaotic . . ."

"Necessary? That's dangerous."

"How so?"

Softly. She feels threatened.

"Necessary postures keep you from adapting. Inevitably, they grow top-heavy, tipping and tipping at a crazier and crazier angle until they come crashing down. It's like bankers

162

thinking they buy the future. "Power in my time! To hell with my descendants!"

"What are descendants doing for me?"

Don't say it! Look at her. She's reacting out of the common insanity. Give her another small taste of our insight.

"Honoured Matres originated as terrorists. Bureaucrats first and terror as your chosen weapon."

"When it's in your hands, use it. But we were rebels. Terrorists? That's too chaotic."

She likes that word chaos. It defines everything on the outside. She doesn't even ask how you know her origins. She accepts our mysterious abilities.

"Isn't it odd, Dama . . ." *No reaction; continue.* ". . . how rebels all too soon fall into old patterns if they are victorious? It's not so much a pitfall in the path of all governments as it is a delusion waiting for anyone who gains power."

"Hah! And I thought you would tell me something new. We know that one: 'Power corrupts. Absolute power corrupts absolutely.'"

"Wrong, Dama. Something more subtle but far more pervasive is at work. We've said it often enough but few hear us. Power attracts the corruptible."

"You dare accuse me of being corrupt?"

Watch the eyes!

"I? Accuse you? The only one who can do that is yourself. I merely give you the Bene Gesserit opinion."

"And tell me nothing! You still conceal."

"Yet, we believe there's a morality above any law; an overview that must stand watchdog on all attempts at unchanging regulation."

You used both words in one sentence and she didn't notice.

"Power always works, witch. That's the law."

"And governments that perpetuate themselves long enough under *that* belief always become packed with corruption."

"Morality!"

She's not very good at sarcasm, especially when she's on the defensive.

"I've really tried to help you, Dama. Laws are dangerous to everyone—innocent and guilty alike. No matter whether you believe yourself powerful or helpless. They have no human understanding in and of themselves."

"There's no such thing as human understanding!"

Our question is answered. Not human. Talk to her unconscious side. She's wide open.

"Laws must always be interpreted. The law-bound want no latitude for compassion. No elbow room. The law is the law!"

"It is!" *Very defensive.*

"That's a dangerous idea, especially for the innocent. People know this instinctively and resent such laws. Little things are done, often unconsciously, to hamstring 'the law' and those who deal in that nonsense."

"How dare you call it nonsense?" Half rising from her chair and sinking back.

"Oh, yes. And the law, personified by all whose livelihoods depend on it, becomes resentful hearing words such as mine."

"Rightly so, witch!" *But she doesn't tell you to be silent.*

"'More law!' you say. 'We need more law!' So you make new instruments of non-compassion and, incidentally, new niches of employment for those who feed on the system."

"That's the way it's always been and always will be."

"Wrong again. It's a rondo. It rolls and rolls until it injures the wrong person or the wrong group. Then you get anarchy. Chaos." *See her jump?* "Rebels, terrorists, increasing outbursts of raging violence. A jihad! And all because you created something non-human."

Hand on her chin. Watch it!

"How did we wander so far away from politics, witch? Was this your intention?"

"We haven't wandered a fraction of a millimetre!"

"I suppose you're going to tell me you witches practise a form of democracy."

"With an alertness you cannot imagine."

"Try me." *She thinks you'll tell her a secret. Tell her one.*

"Democracy is susceptible to being led astray by having scapegoats paraded in front of the electorate. Get the rich, the greedy, the criminals, the stupid leader and so on ad nauseam."

164

"You believe as we do." *My! How desperately she wants us to be like her.*

"You said you were bureaucrats who rebelled. You know the flaw. A top-heavy bureaucracy the electorate cannot touch always expands to the system's limit of energy. Steal it from the aged, from the retired, from anyone. Especially from those we once called middle-class because that's where most of the energy originates."

"You think of yourselves as . . . as middle-class?"

"We don't think of ourselves in any fixed way. But Other Memory tells us the flaws of bureaucracy. I presume you have some form of civil service for the 'lower orders'."

"We take care of our own." *That's a nasty echo.*

"Then you know how that dilutes the vote. Chief symptom: people don't vote. Instinct tells them it's useless."

"Democracy is a stupid idea anyway!"

"We agree. It's demagogue prone. That's a disease to which electoral systems are vulnerable. Yet, demagogues are so easy to identify. They gesture a lot and speak with pulpit rhythms, using words that ring of religious fervour and god-fearing sincerity."

She's chuckling!

"Sincerity with nothing behind it takes so much practice, Dama. The practice can always be detected."

"By Truthsayers?"

See how she leans forward? We have her again.

"By anyone who learns the signs: Repetition. Great attempts to keep your attention on words. You must pay no attention to words. Watch what the person does. That way you learn the motives."

"Then you don't have democracy." *Tell me more Bene Gesserit secrets.*

"But we do."

"I thought you said . . ."

"We guard it well, watching for the things I've just described. The dangers are great but so are the rewards."

"Do you know what you've told me? That you're a pack of fools!"

"Nice lady!" the Futar said.

"Shut up or I'll send you back to the herd!"

"You not nice, Dama."

"See what you've done, witch? You've ruined him!"

"I suppose there are always others."

Ohhhhh. Look at that smile.

Lucilla matched the smile precisely, pacing her own breaths to those of the Great Honoured Matre. *See how alike we are? Of course I tried to injure you. Wouldn't you have done the same in my place?*

"So you know how to make a democracy do whatever you want." A gloating expression.

"The technique is quite subtle but easy. You create a system where most people are dissatisfied, vaguely or deeply."

That's how she sees it. Look at her nod in time to your words.

Lucilla held herself to the rhythm of Great Honoured Matre's nodding head. "This builds up widespread feelings of vindictive anger. Then you supply targets for that anger as you need them."

"A diversionary tactic."

"I prefer to think of it as distraction. Don't give them time to question. Bury your mistakes in more laws. You traffic in illusion. Bullring tactics."

"Oh, yes! That's good!" *She's almost gleeful. Give her more bullring.*

"Wave the pretty cape. They'll charge it and be confused when there's no matador behind the thing. That dulls the electorate just as it dulls the bull. Fewer people use their vote intelligently next time."

"And that's why we do it!"

We do it! Does she listen to herself?

"Then you rail against the apathetic electorate. Make them feel guilty. Keep them dull. Feed them. Amuse them. Don't overdo it!"

"Oh, no! Never overdo it."

"Let them know hunger awaits them if they don't fall into line. Give them a look at the boredom imposed on boat rockers." *Thank you, Mother Superior. It's an appropriate image.*

"Don't you let the bull get an occasional matador?"

166

"Of course. Thump! Got that one! Then you wait for the laughter to subside."

"I knew you didn't allow a democracy!"

"Why won't you believe me?" *You're tempting fate!*

"Because you'd have to permit open voting, juries and judges and . . ."

"We call them Proctors. A sort of Jury of the Whole."

Now, you've confused her.

"And no laws . . . regulations, whatever you want to call them?"

"Didn't I say we defined them separately? Regulation— past. Law—future."

"You limit these . . . these Proctors, somehow!"

"They can arrive at any decision they desire, the way a jury should function. The law be damned!"

"That's a very disturbing idea." *She's disturbed all right. Look at how dull her eyes are.*

"The first rule of our democracy: no laws restricting juries. Such laws are stupid. It's astonishing how stupid humans can be when acting in small, self-serving groups."

"You're calling me stupid, aren't you!"

Beware the orange.

"There appears to be a rule of nature that says it's almost impossible for self-serving groups to act enlightened."

"Enlightened! I knew it!"

That's a dangerous smile. Be careful.

"It means flowing with the forces of life, adjusting your actions that life may continue."

"With the greatest amount of happiness for the greatest number, of course."

Quick! We've been too clever! Change the subject!

"That was an element the Tyrant left out of his Golden Path. He didn't consider happiness, only survival of humankind."

We said change the subject! Look at her! She's in a rage!

Great Honoured Matre dropped her hand away from her chin. "And I was going to invite you into our order, make you one of us. Release you."

Get her off this! Quick!

167

"Don't speak," Great Honoured Matre said. "Don't even open your mouth."

Now you've done it!

"You'd help Logno or one of the others and she'd be in my seat!!" She glanced at the crouching Futar. "Eat, darling?"

"Not eat nice lady."

"Then I'll throw her carcass to the herd!"

"Great Honoured Matre . . ."

"I told you not to speak! You *dared* call me Dama."

She was out of her chair in a blur. Lucilla's cage door slammed open with a crash against the wall. Lucilla tried to dodge but the shigawire confined her. She did not see the kick that crushed her temple.

As she died, Lucilla's awareness was filled with a scream of rage—the horde of Lampadas venting emotions it had confined for so many generations.

> *Some never participate. Life happens to them. They get by on little more than dumb persistence and resist with anger or violence all things that might lift them out of resentment-filled illusions of security.*
>
> —Alma Mavis Taraza

Back and forth, back and forth. All day long, back and forth. Odrade shifted from one comeye record to another, searching, undecided, uneasy. First a look at Scytale, then young Teg out there with Duncan and Murbella, then a long stare out a window while she thought about Burzmali's last report from Lampadas.

How soon could they try to restore the Bashar's memories? Would a restored ghola obey?

Why no more word from the Rabbi? Should we begin Extremis Progressiva, Sharing among ourselves as far as possible? The effect on morale would be devastating.

Records were projected above her table while aides and advisers entered and departed. Necessary interruptions. Sign this. Approve this. Decrease melange for this group?

Bellonda was here, seated at the table. She had stopped

asking what Odrade sought and merely watched with that unwavering stare. Merciless.

Bell wanted a return to the question of whether a new sandworm population in the Scattering might restore the Tyrant's malign influence. That *endless dream* in each revenant of the worm still worried her. But numbers alone said the Tyrant's hold on their destiny was ended.

It had been a protracted argument.

"We don't know his powers!"

"Exponential growth of humankind!"

"Kwisatz haderach!"

There it is: our bête noire. Control of our future.

Late evening already, Odrade realized. Lights had come on automatically without her noticing. She stood and went to the bow window, pausing to touch the bust of Chenoeh in passing. *What would you have done, had you not died in the Agony, Chenoeh?*

Bellonda turned to watch these movements.

Tamalane had come in earlier seeking some record from Bellonda. Fresh from a new accumulation of Archives, Bellonda had launched herself into a diatribe about Sisterhood population shifts, the drain on resources.

"Not to mention the no-ships! This whole Scattering commits us to service contracts with Ix for hundreds of SY!"

We may not have those hundreds of Standard Years, Bell. I can feel the hunter with the axe coming closer.

Tam had a second verse: "We're a last-man club."

"Tontine!" Bellonda sneered.

They would put it in terms of survivor-take-all.

Tamalane left on that note, records in hand.

Odrade stared out the window as dusk moved across the landscape. It became darker in almost imperceptible shadings. As full dark fell, she became aware of lights far out in the plantation houses. She knew those lights had been turned on much earlier but she had the sensation that night created the lights. Some blanked out occasionally as people moved about in their dwellings. *No people—no lights. Don't waste energy.*

Winking lights held her attention for a moment. A variation on the old question about a tree falling in the forest: Was there sound if no one heard? Odrade voted on the side of those who said vibrations existed no matter whether a sensor recorded them.

Do secret sensors follow our Scattering? What new talents and inventions do the first Scattered Ones use?

Bellonda had allowed long enough silence. "Dar, you're sending worrisome signals through Chapter House."

Odrade accepted this without comment.

"Whatever you're doing, it's being interpreted as indecision." *How sad Bell sounds.* "Important groups are discussing whether to replace you. Proctors are voting."

"Only the Proctors?"

"Dar, did you really wave at Praska the other day and tell her it was good to be alive?"

"I did."

"What *have* you been doing?"

"Reassessing. No word yet from Dortujla?"

"You've asked that at least a dozen times today!" Bellonda gestured at the worktable. "You keep going back to Burzmali's last report from Lampadas. Something we've overlooked?"

"Why do our enemies hold fast on Gammu? Tell me, Mentat."

"I've insufficient data and you know it!"

"Burzmali was no Mentat but his picture of events has a persistent force, Bell. I tell myself, well, after all, he was the Bashar's favourite student. It's understandable that Burzmali would show characteristics of his teacher."

"Out with it, Dar. What do you see in Burzmali's report?"

"He fills in an empty picture. Not completely but . . . tantalizing the way he keeps referring to Gammu. Many economic forces have powerful connections there. Why are those threads not cut by our enemies?"

"They're in that same system, obviously."

"What if we mounted an all-out attack on Gammu?"

"No one wants to do business in violent surroundings. That what you're saying?"

"Partly."

"Most parties to that economic system probably would want

170

to move. Another planet, another subservient population."

"Why?"

"They could predict with more reliability. They would increase defences, of course."

"This alliance we sense there, Bell, they would redouble their efforts to find and obliterate us."

"Certainly."

Bellonda's terse comment forced Odrade's thoughts outward. She lifted her gaze to the distant snow-tonsured mountains glimmering in starlight. Would attackers come from that direction?

The thrust of that thought might have dulled a lesser intellect. But Odrade needed no Litany Against Fear to remain clear-headed. She had a simpler formula.

Face your fears or they will climb over your back.

Her attitude was direct: The most terrifying things in the universe came from human minds. The nightmare (the white horse of Bene Gesserit extinction) possessed both mythic and reality forms. The hunter with the axe could strike mind or flesh. But you could not flee the terrors of the mind.

Face them then!

What did she confront in this darkness? Not that faceless hunter with her axe, not the drop into the unknown chasm (both visible to her *bit of talent*), but the very tangible Honoured Matres and whoever supported them.

And I dare not use even my small prescience to guide us. I could lock our future into unchanging form. Muad'Dib and his Tyrant son did that and then the Tyrant spent thirty-five hundred years extricating us.

Moving lights in the middle distance caught her attention. Gardeners working late, still pruning the orchards as though those venerable trees would go on forever. Ventilators gave her a faint odour of smoke from fires where orchard trimmings were being burned. Very attentive to such details, the Bene Gesserit gardeners. Never leave deadwood around to attract parasites that might then take the next step into living trees. Clean and neat. Plan ahead. Maintain your habitat. This moment is part of forever.

Never leave deadwood around?

171

Was Gammu deadwood?

"What is it about orchards that fascinates you so much?" Bellonda wanted to know.

Odrade spoke without turning. "They restore me."

Only two nights ago she had gone walking out there, the weather cold and bracing, a touch of mist close to the ground. Her feet stirred leaves. Faint smell of compost where a sparse rain had settled in warmer low places. A rather attractive, marshy smell. Life in its usual ferment even at that level. Empty limbs above her stood out starkly against starlight. Depressing, really, when compared with springtime or harvest season. But beautiful in its flow. Life once more waiting for its call to action.

"Aren't you worried about the Proctors?" Bellonda asked.

"How will they vote, Bell?"

"It's very close."

"Will others follow them?"

"There's concern about your decisions. Consequences."

Bell was very good at that: a great deal of data in a few words. Most Bene Gesserit decisions moved through a triple maze: Effectiveness, Consequences and (most vital) Who Can Carry Out Orders? You matched deed and person with great care, precise attention to details. This had a heavy influence on Effectiveness and that, in turn, ruled Consequences. A good Mother Superior could wend her way through decision mazes in seconds. Liveliness in Central then. Eyes brightened. Word was passed that "she acted without hesitation". That created confidence among acolytes and other students. Reverend Mothers (Proctors especially) waited to assess Consequences.

Odrade spoke to her reflection in the window as much as to Bellonda. "Even Mother Superior must take her own time."

"But what has you in such turmoil?"

"Are you urging speed, Bell?"

Bellonda drew back in her chairdog as though Odrade had pushed her.

"Patience is extremely difficult in these times," Odrade said. "But choosing the right moment influences my choices."

"What do you intend with our new Teg? That's the question you must answer."

"If our enemies removed themselves from Gammu, where would they go, Bell?"

"You would attack them there?"

"Push them a bit."

Bellonda spoke softly. "That's a dangerous fire to feed."

"We need another bargaining chip."

"Honoured Matres don't bargain!"

"But their associates do, I think. Would they remove themselves to . . . let us say, Junction?"

"What is so interesting about Junction?"

"Honoured Matres are based there in force. And our beloved Bashar kept a memory-dossier of the place in his lovely Mentat mind."

"Ohhhhhhh." It was as much a sigh as a word.

Tamalane entered then and demanded attention by standing silently until Odrade and Bellonda looked at her.

"The Proctors support Mother Superior." Tamalane held up a clawed finger. "By one vote!"

Odrade sighed. "Tell us, Tam, the Proctor I greeted in the hallway, Praska, how did she vote?"

"She voted for you."

Odrade aimed a tight smile at Bellonda. "Send out spies and agents, Bell. We must goad the hunters into meeting us on Junction."

Bellonda stared back but not challenging. Mother Superior's decisive orders carried great weight. It could be assumed now that Odrade had been working out a plan. They all accepted that Bene Gesserit muscle lay in this ability to surround problems, to look at them from all sides, even from the perspective of enemies. It was a pragmatism that Mentats often used as *Projection Base*, the pragmatic lifted to sophisticated heights.

Bell will deduce my plan by morning.

When Bellonda and Tamalane had gone, muttering to each other, worry in the sound of their voices, Odrade went out into the short corridor to her private quarters. The corridor was patrolled by its usual acolytes and Reverend Mother servitors. A few acolytes smiled at her. So word of the Proctors' vote had reached them. Another crisis passed.

173

Odrade went through her sitting room to her sleeping cell where she stretched out on her cot fully clothed. One glow-globe bathed the room in pale yellow light. Her gaze went past the desert map to the Van Gogh painting in its protective frame and cover on the wall at the foot of her cot.

Cottages at Cordeville.

A better map than the one marking the growth of the desert, she thought. *Remind me, Vincent, of where I came from and what I yet may do.*

This day had drained her. She had gone beyond fatigue into a place where the mind caught itself in tight circles.

Responsibilities!

They hemmed her in and she knew she could be her most disagreeable self when beset by duties. Forced to expend energy just maintaining a semblance of calm demeanour. *Bell saw this in me.* It was maddening. The Sisterhood was cut off at every passage, made almost ineffectual.

We provide the best Suk doctors, the best Truthsayers, the best negotiators . . .

She brought herself up short. *Dangerous thinking!* A constant Bene Gesserit peril. Never weaken humankind by taking over all responsibilities. Best? What was best when they were in danger of extermination?

How can I look at Honoured Matres with sufficient detachment and still get into their psyches?

She closed her eyes and tried to construct an image of an Honoured Matre commander to address. *Old . . . steeped in power. Sinewy. Strong and with that blinding speed they have.* No face on her but the visualized body stood there in Odrade's mind.

Forming the words silently, Odrade spoke to the faceless Honoured Matre.

"It is difficult for us to let you make your own mistakes. Teachers always find this hard. Yes, we consider ourselves teachers. We do not so much teach individuals as the species. We provide lessons for all. If you see the Tyrant in us, you are right."

The image in her mind made no reply.

How could teachers teach when they could not emerge from

174

hiding? Burzmali dead, ghola Teg an unknown quantity. Odrade felt invisible pressures converging on Chapter House. No wonder Proctors voted. A web enclosed the Sisterhood. The strands held them tightly. And somewhere on that web, a faceless Honoured Matre commander crouched.

Spider Queen.

Her presence was known by actions of her minions. A trap strand of her web trembled and attackers hurled themselves on to entangled victims, insanely violent, uncaring how many of their own died or how many they butchered.

Someone commanded the search: Spider Queen.

Is she sane by our standards? Into what awful perils have I sent Dortujla?

Honoured Matres went beyond megalomania. They made the Tyrant appear a ridiculous pirate by comparison. Leto II, at least, had known what the Bene Gesserit knew: how to balance on the point of the sword, aware that you would be mortally cut when you slid from that position. *The price you pay for seizing such power.* Honoured Matres ignored this inevitable fate, hewing and slashing around them like a giant in the throes of terrible hysteria.

Nothing ever before had opposed them successfully and they chose to respond now with the killing rage of berserkers. Hysteria by choice. Deliberate.

Because we left our Bashar on Dune to spend his pitiful force in a suicidal defence? No telling how many Honoured Matres he killed. And Burzmali at the death of Lampadas. Surely, the hunters felt his sting. Not to mention Idaho-trained males we send out to pass along Honoured Matre techniques of sexual enslavement. And to men!

Was that enough to bring such rage? Possibly. But what of the stories from Gammu? Did Teg display a new talent that terrified Honoured Matres?

If we restore our Bashar's memories, we must watch him carefully.

Would a no-ship contain him?

What really made Honoured Matres so reactive? They wanted blood. Never bring such people bad news. No wonder their minions behaved with frenzy. A powerful person in fright

175

might kill the bearer of bad tidings. Bring no bad tidings. Better to die in battle.

Spider Queen's people went beyond arrogance. Far beyond. No censure possible. You might just as well berate a cow for eating grass. The cow would be justified in looking at you with its moonstruck eyes, inquiring: "Isn't this what I'm supposed to do?"

Knowing probable consequences, why did we ignite them? We aren't like the person who hits out at a round grey object with a stick and finds that the object was a hornets' nest. We knew what we struck. Taraza's plan and none of us questioned. You see, Tar? Your mistake. And I could do no better than follow your orders.

The Sisterhood faced an enemy whose deliberate policy was hysterical violence. "We will run amok!"

And what would happen if Honoured Matres met painful defeat? What would their hysteria become?

I fear it.

Did the Sisterhood dare feed this fire?

We must!

Spider Queen would redouble her efforts to find Chapter House. Violence would escalate to an even more repulsive stage. What then? Would Honoured Matres suspect everyone and anyone of being sympathetic to the Bene Gesserit? Might they not turn against their own supporters? Did they contemplate being alone in a universe devoid of other sentient life? More likely this did not even enter their minds.

What do you look like, Spider Queen? How do you think?

Murbella said she did not know her supreme commander nor even sub-commanders of her Hormu Order. But Murbella provided a suggestive description of a sub-commander's quarters. Informative. What does a person call home? Who does she keep close to share life's little homilies?

Most of us choose our companions and surroundings to reflect ourselves.

Murbella said: "One of her personal servants took me into the private area. Showing off, demonstrating that she had access to the sanctum. The public area was neat and clean but the private rooms were messy—clothing left where it had been

176

dropped, unguent jars open, bed unmade, food drying in dishes on the floor. I asked why they had not cleaned up this mess. She said it was not her job. The one who cleaned was allowed into the quarters just before nightfall."

Secret vulgarities.

Such a one would have a mind to match that private display.

Odrade's eyes snapped open. She focused on the Van Gogh painting. *My choice.* It put tensions on the long span of human history that Other Memory could not. *You sent me a message, Vincent. And because of you, I will not cut off my ear . . . or send useless love messages to ones who do not care. That's the least I can do to honour you.*

The sleeping cell had a familiar odour, peppery pungency of carnation. Odrade's favourite floral perfume. Attendants kept it here as a nasal background.

My own truth?

Once more, she closed her eyes and her thoughts snapped back to Spider Queen. Odrade felt this exercise creating another dimension to that faceless woman.

Wealth.

Murbella said an Honoured Matre commander had but to give an order and anything she wanted was brought.

"Anything?"

Murbella described known instances: grossly distorted sexual partners, cloying sweetmeats, emotional orgies ignited by performances of extraordinary violence.

"They're always looking for extremes."

Romans live!

Reports of spies and agents fleshed out Murbella's semi-admiring accounts.

"Everyone says they have a right to rule."

Those women evolved from an autocratic bureaucracy.

Much evidence confirmed it. Murbella spoke of history lessons that said early Honoured Matres conducted research to gain sexual dominance over their populations "when taxation became too threatening to those they governed".

A right to rule?

It did not appear to Odrade that these women insisted on

such a right. No. They assumed that their rightness must never be questioned. Never! No decisions wrong. Disregard consequences. It never happened.

Odrade sat upright on her cot, knowing she had found the insight she sought.

Mistakes never happen.

That would require an extremely large bag of unconsciousness to contain it. Very tiny consciousness then peering out at a tumultuous universe they themselves created!

Ohhhh, lovely!

Odrade summoned her night attendant, a first stage acolyte, and asked for melange tea containing a dangerous stimulant, something to help her delay the body's demands for sleep. But at a cost.

The acolyte hesitated before obeying. She returned in a moment with the mug steaming on a small tray.

Odrade had decided long ago that melange tea made with the deep cold water of Chapter House had a taste that worked its way deep into her psyche. The bitter stimulant deprived her of that refreshing taste and gnawed at her conscience. Word would go out from the ones who watched. *Worry, worry, worry.* Would Proctors take another vote?

She sipped slowly, giving the stimulant time to work. *Condemned woman rejects last dinner. Sips tea.*

Presently, she put aside the empty mug and called for warm clothing. "I'm going for a walk in the orchards." The night attendant made no comment. Everyone knew she often went walking there, even at night.

"She says it helps her think."

The walk would not alarm the watchdogs as much as the stimulant. Reverend Mothers didn't often resort to such things.

Within minutes she was in the narrow, link-fenced path to her favourite orchard, her way lighted by a miniglobe fixed on a short cord to her right shoulder. A small herd of the Sisterhood's black cattle came up to the fence beside Odrade and gazed at her as she passed. She looked at the wet muzzles, inhaled the rich smell of alfalfa in the steam of their breathing and paused. The cows sniffed and sensed the pheromone that

178

told them to accept her. They went back to eating forage piled near the fence by herdsmen.

Turning her back on the cattle, Odrade looked at leafless trees across from the pasture. Her miniglobe drew a circle of yellow light that emphasized winter starkness.

Few understood why this place attracted her. It was not enough to say she found troubled thoughts soothed here.

"Even in winter?" Bellonda disliked the cold.

Odrade continued along the path. Yes, even in winter with frost on the ground crunching underfoot. This orchard was a hard-bought silence between storms. She extinguished her miniglobe and let her feet follow the familiar way in darkness. Occasionally, she glanced up at starlight defined by leafless branches. *Storms.* She felt one approaching that no meteorologist could anticipate. *Storms beget storms. Rage begets rage. Revenge begets revenge. Wars beget wars.*

The old Bashar had been a master at breaking those circles. Would his ghola still have that talent?

What a perilous gamble.

Odrade looked back at the cattle, a dark blob of movement and starlighted steam. They had herded close for warmth and she heard a familiar grinding as they chewed their cuds.

I must go south into the desert. Face to face with Sheeana there. The sandtrout thrive. Why are there no sandworms?

She spoke aloud to the cattle clustered by the fence. "Eat your grass. It's what you're supposed to do."

If a spying watchdog chanced on that remark, Odrade knew she would have serious explaining to do.

But I have seen through to the heart of our enemy this night. And I pity them.

> *To know a thing well, know its limits. Only when pushed beyond its tolerances will true nature be seen. (The Amtal Rule) Do not depend only on theory if your life is at stake. (Bene Gesserit Commentary)*

Duncan Idaho stood almost in the centre of the no-ship's practice floor and three paces from the ghola child. Sophisticated training instruments were near at hand, some exhausting, some dangerous.

The child looked so admiring and trusting this morning.

Do I understand him better because I, too, am a ghola? A questionable assumption. *This one has been brought up in a much different way than the one they designed for me. Designed! The precise term.*

The Sisterhood had copied as much of Teg's original childhood as possible. Even to an adoring younger companion standing in for the long lost brother. And Odrade giving him the deep teaching! As Teg's birth mother did.

Idaho remembered the aged Bashar whose cells had produced this child. A thoughtful man whose comments were to be heeded. With only a slight effort, Idaho recalled the man's manner and words:

"The true warrior often understands his enemy better than he understands his friends. A dangerous pitfall if you let understanding lead to sympathy as it will naturally do when left unguided."

Difficult to think of the mind behind those words as latent somewhere in this child. The Bashar had been so insightful, teaching about sympathies on that long ago day in the Gammu Keep.

"Sympathy for the enemy—a weakness of police and armies alike. Most perilous are the unconscious sympathies directing you to preserve your enemy intact because the enemy is your justification for existence."

"Sir?"

How could that piping voice become the commanding tones of the old Bashar?

"What is it?"

"Why are you just standing there looking at me?"

"They called the Bashar 'Old Reliability'. Did you know that?"

"Yes, sir. I've studied the story of his life."

Was it "Young Reliability" now? Why did Odrade want his original memories restored so quickly?

"Because of the Bashar, the entire Sisterhood has been digging into Other Memory, revising their views of history. Did they tell you that?"

"No, sir. Is it important for me to know? Mother Superior said you would train my muscles."

"You like to drink Danian Marinete, a very fine brandy, I recall."

"I'm too young to drink, sir."

"You were a Mentat. Do you know what that means?"

"I'll know when you restore my memories, won't I?"

No respectful *sir*. Calling the teacher to task for unwanted delays.

Idaho smiled and got a grin in response. An engaging child. Easy to show him natural affection.

"Watch out for him," Odrade had said. "He's a charmer."

For some reason he did not care to explore, Idaho recalled Odrade's briefing before bringing the child. She obviously had been digging into Bene Gesserit concepts of education but there was more to it than that.

"Since every individual is accountable ultimately to the self," she said, "the formation of that self demands our utmost care and attention."

"Is that necessary with a ghola?"

They had been in Idaho's sitting room that night, Murbella a fascinated listener.

"He will remember everything you teach him."

"So we do a little editing of the original."

"Careful, Duncan! Give a bad time to an impressionable child, teach that child not to trust anyone, and you create a suicide—slow or fast suicide, doesn't make any difference."

"Are you forgetting that I knew the Bashar?"

"Don't you remember, Duncan, how it was before your memories were restored?"

"I knew the Bashar could do it and I thought of him as my salvation."

"And that's how he sees you. It's a special kind of trust."

"I'll treat him honestly."

"You may think you act from honesty but I advise you to

181

look deeply into yourself every time you come face to face with his trust."

"And if I make a mistake?"

"We will correct it if possible." She glanced up at the comeyes and back to him.

"I know you'll be watching us!"

"Don't let it inhibit you. I'm not trying to make you self conscious. Just cautious. And remember that my Sisterhood has efficient methods of healing."

"I'll be cautious."

"You might remember it was the Bashar who said: 'The ferocity we display to our foes is always tempered by the lesson we hope to teach.'"

"I can't think of him as a foe. The Bashar was one of the finest men I've ever known."

"Excellent. I place him in your hands."

And here the child was on the practice floor getting more than a little impatient with his teacher's hesitations.

"Sir, is this part of a lesson, just standing here? I know sometimes . . ."

"Be still."

Teg came to military attention. No one had taught him that. This was from his original memories. Idaho was suddenly fascinated by this glimpse of the Bashar.

They knew he would catch me this way!

Never underestimate Bene Gesserit persuasiveness. You could find yourself doing things for them without knowing pressures had been applied. Subtle and damnable! There were compensations, of course. You lived in interesting times, as the ancient curse/benison had it. All in all, Idaho decided, he preferred interesting times, even these times.

He took a deep breath. "Restoring your original memories will cause pain—physical and mental. In some ways, the mental pains are worse. I am to prepare you for that."

Still at attention. No comment.

"We will begin without weapons, using an imaginary blade in your right hand. This is a variation on the 'five attitudes'. Each response arises before the need. Drop your arms to your sides and relax."

Moving behind Teg, Idaho grasped the child's right arm below the elbow and demonstrated the first movements.

"Each attacker is a feather floating on an infinite path. As the feather approaches, it is diverted and removed. Your response is like a puff of air blowing the feather away."

Idaho stepped aside and observed as Teg repeated the movements, correcting occasionally with a sharp blow to an offending muscle.

"Let your body do the learning!" When Teg asked why he did that.

In a rest period, Teg wanted to know what Idaho meant by "mental pains".

"You have ghola-imposed walls around your original memories. At the proper moment, some of those memories will come flooding back. Not all memories will be pleasant."

"Mother Superior says the Bashar restored your memories."

"Gods of the deep, child! Why do you keep saying 'the Bashar'? That was you!"

"But I don't know that yet."

"You present a special problem. For a ghola to reawaken, there should be memory of death. But the cells for you do not carry death memory."

"But the . . . Bashar is dead."

"The Bashar! Yes, he's dead. You must feel that where it hurts most and know that *you* are the Bashar."

"Can you really give me back that memory?"

"If you can stand the pain. Do you know what I said to *you* when you restored my memories? I said: 'Atreides! You're all so damned alike!'"

"You hated . . . me?"

"Yes, and you were disgusted with yourself for what you did to me. Does that give you any idea of what I must do?"

"Yes, sir." Very low.

"Mother Superior says I must not betray your trust . . . yet, you betrayed my trust."

"But I restored your memories?"

"See how easy it is to think of yourself as Bashar? You were

183

shocked. And yes, you restored my memories."

"That's all I want."

"So you say."

"Mother . . . Superior says you're a Mentat. Will that help . . . that I was a Mentat, too?"

"Logic says, 'Yes'. But we Mentats have a saying, that logic moves blindly. And we're aware there's a logic that kicks you out of the nest into chaos."

"I know what chaos means!" Very proud of himself.

"So you think."

"And I trust you!"

"Listen to me! We are servants of the Bene Gesserit. Reverend Mothers did not build their order on trust."

"Shouldn't I trust Mother . . . Superior?"

"Within limits you will learn and appreciate. For now, I warn you the Bene Gesserit work under a system of organized *distrust*. Have they taught you about democracy?"

"Yes, sir. That's where you vote for . . ."

"That's where you distrust anyone with power over you! The sisters know it well. Don't trust too much."

"Then I should not trust you, either?"

"The only trust you can place in me is that I will do my best to restore your original memories."

"Then I don't care how much it hurts." He looked up at the comeyes, knowledge of their purpose in his expression. "Do they mind that you say these things about them?"

"Their feelings don't concern a Mentat except as data."

"Does that mean fact?"

"Facts are fragile. A Mentat can get tangled in them. Too much *reliable* data. It's like diplomacy. You need a few good lies to get at your projections."

"I'm . . . confused." He used the word hesitantly, not sure it was what he meant.

"I said that once to Mother Superior. She said: 'I've been behaving badly.'"

"You're not supposed to . . . confuse me?"

"Unless it teaches." And when Teg still looked puzzled, Idaho said: "Let me tell you a story."

Teg immediately sat on the floor, an action revealing that

184

Odrade often used the same technique. Good. Teg already was receptive.

"In one of my lives I had a dog that hated clams," Idaho said.

"I've had clams. They come from the Great Sea."

"Yes, well my dog hated clams because one of them had the temerity to spit in his eye. That stings. But even worse, it was an innocent hole in the sand that did the spitting. No clam visible."

"What'd your dog do?" Leaning forward, chin on fist.

"He dug up the offender and brought it to me." Idaho grinned. "Lesson one: Don't let the unknown spit in your eye."

Teg laughed and clapped his hands.

"But look at it from the dog's viewpoint. Go after the spitter! Then—glorious reward: Master is pleased."

"Did your dog dig more clams?"

"Every time we went to the beach. He went growling after spitters and Master took them away never to be seen again except as empty shells with bits of meat still clinging to the insides."

"You ate them."

"See it as the dog did. Spitters get their just punishment. He has a way to rid his world of offensive things and Master is pleased with him."

Teg demonstrated his brightness. "Do the sisters think of us as dogs?"

"In a way. Never forget it. When you get back to your rooms, look up 'Lèse Majesté'. It helps place our relationship to our Masters."

Teg looked up at the comeyes and back to Idaho but said nothing.

Idaho lifted his attention to the door behind Teg and said: "That story was for you, too."

Teg jumped to his feet, turning and expecting to see Mother Superior. But it was only Murbella.

She was leaning against the wall near the door.

"Bell won't like you talking about the Sisterhood that way," she said.

185

"Odrade told me I have a free hand." He looked at Teg. "We've wasted enough time on stories! Let me see if your body has learned anything."

An odd feeling of excitement had come over Murbella as she entered the training area and saw Duncan with the child. She watched for a time, aware that she was seeing him in a new and almost Bene Gesserit light. Mother Superior's briefing came out in Duncan's candour with Teg. Extremely odd sensation, this new awareness, as though she had come a full step away from her former associates. The feeling was poignant with loss.

Murbella found herself missing strange things in her former life. Not the hunting in the streets, seeking new males to captivate and bring under Honoured Matre control. The powers that came from creating sexual addicts had lost their savour under Bene Gesserit teaching and her experiences with Duncan. She admitted to missing one element of that power, though: the sense of belonging to a force nothing could stop.

It was both abstract and specific. Not the recurrent conquests but the expectation of inevitable victory that came in part from the drug she shared with Honoured Matre sisters. As the need waned in the shift to melange, she saw the old addiction from a different perspective. Bene Gesserit chemists, tracing the adrenalin substitute from samples of her blood, held it ready if she required it. She knew she did not. Another withdrawal plagued her. Not the captivated males but the flow of them. Something within her said this was gone forever. She would never re-experience it. New knowledge had changed her past.

She had prowled the corridors between her quarters and the practice floor this morning, wanting to watch Duncan with the child, afraid her presence might interfere. This prowling was a thing she often did these days after the more strenuous of her morning lessons with a Reverend Mother teacher. Thoughts of Honoured Matres were much with her at these times.

She could not escape this feeling of loss. It was an emptiness such that she wondered if anything could possibly fill it. The sensation was worse than that of growing old. Growing old as an Honoured Matre had offered its compensations. Powers gathered in *that* sisterhood had a tendency to grow rapidly with age. Not that. It was an *absolute* loss.

I have been defeated.

Honoured Matres never contemplated defeat. Murbella felt herself forced to it. She knew Honoured Matres were sometimes slain by enemies. Those enemies always paid. It was the law: Whole planets blackened to get one offender.

Murbella knew Honoured Matres hunted for Chapter House. As a matter of former loyalties, she was aware that she should be assisting those hunters. The poignancy of her personal defeat lay in the fact that she did not want the Bene Gesserit to pay the remembered price.

The Bene Gesserit are too valuable.

They were infinitely valuable to Honoured Matres. Murbella doubted that any other Honoured Matre even suspected this.

Vanity.

That was the judgment she attached to her former sisters. *And to myself as I was.* A terrible pride. It had grown out of being subjugated so many generations before they gained their own ascendancy. Murbella had tried to convey this to Odrade, recounting from history taught by Honoured Matres.

"The slave makes an awful master," Odrade said.

There was an Honoured Matre pattern, Murbella realized. She had accepted it once but now rejected it and could not give all of her reasons for this change.

I have grown out of those things. They would be childish to me now.

Duncan once more had stopped the practice session. Perspiration poured from both teacher and student. They stood panting, regaining breath, an odd exchange of looks between them. *Conspiracy?* The child looked strangely mature.

Murbella recalled Odrade's comment: "Maturity imposes its own behaviour. One of our lessons—make those imperatives available to consciousness. Modify instincts."

They have modified me and will do so even more.

She could see the same thing at work in Duncan's behaviour with the ghola child.

"This is an activity that creates many stresses in the societies we influence," Odrade said. "That forces us to constant adjustments."

But how can they adjust to my former sisters?

Odrade revealed characteristic sang-froid when braced with this question.

"We face major adjustments because of our past activities. It was the same during the reign of the Tyrant."

Adjustments?

Duncan was talking to the child. Murbella moved closer to listen.

"You've been exposed to the story of Muad'Dib? Good. You're an Atreides and that includes flaws."

"Does that mean mistakes, sir?"

"You're damned right it does! Never choose a course just because it offers the opportunity for a dramatic gesture."

"Is that how I died?"

He has the child thinking of his former self in the first person.

"You be the judge. But it was always an Atreides weakness. Attractive things, gestures. Die on the horns of a great bull as Muad'Dib's grandfather did. A grand spectacle for his people. The stuff of stories for generations! You can even hear bits of it around after all of these eons."

"Mother Superior told me that story."

"Your birth mother probably told it to you, too."

The child shuddered. "It gives me a funny feeling when you say birth mother." Awe in his young voice.

"Funny feelings are one thing; this lesson is another. I'm talking about something with a persistent label: *The Desian Gesture*. It used to be *Atreidesian* but that's too cumbersome."

Once more the child touched that core of mature awareness. "Even a dog's life has its price."

Murbella caught her breath, glimpsing how it would be—an adult mind in that child's body. Disconcerting.

"Your birth mother was Janet Roxbrough of the Lernaeus Roxbroughs," Idaho said. "She was Bene Gesserit. Your father was Loschy Teg, a CHOAM station factor. In a few minutes I'm going to show you the Bashar's favourite picture of his home on Lernaeus. I want you to keep it with you and study it. Think of it as your favourite place."

188

Teg nodded but the expression on his face said he was afraid.

Was it possible the great Mentat Warrior had known fear? Murbella shook her head. She had an intellectual knowledge of what Duncan was doing but felt gaps in the accounts. This was something she might never experience. What would the feeling be—reawakening to new life with the memories of another lifetime intact? Much different from a Reverend Mother's Other Memory, she suspected.

"Mind at its beginning," Duncan called it. "Awakening of your True Self. I felt I had been plunged into a magic universe. My awareness was a circle and then a globe. Arbitrary forms became transient. The table was not a table. Then I fell into a trance—everything around me had a shimmering quality. Nothing was real. This passed and I felt I had lost the one reality. My table was a table once more."

She had studied the Bene Gesserit manual "On Awakening a Ghola's Original Memories". Duncan was diverging from those instructions. Why?

He left the child and approached Murbella.

"I have to talk to Sheeana," he said as he passed her. "There's got to be a better way."

> *Ready comprehension is often a knee-jerk response and the most dangerous form of* understanding. *It blinks an opaque screen over your ability to learn. The judgmental precedents of law function that way, littering your path with dead ends. Be warned. Understand nothing. All comprehension is temporary.*
>
> —Mentat Fixe (adacto)

Idaho, seated alone at his console, encountered an entry he had stored in Shipsystems during his first days of confinement, and found himself dumped (he applied the word later) into attitudes and sensory awareness of that earlier time. It no longer was afternoon of a frustrating day in the no-ship. He was back *there*, stretched between *then* and *now* the way serial ghola lives linked this incarnation to his original birth.

189

Immediately, he saw what he had come to call "the net" and the elderly couple defined by criss-crossed lines, bodies visible through a shimmering of jewelled ropes—green, blue, gold and a silver so brilliant it made his eyes ache.

He sensed godlike stability in these people, but something common about them. The word *ordinary* came to mind. The by now familiar garden landscape stretched out behind them: floral bushes (roses, he thought), rolling lawns, tall trees.

The couple stared back at him with an intensity that made Idaho feel naked.

New power in the vision! It no longer was confined to the Great Hold, an increasingly compulsive magnet drawing him down there so frequently he knew the watchdogs were alerted.

Is he another kwisatz haderach?

There was a level of suspicion the Bene Gesserit could achieve that would kill him if it grew. And they were watching him now! Questions, worried speculations. Despite this, he could not turn away from the vision.

Why did that elderly couple look so familiar? Someone from his past? Family?

Mentat riffling of his memories produced nothing to fit the speculation. Round faces. Abbreviated chins. Fat wrinkles at the jowls. Dark eyes. The net obscured their colour. The woman wore a long blue and green dress that concealed her feet. A white apron stained with green covered the dress from ample bosom to just below her waist. Garden tools dangled from apron loops. She carried a trowel in her left hand. Her hair was grey. Wisps of it had escaped a confining green scarf and blew around her eyes, emphasizing laughter lines there. She appeared . . . grandmotherly.

The man suited her as though created by the same artist as a perfect match. Bib overalls over a mounded stomach. No hat. Those same dark eyes with reflections twinkling in them. A brush of close-cropped wiry grey hair.

He had the most benign expression Idaho had ever seen. Upcurved smile creases at the corners of his mouth. He held a small shovel in his left hand, and on his extended right palm he balanced what appeared to be a small metal ball. The ball emitted a piercing whistle that made Idaho clap his hands over his ears. This did not stop the sound. It faded away of itself. He lowered his hands.

Reassuring faces. That thought aroused Idaho's suspicions because now he recognized the familiarity. They looked somewhat like Face Dancers, even to the pug noses.

He leaned forward but the vision kept its distance. "Face Dancers," he whispered.

Net and elderly couple vanished.

They were replaced by Murbella in practice-floor leotards of glistening ebony. He had to reach out and touch her before he could believe she really stood there.

"Duncan? What is it? You're all sweaty."

"I . . . think it's something the damned Tleilaxu planted in me. I keep seeing . . . I think they're Face Dancers. They . . . they look at me and just now . . . a whistle. It hurt."

She glanced up at the comeyes but did not appear worried. This was something the sisters could know without it presenting immediate dangers . . . except possibly to Scytale.

She sank to her haunches beside him and put a hand on his arm. "Something they did to your body in the tanks?"

"No!"

"But you said . . ."

"My body's not just a piece of new baggage for this trip. It has all of the chemistry and substance I ever had. It's my mind that's different."

That worried her. She knew the Bene Gesserit concern over wild talents. "Damn that Scytale!"

"I'll find it," he said.

He closed his eyes and heard Murbella stand. Her hand went away from his arm.

"Maybe you shouldn't do that, Duncan."

She sounded far away.

Memory. Where did they hide the secret thing? Deep in the original cells? Until this moment, he had thought of his memory as a Mentat tool. He could call up his own images from long ago moments in front of mirrors. Close up, examining an age wrinkle. Looking at a woman behind him—two faces in the mirror and his face full of questions.

Faces. A succession of masks, different views of this person he called *myself*. Slightly imbalanced faces. Hair sometimes grey, sometimes the jet karakul of his current life. Sometimes humorous, sometimes grave and seeking inward for wisdom to meet a new day. Somewhere in all of that lay a consciousness that observed and deliberated. Someone who made choice. The Tleilaxu had tampered with that.

He knew there were styles in acceptable character. His had always been an enduring style—always somewhat out of fashion; never trendy, but not so far out of date as to be unacceptable. He could see it there in those memories of his mirrored faces. Ancient. Even when young.

Idaho felt his blood pumping hard and knew danger was present. This was what he was intended to experience . . . but not by the Tleilaxu. He had been born with it.

This is what it means to be alive.

No memory from his other lives, nothing the Tleilaxu had done to him, none of that changed his deepest awareness one whit.

He opened his eyes. Murbella still stood near but her expression was veiled. *So that's how she will look as a Reverend Mother.*

He did not like this change in her.

"What happens if the Bene Gesserit fail?" he asked.

When she did not reply, he nodded. *Yes. That's the worst assumption. The Sisterhood down history's sewerpipe. And you don't want that, my beloved.*

He could see it in her face when she turned and left him.

Looking up at the comeyes, he said: "Dar. I must talk to you, Dar."

No response from any of the mechanisms around him. He had not expected one. Still, he knew he could talk to her and she would have to listen.

"I've been coming at our problem from the other direction," he said. And he imagined the busy whirring of recorders as they spun the sounds of his voice into ridulian crystals. "I've been getting into the minds of Honoured Matres. I know I've done it. Murbella resonates."

That would alert them. He had an Honoured Matre of his own. But *had* was not the proper word. He did not *have*

Murbella. Not even in bed. They had each other. Matched the way those people in his vision appeared to be matched. Was that what he saw there? Two older people sexually trained by Honoured Matres?

"I look at another issue now," he said. "How to overcome the Bene Gesserit."

That threw down the gauntlet.

"Episodes," he said. A word Odrade was fond of using.

"That's how we have to see what's happening to us. Little episodes. Even the worst-case assumption has to be screened against that background. The Scattering has a magnitude that dwarfs anything we do."

There! That demonstrated his value to the sisters. It put Honoured Matres in a better perspective. They were back here in the Old Empire. Fellow dwarfs. He knew Odrade would see it. Bell would make her see it.

Somewhere out there in the Infinite Universe, a jury had brought in a verdict against Honoured Matres. Law and its managers had not prevailed for the hunters. He suspected that his vision had shown him two of the jurors. And if they were Face Dancers, they were not Scytale's Face Dancers. Those two people behind the shimmering net belonged to no one but themselves.

Major flaws in government arise from a fear of making radical internal changes even though a need is clearly seen.

—**Darwi Odrade**

For Odrade, the first melange of the morning was always different. Her flesh responded like a starveling who clutched at sweet fruit. Then followed the slow, penetrating and painful restoration.

This was the fearful thing about melange addiction.

She stood at the window of her sleeping chamber waiting for the effect to run its course. Weather Control, she noted, had achieved another morning rain. The landscape was washed clean, everything immersed in a romantic haze, all edges blurred and reduced to essences like old memories. She opened the window. Damp cold air blew across her face, drawing recollections around her the way one put on a familiar garment.

She inhaled deeply. Smells after a rain! She remembered the essentials of life amplified and smoothed by falling water but these rains were different. They left a flinty aftersmell she could taste. Odrade did not like it. The message was not of things washed clean but of life resentful, wanting all rain stopped and locked away. This rain no longer gentled and brought fullness. It carried inescapable awareness of change.

Odrade closed the window. At once, she was back in the familiar odours of her quarters, and that constant smell of shere from the metering implants required of everyone who knew the location of Chapter House. She heard Streggi enter, the slip-slip sounds of the desert map being changed.

I was fortunate to find Streggi. The replacement she's training is not as good but "adequate".

An efficient sound in Streggi's movements. Weeks of close association had confirmed Odrade's first judgment. Reliable. Not brilliant but supremely sensitive to Mother Superior's needs. Look how quietly she moved. Transfer Streggi's sensitivity to the needs of young Teg and they had his required height and mobility. *A horse? Much more.*

Odrade's melange assimilation reached its peak and subsided. Streggi's reflection in the window showed her waiting for assignment. She knew these moments were given over to the spice. At her stage, she would be looking forward to the day when she entered this mysterious enhancement.

I wish her well of it.

Most Reverend Mothers followed the teaching and seldom thought of their spice as addiction. Odrade knew it every morning for what it was. You took your spice during the day as your body demanded, following a pattern of early training: dosage minimal, just enough to whet the metabolic system and drive it into peak performance. Biological necessities meshed more smoothly with melange. Food tasted better. Barring accident or fatal assault, you lived much longer than you could without it. But you were addicted.

Her body restored, Odrade blinked and considered Streggi. Curiosity about the morning's long ritual was plain in her. Speaking to Streggi's reflection in the window, Odrade said: "Have you learned about melange withdrawal?"

"Yes, Mother Superior."

Despite warnings to keep awareness of addiction low key, it was never more than an eyeblink away from Odrade and she felt the accumulated resentments. Mental preparations as an acolyte (firmly impressed in the Agony) had been eroded by Other Memory and accumulations of time. The admonition: "Withdrawal removes an essential of your life and, if it occurs in late middle age, can kill you." How little that meant now.

Streggi signalled impatience by clearing her throat. A telling mannerism that would have to be cured.

"Withdrawal has intense meaning for me," Odrade said. "I am one of those for whom the morning melange is painful. I'm sure they told you this happens."

"I'm sorry, Mother Superior."

Odrade studied the map. It showed a longer finger of desert thrusting northward and a pronounced widening of drylands to the southeast of Central where Sheeana had her station. Presently, Odrade returned her attention to Streggi who was watching Mother Superior with new interest.

Brought up short by thoughts of the spice's darker side!

"The uniqueness of melange is seldom considered in our age," Odrade said. "All of the old narcotics in which humans have indulged possess a remarkable factor in common—all except the spice. Do you know what that is?"

"I've . . . we never . . ."

"In common, Streggi! Nicotine, cocaine, heroin, the d-morphias, angel dust (awful name!), uncounted ones known generally by their initials—all brought shorter life and pain."

"Oh, I see. We were told, Mother Superior."

"But you probably were not told that a fact of governance could be obscured by our concern with Honoured Matres. There's an energy greed in governments (yes, even in ours) that can dump you into a trap."

"Proctors tell us the energy of . . ."

"Words are not enough, Streggi! If you serve me, you will

feel it in your guts because every morning you will watch me suffer. Let knowledge of it sink into you, this deadly trap. Don't become uncaring pushers, caught in a system that displaces life with careless death as Honoured Matres do. Remember: acceptable narcotics can be taxed to pay salaries or otherwise create jobs for uncaring functionaries."

"But melange . . ."

"The spice! Each side supporting the other as we totter toward extinction."

Streggi was puzzled. "But melange extends our lives, increases health and arouses appetites for . . ."

She was stopped by Odrade's scowl.

Right out of the Acolyte Manual!

"It has this other side, Streggi, and you see it in me. The Acolyte Manual does not lie. But melange is a narcotic and we are addicted."

"I know it's not gentle with everyone, Mother Superior. But you said Honoured Matres were . . ."

"The substitute they employ replaces melange with few benefits except to prevent withdrawal agonies and death. It is parallel addictive."

"Does the captive . . ."

"Murbella used it and now she uses melange. They are interchangeable. Interesting?"

"I . . . suppose we will learn more of this. I notice, Mother Superior, that you never call them whores."

"As Acolytes do? Ahh, Streggi, Bellonda has been a bad influence. Oh, I recognize the pressures." As Streggi started to protest. "Acolytes feel the threat. They look at Chapter House and think of it as their fortress for the long night of the whores."

"Something like that, Mother Superior." Extremely hesitant.

"Streggi, this planet is only another temporary place. Today we go south and impress that upon you. Find Tamalane, please, and tell her to make the arrangements we discussed for our visit to Sheeana. Speak to no one else about it."

"Yes, Mother Superior. Do you mean I will accompany . . ."

"I want you by my side. Tell the one you are training that she now has full charge of my map."

As Streggi left, Odrade thought of Sheeana and Idaho. *She wants to talk to him and he wants to talk to her.*

Comeye analysis noted that these two sometimes conversed by hand signals while hiding most of the movements with their bodies. It had the look of an old Atreides battle language. Odrade recognized some of it but not enough to determine content. Bellonda wanted an explanation from Sheeana. "Secrets!" Odrade was more cautious. "Let it go a bit. Perhaps something interesting will come of it."

What does Sheeana want?

Whatever Duncan had in mind it concerned Teg. Creating the pain required for Teg to recover his original memories went against Duncan's grain.

Odrade had noted this when she interrupted Duncan at his console yesterday.

"You're late, Dar." Not looking up from whatever it was he did there. *Late? It was early evening.*

He had been calling her Dar frequently for several years, a goad, a reminder that he resented his fishtank existence. The goad irritated Bellonda who argued against "his damned familiarities". He called Bellonda "Bell", of course. Duncan was generous with his needle.

Remembering this, Odrade paused before entering her workroom. Duncan had slammed a fist on to the counter beside his console. "There's got to be a better way for Teg!"

A better way? What does he have in mind?

Movement down the corridor beyond the workroom brought her out of this reflection. Streggi returning from Tamalane. Streggi entered the Acolyte Ready Room. *Giving the word to her replacement on the desert map.*

A stack of Archival records waited on Odrade's table. *Bellonda!* Odrade stared at the pile. No matter how much she tried to delegate there was always this organized residue that her councillors insisted only Mother Superior could handle. Much of this new lot came from Bellonda's demand for "suggestions and analyses".

"We must actively seek new ideas. Our decisions concern the very destiny of the Sisterhood!"

Destiny. What a sad little word.

After sorting through the pile, Odrade showed her anger by pushing it away. *Barn sweepings trampled by cattle! Not one good idea. Nothing even suggestive.*

"No trails, no tracks," one of the *analyses* admonished. *Pull in our necks even farther? Emulate the turtle?*

Bellonda was becoming positively malign! *She and her staff are trying to control me by deluging me with trivia!*

A typical Archives ploy. At least, they wanted her to think it typical. *Don't avoid telltale behaviour with sisters! Oh, no. Watchdogs must know what every sister does.*

Odrade touched her console. "Bell!"

The voice of an Archives clerk responded: "Mother Superior?"

"Get Bell up here! I want her in front of me as fast as her fat legs can move!"

It was less than a minute. Bellonda stood in front of the worktable like a chastened acolyte. They all knew that tone in Mother Superior's voice.

Odrade touched the stack on her table and jerked her hand back as though shocked. "What in the name of Shaitan is all of that?"

"We judged it significant for . . ."

"You think I have to see everything and anything? Where's the keynoting? This is sloppy work, Bell! I'm not stupid and neither are you. But this . . . in the face of this . . ."

"I delegate as much as . . ."

"Delegate? Look at this! Which must I see and which may *I* delegate? Not one keynote!"

"I'll see that it's corrected immediately."

"Indeed you will, Bell. Because Tam and I are going south today, an unannounced inspection tour and a visit with Sheeana. And while I'm gone, you will sit in my chair. See how *you* like this daily deluge!"

"Will you be out of touch with . . ."

"I'll have a lightline and Ear-C at all times."

Bellonda breathed easier.

"I suggest, Bell, that you get back to Archives and put someone in charge who will take responsibility. I'm damned if you're not beginning to act like bureaucrats. Covering your asses!"

"Real boats rock, Dar."

Was that Bell attempting humour? All was not lost!

When Bellonda had gone, Odrade contemplated this room of so many decisions. *We are getting sloppy.* Fear of emotions—suppression itself—created a dangerous gap.

I must remind Bell that bureaucracy loathes emotions. They interfere with proper administration of rules!

It was quite natural that laws had no feelings, Odrade thought. *And that puts us in danger!* Good bureaucrats emulated rules, not fellow humans. The best bureaucrats achieved a cool non-humanity. "Compassion is not in my job description." That was the way to advancement.

Odrade waved a hand over her projector and there was Tamalane in the Transport Hall. "Tam?"

"Yes?" Without turning from an assignment list.

"How soon can we leave?"

"About two hours."

"Call me when you're ready. Oh, and Streggi goes with us. Make room for her." Odrade blanked the projection before Tamalane could respond.

There were things she should be doing, Odrade knew. Tam and Bell were not the only sources of Mother Superior's concerns.

Sixteen planets remaining to us . . . and that includes Buzzell, definitely a place in peril. Only sixteen! She pushed that thought aside. No time for it. Compassion drained away energy, too.

Murbella. Should I call her and . . . No. That can wait. The new Board of Proctors? Let Bell deal with that. Community disbandings?

Siphoning personnel into a new Scattering had forced consolidations. *Staying ahead of the desert!* It was depressing and she did not feel she could face it today. *I'm always fidgety before a trip.*

Abruptly, Odrade fled the workroom and went stalking the

corridors, looking into how her charges were performing, pausing in doorways, noting what the students read, how they behaved in their everlasting prana-bindu exercises.

"What are you reading there?" demanded of a young second stage acolyte at a projector in a semi-darkened room.

"The diaries of Tolstoy, Mother Superior."

That knowing look in the acolyte's eyes said: "Do you have his words directly in Other Memory?" The question was right there on the edge of the girl's tongue! They were always trying such petty gambits when they caught her alone.

"Tolstoy was a *family* name!" Odrade snapped. "By your mention of diaries, I presume you refer to Count Leo Nikolayevich."

"Yes, Mother Superior." Abashedly aware of censure.

Softening, Odrade threw a quotation at the girl: "'I am not a river, I am a net.' He spoke those words at Yasnaya Polyana when he was only twelve. You'll not find them in his diaries but they are probably the most significant words he ever uttered."

Odrade turned away before the acolyte could thank her. *Always teaching!*

She wandered down to the main kitchens then and inspected them, tracing inner edges of racked pots for grease, noting the cautious way even the teaching chef observed her progress.

The kitchen was steamy with good smells from lunch preparations. There was a restorative sound of chopping and stirring but the usual banter stopped at her entrance.

Odrade found nothing to require severe complaint (although they were being too lavish with salt in the soup and there was a spill of chopped parsley ignored on the floor). The sous-chef noticed her look at the parsley and gestured to a postulant on clean-up: Odrade was glad she did not have to censure anyone. It made her next move easier.

She went around the long counter with its busy cooks to the teaching chef's raised platform. He was a great beefy man with prominent cheekbones, his face as florid as the meats over which he ministered. Odrade had no doubts he was one of history's great chefs. His name suited him: Placido Salat. He was assured of a warm place in her thoughts for several reasons, including the fact that he had trained her personal chef. Important visitors in the days before Honoured Matres had received a kitchen tour and a taste of specialities.

"May I introduce our senior chef, Placido Salat?"

His beef placido (lower case his choice) was the envy of many. Almost raw and served with a herbed and spicy mustard sauce that did not obscure the meat.

Odrade thought the dish too exotic but never judged it aloud.

When she had Salat's full attention (after a slight interruption to correct a sauce) Odrade said: "I'm hungry for something special, Placido."

He recognized the opening. This was how she always began a request for her "special dish".

"Perhaps an oyster stew," he suggested.

It's a dance, Odrade thought. They both knew what she wanted.

"Excellent!" she agreed and went into the required performance. "But it must be treated gently, Placido, the oysters not overcooked. Some of our own powdered dry celery in the broth."

"And perhaps a bit of paprika?"

"I always prefer it that way. Be extremely careful with the melange. A breath of it and no more."

"Of course, Mother Superior!" Eyes rolling in horror at the thought he might use too much melange. "So easy for the spice to dominate."

"Cook the oysters in clam nectar, Placido. I would prefer you watch over them yourself, stirring gently until the edges of the oysters just start to curl."

"Not a second longer, Mother Superior."

"Heat some quite creamy milk on the side. Don't boil it!"

Placido displayed astonishment that she might suspect him of boiling the milk for her oyster stew.

"A small pat of butter in the serving bowl," Odrade said. "Pour the combined broth over it."

"No sherry?"

"How glad I am that you are taking personal charge of my special dish, Placido. I forgot the sherry." (Mother Superior never forgot anything and they all knew it but this was a required step in the dance.)

"Three ounces of sherry in the cooking broth," he said.

"Heat it to get rid of the alcohol."

"Of course! But we must not bruise the flavours. Would you like croutons or saltiness?"

"Croutons, please."

Seated at an alcove table, Odrade ate two bowls of oyster stew, remembering how Sea Child had savoured it. Papa had introduced her to this dish when she was barely capable of conveying spoon to mouth. He had made the stew himself, his own speciality. Odrade had taught it to Salat.

She complimented him on the wine.

"I particularly enjoyed your choice of a chablis for accompaniment."

"A flinty chablis with a sharp edge on it, Mother Superior. One of our better vintages. It sets off the oyster flavours admirably."

Tamalane found her in the alcove. They always knew where to find Mother Superior when they wanted her.

"We are ready." Was that displeasure on Tam's face?

"Where will we stop tonight?"

"Eldio."

Odrade smiled. She liked Eldio.

Tam catering to me because I'm in a critical mood? Perhaps we have the makings of a small diversion.

Following Tamalane to the transport docks, Odrade thought how characteristic it was that the older woman preferred to travel by tube. Surface trips annoyed her. "Who wants to waste time at my age?"

Odrade disliked tubes for personal transport. You were so closed in and helpless! She preferred surface or air and used tubes only when speed was urgent. She had no hesitation about using smaller tubes for chits and notes. *Notes don't care just as long as they get there*.

This thought always made her conscious of the network that adjusted to her movements wherever she went.

Somewhere in the heart of things (there was always a "heart of things") an automated system routed communications and

202

made sure (most of the time) that important missives arrived where addressed.

When Private Dispatch (they all called it PD) was not needed, stat or viz was available along scrambled sorters and lightlines. Off planet was another-matter, especially in these hunted times. Safest to send a Reverend Mother with memorized message or distrans implant. Every messenger took heavier doses of shere these days. T-probes could read even a dead mind not guarded by shere. Every off-planet message was encrypted but an enemy might hit on the one-time cover concealing it. Great risk off planet. Perhaps that was why the Rabbi remained silent.

Now why am I thinking such things at this moment?

"No word yet from Dortujla?" she asked as Tamalane prepared to enter the Dispatch roundalay where the others in their party waited. So many people. Why so many?

Odrade saw Streggi up ahead at the edge of the dock talking to a Communications acolyte. There were at least six other people from Communications nearby.

Tamalane turned in obvious pique. "Dortujla! We have all said we will notify you the instant we hear!"

"I was just asking, Tam. Just asking."

Meekly, Odrade followed Tamalane into Dispatch. *I should put a monitor on my mind and question everything that rises there.* Mental intrusions always had good reason behind them. That was the Bene Gesserit way, as Bellonda often reminded her.

Odrade felt surprise at herself then, realizing that she was more than a little sick of Bene Gesserit ways.

Let Bell worry about such things for a change!

This was a time for floating free, for responding like a will o' the wisp to the currents moving around her.

Sea Child knew about currents.

> *Time does not count itself. You have only to look at a circle and this is apparent.*
>
> —Leto II (The Tyrant)

"Look! Look what we have come to!" the Rabbi wailed. He sat cross-legged on the cold curved floor with his shawl pulled up over his head and almost concealing his face.

The room around him was gloomy and resonating with small machinery sounds that made him feel weak. If those sounds should stop!

Rebecca stood in front of him, hands on her hips, a look of weary frustration on her face.

"Do not stand there like that!" the Rabbi commanded. He peered up at her from beneath the shawl.

"If you despair, then are we not lost?" she asked.

The sound of her voice angered him and he was a moment putting this unwanted emotion aside.

She dares to instruct me? But was it not said by wiser men that knowledge can come from a weed? A great shuddering sigh shook him and he dropped the shawl to his shoulders. Rebecca helped him stand.

"A no-chamber," the Rabbi muttered. "In here, we hide from . . ." His gaze searched upward at a dark ceiling. "Better left unspoken even here."

"We hide from the unspeakable," Rebecca said.

"The door cannot even be left open at Passover," he said. "How will the Stranger enter?"

"Some strangers we do not want," she said.

"Rebecca." He bowed his head. "You are more than a trial and a problem. This little cell of Secret Israel shares your exile because we understand that . . ."

"Stop saying that! You understand nothing of what has happened to me. My problem?" She leaned close to him. "It is to remain human while in contact with all of those past lives."

The Rabbi recoiled.

"So you are no longer one of us? Are you a Bene Gesserit then?"

"You will know when I'm Bene Gesserit. You will see me looking at myself as I look at myself."

His brows drew down in a scowl. "What are you saying?"

"What does a mirror look at, Rabbi?"

"Hmmmmph! Riddles now." But a faint smile twitched at his mouth. A look of determination returned to his eyes. He stared around him at the room. There were eight of them here—more than this space should hold. *A no-chamber!* It had been assembled painstakingly with smuggled bits and pieces. So small. Twelve and half metres long. He had measured it himself. A shape like an ancient barrel laid on its side, oval in cross section and with half-globe closures at the ends. The ceiling was no more than a metre above his head. The widest point here at the centre was only five metres and the curve of floor and ceiling made it seem even narrower. Dried food and recycled water. That was what they must live on and for how long? One SY maybe if they were not found. He did not trust the security of this device. Those peculiar sounds in the machinery.

It had been late in the day when they crept into this hole. Darkness up there now for sure. And where were the rest of his people? Fled to whatever sanctuary they could find, drawing on old debts and honourable commitments for past services. Some would survive. Perhaps they would survive better than this remnant in here.

The entrance to the no-chamber lay concealed beneath an ash pit with a free-standing chimney beside it. The reinforcing metal of the chimney contained threads of ridulian crystal to relay exterior scenes into this place. Ashes! The room still smelled of burned things and it already had begun to take on a sewer stink from the small recycling chamber. What a euphemism for a toilet!

Someone came up behind the Rabbi. "The searchers are leaving. Lucky we were warned in time."

It was Joshua, the one who had built this chamber. He was a short, slender man with a sharply triangular face narrowing to a thin chin. Dark hair swept over his broad forehead. He had widely-spaced brown eyes that looked out at his world with a brooding inwardness the Rabbi did not trust. *He looks too young to know so much about these things*.

"So they are leaving," the Rabbi said. "They will be back. You will not think us lucky then."

"They will not guess we hid so near the farm," Rebecca said. "The searchers were mostly looting."

"Listen to the Bene Gesserit," the Rabbi said.

"Rabbi." What a chiding sound in Joshua's voice! "Have I not heard you say many times that the blessed ones are they who hide the flaws of others even from themselves?"

"Everybody's a teacher now!" the Rabbi said. "But who can tell us what will happen next?"

He had to admit the truth of Joshua's words, though. *It is the anguish of our flight that troubles me. Our little diaspora. But we do not scatter from Babylon. We hide in a . . . a cyclone cellar!*

This thought restored him. *Cyclones pass.*

"Who is in charge of the food?" he asked. "We must ration ourselves from the start."

Rebecca heaved a sigh of relief. The Rabbi was at his worst in the wide oscillations—too emotional or too intellectual. He had himself in hand once more. He would become intellectual next. That would have to be dampened, too. Bene Gesserit awareness gave her a new view of the people around her. *Our Jewish susceptibility. Look at the intellectuals!*

It was a thought peculiar to the Sisterhood. The drawbacks of anyone placing considerable reliance on intellectual achievements were large. She could not deny all of that evidence from the Lampadas horde. Speaker paraded it for her whenever she wavered.

Rebecca had come almost to enjoy the pursuit of memory fancies, as she thought of them. Knowing earlier times forced her to deny her own earlier times. She had been required to believe so many things she now knew were nonsense. Myths and chimeras, impulses of extremely childish behaviour.

"Our gods should mature as we mature."

Rebecca suppressed a smile. Speaker did that to her often— a little nudge in the ribs from someone who knew you would appreciate it.

Joshua had gone back to his instruments. She saw that someone was reviewing the catalogue of food stores. The Rabbi watched this with his normal intensity. Others had rolled themselves into blankets and were sleeping on the cots in the darkened end of the chamber. Seeing all of this, Rebecca knew what her function must be. *Keep us from boredom.*

"The games master?"

Unless you have something better to suggest, don't try to tell me about my own people, Speaker.

Whatever else she might say about these inner conversations, there was no doubt that all of the pieces were connected—the past with this room, this room with her projections of consequences. And that was a great gift from the Bene Gesserit. *Do not think of "The Future". Predestination? Then what happens to the freedom you are given at birth?*

Rebecca looked at her own birth in a new light. It had embarked her on movement toward an unknown destiny. Fraught with unseen perils and joys. So they had come around a bend in the river and found attackers. The next bend might reveal a cataract or a stretch of peaceful beauty. And here lay the magical enticement of prescience, the lure to which Muad'Dib and his Tyrant son had succumbed. *The oracle knows what is to come!* The horde of Lampadas had taught her not to seek oracles. The known could beleaguer her more than the unknown. The sweetness of the new lay in its surprises. Could the Rabbi see it?

"Who will tell us what happens next?" he asks.

Is that what you want, Rabbi? You will not like what you hear. I guarantee it. From the moment the oracle speaks your future becomes identical to your past. How you would wail in your boredom. Nothing new, not ever. Everything old in that one instant of revelation.

"But this is not what I wanted!" *I can hear you saying it.*

No brutality, no savagery, no quiet happiness nor exploding joy can come upon you unexpectedly. Like a runaway tube train in its wormhole, your life will speed through to its final moment of confrontation. Like a moth in the car you will beat your wings against the sides and ask Fate to let you out. "Let the tube undergo a magical change of direction. Let something new happen! Don't let the terrible things I have seen come to pass!"

Abruptly, she saw that this must have been Muad'Dib's travail. To whom had he uttered his prayers?

"Rebecca!" It was the Rabbi calling her.

She went to where he stood beside Joshua now, looking at

the dark world outside of their chamber as it was revealed in the small projection above Joshua's instruments.

"There is a storm coming," the Rabbi said. "Joshua thinks it will make a cement of the ash pit."

"That is good," she said. "It is why we built here and left the cover off the pit when we entered."

"But how do we get out?"

"We have tools for that," she said. "And even without tools, there's always our hands."

A major concept guides the Missionaria Protectiva: Purpose-ful instruction of the masses. This is firmly seated in our belief that the aim of argument should be to change the nature of truth. In such matters, we prefer the use of power rather than force.

—The Coda

To Duncan Idaho, life in the no-ship had taken on the air of a peculiar game since the advent of his vision and insights into Honoured Matre behaviour. Entry of Teg into the game was a deceptive move, not just the introduction of another player.

He stood beside his console this morning and recognized elements in this game parallel to his own ghola childhood at the Bene Gesserit Keep on Gammu with the ageing Bashar as weapons master-guardian.

Education. That had been a primary concern then as it was now. And the guards, mostly unobtrusive in the no-ship but always there as they had been on Gammu. Or their spy devices present, artfully camouflaged and blended into the decor. He had become an adept at evading them on Gammu. Here, with Sheeana's help, he had raised evasion to a fine art.

Activity around him was reduced to low background. Guards carried no weapons. But they were mostly Reverend Mothers with a few senior acolytes. They would not believe they needed weapons.

Some things in the no-ship contributed to an illusion of freedom, chiefly its size and complexity. The ship was large, how large he could not determine but he had access to many floors and to corridors that ran for more than a thousand paces.

Tubes and tunnels, access piping that conveyed him in suspensor pods, dropchutes and lifts, conventional hallways and wide corridors with hatches that hissed open at a touch (or remained sealed: *Forbidden!*)—all of it was a place to lock in memory, becoming there his own turf, private to him in a way far different from what it was to guards.

The energy required to bring the ship down to the planet and maintain it spoke of a major commitment. The Sisterhood could not count the cost in any ordinary way. The comptroller of the Bene Gesserit treasury did not deal merely in monetary counters. Not for them the Solar or comparable currencies. They banked on their people, on food, on payments due sometimes for millennia, payments often in kind—both materials and loyalties.

Pay up, Duncan! We're calling in your note!

This ship was not just a prison. He had considered several Mentat projections. Prime: it was a laboratory where Reverend Mothers sought a way to nullify a no-ship's ability to confuse human senses.

A no-ship gameboard—puzzle and warren. All to confine three prisoners? No. There had to be other reasons.

The game had secret rules, some he could only guess. But he had found it reassuring when Sheeana entered into the spirit of it. *I knew she would have her own plans. Obvious when she began practising Honoured Matre techniques. Polishing my trainees!*

Sheeana wanted intimate information about Murbella and much more—his memories of people he had known in his many lives, especially memories of the Tyrant.

And I want information about the Bene Gesserit.

The Sisterhood kept him in minimal activity. Frustrating him to increase Mentat abilities. He was not at the heart of that larger problem he sensed outside the ship. Tantalizing fragments came to him when Odrade gave him glimpses of their predicament through her questions.

Enough to offer new premises? Not without access to data that his console refused to display.

It was his problem, too, damn them! He was in a box within their box. All of them trapped.

Odrade had stood beside this console one afternoon a week ago and blandly assured him the Sisterhood's data sources were "opened wide" to him. Right there she had stood, her back to the counter, leaning on it casually, arms folded across her breast. Her resemblance to the adult Miles Teg was uncanny at times. Even to that need (Was it a compulsion?) to stand while talking. She disliked chairdogs, too.

He knew he had an extremely loose comprehension of her motives and plans. But he didn't trust them. Not after Gammu.

Decoy and bait. That was how they had used him. He was lucky not to have gone the way of Dune—a dead husk. Used up by the Bene Gesserit.

The no-ship game had rules Odrade's visits did not supply. He could only speculate.

When he fidgeted this way, Idaho preferred to slump into the chair at his console. Sometimes, he sat here for hours, immobile, his mind trying to encompass complexities of the ship's powerful data resources. The system could identify any human in it. *So it has automatic monitors.* It had to know who was speaking, making demands, assuming temporary command.

Flight circuits defy my attempts to break through the locks. Disconnected? That was what his guards said. But the ship's way of identifying who tapped the circuits—he knew his key lay there.

Would Sheeana help? It was a dangerous gamble to trust her too much. Sometimes when she watched him at his console he was reminded of Odrade. *Sheeana was Odrade's student.* That was a sobering memory.

What was their interest in how he used Shipsystems? As if he needed to ask!

During his third year here he had made the system hide data for him, doing this with his own keys. To thwart the prying comeyes, he hid his actions in plain sight. Obvious insertions for later retrieval but with an encrypted second message. Easy for a Mentat and useful mostly as a trick, exploring the potentials of shipsystems. He had booby-trapped his data to a random dump without hope of recovery.

Bellonda suspected, but when she questioned him about it, he only smiled.

I hide my history, Bell. My serial lives as a ghola—all of them back to the original non-ghola. Intimate things I remember about those experiences: a dumping ground for poignant memories.

Sitting now at the console, he experienced mixed feelings. Confinement galled him. No matter the size and richness of his prison, it still was a prison. He had known for some time that he very likely could escape but Murbella and his increasing knowledge about their predicament held him. He felt as much a prisoner of his thoughts as of the elaborate system represented by guards and this monstrous device. The noship was a device, of course. A tool. A way to move unseen in a dangerous universe. A means of concealing yourself and your intentions even from prescient searchers.

With accumulated skills of many lifetimes, he looked on his surroundings through a screen of sophistication and naivete. Mentats cultivated naivete. Thinking you knew something was a sure way to blind yourself. It was not *growing up* that slowly applied brakes to learning (Mentats were taught) but an accumulation of "things I know".

Guilds and assemblages of experts demonstrate a sure way to lock up the keys to learning.

New data sources the Sisterhood had opened to him (if he could rely on them) raised questions. How was opposition to Honoured Matres organized in the Scattering? Obviously there were groups (he hesitated to call them powers) who hunted Honoured Matres the way Honoured Matres hunted the Bene Gesserit. Killed them, too, if you accepted Gammu evidence.

Futars and Handlers? He made a Mentat Projection: A Tleilaxu offshoot in the first Scattering had engaged in genetic manipulation. Those two he saw in his vision: were they the ones who created Futars? Could that couple be Face Dancers? Independent of Tleilaxu Masters? All was not singular in the Scattering.

Dammit! He needed access to more data, to potent sources. His present sources were not even remotely adequate. A tool of limited purpose, his console could be adapted to larger requirements but his adaptations limped. He needed to stride out as a Mentat!

I've been hobbled and that's a mistake. Doesn't Odrade trust me? She's an Atreides, damn her! She knows what I owe her Family.

More than one lifetime and the debt never paid!

He knew he was fidgeting. He felt there was nothing of any interest in the ship. Outside. That was what drew his attention.

They would never let him out. His mixture of Siona and non-Siona genes worried them. He sensed this in the odd ways they employed him. Occasionally, he was called on to lecture groups of acolytes and Reverend Mothers. He did not believe those lectures revealed startling new things about Honoured Matres and their sexual techniques. It was background. "Here is our tame ghola-Mentat. Watch him perform!"

How did they select audiences? Mandatory? Or did they simply make an announcement? *"The Mentat will lecture on such and such a night. All of those interested may attend. Leave your name with Proctor X to facilitate provisions for adequate seating."*

Attendance varied. Sometimes only ten or twelve. On one occasion, he had looked out over an audience of more than a thousand. They had been forced to meet in the Great Hold.

He was still fidgeting. Abruptly, his mind locked on that. Mentat fidgeting! A signal that he stood poised at the edge of breakthrough. *A Prime Projection!* Something they had *not* told him about Teg?

Questions! There were unasked questions lashing at him.

I need perspective! Not necessarily a matter of distance. You could gain perspective from within if your questions carried few distortions.

He sensed that somewhere in Bene Gesserit experiences (perhaps even in Bell's jealously-guarded Archives) lay missing pieces. Bell should appreciate this! A fellow Mentat *must* know the excitement of this moment. His thoughts were like

212

tesserae, most of the pieces at hand and ready to fit into a mosaic. It was not a matter of solutions.

He could hear his first Mentat teacher, the words rumbling in his mind: *"Assemble your questions in counterpoise and toss your temporary data on to one side of the scales or the other. Solutions unbalance any situation. Imbalances reveal what you seek."*

Yes! Achieving imbalances with sensitized questions was a Mentat's juggling act.

Where were the missing pieces? What he needed might be found in Bene Gesserit folklore, if they went in for that. The "Oh, by the way!" stuff that humans gathered in passing.

Something Murbella had said the night before—What? They had been in her bed. He recalled seeing the time projected on the ceiling: 9:47. And he had thought: *That projection takes energy.*

He could almost feel the flow of the ship's power, this giant enclosure cut out of Time. Frictionless machinery to create a mimetic presence no instrument could distinguish from natural background. Except for now when it was on standby, shielded not from eyes but from prescience.

Murbella beside him: another kind of power, both aware of the force trying to pull them together. The energy it took to suppress that mutual magnetism! Sexual attraction building and building and building.

Murbella talking. Yes, that was it. Oddly self analytic. She approached her own life with a new maturity, a Bene Gesserit-heightened awareness and confidence that something of great strength grew in her.

Every time he recognized this Bene Gesserit change, he felt sad. *Nearer the day of our parting.*

But Murbella was talking. "She (Odrade was often 'she') keeps asking me to assess my love for you."

Remembering this, Idaho allowed it to replay.

"She has tried the same approach with me."

"What do you say?"

"Odi et amo. Excrucior."

She lifted herself on one elbow and looked down at him. "What language is that?"

213

"A very old one Leto had me learn once."

"Translate." Peremptory. Her old Honoured Matre self.

"'I hate her and I love her. And I am racked.'"

"Do you really hate me?" Unbelieving.

"What I hate is being tied this way, not the master of my self."

"Would you leave me if you could?"

"I want the decision to recur moment by moment. I want control of it."

"It's a game where one of the pieces can't be moved."

There it was! Her words.

Remembering, Idaho felt no elation but as though his eyes had suddenly been opened after a long sleep. *A game where one of the pieces can't be moved. Game.* His view of the no-ship and what the Sisterhood did here.

There was more to the exchange.

"The ship is our own special school," Murbella said.

He could only agree. The Sisterhood reinforced his Mentat capacities to screen data and display what had not gone through. He sensed where this might lead and felt leaden fear.

"You clear the nerve passages. You block off distractions and useless mind-wanderings."

You redirected your responses into that dangerous mode every Mentat was warned to avoid. "You can lose yourself there."

Students were taken to see human vegetables, "failed Mentats", kept alive to demonstrate the peril.

How tempting, though. You could sense the power in that mode. *Nothing hidden. All things known.*

Known to wasted human bodies motionless on their mattresses, a faint odour of bedsores around them.

In the midst of that fear, Murbella turning toward him on the bed, he felt the sexual tensions become almost explosive.

Not yet. Not yet!

One of them had said something else. What? He had been thinking about the limits of logic as a tool to expose the Sisterhood's motives.

"Do you often try to analyse them?" Murbella asked.

Uncanny how she did that, addressing his unspoken

thoughts. She denied she read minds. "I just read you, ghola mine. You are mine, you know."

"And vice versa."

"Too true." Almost bantering but it covered something deeper and convoluted.

There was a pitfall in any analysis of human psyches and he said this. "Thinking you know why you behave as you do gives you all sorts of excuses for extraordinary behaviour."

Excuses for extraordinary behaviour! There was another piece in his mosaic. More of the game but these counters were guilt and blame.

Murbella's voice was almost musing. "I suppose you can rationalize almost anything by laying it on some trauma."

"Rationalize such things as burning entire planets?"

"There's a kind of brutal self-determination in that. *She* says making determined choices firms up the psyche and gives you a sense of identity you can rely on under stress. Do you agree, Mentat mine?"

"The Mentat is not yours." No force in his voice.

Murbella laughed and slumped back on to her pillow. "You know what the sisters want of us, Mentat mine?"

"They want our children."

"Oh, much more than that. They want our willing participation in their dream."

Another piece of the mosaic!

But who other than a Bene Gesserit knew that dream? The sisters were actresses, always performing, letting little that was real come through their masks. The real person was walled in and metered out as needed.

"Why does she keep that old painting?" Murbella asked.

Idaho felt his stomach muscles tighten. Odrade had brought him a holorecord of the painting she kept in her sleeping chamber. *Cottages at Cordeville by Vincent Van Gogh.* Awakening him in this bed at some witching hour of the night almost a month ago.

"You asked for my hold on humanity and here it is." Thrusting the holo in front of his sleep-fogged eyes. He sat up and stared at the thing, trying to comprehend. What was wrong with her? Odrade sounded so excited.

215

She left the holo in his hands while she turned on all of the lights, giving the room a sense of hard and immediate shapes, everything vaguely mechanical the way you would expect it in a no-ship. Where was Murbella? They had gone to sleep together.

He focused on the holo and it touched him in an unaccountable way, as though it linked him to Odrade. *Her hold on her humanity?* The holo felt cold to his hands. She took it from him and propped it on the side table where he stared at it while she found a chair and sat near his head. Sitting? Something compelled her to be near him!

"It was painted by a madman on Old Terra," she said, bringing her cheek close to his while both looked at the copy of the painting. "Look at it! An encapsulated human moment."

In a landscape? Yes, dammit. She was right.

He stared at the holo. *Those marvellous colours!* It was not just the colours. It was the totality.

"Most modern artists would laugh at the way he created that," Odrade said.

Couldn't she be silent while he looked at it?

"That was a human being as ultimate recorder," Odrade said. "The human hand, the human eye, the human essence brought to focus in the awareness of one person who tested the limits."

Tested the limits! More of the mosaic.

"Van Gogh did that with the most primitive materials and equipment." She sounded almost drunk. "Pigments a caveman would have recognized! Painted on a fabric he could have made with his own hands. He might have made the tools himself from fur and wild twigs."

She touched the surface of the holo, her finger placing a shadow across the tall trees. "The cultural level was crude by our standards, but see what he produced?"

Idaho felt he should say something but words would not come. Where was Murbella? Why wasn't she here?

Odrade pulled back and her next words burned themselves into him.

"That painting says you cannot suppress the wild thing, the

216

uniqueness that *will* occur among humans no matter how much we try to avoid it."

Idaho tore his gaze away from the holo and looked at Odrade's lips when she spoke.

"Vincent told us something important about our fellows in the Scattering."

This long-dead painter? About the Scattering?

"They have done things out there and are doing things we cannot imagine. Wild things! The explosive size of that Scattered population ensures it."

Murbella entered the room behind Odrade, belting a soft white robe, her feet bare. Her hair was damp from a shower. So that was where she had gone.

"Mother Superior?" Murbella's voice was sleepy.

Odrade spoke over her shoulder without fully turning. "Honoured Matres think they can anticipate and control every wildness. What nonsense. They cannot even control it in themselves."

Murbella came around to the foot of the bed and stared questioningly at Idaho. "I seem to have come in on the middle of a conversation."

"Balance, that's the key," Odrade said.

Idaho kept his attention on Mother Superior.

"Humans can balance on strange surfaces," Odrade said. "Even on unpredictable ones. It's called 'getting in tune'. Great musicians know it. Surfers I watched when I was a child on Gammu, they knew it. Some waves throw you but you're prepared for that. You climb back up and go at it once more."

For no reason he could explain, Idaho thought of another thing Odrade had said: "We have no attic storerooms. We recycle everything."

Recycle. Cycle. Pieces of the circle. Pieces of the mosaic.

He was random hunting and knew better. Not the Mentat way. Recycle, though—Other Memory was not an attic storeroom then but something they considered as recycling. It meant they used their past only to change it and renew it.

Getting in tune.

A strange allusion from someone who claimed she avoided music.

217

Remembering, he sensed his mental mosaic. It had become a jumble. Nothing fitted anywhere. Random pieces that probably did not go together at all.

But they did!

Mother Superior's voice continued in his memory. *So there is more.*

"People who know this go to the heart of it," Odrade said. "They warn that you cannot think about what you're doing. That's a sure way to fail. You just do it!"

Don't think. Do it. He sensed anarchy. Her words threw him back on to resources other than Mentat training.

Bene Gesserit trickery! She did this deliberately, knowing the effect. Where was the affection he sometimes felt radiating from her? Could she have concern for the wellbeing of someone she treated this way?

When Odrade left them (he barely noticed her departure), Murbella sat on the bed and straightened the robe around her knees.

Humans can balance on strange surfaces. Movement in his mind: the pieces of the mosaic trying to find relationships.

He felt a new surge in the universe. Those two strange people in his vision? They were part of it. He knew this without being able to say why. What was it the Bene Gesserit claimed? "We modify old fashions and old beliefs."

"Look at me!" Murbella said.

Voice? Not quite but now he was sure she tried it on and she had not told him they were training her in this witchery.

He saw the alien look in her green eyes that told him she was thinking about her former associates.

"Never try to be more clever than the Bene Gesserit, Duncan."

Speaking for the comeyes?

He could not be sure. It was the intelligence behind her eyes that gripped him these days. He could feel it growing there, as though her teachers blew into a balloon and Murbella's intellect expanded the way her abdomen expanded with new life.

Voice! What were they doing to her?

That was a stupid question. He knew what they were doing. They were taking her away from him, making a sister of her.

218

No longer my lover, my marvellous Murbella. A Reverend Mother then, remotely calculating in everything she did. *A witch.* Who could love a witch?

I could. And always will.

"They grab you from your blind side to use you for their own purposes," he said.

He could see his words take hold. She had awakened to this trap after the fact. The Bene Gesserit were so damnably clever! They had enticed her into their trap, giving her small glimpses of things as magnetic as the force binding her to him. It could only be an enraging realization to an Honoured Matre.

We trap others! They do not trap us!

But this had been done by the Bene Gesserit. They were in a different category. Almost sisters. Why deny it? And she wanted their abilities. She wanted out of this probation into the full teaching she could sense just beyond the ship's walls. Didn't she know why they still kept her on probation?

They know she still struggles in their trap.

Murbella slipped out of her robe and climbed into the bed beside him. Not touching. But keeping that warmed sense of nearness between their bodies.

"They originally intended me to control Sheeana for them," he said.

"As you control me?"

"Do I control you?"

"Sometimes I think you're a comic, Duncan."

"If I can't laugh at myself I'm really lost."

"Laugh at your pretensions to humour, too?"

"Those first." He turned toward her and cupped her left breast in his hand, feeling the nipple harden under his palm. "Did you know I was never weaned?"

"Never in all of those . . .?"

"Not once."

"I might have guessed." A smile formed fleetingly on her lips and abruptly, both of them were laughing, clutching each other, helpless with it. Presently, Murbella said, "Damn, damn, damn."

"Damn who?" as his laughter subsided and they pulled apart, forcing the separation.

"Not who, what. Damn fate!"

"I don't think fate cares."

"I love you and I'm not supposed to do that if I'm to be a proper Reverend Mother."

He hated these excursions so close to self pity. *Joke then!* "You've never been a proper anything." He massaged the pregnant swelling of her abdomen.

"I *am* proper!"

"That's a word they left out when they made you."

She pushed his hand away and sat up to look down at him. "Reverend Mothers are never supposed to love."

"I know that." *Did my anguish reveal itself?*

She was too caught up in her own worries. "When I get to the Spice Agony . . ."

"Love! I don't like the idea of agony associated with you in any way."

"How can I avoid it? I'm already in the chute. Very soon they'll have me up to speed. I'll go very fast then."

He wanted to turn away but her eyes held him.

"Truly, Duncan. I can feel it. In a way, it's like pregnancy. There comes a point when it's too dangerous to abort. You must go through with it."

"So we love each other!" Forcing his thoughts away from one danger into another.

"And they forbid it."

He looked up at the comeyes. "The watchdogs are watching us and they have fangs."

"I *know*. I'm talking to *them* right now. My love for you is not a flaw. Their coldness is the flaw. They're just like Honoured Matres!"

A game where one of the pieces can't be moved.

He wanted to shout it but listeners behind the comeyes would hear more than spoken words. Murbella was right. It was dangerous to think you could gull Reverend Mothers.

Something veiled in her eyes as she looked down at him. "How very strange you looked just then." He recognized the Reverend Mother she might become.

Veer away from that thought!

Thinking about the strangeness of his memories sometimes diverted her. She thought his previous incarnations made him somehow similar to a Reverend Mother.

"I've died so many times."

"You remember it?" The same question every time.

He shook his head, not daring to say anything more for the watchdogs to interpret.

Not the deaths and reawakenings.

Those became dulled by repetition. Sometimes he didn't even bother to put them into his secret data-dump. No . . . it was the unique encounters with other humans, the long collection of recognitions.

That was a thing Sheeana claimed she wanted from him. "Intimate trivia. It's the stuff all artists want."

Sheeana did not know what she asked. All of those living encounters had created new meanings. Patterns within patterns. Minuscule things gained a poignancy he despaired of sharing with anyone . . . not even with Murbella.

The touch of a hand on my arm. A child's laughing face. The glitter in an attacker's eyes.

Mundane things without counting. A familiar voice saying: "I just want to put my feet up and collapse tonight. Don't ask me to move."

All had become part of him. They were bound into his character. Living had cemented them inextricably and he could not explain it to anyone.

Murbella spoke without looking at him. "There were many women in those lives of yours."

"I've never counted them."

"Did you love them?"

"They're dead, Murbella. All I can promise is that there are no jealous ghosts in my past."

Murbella extinguished the glowglobes. He closed his eyes and felt darkness close in as she crept into his arms. He held her tightly, knowing she needed it, but his mind rolled of its own volition.

An old memory produced a Mentat teachers' saying: *"The greatest relevancy can become irrelevant in the space of a heartbeat. Mentats should look upon such moments with joy."*

He felt no joy.

All of those serial lives continued within him in defiance of Mentat relevancies. A Mentat came at his universe fresh in each instant. Nothing old, nothing new, nothing set in ancient adhesives, nothing truly *known*. You were the net and you existed only to examine the catch.

What did not go through? How fine a mesh did I use on this lot?

That was the Mentat view. But there was no way the Tleilaxu could have included all of those ghola-Idaho cells to recreate him. There had to be gaps in their serial collection of his cells. He had identified many of those gaps.

But no gaps in my memory. I remember them all.

He was a network linked outside of Time. That is how I can see the people of that vision . . . the net. It was the only explanation Mentat awareness could provide and if the Sisterhood guessed, they would be terrified. No matter how many times he denied it, they would say: "Another kwisatz haderach! Kill him!"

So work for yourself, Mentat!

He knew he had most of the mosaic pieces but still they did not go together in that *Ahh, hah!* assembly of questions Mentats prized.

A game where one of the pieces can't be moved.

Excuses for extraordinary behaviour.

"They want our willing participation in their dream."

Test the limits!

Humans can balance on strange surfaces.

Get in tune. Don't think. Do it.

> The best art imitates life in a compelling way. If it imitates a dream, it must be a dream of life. Otherwise, there is no place where we can connect. Our plugs don't fit.
>
> —Darwi Odrade

As they travelled south toward the desert in the early after-noon, Odrade found the countryside disturbingly changed from her previous inspection three months earlier. She felt vindicated in having chosen ground vehicles. Views framed by the thick plaz protecting them from the dust revealed more details at this level.

Much drier.

Her immediate party rode in a relatively light car—only fifteen passengers including the driver. Suspensors and sophisticated jet drive when they were not on ground-effect. Capable of a smooth three hundred klicks an hour on the glaze. Her escort (too large, thanks to an overzealous Tamalane) followed in a bus that also carried changes of clothing, foods and drinks for wayside stops.

Streggi, seated beside Odrade and behind the driver, said: "Could we not manage a small rain here, Mother Superior?"

Odrade's lips thinned. Silence was the best answer.

They had been late starting. All of them assembled on the loading dock and ready to leave when a message came down from Bellonda. Another disaster report requiring Mother Superior's personal attention at the last minute!

It was one of those times when Odrade felt her only possible role was that of official interpreter. Walk to the edge of the stage and tell them what it meant: "Today, sisters, we learned that Honoured Matres have obliterated four more of our planets. We are that much smaller."

Only twelve planets left (including Buzzell) and the faceless hunter with the axe is that much closer.

Odrade felt the chasm yawning beneath her.

Bellonda had been ordered to contain this latest bad news until a more appropriate moment.

Odrade looked out the window beside her. What was an appropriate moment for such news?

They had been driving south a little more than three hours, the burner-glazed roadway like a green river ahead of them. This passage led them through hillsides of cork oaks that stretched out to ridge-enclosed horizons. The oaks had been allowed to grow gnome-like in less regimented plantations than orchards. There were meandering rows up the hills. The original plantation had been laid out on existing contours, semi-terraces now obscured by long brown grass.

"We grow truffles in there," Odrade said.

Streggi had more bad news. "I am told the truffles are in trouble, Mother Superior. Not enough rain."

No more truffles? Odrade hesitated on the edge of bringing a Communications acolyte from the rear and asking Weather if this dryness could be corrected.

She sat back without speaking. *Complexities!* Easy to be snared by them. Your path so tangled you could see no way out. *Cut them then!* Follow the example of Alexander when dealing with Gordian complexities. Alexander and his handy snickersnee. Or was it a sword? She did not want to go digging for accuracy. Something else demanded her attention.

"Why haven't they mown that grass under the oaks? We should have gathered it for winter cattle feed. My orders were explicit."

People around her withdrew a bit at her tone. Odrade could be peppery when aroused. *Look at how she treated Tam this morning.* All of them knew what aroused her quickest: hiding mistakes. Someone would be called to task because that grass had not been gathered.

Mother Superior can overlook nothing.

Odrade glanced back at her attendants. Three rows, four people in each row, specialists to extend her observational powers and carry out orders. And look at that bus following them! One of the larger such vehicles on Chapter House. Thirty metres long, at least! Crammed with people! Dust whirled across and around it.

Tamalane rode back there at Odrade's orders. More of Mother Superior's pepper, everyone thought. Tam had brought too many people but Odrade had discovered it too late for changes.

"Not an inspection! A damned invasion!" *Follow my lead, Tam. A little political drama. Make transition easier.*

She returned her attention to the driver, only male in this car. Clairby, a vinegary little transport expert. Pinched-up face, skin the colour of newly-turned damp earth. Odrade's favourite driver. Fast, safe and wary of limits in his machine.

They crested a hill and cork oaks thinned out, replaced ahead by fruit orchards surrounding a community.

Beautiful in this light, Odrade thought. Low buildings of white walls and orange-tiled roofs. An arch-shaded entrance street could be seen far down the slope and, in a line behind it, the tall central structure containing regional overview offices.

The sight reassured Odrade. The community had a glowing look softened by distance and a haze rising from its ring orchards. Branches still bare up here in this winter belt but surely capable of at least one more crop.

The Sisterhood demanded a certain beauty in its surroundings, she reminded herself. A cosseting that provided support for the senses without subtracting from needs of the stomach. Comfort where possible . . . but not too much!

Someone behind Odrade said: "I do believe some of those trees are starting to leaf."

Odrade took a more careful look. Yes! Tiny bits of green on dark boughs. Winter had slipped here. Weather Control, struggling to make seasonal shifts, could not prevent occasional mistakes. The expanding desert was creating higher temperatures too early here, odd warming patches that caused plants to leaf or bloom just in time for an abrupt frost. Die-back of plantations was becoming much too common.

A Field Adviser had dredged up the ancient term, "Indian Summer", for a report illustrated by projections of an orchard in full blossom being assaulted by snow. Odrade had felt memory stirring at the adviser's words.

Indian Summer. How appropriate!

Her councillors sharing that little view of their planet's travail recognized the metaphor of a marauding freeze coming on the heels of inappropriate warmth: an unexpected revival of warm weather, a time when raiders could plague their neighbours.

Remembering, Odrade felt the chill of the hunter's axe. *How soon?* She dared not seek the answer. *I'm not a kwisatz haderach!*

She found herself close to self pity. *Why me? Why is all of this on my shoulders? Why must I be the one to walk the tightrope across the chasm?*

Other Memories did not let this continue. Acid comments poured from the dead who experienced life through her senses. *"It was your own choice, Sister! And who better?"*

Without turning, Odrade spoke to Streggi. "This place, Pondrille, have you ever been here?"

"It was not my postulant centre, Mother Superior, but I presume it is similar."

Yes, these communities were much alike: mostly low structures set in garden plots and orchards; school centres for specific training. It was a screening system for prospective sisters, the mesh finer the closer you got to Central.

Some of these communities such as Pondrille concentrated on toughening their charges. They sent women out for long hours every day to manual labour. Hands that grubbed in dirt and became stained with fruit seldom balked at muckier tasks later in life.

Now that they were out of the dust, Clairby opened the windows. Heat poured in! What was Weather doing?

Two buildings at the edge of Pondrille had been joined one storey above the street, forming a long tunnel. All it needed, Odrade thought, was a portcullis to duplicate a town gate out of pre-space history. Armoured knights would not find the dusky heat of this entry unfamiliar. It was defined in dark plastone, visually identical to stone. Comeye apertures overhead surely were places were guardians lay in wait.

The long, shaded entry to the community was clean, she saw. Nostrils were seldom assailed by rot or other offensive odours in Bene Gesserit communities. No slums. Few cripples hobbling along the walks. Much healthy flesh. Good management took care to keep a healthy population happy.

We have our disabled, though. And not all of them physically disabled.

Clairby parked just within the exit from the shaded street and they emerged. Tamalane's bus pulled to a stop behind them.

Odrade had hoped the entry passage would provide relief from the heat but perversity of nature had made an oven of the place and the temperature actually increased here. She was glad to pass through into the clear light of the central square where sweat burning off her body provided a few seconds of coolness.

The illusion of relief passed abruptly as the sun scorched her head and shoulders. She was forced to call on metabolic control to adjust her body heat.

Water splashed in a reflecting circle at the central square, a careless display that soon would have to end.

Leave it for now. Morale!

She heard her companions following, the usual groans against "sitting too long in one position". A greeting delegation could be seen hurrying from the far side of the square. Odrade recognized Tsimpay, Pondrille's leader, in the van.

Mother Superior's attendants moved on to the blue tiles of the fountain plaza—all except Streggi, who stood at Odrade's shoulder. Tamalane's group, too, was attracted to splashing water.

Our own form of Fancy, Odrade thought. *Fountains.* You found them often where Bene Gesserit avenues met in a roundabout. Never a statue or relic from the past.

Not for us casual reminders of famous predecessors. Only the bust of Chenoeh in her niche on my wall.

The Sisterhood made its own choices in these matters, she thought, but the goad of history was here. Reverend Mothers felt their history in such immediacy it created its own patterns, its own legends and myths. All part and parcel of a human dream so ancient it could never be completely discarded.

Fertile fields and open water—clear, potable water you can dip your face into for thirst-quenching relief.

Indeed, some of her party were doing just that at the fountain. Their faces glistened with dampness.

The Pondrille delegation came to a stop near Odrade while still on the blue tiles of the fountain plaza. Tsimpay had brought three other Reverend Mothers and five older acolytes.

Near the Agony, all of those acolytes, Odrade observed. Showing their awareness of the trial in directness of gaze.

Tsimpay was someone Odrade saw infrequently at Central where she came sometimes as a teacher. She was looking fit:

brown hair so dark it appeared reddish-black in this light. The narrow face was almost bleak in its austerity. Her features centred on all-blue eyes under heavy brows.

"We are glad to see you, Mother Superior." Sounded as though she meant it.

Odrade inclined her head, a minimal gesture. *I hear you. Why are you so glad to see me?*

Tsimpay understood. She gestured to a tall, hollow-cheeked Reverend Mother beside her. "You remember Fali, our Orchard Mistress? Fali has just been to me with a delegation of gardeners. A serious complaint."

Odrade spared Fali a brief glance. One of those middle-echelon specialists whose abilities had been aimed into a prime requirement for Bene Gesserit survival: knowledge of plant life and how it supported your people. Fali's weathered face looked a bit grey. *Overworked?* She had a thin mouth above a sharp chin. Dirt under her fingernails. Odrade noted it with approval. *Not afraid to join in the grubbing.*

Delegation of gardeners. So there was an escalation of complaints. Must have been serious. Not like Tsimpay to dump it on Mother Superior.

"Let's hear it," Odrade said.

With a glance at Tsimpay, Fali went through a detailed recital, even providing qualifications of delegation leaders. All of them good people, of course.

Odrade recognized the pattern. There had been conferences concerning this inevitable consequence, Tsimpay in attendance at some of them. How could you explain to your people that a distant sandworm (perhaps not even in existence yet) required this change? How could you explain to farmers that it was *not* a matter of "just a bit more rain" but went straight to the heart of the planet's total weather. More rain here could mean a diversion of high-altitude winds. That in its turn would change things elsewhere, cause moisture-laden sciroccos where they not only would be upsetting but dangerous. Too easy to bring on great tornadoes if you inserted the wrong conditions. A planet's weather was no simple thing to treat with easy adjustments. *As I have sometimes demanded.* Each time, there was a total equation to be scanned.

"The planet casts the final vote," Odrade said. It was an old reminder in the Sisterhood of human fallibility.

"Does Dune still have a vote?" Fali asked. More bitterness in the question than Odrade had anticipated.

"I feel the heat. We saw the leaves on your orchards as we arrived," Odrade said. *I know what concerns you, Sister.*

"We will lose part of the crop this year," Fali said. Accusation in her words: *This is your fault!*

"What did you tell your delegation?" Odrade asked.

"That the desert must grow and Weather no longer can make every adjustment we need."

Truth. The agreed response. Inadequate, as truth often was, but all they had now. Something would have to give soon. Meanwhile, more delegations and loss of crops.

"Will you take tea with us, Mother Superior?" Tsimpay, the diplomat intervening. *You see how it is escalating, Mother Superior? Fali will now go back to dealing with fruits and vegetables. Her proper place. Message delivered.*

Streggi cleared her throat.

That damnable gesture will have to be suppressed! But the meaning was clear. Streggi had been put in charge of their schedule. *We must be going.*

"We got a late start," Odrade said. "We stopped only to stretch our legs and see if you have problems you cannot meet on your own."

"We can handle the gardeners, Mother Superior."

Tsimpay's brisk tone said much more and Odrade almost smiled.

Inspect if you wish, Mother Superior. Look anywhere. You will find Pondrille in Bene Gesserit order.

Odrade glanced at Tamalane's bus. Some of the people already were returning to the air-conditioned interior. Tamalane stood by the door, well within earshot.

"I hear good reports of you, Tsimpay," Odrade said. "You can do without our interference. I certainly don't want to intrude on you with an entourage that is far too large." This last loud enough that all would be certain to hear.

"Where will you spend the night, Mother Superior?"

"Eldio."

229

"I've not been down there for some time but I hear the sea is much smaller."

"Overflights confirm what you've heard. No need to warn them that we're coming, Tsimpay. They already know. We had to prepare them for this invasion."

Orchard Mistress Fali took a small step forward. "Mother Superior, if we could get just . . ."

"Tell your gardeners, Fali, that they have a choice. They can grumble and wait here until Honoured Matres arrive to enslave them or they can elect to go Scattering."

Odrade returned to her car and sat, eyes closed, until she heard the doors sealed and they were well on their way. Presently, she opened her eyes. They already were out of Pondrille and on to the glassy lane through the southern ring orchards. There was charged silence behind her. Sisters were looking deeply into questions about Mother Superior's behaviour back there. An unsatisfactory encounter. Acolytes naturally picked up the mood. Streggi looked glum.

This weather demanded notice. Words no longer could smooth over the complaints. Good days were measured by lower standards. Everyone knew the reason but changes remained a focal point. Visible. You could not complain about Mother Superior (not without good cause!) but you could grumble about the weather.

Why did they have to make it so cold today? Why today when I have to be out in it? Quite warm when we came out but look at it now. And me without proper clothing!

Streggi wanted to talk. *Well, that's why I brought her.* But she had become almost garrulous as enforced intimacy eroded her awe of Mother Superior.

"Mother Superior, I've been searching in my manuals for an explanation of . . ."

"Beware of manuals!" How many times in her life had she heard or spoken those words? "Manuals create habits."

Streggi had been lectured often about habits. The Bene Gesserit had them—those things the Folk preserved as "Typical of the Witches!" But patterns that allowed others to predict behaviour, those must be carefully excised.

"Then why do we have manuals, Mother Superior?"

"We have them mainly to disprove them. The Coda is for novices and others in primary training."

"And the histories?"

"Never ignore the banality of recorded histories. As a Reverend Mother, you will relearn history in each new moment."

"Truth is an empty cup." Very proud of her remembered aphorism.

Odrade almost smiled.

Streggi is a jewel.

It was a cautioning thought. Some precious stones could be identified by their impurities. Experts mapped impurities within the stones. A secret fingerprint. People were like that. You often knew them by their defects. The glittering surface told you too little. Good identification required you to look deep inside and see the impurities. *There* was the gem quality of a total being. What would Van Gogh have been without impurities?

"Then all of the histories we study . . ."

"Careful, Streggi."

The acolyte knew that tone.

In her most deliberate moments, Odrade's voice became creamy, compelling and with softly articulated sounds flowing from her as from a great pitcher where only the best had been stored.

"It is comments of perceptive cynics, Streggi, things *they* say *about* history, that should be your guides before the Agony. Afterward, you will be your own cynic."

"No value in histories at all?" Streggi was outraged, thinking she had wasted all of those study hours.

"You will discover your own values later. For now, they reveal dates and tell you something occurred. Something! Reverend Mothers search out the *somethings* and learn the prejudices of historians."

"That's all?" Still deeply offended. *Why did they waste my time that way?*

"Many histories are largely worthless because prejudiced, written to please one powerful group or another. Wait for your eyes to be opened, my dear. We are the best historians. We were there."

"And my viewpoint will change daily?" Very introspective.

"That's a lesson the Bashar reminded us to keep fresh in our minds. The past must be reinterpreted by the present."

"I'm not sure I will enjoy that, Mother Superior. So many moral decisions."

Ahhhh, this jewel saw to the heart of it and spoke her mind like a true Bene Gesserit. There were brilliant facets among Streggi's impurities.

Odrade looked sideways at the pensive acolyte. Long ago, the Sisterhood had ruled that each sister must make her own moral decisions. *Never follow a leader without asking your own questions.* That was why moral conditioning of the young took such high priority.

That is why we like to get our prospective sisters so young. And it may be why a moral flaw has crept into Sheeana. We got her too late. What do she and Duncan talk about so secretly with their hands?

"Moral decisions are always easy to recognize," Odrade said. "They are where you abandon self interest."

Yes, any educational system that failed to provide a moral-ethical foundation was feeding forces that would destroy it.

Streggi looked at Odrade with awe. "The courage you must have to . . ."

"Not courage! Not even desperation. What we do is, in its most basic sense, natural. Things done because there is no other choice."

"Sometimes you make me feel ignorant, Mother Superior."

"Excellent! That's beginning wisdom. There are many kinds of ignorance, Streggi. You will always find new ones. Oh, yes!" as Streggi started to interrupt. "The basest ignorance is to follow your own desires without examining them. Sometimes, we do it unconsciously. Hone your sensitivity. Be aware of what you do unconsciously. Always ask: 'When I did that, what was I trying to gain?'"

After a long silence, Streggi said: "I find it difficult not to hate historians who . . ."

"That was the Tyrant's flaw, Streggi. He killed some of them, you know."

Again, Streggi fell silent.

They crested the final hill before Eldio and Odrade welcomed a reflective moment.

Someone behind her murmured, "There's the sea."

"Stop here," Odrade ordered as they neared a wide turnout at a curve overlooking the sea. Clairby knew the place and was prepared for it. Odrade often asked him to stop here. He brought them to a halt where she wanted. The car creaked as it settled. They heard the bus pull up behind, a loud voice back there calling on companions to "Look at that!"

Eldio lay off to Odrade's left far down there: delicate buildings, some raised off the ground on slender pipes, wind passing under and through them. This was far enough south and down off the heights where Central perched that it was always much warmer. Small vertical-axis windmills, looking like toys from this distance, whirled at the corners of Eldio's buildings to power the community. Odrade pointed them out to Streggi.

"We thought of them as independence from bondage to a complex technology controlled by others."

As she spoke, Odrade shifted her attention to the right. *The sea!* It was a dreadfully condensed remnant of its once glorious expanse. Sea Child hated what she saw.

Warm vapour lifted from the sea. The dim purple of dry hills drew a blurred outline of horizon on the far side of the water. She saw that Weather had introduced a wind to disperse saturated air. The result was a choppy froth of waves beating against the shingle below this vantage.

There had been a string of fishing villages here, Odrade recalled. Now that the sea had receded, villages lay farther back up the slope. Once, the villages had been a colourful accent along the shore. Much of their population had been siphoned off in the new Scattering. People who remained had built a tram to get their boats to and from the water.

She approved of this and deplored it. Energy conservation. The whole situation struck her suddenly as grim—like one of

233

those Old Empire geriatric installations where people waited around to die.

How long until these places die?

"The sea is so small!" It was a voice from the rear of the car. Odrade recognized it. An Archives clerk. *One of Bell's damned spies.*

Leaning forward, Odrade tapped Clairby on the shoulder. "Take us down to the near shore, that cove almost directly below us."

"Not into the hamlet?" (Now why did Clairby cling to that archaic term? Showing off for Mother Superior?)

"I wish to swim in our sea, Clairby, while it still exists."

Streggi and two other acolytes joined her in the warm waters of the cove. The others walked along the shore or watched this odd scene from the car and bus.

Mother Superior swimming nude in the sea!

Sea Child did not mind. She floated on this last large body of water remaining to Chapter House, recapturing those recalcitrant sensations of her earliest sea experiences.

Gammu—far away and long ago.

She felt energizing water around her. Swimming was required because of command decisions she must make.

How much of this last great sea could they afford to maintain during these final days of their planet's temperate life? The desert was coming—*total desert* to match that of lost Dune. *If the axe-bearer gives us time.* The threat felt very close and the chasm deep. *Damn this wild talent! Why do I have to know?*

Slowly, Sea Child and wave motions restored her sense of balance. This body of water was a major complication—much more important than scattered small seas and lakes. Moisture lifted from here in significant amounts. Energy to charge unwanted deviations in Weather's barely-controlled management. Yet, this sea still fed Chapter House. It was a communication and transport route. Sea carriers were cheapest. Energy costs must be balanced against other elements in her decision. But the sea would vanish. That was sure. Whole populations faced new displacements.

Sea Child's memories interfered. Nostalgia. It blocked paths of proper judgment. *How fast must the sea go?* That was the question. All of the inevitable relocations and resettlements waited on that decision.

Best it were done quickly. The pain banished into our past. Let us get on with it!

She swam to the shallows and looked up at a puzzled Tamalane. Tam's robed skirts were dark with splashings from an unexpected wave. Odrade lifted her head clear of the small surges.

"Tam! Eliminate the sea as fast as possible. Get Weather to plot a swift dehydration scheme. Food and Transport will have to be brought into it. I'll approve the final plan after our usual review."

Tamalane turned away without speaking. She beckoned appropriate sisters to accompany her, glancing only once at Mother Superior as she did this. *See! I was right to bring along the necessary cadre!*

Odrade climbed from the water. Wet sand gritted under her feet. *Soon, it will be dry sand.* She dressed without bothering to towel herself. Clothing gripped her flesh uncomfortably but she ignored this, walking up the strand away from the others, not looking back at the sea.

Souvenirs of memory must be only that. Things to be taken up and fondled occasionally for evocation of past joys. No joy can be permanent. All is transient. "This, too, shall pass away," applies to all of our living universe.

Where the beach became loamy dirt and a few sparse plants, she turned finally and looked back at the sea she had just condemned.

You see, Alexander? I didn't even need a sword. A few words did it.

Only life itself mattered, she told herself. And life could not endure without an ongoing thrust of procreation.

Survival. Our children must survive. The Bene Gesserit must survive!

No single child was more important than the totality. She accepted this, recognizing it as the species talking to her from her deepest self, the self she had first encountered as Sea Child.

Odrade allowed Sea Child one last sniff of salt air as they

returned to their vehicles and prepared to drive into Eldio. She felt herself grow calm. That essential balance, once learned, did not require a sea to maintain it.

> *Uproot your questions from their ground and the dangling roots will be seen. More questions!*
>
> **—Mentat Zensufi**

Dama was in her element.

Spider Queen!

She liked the witches' title for her. This was the heart of her web, this new control centre on Junction. The exterior of the building still did not suit her. Too much Guild complacency in its design. Conservative. But the interior had begun to take on a familiarity that soothed her. She could almost imagine she had never left Dur, that there had been no Futars and the harrowing flight back into the Old Empire.

She stood in the open door of the Assembly Room looking out at the Botanical Garden. Logno waited four paces behind. *Not too close behind me, Logno, or I shall have to kill you.*

There was still dew on the lawn beyond the tiles where, when the sun had risen far enough, servants would distribute comfortable chairs and tables. She had ordered a sunny day and Weather had damned well better produce it. Logno's report was interesting. So the old witch had returned to Buzzell. And she was angry, too. Excellent. Obviously, she knew she was being watched and she had visited her supreme witch to ask for removal from Buzzell, for sanctuary. And she had been refused.

They don't care that we destroy their limbs just as long as the central body remains hidden.

Speaking over her shoulder to Logno, Dama said: "Bring that old witch to me. And all of her attendants."

As Logno turned to obey, Dama added: "And begin starving some Futars. I want them hungry."

"Yes, Dama."

236

Someone else moved into Logno's attendant position. Dama did not turn to identify the replacement. There were always enough aides to carry out necessary orders. One was much like another except in the matter of threat. Logno was a constant threat. *Keeps me alert.*

Dama inhaled deeply of the fresh air. It was going to be a good day precisely because that was what she desired. She gathered in her secret memories then and let them soothe her.

Guldur be blessed! We've found the place to rebuild our strength.

Consolidation of the Old Empire was proceeding as planned. There could not be many witches' nests left out there and, once that damnable Chapter House was found, the limbs could be destroyed at leisure.

Ix, now. There was a problem. *Perhaps I should not have killed those two Ixian scientists yesterday.*

But the fools had dared demand "more information" from her. Demand! And after saying they still had no solution to rearming The Weapon. Of course, they did not know it was a weapon. Did they? She could not be sure. So it had been a good thing to kill those two after all. Teach them a lesson.

Bring us answers, not questions.

She liked the order she and her sisters were creating in the Old Empire. There had been too much wandering about and too many different cultures, too many unstable religions.

Worship of Guldur will serve them as it serves us.

She felt no mystical affinity to her religion. It was a useful tool of power. The roots were well-known: Leto II, the one those witches called "The Tyrant", and his father, Muad'Dib. Consummate power brokers, both of them. Lots of schismatic cells around but those could be weeded out. Keep the essence. It was a well-lubricated machine.

Oligarchic laissez-faire is not for us.

Everything reduced to manageable essence. Politics. Who holds the power? Conspiracies everywhere, naturally. Even here in the core. All carried out with a false air of open behaviour and compliance with "the good of our order". Nothing more insidious in the universe and nothing more apparent to a watchful Great Honoured Matre.

The tyranny of the minority cloaked in the mask of the majority.

That was what the witch Lucilla had recognized. No way to let her live after discovering she knew how to manipulate the masses. The witch nests would have to be found and burned. Lucilla's perceptiveness clearly was not an isolated example. Her actions betrayed the workings of a school. They taught this thing! Fools! You had to manage reality or things really got out of control.

Logno returned. Dama could always tell the sound of her footsteps. Furtive.

"The old witch will be brought from Buzzell," Logno said. "And her attendants."

"Don't forget about the Futars."

"I have given the orders, Dama."

Oily voice! You'd like to feed me to the herd, wouldn't you, Logno?

"And tighten up security on the cages, Logno. Three more of them escaped last night. They were wandering around in the garden when I awoke."

"I was told, Dama. More cage guards have been assigned."

"And don't tell me they're harmless without a Handler."

"I do not believe that, Dama."

And that's truth from her, for once. Futars terrify her. Good.

"I believe we have our power base, Logno." Dama turned, noting that Logno had encroached at least two millimetres into the danger zone. Logno saw it, too, and retreated. *As close as you want in front where I can see you, Logno, but not behind my back.*

Logno saw the orange blaze in Dama's eyes and almost knelt. *Definite bending of the knees.* "It is my eagerness to serve you, Dama!"

Your eagerness to replace me, Logno.

"What of that woman from Gammu? Odd name. What was it?"

"Rebecca, Dama. She and some of her companions have . . . ahhh, temporarily eluded us. We will find them. They cannot get off the planet."

"You think I should have kept her here, don't you?"

"It was wise to think of her as bait, Dama!"

"She's still bait. That witch we found on Gammu did not go to those people by accident. Schismatics! Weed them out, Logno."

"Yes, Dama."

Yes, Dama! But the subservient sound in Logno's voice was enjoyable. "Well, get on with it!"

Logno scurried away.

There were always those little cells of potential violence meeting secretly somewhere. Building up their mutual charges of hate, swarming out to disrupt the orderly lives around them. Someone always had to clean up after those disruptions. Dama sighed. Terror tactics were so . . . so temporary!

Success, that was the danger. It had cost them an empire. If you waved your success around like a banner someone always wanted to cut you down. Jealousy!

We will hold our success more cautiously this time.

She fell into a semi-reverie, still alert to the sounds behind her, but relishing the evidence of new victories that had been displayed to her this morning. She liked to roll the names of captive planets silently on her tongue.

Wallach, Kronin, Reenol, Ecaz, Bela Tegeuse, Gammu, Gamont, Niushe . . .

> *Humans are born with a susceptibility to that most persistent and debilitating disease of intellect: self-deception. The best of all possible worlds and the worst get their dramatic colouration from it. As nearly as we can determine, there is no natural immunity. Constant alertness is required.*
>
> —**The Coda**

With Odrade away from Central (and probably only for a short time) Bellonda knew swift action was required. *That damned Mentat-ghola is too dangerous to live!*

Mother Superior's party was barely out of sight into the lowering afternoon before Bellonda was on her way to the no-ship.

Not for Bellonda a thoughtful approach through ring orchards. She ordered space on a tube, windowless, automatic and fast. Odrade, too, had observers who might send unwanted messages.

En route, Bellonda reviewed her assessment of Idaho's many lives, a record she had kept in Archives ready for quick retrieval. In the original and early gholas, his character had been dominated by impulsiveness. Quick to hate, quick to give loyalty. Later Idaho gholas tempered this with cynicism but the underlying impulsiveness remained. The Tyrant had called it to action many times. Bellonda recognized a pattern.

He can be goaded by pride.

His long service to the Tyrant fascinated her. Not only had he been a Mentat several times but there was evidence he had been a Truthsayer in more than one incarnation.

Idaho's appearance reflected what she saw in her records. Interesting character lines, a look around the eyes and a set to his mouth that went with complex inner development.

Why would Odrade not accept the danger in this man? Truthsayer powers linked to a Mentat of unknown potential! Let him act just once to betray proscribed abilities and no one in the Sisterhood could ignore the peril. Not even Odrade. *No more kwisatz haderachs to hold us in bondage!*

Bellonda had felt frequent misgivings when Odrade spoke of Idaho with such flaunting of her emotions.

"He thinks clearly and directly. There's a fastidious cleanliness about his mind. It's restorative. I like him and I know that's a trivial thing to influence my decisions."

She admits his influence!

Bellonda found Idaho alone and seated at his console. His attention was fixed on a linear display she recognized: the no-ship's operational schematics! He washed the projection when he saw her.

"Hello, Bell. Been expecting you."

He touched his console field and a door opened behind him. Young Teg entered and took up a position near Idaho, staring silently at Bellonda.

Idaho did not invite her to sit or find a chair for her, forcing her to bring one from his sleeping chamber and place it facing him. When she was seated, he turned a look of wary amusement on her.

Bellonda remained taken aback by his greeting. *Why did he expect me?*

He answered her unspoken question. "Dar projected earlier, told me she was off to see Sheeana. I knew you'd waste no time getting to me when she was gone."

Simple Mentat projection or . . . "She warned you!"

"Wrong."

"What secrets do you and Sheeana share?" Demanding.

"She uses me the way you want her to use me."

"The Missionaria!"

"Bell! Two Mentats together. Must we play these stupid games?"

Bellonda took a deep breath and sought Mentat mode. Not easy under these circumstances, that child staring at her, the amusement on Idaho's face. Was Odrade displaying an unsuspected slyness? Working against a sister with this ghola?

Idaho relaxed when he saw Bene Gesserit intensity become that doubled focus of the Mentat. "I've known for a long time that you want me dead, Bell."

Yes . . . I have been readable in my fears.

It had been very close there, he thought. Bellonda had come to him with death in mind, a little drama to create "the necessity" all prepared. He entertained few illusions about his ability to match her in violence. But Bellonda-Mentat would observe before acting.

"It's disrespectful the way you use our first names," she said, goading.

"Different recognition, Bell. You're no longer Reverend Mother and I'm not 'the ghola'. Two human beings with common problems. Don't tell me you're unaware of this."

She glanced around his workroom. "If you expected me why didn't you have Murbella here?"

"Force her to kill you while protecting me?"

Bellonda assessed this. *The damned Honoured Matre probably could kill me, but then . . .* "You sent her away to protect her."

"I've a better protector." He gestured at the child.

241

Teg? A protector? There were those stories from Gammu about him. Does Idaho know something?

She wanted to ask but did she dare risk diversion? Watchdogs must receive a clear scenario of danger.

"Him? How could . . ."

"Would he serve the Bene Gesserit if he saw you kill me?"

When she did not answer, he said: "Put yourself in my place, Bell. I'm a Mentat caught not only in your trap but in that of the Honoured Matres."

"Is that all you are, a Mentat?"

"No. I'm a Tleilaxu experiment but I don't see the future. I'm not a kwisatz haderach. I'm a Mentat with memories of many lives. You, with your Other Memories—think about the leverage that gives me."

While he was speaking, Teg came to lean against the console at Idaho's elbow. The boy's expression was one of curiosity but she saw no fear of her.

Idaho gestured at the projection focus over his head, silver motes dancing there ready to create their images. "A Mentat sees his relays producing discrepancies—winter scenes in summer, sunshine when his visitors have come through rain . . . Didn't you expect me to discount your little playlets?"

She heard Mentat summation. To that extent, they shared common teaching. She said: "You naturally told yourself not to minimize the Tao."

"I asked different questions. Things that happen together can have underground links. What is cause and effect when confronted with simultaneity?"

"You had good teachers."

"And not just in one life."

Teg leaned toward her. "Did you really come here to kill him?"

No sense lying. "I still think he is too dangerous." Let watchdogs argue that!

"But he's going to give me back my memories!"

"Dancers on a common floor, Bell," Idaho said. "Tao. We may not appear to dance together, may not use the same steps or rhythms but we are seen together."

She began to suspect where he might be leading and wondered if there might be another way to destroy him.

"I don't know what you're talking about," Teg said.

"Interesting coincidences," Idaho said.

Teg turned to Bellonda. "Maybe you would explain, please?"

"He's trying to tell me we need each other."

"Then why doesn't he say so?"

"It's more subtle than that, boy." And she thought: *The record must show me warning Idaho*. "The nose of the donkey doesn't cause the tail, Duncan, no matter how often you see the beast pass that thin vertical space limiting your view of it."

Idaho met Bellonda's fixed gaze. "Dar came here once with a sprig of apple blossoms, but my projection showed harvest time."

"It's riddles, isn't it!" Teg said, clapping his hands.

Bellonda recalled the record of that visit. Precise movements by Mother Superior. "You didn't suspect a hothouse?"

"Or that she just wanted to please me?"

"Am I supposed to guess?" Teg asked.

After a long silence, Mentat gaze locked to Mentat gaze, Idaho said: "There's anarchy behind my confinement, Bell. Disagreement in your highest councils."

"There can be deliberation and judgment even in anarchy," she said.

"You're a hypocrite, Bell!"

She drew back as though he had struck her, a purely involuntary movement that shocked her by the forced reaction. *Voice?* No . . . something reaching deeper. She was suddenly terrified of this man.

"I find it marvellous that a Mentat *and a Reverend Mother* could be such a hypocrite," he said.

Teg tugged at Idaho's arm. "Are you fighting?"

Idaho brushed the hand away. "Yes, we're fighting."

Bellonda could not tear her gaze from Idaho's. She wanted to turn and flee. What was he doing? This had gone completely awry!

"Hypocrites and criminals among you?" he asked.

243

Once more, Bellonda remembered the comeyes. He not only was playing her but the watchers as well! And doing it with exquisite care. She was suddenly filled with admiration for his performance but this did not allay her fear.

"I ask why your sisters tolerate you?" His lips moved with such delicate precision! "Are you a necessary evil? A source of valuable data and, occasionally, good advice?"

She found her voice. "How dare you?" Guttural and containing all of her vaunted viciousness.

"It could be that you strengthen your sisters." Voice flat, not changing tone in the slightest. "Weak links create places others must reinforce and that would strengthen those others."

Bellonda realized she was barely keeping her hold on Mentat mode. Could any of this be true? Was it possible Mother Superior saw her that way?

"You came with criminal disobedience in mind," he said. "All in the name of necessity! A little drama for the comeyes, proving you had no other choice."

She found his words restoring Mentat abilities. Did he do that knowingly? She was fascinated by the need to study his manner as well as his words. Did he really read her that well? The record of this encounter might be far more valuable than her little playlet. And the outcome no different!

"You think Mother Superior's wishes are law?" she asked.

"Do you really think me unobservant?" Waving a hand at Teg who started to interrupt. "Bell! Be only a Mentat."

"I hear you." *And so do many others!*

"I'm deep into your problem."

"We've given you no problem!"

"But you have. *You* have, Bell. You're misers the way you parcel out the pieces but I see it."

Bellonda abruptly remembered Odrade saying: "I don't need a Mentat! I need an inventor."

"You . . . need . . . me," Idaho said. "Your problem is still in its shell but the meat's there and must be extracted."

"Why would we possibly need you?"

"You need my imagination, my inventiveness, things that kept me alive in the face of Leto's wrath."

"You've said he killed you so many times you lost count."
Eat your own words, Mentat!

He gave her an exquisitely controlled smile, so precise that neither she nor the comeyes could mistake its intent. "But how can you trust me, Bell?"

He condemns himself!

"Without something new you're doomed," he said. "Only a matter of time and you all know it. Perhaps not this generation. Perhaps not even the next one. But inevitably."

Teg pulled sharply at Idaho's sleeve. "The Bashar could help couldn't he?"

So the boy really listened. Idaho patted Teg's arm. "The Bashar's not enough." Then to Bellonda: "Underdogs together. Must we growl over the same bone?"

"You've said that before." *And doubtless will say it again.*

"Still Mentat?" he asked. "Then discard drama! Get the romantic haze off our problem."

Dar's the romantic! Not me!

"What's romantic," he asked, "about little pockets of Scattered Bene Gesserits waiting to be slaughtered?"

"You think none will escape?"

"You're seeding the universe with enemies," he said. "You're feeding Honoured Matres!"

She was fully (and only) Mentat then, required to match this ghola ability for ability. Drama? Romance? The body got in the way of Mentat performance. Mentats must use the body, not let it interfere.

"No Reverend Mother you've Scattered has ever returned or sent a message," he said. "You try to reassure yourselves by saying only the Scattered ones know where they go. How can you ignore the message they send in this other fact? Why has not one tried to communicate with Chapter House?"

He's chiding all of us, damn him! And he's right.

"Have I stated our problem in its most elemental form?"

Mentat questioning!

"Simplest question, simplest projection," she agreed.

"Amplified sexual ecstasy: Bene Gesserit imprint?"

"Murbella?" A one-word challenge. *Assess this woman you say you love!*

"They're conditioned against raising their own enjoyment to addictive levels but they are vulnerable."

"She denies their knowledge is based on Bene Gesserit sources."

"As she was conditioned to do."

"A lust for power instead?"

"At last, you have asked a proper question." And when she did not reply, he said: "Mater Felicissima." Addressing her by the ancient term for Bene Gesserit Council members.

She knew why he did it and felt the word produce the wanted effect. She was firmly balanced now, Mentat Reverend Mother encompassed by the *mohalata* of her own Spice Agony—that union of benign Other Memory protecting her from domination by malignant ancestors.

How did he know to do that? Every observer behind the comeyes would be asking that question. *Of course! The Tyrant trained him thus, time and time again. What do we have here? What is this talent Mother Superior dares employ? Dangerous, yes, but far more valuable than I suspected. By the gods of our own creation! Is he the tool to free us?*

How calm he was. He knew he had caught her.

"In one of my lives, Bell, I visited your Bene Gesserit house on Wallach IX and there talked to one of your ancestors, Tersius Helen Anteac. Let her guide you, Bell. She knows."

Bellonda felt familiar prodding in her mind. *How could he know Anteac was my ancestor?*

"I went to Wallach IX at the Tyrant's command," he said. "Oh, yes! I often thought of him as Tyrant. My orders were to suppress the Mentat school you thought you had hidden there."

Anteac-simulflow intruded: *"I show you now the event of which he speaks."*

"Consider," he said. "I, a Mentat, forced to suppress a school that trained people the way I was trained. I knew why he ordered it, of course, and so do you."

Simulflow poured it through her awareness: *Order of Mentats, founded by Gilbertus Albans; temporary sanctuary with Bene Tleilax who hoped to incorporate them into Tleilaxu hegemony; spread into uncounted "seed schools"; suppressed*

246

by Leto II because they formed a nucleus of independent opposition; spread into the Scattering after the Famine.

"He kept a few of the finest teachers on Dune, but the question Anteac forces you to confront now does not go there. Where have your sisters gone, Bell?"

"We have no way of knowing yet, do we?" She looked at his console with new awareness. It was wrong to block such a mind. If they were to use him, they must use him fully.

"By the way, Bell," as she stood to leave. "Honoured Matres could be a relatively small group."

Small? Didn't he know how the Sisterhood was being overwhelmed by terrifying numbers on planet after planet?

"All numbers are relative. Is there something in the universe truly immovable? Our Old Empire could be a last retreat for them, Bell. A place to hide and try to regroup."

"You suggested that before . . . to Dar."

Not Mother Superior. Not Odrade. Dar. He smiled. "And perhaps we could help with Scytale."

"We?"

"Murbella to gather information, I to assess it."

He did not like the smile this produced.

"Precisely what are you suggesting?"

"Let our imaginations roam and fashion our experiments accordingly. Of what use would even a no-planet be if someone could penetrate the shielding?"

She glanced at the boy. Idaho knew their suspicion that the Bashar had *seen* the no-ships? Naturally! A Mentat of his abilities . . . bits and pieces assembled into a masterful projection.

"It would require the entire output of a G-3 sun to shield any half-way livable planet." Dry and very cool the way she looked down at him.

"Nothing is out of the question in the Scattering."

"But not within our present capabilities. Do you have something less ambitious?"

"Review the genetic markers in the cells of your people. Look for common patterns in Atreides inheritance. There may be talents you have not even guessed."

"Your inventive imagination bounces around."

"G-3 suns to genetics. There may be common factors."

Why these mad suggestions? No-planets and people for whom prescient shields are transparent? What is he doing?

She did not flatter herself that he spoke only for her benefit. There were always the comeyes.

He remained silent, one arm thrown negligently across the boy's shoulders. Both of them watching her! A challenge?

Be a Mentat if you can!

No-planets? As the mass of an object increased, energy to nullify gravitation passed threshholds matched to prime numbers. No-shields met even greater energy barriers. Another magnitude of exponential increase. Was Idaho suggesting that someone in the Scattering might have found a way around the problem? She asked him.

"Ixians have not penetrated Holtzmann's unification concept," he said. "They merely use it—a theory that works even when you don't understand it."

Why does he direct my attention to the technocracy of Ix? Ixians had their fingers in too many pies for the Bene Gesserit to trust them.

"Aren't you curious why the Tyrant never suppressed Ix?" he asked. And when she continued to stare at him: "He only bridled them. He was fascinated by the idea of human and machine inextricably bound to each other, each testing the limits of the other."

"Cyborgs?"

"Among other things."

Didn't Idaho know the residue of revulsion left by the Butlerian Jihad even among the Bene Gesserit? Alarming! The convergence of what each—human *and* machine—could do. Considering machine limitations, that was a succinct description of Ixian short-sightedness. Was Idaho saying the Tyrant subscribed to the idea of Machine Intelligence? Foolishness! She turned away from him.

"You're leaving too quickly, Bell. You should be more interested in Sheeana's immunity to sexual bonding. The young men I send for polishing are *not* imprinted and neither is she. Yet, no Honoured Matre is more of an adept."

Bellonda saw now the value Odrade placed in this ghola.

Priceless! And I might have killed him. The nearness of that error filled her with dismay.

When she reached the doorway, he stopped her once more. "The Futars I saw on Gammu—why were we told they hunt and kill Honoured Matres? Murbella knows nothing of this."

Bellonda left without looking back. Everything she had learned about Idaho today increased his danger . . . but they had to live with it . . . for now.

Idaho took a deep breath and looked at the puzzled Teg. "Thank you for being here and I do appreciate the fact that you remained silent in the face of great provocation."

"She wouldn't really have killed you . . . would she?"

"If you had not gained me those first few seconds, she might have."

"Why?"

"She has the mistaken idea that I might be a kwisatz haderach."

"Like Muad'Dib?"

"And his son."

"Well, she won't hurt you now."

Idaho looked at the door where Bellonda had gone. Reprieve. That was all he had achieved. Perhaps he no longer was *just* a cog in the machinations of others. They had achieved a new relationship, one that could keep him alive if carefully exploited. Emotional attachments had never figured in it, not even with Murbella . . . nor with Odrade. Deep down, Murbella resented sexual bondage as much as he did. Odrade might hint at ancient ties of Atreides loyalty but emotions in a Reverend Mother could not be trusted.

Atreides! He looked at Teg, seeing family appearance already beginning to shape the immature face.

And what have I really achieved with Bell? They no longer were likely to provide him with false data. He could place a certain reliance in what a Reverend Mother told him, colouring this by awareness that any human might make mistakes.

I'm not the only one in a special school. The sisters are in my school now!

"May I go find Murbella?" Teg asked. "She promised to

249

teach me how to fight with my feet. I don't think the Bashar ever learned that."

"*Who* never learned it?"

Head down, abashed. "*I* never learned it."

"Murbella's on the practice floor. Run along. But let me tell her about Bellonda."

Schooling in a Bene Gesserit environment never stopped, Idaho thought as he watched the boy leave. But Murbella was right when she said they were learning things available only from the sisters.

This thought stirred misgivings. He saw an image in memory: Scytale standing behind the field barrier in a corridor. What was their fellow prisoner learning? Idaho shuddered. Thinking of the Tleilaxu always called up memories of Face Dancers. And that recalled Face Dancer ability to "reprint" the memories of anyone they killed. This in its turn filled him with fears of his visions. Face Dancers?

And I am a Tleilaxu experiment.

This was not something he dared explore with a Reverend Mother or even within the sight or hearing of one.

He went out in the corridors then and into Murbella's quarters where he settled himself in a chair and examined the residue of a lesson she had studied. Voice. There was the clairtone she used to echo her vocal experiments. The breathing harness to force prana-bindu responses lay across a chair, carelessly discarded in a tangle. She had bad habits from Honoured Matre days.

Murbella found him there when she returned. She wore skintight white leotards blotched with perspiration and was in a hurry to remove this clothing and make herself comfortable. He stopped her on her way to the shower, using one of the tricks he had learned.

"I've discovered some things about the Sisterhood that we didn't know before."

"Tell me!" It was *his* Murbella demanding this, perspiration glistening on her oval face, green eyes admiring. *My Duncan saw through them again!*

"A game where one of the pieces cannot be moved," he reminded her. *Let the comeye watchdogs play with that one!*

"They not only expect me to help them create a new religion around Sheeana, *our willing participation in their dream*, I'm supposed to be their gadfly, their conscience, making them question their own excuses for *extraordinary behaviour*."

"Has Odrade been here?"

"Bellonda."

"Duncan! That one is dangerous. You should never see her alone."

"The boy was with me."

"He never said!"

"He obeys orders."

"All right! What happened?"

He gave her a brief account, even to describing Bellonda's facial expressions and other reactions. (And wouldn't the comeye watchers have great sport with that!)

Murbella was enraged. "If she harms you I will never again cooperate with any of them!"

Right on cue, my darling. Consequences! You Bene Gesserit witches should re-examine your behaviour with great care.

"I'm still stinking from the practice floor," she said. "That boy! He is a quick one. I've never seen a child that bright."

He stood. "Here, I'll scrub you."

In the shower, he helped her out of the sweaty leotards, his hands cool on her skin. He could see how much she enjoyed his touch.

"So gentle and yet so strong," she whispered.

Gods below! The way she looked at him, as though she could devour him.

For once, Murbella's thoughts of Idaho were free of self accusation. *I remember no moment when I awakened and said: "I love him!"* No, it had wormed its way into this deeper and deeper addiction until, accomplished fact, it must be accepted in every living moment. Like breathing . . . or heartbeats. *A flaw? The Sisterhood is wrong!*

"Wash my back," she said and laughed when the shower drenched his clothing. She helped him undress and there in the shower it happened once more: this uncontrollable compulsion, this male-female mingling that drove away everything except sensation. Only afterward could she remember and say to herself: *He knows every technique I do.* But it was more than technique. *He wants to please me! Dear Gods of Dur! How was I ever this fortunate?*

She clung to his neck while he carried her out of the shower and dropped her still wet on to her bed. She pulled him down beside her and they lay there quietly, letting their energies rebuild.

Presently, she whispered: "So the Missionaria will use Sheeana."

"Very dangerous."

"Puts the Sisterhood in an exposed position. I thought they always tried to avoid that."

"From my point of view, it's ludicrous."

"Because they intended you to control Sheeana?"

"No one can control her! Perhaps no one should." He looked up at the comeyes. "Hey, Bell! You have more than one tiger by the tail."

Bellonda, returning to Archives, stopped at the door of Comeye-Recording and looked a question at the Watch Mother.

"In the shower again," the Watch Mother said. "It gets boring after a while."

"Participation Mystique!" Bellonda said and strode off to her quarters, her mind roiling with changed perceptions that needed reorganizing. *He's a better Mentat than I am!*

I'm jealous of Sheeana, damn her! And he knows it!

Participation Mystique! The orgy as energizer. Honoured Matre sexual knowledge was having an effect on the Bene Gesserit akin to that primitive submersion in shared ecstasy. We take one step toward it and one step away.

Just knowing this thing exists! How repellent, how dangerous . . . and yet, how magnetic.

And Sheeana is immune! Damn her! Why did Idaho have to remind them of that just now?

*Give me the judgment of balanced minds in preference to
laws every time. Codes and manuals create patterned behaviour. All patterned behaviour tends to go unquestioned,
gathering destructive momentum.*

—Darwi Odrade

Tamalane appeared in Odrade's quarters at Eldio just before
dawn, bringing news about the glazeway ahead of them.

"Drifting sand has made the road dangerous or impassable
in six places beyond the sea. Very large dunes."

Odrade had just completed her daily regimen: mini-Agony
of spice followed by exercise and cold shower. Eldio's guest
sleeping cell had only one sling chair (they knew her preferences) and she had seated herself to await Streggi and the
morning report.

Tamalane's face appeared sallow in the light of two silvery
glowglobes but there was no mistaking her satisfaction. *If you
had listened to me in the first place!*

"Get us 'thopters," Odrade said.

Tamalane left, obviously disappointed at Mother Superior's
mild reaction.

Odrade summoned Streggi. "Check alternative roads. Find
out about passage around the sea's western end."

Streggi hurried away, almost colliding with Tamalane who
was returning.

"I regret to inform you that Transport cannot give us
enough 'thopters immediately. They are relocating five
communities east of us. We probably can have them by
noon."

They all knew Tam used that mincing tone when she wished
to reprimand Odrade for bad planning.

"Isn't there an observation terminal at the edge of that
desert spur south of us?" Odrade asked.

"The first obstruction is just beyond it." Tamalane still was
too pleased with herself.

"Have the 'thopters meet us there," Odrade said. "We will
leave immediately after breakfast."

"But Dar . . ."

253

"Tell Clairby you are riding with me today. Yes, Streggi?" The acolyte stood in the doorway behind Tamalane.

The set of her shoulders as she left said Tamalane did not take the new seating arrangement as forgiveness. *On the coals!* But Tam's behaviour fitted itself to their need.

"We can get to the observation terminal," Streggi said, indicating she had heard. "We'll stir up dust and sand but it's safe."

"Let's hurry breakfast."

The closer they came to the desert, the more barren the country and Odrade commented on this as they sped south.

Within one hundred klicks of the last reported desert fringe, they saw signs of communities uprooted and removed to colder latitudes. Bare foundations, unsalvageable walls damaged in dismantling and left behind. Pipes cut off at foundation level. Too expensive to dig them out. Sand would cover all of this unsightly mess before long.

They had no Shield Wall here as there had been on Dune, Odrade observed to Streggi. Someday soon, the population of Chapter House would remove itself to polar regions and mine the ice for water.

"Is it true, Mother Superior," someone in the back with Tamalane asked, "that we're already making spice harvesting equipment?"

Odrade turned in her seat. The question had come from a Communications clerk, senior acolyte: an older woman with responsibility wrinkles deep in her forehead; dark and squinty from long hours at her equipment.

"We must be ready for the worms," Odrade said.

"If they come," Tamalane said.

"Have you ever walked on the desert, Tam?" Odrade asked.

"I was on Dune." Very short answer.

"But did you go out into open desert?"

"Only to some small drifts near Keen."

"That is not the same." A short answer deserved an equally short rejoinder.

"Other Memory tells me what I need to know." That was for the acolytes.

"It's not the same, Tam. You have to do it yourself. A very curious sensation on Dune, knowing a worm could come at any instant and consume you."

"I've heard about your Dune . . . exploit."

Exploit. Not "experience". Exploit. Very precise with her censure. Quite like Tam. "Too much of Bell has rubbed off on her," some will say.

"Walking on that sort of desert changes you, Tam. Other Memory becomes clearer. It's one thing to tap experiences of a Fremen ancestor. It's quite different walking there as a Fremen yourself if only for a few hours."

"I did not enjoy it."

So much for Tam's venturesome spirit and everyone in the car had seen her in a bad light. Word would spread.

On the coals, indeed!

But the shift to Sheeana on the Council (*if she suits*) would have an easy explanation. *And damn the need for our little dramas!*

They had an al fresco picnic at the observation terminal and looked out on to the first dunes from a hill sere with dead grass.

The terminal was a fused expanse of silica, green and glassy with heat bubbles through it. Odrade stood at the fused edge and noted how grass below her ended in patches, sand already invading the lower slopes of this once verdant hill. There were new saltbushes (planted by Sheeana's people, one of Odrade's entourage said) forming a random grey screen along the encroaching fingers of desert. A silent war. Chlorophyll-based life fighting a rear-guard action against the sand.

A low dune lifted above the terminal to her right. Waving for the others not to follow, she climbed the sandhill and just beyond its concealing bulk, there was the desert of memory.

So this is what we are creating.

No signs of habitation. She did not look back at growing things making their last desperate struggle against invading dunes but kept her attention focused outward to the horizon. There was the boundary desert dwellers watched. Anything moving in that dry expanse was potentially dangerous.

Keep your attention where it belongs! Look ahead. Don't look back.

When she returned to the others, she kept her gaze for a time on the glazed surface of the terminal.

The older Communications acolyte came up to Odrade with a request from Weather.

Odrade scanned it. Concise and inescapable. Nothing sudden about the changes spelled out in these words. They were asking for more ground equipment. This did not come with the abruptness of an accidental storm but with Mother Superior's decision.

Yesterday? Did I decide to phase out the sea only yesterday?

Weather compared the desert to a growing cancer.

The banality of this comparison offended Odrade. Of course it was a cancer! Another kind of cell was taking over the future of Chapter House.

Accountants! She could smell them in this report. Archives and Accountants! Sometimes useful but Odrade abhorred the need for them.

She returned the report to the Communications acolyte and looked beyond her at the sand-marked glaze.

"Request approved." Then: "It saddens me to see all of those buildings gone back there."

The acolyte shrugged. *She shrugged!* Odrade felt like striking her. (And wouldn't that send upsets rumbling through the Sisterhood!)

Odrade turned her back on the woman.

What could I possibly say to her? We have been on this ground five times the lifetime of our oldest sisters. And this one shrugs.

Yet . . . by some standards, she knew the Sisterhood's installations had barely reached maturity. Plaz and plasteel tended to maintain an orderly relationship between buildings and their settings. *Fixed in land and memory.* Towns and cities did not submit easily to other forces . . . except to human whims.

Another natural force.

The concept of respect for age was an odd one, she decided. Humans carried it inborn. She had seen it in the old Bashar when he spoke of his Family holdings on Lernaeus.

"We thought it fitting to keep my mother's decor."

Continuity. Would a revived ghola revive those feelings as well?

This is where my kind have been.

That took on a peculiar patina when "my kind" were blood-related ancestors.

Look how long we Atreides persisted on Caladan, restoring the old castle, polishing deep carvings in ancient wood. Whole teams of retainers just to keep the creaking old place at a level of barely tolerable functionalism.

But those retainers had not thought themselves ill-used. There had been a sense of privilege in their labours. Hands that polished the wood almost caressed it.

"Old. Been with the Atreides a long time now."

People and their artifacts. She felt tool sense as a living part of herself.

"I'm better because of this stick in my hand . . . because of this fire-sharpened spear to kill my meat . . . because of this shelter against the cold . . . because of my stone cellar to store our winter food . . . because of this swift sailing vessel . . . this giant ocean liner . . . this ship of metal and ceramics that carries me into space . . ."

Those first human venturers into space—how little they suspected of where the voyage would extend. How isolated they were in those ancient times! Little capsules of liveable atmosphere linked to cumbersome data sources by primitive transmission systems. Solitude. Loneliness. Limited opportunity for anything but surviving. Keep the air washed. Be sure of potable water. Exercise to prevent the debilitation of weightlessness. Stay active. Healthy mind in a healthy body. What was a healthy mind, anyway?

"Mother Superior?"

That damned Communications acolyte again!

"Yes?"

"Bellonda says to tell you immediately there has been a messenger from Buzzell. Strangers came and took all of the Reverend Mothers away."

Odrade whirled. "Her entire message?"

"No, Mother Superior. The strangers are described as commanded by a woman. The messenger says she had the look

257

of an Honoured Matre but was not wearing one of their robes."

"Nothing from Dortujla or the others?"

"They were not given the opportunity, Mother Superior. The messenger is a First Stage acolyte. She came in the small no-ship following explicit orders from Dortujla."

"Tell Bell that acolyte must not be allowed to leave. She has dangerous information. I will brief a messenger when I return. It must be a Reverend Mother. Do you have that?"

"Of course, Mother Superior." Hurt at the suggestion of doubt.

It was happening! Odrade contained her excitement with difficulty.

They have taken the bait. Now . . . are they on the hook?

Dortujla did a dangerous thing depending on an acolyte that way. Knowing Dortujla, that must be an extremely reliable acolyte. Prepared to kill herself if captured. I must see this acolyte. She may be ready for the Agony. And perhaps that's a message Dortujla sends me. It would be like her.

Bell would be incensed, of course. *Foolish to depend on someone from a punishment station!*

Odrade summoned a Communications team. "Set up a link with Bellonda."

The portable projector was not as clear as a fixed installation but Bell and her setting were recognizable.

Sitting at my table as though she owned it. Excellent!

Not giving Bellonda time for one of her outbursts, Odrade said: "Determine if that messenger acolyte is ready for the Agony."

"She is." *Gods below! That was terse for Bell.*

"Then see to it. Perhaps she can be our messenger."

"Already have."

"Is she resourceful?"

"Very."

What in the name of all the devils has happened to Bell? She's acting extremely odd. Not like her usual self at all. Duncan!

"Oh, and Bell, I want Duncan to have an open link with Archives."

"Did that this morning."

258

Well, well. Contact with Duncan is having its effect.

"I'll talk to you after I've seen Sheeana."

"Tell Tam she was right."

"About what?"

"Just tell her."

"Very well. I must say, Bell, I couldn't be more satisfied with the way you're handling matters."

"After the way you've handled me, how could I fail?"

Bellonda was actually smiling as they broke the connection. Odrade turned to find Tamalane standing behind her.

"Right about what, Tam?"

"That there's more to contacts between Idaho and Sheeana than we've suspected." Tamalane moved close to Odrade and lowered her voice. "Don't put her in my chair without discovering what they keep secret."

"I'm aware you knew my intentions, Tam. But . . . am I that transparent?"

"In some things, Dar."

"I'm fortunate to have you as a friend."

"You have other supporters. When the Proctors voted, it was your creativity that worked for you. 'Inspired' is the way one of your defenders put it."

"Then you know I'll have Sheeana on the coals quite thoroughly before I make one of my *inspired* decisions."

"Of course."

Odrade signalled Communications to remove the projector and went to wait at the edge of the glassy area.

Creative imagination.

She knew the mixed feelings of her associates.

Creativity!

Always dangerous to entrenched power. Always coming up with something new. New things could destroy the grip of authority. Even the Bene Gesserit approached creativity with misgivings. Maintaining an even keel inspired some to shunt boat-rockers aside. That was an element behind Dortujla's posting. The trouble was that creative ones tended to welcome backwaters. They called it *privacy*. It had taken quite a force to bring Dortujla out.

Be well, Dortujla. Be the best bait we ever used.

259

The 'thopters came then—sixteen of them, pilots showing displeasure at this added assignment after all the trouble they had been through. *Moving whole communities!*

In a fragile mood, Odrade watched the 'thopters settle to the hard-glazed surface, wing fans folding back into pod sleeves—each craft like a sleeping insect.

An insect designed in its own likeness by a mad robot.

When they were airborne, Streggi once more seated beside Odrade, Streggi asked: "Will we see sandworms?"

"Possibly. But there are no reports of them yet."

Streggi sat back, disappointed by the answer but unable to lever it into another question. Truth could be upsetting at times and they had such high expectations invested in this evolutionary gamble.

Else why destroy everything we loved on Chapter House?

As with most acolytes at her level, Streggi knew "the tool of candour." She had been provided with a reliable reason: *"Because honesty cuts through immature attention barriers."*

They came to expect straight answers, accurate comment, and that kept interest high. Acolytes learned that civilization foundered on euphemisms, innuendo, circumlocutions and outright lies masked by smiling faces. That was a mistake the Sisterhood seldom made with its own people.

We make other mistakes.

Simulflow intruded with an image of a long-ago sign arching over a narrow entry to a pink brick building: *HOSPITAL FOR INCURABLE DISEASES.*

Was that where the Sisterhood found itself? Or was it that they tolerated too many failures? Intrusive Other Memory had to have its purpose.

Failures?

Odrade searched it out: *If it comes, we must think of Murbella as a sister.* Not that their captive Honoured Matre was an incurable failure. But she was a misfit and undergoing the deep training at a very late age.

How quiet they were all around her, everyone looking out at windswept sand—whaleback dunes giving way at times to dry wavelets. Early afternoon sun had just begun to provide

260

sufficient sidelighting to define near vistas. Dust obscured the horizon ahead.

Odrade curled up in her seat and slept. *I've seen this before. I survived Dune.*

The stir as they came down and circled over Sheeana's Desert Watch Centre awakened her.

Desert Watch Centre. We're at it again. We haven't really named it . . . no more than we gave a name to this planet. Chapter House! What kind of a name is that? Desert Watch Centre! Description, not a name. Accent on the temporary.

As they descended, she saw confirmations of her thought. The sense of temporary housing was amplified by spartan abruptness in all junctures. No softness, no rounding of any connection. *This attaches here and that goes over there.* All joined by removable connectors.

It was a bumpy landing, the pilot telling them that way: "Here you are and good riddance."

Odrade went immediately to the room always set aside for her and summoned Sheeana. Temporary quarters: another spartan cubicle with hard cot. Two chairs this time. A window looked westward on to desert. The temporary nature of these rooms grated on her. Anything here could be dismantled in hours and carted away. She washed her face in the adjoining bathroom, getting the most out of movement. She had slept in a cramped position on the 'thopter and her body complained.

Refreshed, she went out to a window, thankful that the erection crew had included this tower: ten floors, and this the ninth. Sheeana occupied the top floor, a vantage for doing what the name of the place described.

While waiting, Odrade made necessary preparations.

Open the mind. Shed preconceptions.

First impressions when Sheeana arrived must be seen with naive eyes. Ears must not be prepared for a particular voice. Nose must not expect remembered odours.

I chose this one. I, her first teacher, am susceptible to mistakes.

Odrade turned at a sound from the doorway. Streggi.

"Sheeana has just returned from the desert and is with her

people. She asks Mother Superior to meet her in the upper quarters which are more comfortable."

Odrade nodded.

Sheeana's quarters on the top floor still had that prefab look at the edges. Quick shelter ahead of the desert. A large room, six or seven times the size of the guest cubicle, but then it was both workroom and sleeping chamber. Windows on two sides—west and north. Odrade was struck by the mixture of functional and non-functional.

Sheeana had managed to make her rooms reflect herself. A standard BG cot had been covered with a bright orange and umber spread. A black-on-white line drawing of a sandworm, head-on with all of its crystal teeth displayed, filled an end wall. Sheeana had drawn it, relying on Other Memory and her Dune childhood to guide her hand.

It said something about Sheeana that she had not attempted a more ambitious rendering—full colour, perhaps, and in traditional desert setting. Just the worm and a hint of sand beneath it, a tiny robed human in the foreground.

Herself?

Admirable restraint and a constant reminder of why she was here. A deep impression of nature.

Nature makes no bad art?

It was a statement too glib to accept.

What do we mean by "nature?"

She had seen atrocious *natural* wilderness: brittle trees looking as though they had been dipped in faulty green pigment and left on a tundra's edge to dry into ugly parodies. Repellent. Hard to imagine such trees having any purpose. And blindworms . . . slimy yellow skins. Where was the art in them? Temporary stopping place on evolution's journey elsewhere. Did the intervention of humans always make a difference? Sligs! The Bene Tleilax had produced something disgusting there.

Admiring Sheeana's drawing, Odrade decided certain combinations offended particular human senses. Sligs as food were delectable. Ugly combinations touched early experiences. Experiences judged.

Bad thing!

Much of what we think of as art caters to desires for reassurance. Don't offend me! I know what I can accept.

How did this drawing reassure Sheeana?

Sandworm: blind power guarding hidden riches. Artistry in mystic beauty.

It was reported that Sheeana joked about her assignment. "I am shepherd to worms that may never exist."

And even if they did appear, it would be years before any achieved the size indicated by her drawing. Was it her voice from the tiny figure in front of the worm?

"This will come in time."

An odour of melange pervaded the room, stronger than usual in a Reverend Mother's quarters. Odrade passed a searching look across the furnishings: chairs, worktable, illumination from anchored glowglobes—everything placed where it would serve to advantage. But what was that oddly shaped mound of black plaz in the corner? More of Sheeana's work?

These rooms fitted Sheeana, Odrade decided. Little other than the drawing to recall her origins but the view out of any window might have been from Dar-es-Balat deep in Dune's drylands.

A small rustling sound at the doorway alerted Odrade. She turned and there was Sheeana. Almost shy the way she peered around the door before entering Mother Superior's presence.

Motions as words: *"So she did come to my rooms. Good. Someone might have been careless with my invitation."*

Odrade's readied senses tingled with Sheeana's presence. The youngest-ever Reverend Mother. You often thought of *Quiet Little Sheeana.* She was not always quiet nor was she small but the label stuck. She was not even mousy, but frequently quiet like a rodent waiting at the edge of a field for the farmer to leave. Then the mouse would come darting out to glean fallen grains.

Sheeana came fully into the room and stopped less than a pace from Odrade. "We've been too long apart, Mother Superior."

Odrade's first impression was oddly jumbled.

Candour and concealment?

Sheeana stood quietly receptive.

This descendant of Siona Atreides had developed an interesting face under the Bene Gesserit patina. Maturity working on her according to both Sisterhood and Atreides designs. Marks of many decisions firmly taken. The slender, dark-skinned waif with sun-streaked brown hair had become this poised Reverend Mother. Skin still dark from long hours in the open. Hair still sun-streaked. The eyes, though—the steely total blue that said: "I have been through the Agony."

What is it I sense in her?

Sheeana saw the look on Odrade's face (Bene Gesserit naivete!) and knew this was the long-feared confrontation.

There can be no defence except my truth and I hope she stops short of a full confession!

Odrade watched her former student with exquisite care, every sense open.

Fear! What do I sense? Something when she spoke?

The steadiness of Sheeana's voice had been shaped into the powerful instrument Odrade had anticipated at their first meeting. Sheeana's original nature (a Fremen nature if there ever was one!) had been curbed and redirected. That core of vindictiveness smoothed out. Her capacity for love and hatred brought under tight reins.

Why do I get the impression she wants to hug me?

Odrade felt suddenly vulnerable.

This woman has been inside my defences. No way to exclude her totally ever again.

Tamalane's judgment came to mind: *"She is one of those who keeps herself to herself. Remember Sister Schwangyu? Like that one but better at it. Sheeana knows where she is going. We'll have to watch her carefully. Atreides blood, you know."*

"I'm Atreides, too, Tam."

"Don't think we ever forget it! You think we'd just stand idly by if Mother Superior chose to breed on her own? There are limits to our tolerance, Dar."

"Indeed, this visit is long overdue, Sheeana."

Odrade's tone alerted Sheeana. She stared back suddenly with that look the Sisterhood called "BG placid", of which there probably was nothing more placid in the universe, nothing more completely a mask of what occurred behind it. This was not just a barrier, it was a *nothing*. Anything on this mask would be transgression. This, in itself, was betrayal. Sheeana realized it immediately and responded with laughter.

"I knew you would come probing! The hand-talk with Duncan, right?" *Please, Mother Superior! Accept this.*

"All of it, Sheeana."

"He wants someone to rescue them if Honoured Matres attack."

"That's all?" *Does she think me a complete fool?*

"No. He wants information about our intentions . . . and what we're doing to meet the Honoured Matre threat."

"What have you told him?"

"Everything I could." *Truth is my only weapon. I must divert her!*

"Are you his friend at court, Sheeana?"

"Yes!"

"So am I."

"But not Tam and Bell?"

"My informants tell me Bell now tolerates him."

"Bell? Tolerant?"

"You misjudge her, Sheeana. It's a flaw in you." *She is hiding something. What have you done, Sheeana?*

"Sheeana, do you think you could work with Bell?"

"Because I tease her?" *Work with Bell? What does she mean? Not Bell to head that damnable Missionaria project!*

A faint twitching lifted the corners of Odrade's mouth. *Another prank? Could that be it?*

Sheeana was a prime gossip subject in Central's dining rooms. Stories of how she teased Breeding Mistresses (especially Bell) and elaborately detailed accounts of seductions fleshed out with Honoured Matre comparisons from Murbella spiced more than the food. Odrade had heard snatches of the latest story only two days ago. "She said, 'I used the *Let-him-misbehave* method. Very effective with men who think they're leading you down the garden path.'"

"Tease? Is that what you do, Sheeana?"

"An appropriate word: reshape by going against the natural

inclination." The instant the words were out of her mouth, Sheeana knew she had made a mistake.

Odrade felt warning stillness. *Reshape?* Her gaze went to that odd black mound in the corner. She stared at it with a fixity that surprised her. It drank vision. She kept probing for coherence, something that *spoke* to her. Nothing responded, not even when she probed to her limits. *And that's its purpose!*

"It's called 'Void'," Sheeana said.

"Yours?" *Please, Sheeana. Say someone else did it. The one who did this has gone where I cannot follow.*

"I did it one night about a week ago."

Is black plaz the only thing you reshape? "A fascinating comment on art in general."

"And not on art specific?"

"I have a problem with you, Sheeana. You alarm some sisters." *And me. There's a wild place in you we have not found. Atreides gene markers Duncan told us to seek are in your cells. What have they given you?*

"Alarm my sisters?"

"Especially when they recall that you're the youngest ever to survive the Agony."

"Except for Abominations."

"Is that what you are?"

"Mother Superior!" *She has never deliberately hurt me except as a lesson.*

"You went through the Agony as an act of disobedience."

"Wouldn't you say rather that I went against mature advice?" *Humour sometimes distracts her.*

Prester, Sheeana's acolyte aide, came to the door and rapped lightly on the wall beside it until she had their attention. "You said I was to tell you immediately when the search teams returned."

"What do they report?"

Relief in Sheeana's voice?

"Team eight wants you to look at their scans."

"They always want that!"

Sheeana spoke with forced frustration. "Do you want to look at the scans with me, Mother Superior?"

"I'll wait here."

266

"This won't take long."

When they had gone, Odrade went to the western window: a clear view across rooftops to the new desert. Small dunes here. Almost sunset and that dry heat so reminiscent of Dune.

What is Sheeana hiding?

A young man, hardly more than a boy, had been sunning nude on a neighbouring rooftop, face up on a sea-green mattress with a golden towel across his face. His skin was a sun-warmed gold to match towel and pubic hair. A breeze touched a corner of the towel and lifted it. One languid hand came up and restored the cover.

How can he be idle? Night worker? Probably.

Idleness was not encouraged and this was flaunting it. Odrade smiled to herself. Anyone could be excused for assuming he was a night worker. He might be depending on that specific guess. The trick would be to remain unseen by those who knew otherwise.

I will not ask. Intelligence deserves some rewards. And, after all, he could be a night worker.

She lifted her gaze. A new pattern emerging here: exotic sunsets. Narrow band of orange drawn along the horizon, bulging where the sun had just dipped below the land. Silvery blue above the orange went darker overhead. She had seen this many times on Dune. Meteorological explanations she did not care to explore. Better to let eyes absorb this transient beauty; better to permit ears and skin feel sudden stillness descend upon this land in the quick darkness after the orange vanished.

Faintly, she saw the young man pick up mattress and towel and vanish behind a ventilator.

A sound of running in the corridor behind her. Sheeana entered almost breathless. "They found a spice mass thirty klicks northeast of us! Small but compact!"

Odrade did not dare hope. "Could it be wind accumulation?"

"Not likely. I've set a round-the-clock watch on it." Sheeana glanced at the window where Odrade stood. *She has seen Trebo. Perhaps . . .*

"I asked you earlier, Sheeana, if you could work with Bell.

267

It was an important question. Tam is getting very old and must be replaced soon. There must be a vote, of course."

"Me?" It was totally unexpected.

"My first choice." *Imperative now. I want you close where I can keep watch on you.*

"But I thought . . . I mean, the Missionaria's plan . . ."

"That can wait. And there must be someone else who can shepherd worms . . . if that spice mass is what we hope."

"Oh? Yes . . . several of our people but no one who . . . Don't you want me to test whether the worms still respond to me?"

"Work on the Council should not interfere with that."

"I . . . you can see I'm surprised."

"I would have said shocked. Tell me, Sheeana, what really interests you these days?"

Still probing. Trebo, serve me now! "Making sure the desert grows well." *Truth!* "And my sex life, of course. You saw the young man on the roof next door? Trebo, a new one Duncan sent me for polishing."

Even after Odrade had gone, Sheeana wondered why those words had aroused such merriment. Mother Superior had been deflected, though.

No need even to waste her fallback position—truth: *"We've been discussing the possibility that I might Imprint Teg and restore the Bashar's memories that way."*

Full confession avoided. *Mother Superior did not learn that I hold the key to reactivating our no-ship prison and defusing the mines Bellonda put in it.*

No sweeteners will cloak some forms of bitterness. If it tastes bitter, spit it out. That's what our earliest ancestors did.

—**The Coda**

Murbella found herself arising in the night to continue a dream although quite awake and aware of her surroundings: Duncan asleep beside her, faint ticking of machinery, the chrono-projection on the ceiling. She insisted on Duncan's presence at night lately, fearful when alone. He blamed the fourth pregnancy.

She sat on the edge of the bed. The room was ghostly in the dim light of the chrono. Dream images persisted.

Duncan grumbled and rolled toward her. An outflung arm draped itself across her legs.

She felt that this mental intrusion was not dreamstuff but it had some of those characteristics. Bene Gesserit teachings did this. Them and their damned suggestions about Scytale and . . . and everything! They precipitated motion she could not control.

Tonight, she was lost in an insane world of words. The cause was clear. Bellonda that morning had learned Murbella spoke nine languages and had aimed the suspicious acolyte down a mental path called "Linguistic Heritage". But Bell's influence on this night-time madness provided no escape.

Nightmare: she was a creature of microscopic size trapped in an enormous echoing place labelled in giant letters wherever she turned: "Data Reservoir". Animated words with grimacing jaws and fearsome tentacles surrounded her.

Predatory beasts and she was their prey!

Awake and knowing she sat on the edge of her bed with Duncan's arm on her legs, she still saw the beasts. They herded her backward. She *knew* she was going backward although her body did not move. They pressed her toward a terrible disaster she could not see. Her head would not turn! Not only did she see these creatures (they hid parts of her sleeping chamber) but she heard them in a cacophony of her nine languages.

They will tear me apart!

Although she could not turn, she sensed what lay behind her: more teeth and claws. Threat all around! If they cornered her, they would pounce and she was doomed.

Done for. Dead. Victim. Torture-captive. Fair game.

Despair filled her. Why would Duncan not awaken and save her? His arm was a lead weight, part of the force holding her and allowing these creatures to herd her into their bizarre trap. She trembled. Perspiration poured from her body. Awful words! They united into giant combinations. A creature with knife-fanged mouth came directly toward her and she saw more words in the gaping blackness between its jaws.

See above.

Murbella began to laugh. She had no control of it. *See above. Done for. Dead. Victim . . .*

The laughter awakened Duncan. He sat up, activated a low glowglobe and stared at her. How tousled he looked after their earlier sexual collision.

His expression hovered between amusement and upset at being awakened. "Why are you laughing?"

Laughter subsided in gasps. Her sides ached. She was afraid his tentative smile would ignite a new spasm. "Oh . . . oh! Duncan! Sexual collision!"

He knew this was their mutual term for the addiction that bound them but why would it make her laugh?

His puzzled expression struck her as ludicrous.

Between gasps, she said: "Two more words." And she had to clamp her mouth closed to prevent another outburst.

"What?"

His voice was the funniest thing she had ever heard. She thrust a hand at him and shook her head. "Ohhh . . . ohhh . . ."

"Murbella, what's wrong with you?"

She could only continue shaking her head.

He tried a tentative smile. It gentled her and she leaned against him. "No!" When his right hand wandered. "I just want to be close."

"Look what time it is." He lifted his chin toward the ceiling projection. "Almost three."

"It was so funny, Duncan."

"So tell me about it."

"When I catch my breath."

He eased her down on to her pillow. "We're like a damned old married couple. Funny stories in the middle of the night."

"No, darling, we're different."

"A question of degree, nothing else."

"Quality," she insisted.

"What was so funny?"

She recounted her nightmare and Bellonda's influence.

"Zensunni. Very ancient technique. The sisters use it to rid

270

you of trauma connections. Words that ignite unconscious responses."

Fear returned.

"Murbella, why are you trembling?"

"Honoured Matre teachers warned us terrible things would happen if we fell into Zensunni hands."

"Bullcrap! I went through the same thing as a Mentat."

His words conjured another dream fragment. A beast with two heads. Both mouths open. Words in there. On the left: "One word" and on the right: "leads to another".

Mirth displaced fear. It subsided without laughter. "Duncan!"

"Mmmmmmm." Mentat distance in the sound.

"Bell said Bene Gesserits use words as weapons—Voice. 'Tools of control', she called them."

"A lesson you must learn almost as instinct. They'll never trust you into the deeper training until you learn this."

And I won't trust you afterward.

She rolled away from him and looked at the comeyes glittering in the ceiling around the time projection.

I'm still on probation.

She was aware her teachers discussed her privately. Conversations were choked off when she approached. They stared at her in their special way, as though she were an interesting specimen.

Bellonda's voice cluttered her mind.

Nightmare tendrils. Midmorning then and the sweat of her own exertions a stink in her nostrils. Probationer a dutiful three paces from Reverend Mother. Bell's voice:

"Never be an expert. That locks you up tight."

All of this because I asked if there were no words to guide the Bene Gesserit.

"Duncan, why do they mix mental and physical teaching?"

"Mind and body reinforce each other." Sleepy. *Damn him! He's going back to sleep.*

Bell's voice: "There's no 'Ours not to reason why' in the Bene Gesserit. Reasoning—an extremely delicate subject. Akin to rationalization. Separate the two carefully. Don't think you can hide things from yourself."

271

Murbella knew she could hide little from her teachers or the comeyes. During her first years of captivity, she had practised deceptions and taken secretive precautions. It had dawned on her one day that precautions themselves betrayed what she sought to hide. She had known then that whatever allowances she made for Bene Gesserit abilities might never be enough. That made her want those skills even more.

She shook Duncan's shoulder. "If words are so damned unimportant, why do they talk about disciplines so much?"

"Patterns," he mumbled. "Dirty word."

"What?" She shook him more roughly.

He turned on to his back, moving his lips, then: "Discipline equals patterns equals bad way to go. They say we're all natural pattern creators . . . means 'order' to them, I think."

"Why is that so bad?"

"Gives others a handle to destroy us or traps us in . . . in things we won't change."

"You're wrong about mind and body."

"Hmmmmph?"

"It's pressures locking one to the other."

"Isn't that what I said? Hey! Are we going to talk or sleep or what?"

"No more 'or what'. Not tonight."

A deep sigh lifted his chest.

"They're not out to improve my health," she said.

"Nobody said they were."

"That comes later, after the Agony." She knew he hated reminders of that deadly trial but there was no avoiding it. The prospect filled her mind.

"All right!" he sat up, punched his pillow into shape and leaned back against it to study her. "What's up?"

"They're so damned clever with their word-weapons! She brought Teg to you and said you were fully responsible for him."

"You don't believe it?"

"He thinks of you as his father."

"Not really."

"No, but . . . did you think that about the Bashar?"

272

"When he restored my memories? Yeah."

"You're a pair of intellectual orphans, always looking for parents who aren't there. He hasn't the faintest idea of how much you will hurt him."

"That tends to split up the family."

"So you hate the Bashar in him and you're glad you'll hurt him.'

"Didn't say that."

"Why is he so important?"

' Th . Bashar? Military genius. Always doing the unexpected. Confounds his foes by appearing where they never expect him to be."

"Can't anyone do that?"

"Not the way he does it. He invents tactics and strategies. Just like that!" Snapping his fingers.

"More violence. Just like Honoured Matres."

"Not always. Bashar had a reputation for winning without battle."

"I've seen the histories."

"Don't trust them."

"But you just said . . ."

"Histories focus on confrontations. Some truth in that but it hides more persistent things that go on in spite of upheavals."

"Persistent things?"

"What history touches the woman in the rice paddy driving her water buffalo ahead of her plough while her husband is off somewhere, most likely a conscript, carrying a weapon?"

"Why is that persistent and more important than . . ."

"Her babies at home need food. Man's away on this perennial madness? Someone has to do the ploughing. She's a true image of human persistence."

"You sound so bitter . . . I find that odd."

"Considering my military *history*?"

"That, yes, and Bene Gesserit emphasis on . . . on their Bashar and elite troops and . . ."

"You think they're just more self important people going on about their self important violence? They'll ride right over the woman with her plough?"

"Why not?"

"Because very little escapes them. The violent ones ride *past* the ploughing woman and seldom see they have touched basic reality. A Bene Gesserit would never miss such a thing."

"Again, why not?"

"The self important have limited vision because they ride a death-reality. Woman and plough are life-reality. Without life-reality there'd be no humankind. My Tyrant saw this. The sisters bless him for it even while they curse him."

"So you're a willing participant in their dream."

"I guess I am." He sounded surprised.

"And you're being completely honest with Teg?"

"He asks, I give him candid answers. I don't believe in doing violence to curiosity."

"And you have full responsibility for him?"

"That isn't exactly what she said."

"Ahhhhh, my love. Not *exactly* what she said. You call Bell hypocrite and don't include Odrade. Duncan, if you only knew . . ."

"As long as we're ignoring the comeyes, spit it out!"

"Lies, cheating, vicious . . ."

"Hey! The Bene Gesserit?"

"They have that hoary old excuse: Sister A does it so if I do it that's not so bad. Two crimes cancel each other."

"What crimes?"

She hesitated. *Should I tell him? No. But he expects some answer.* "Bell's delighted the roles are reversed between you and Teg! She's looking forward to his pain."

"Maybe we should disappoint her." He knew it was a mistake to say this as soon as it was out. *Too soon.*

"Poetic justice!" Murbella was delighted.

Divert them! "They aren't interested in Justice. Fairness, yes. They have this homily: 'Those against whom judgment is passed must accept the fairness of it.'"

"So they condition you to accept their judgment."

"There are loopholes in any system."

"You know, darling, acolytes learn things."

"That's why they're acolytes."

"I mean we talk to each other."

"We? You're an acolyte? You're a proselyte!"

"Whatever I am, I've heard stories. Your Teg may not be what he seems."

"Acolyte gossip."

"There are stories out of Gammu, Duncan."

He stared at her. *Gammu? He could never think of it by any name other than the original: Giedi Prime. Harkonnen hell hole.*

She took his silence as an invitation to continue. "They say Teg moved faster than the eye could see, that he . . ."

"Probably started those stories himself."

"Some sisters don't discount them. They're taking a wait and see attitude. They want precautions."

"Haven't you learned anything about Teg from your precious *histories*? It would be typical of him to start such rumours. Make people cautious."

"But remember I was on Gammu then. Honoured Matres were very upset. Enraged. Something went wrong."

"Sure. Teg did the unexpected. Surprised them. Stole one of their no-ships." He patted the wall beside him. "This one."

"The Sisterhood has its forbidden ground, Duncan. They're always telling me to wait for the Agony. All will become clear! Damn them!"

"Sounds like they're preparing you for the Missionaria teaching. Engineer religions for specific purposes and selected populations."

"You don't see anything wrong in that?"

"Morality. I don't argue that with Reverend Mothers."

"Why not?"

"Religions founder on that rock. BGs don't founder."

Duncan, if you only knew their morality! "It annoys them that you know so much about them."

"Bell only wanted to kill me because of it."

"You don't think Odrade is just as bad?"

"What a question!" *Odrade? A terrifying woman if you let yourself dwell on her abilities. Atreides, for all that. I've known Atreides and Atreides. This one is Bene Gesserit first. Teg's the Atreides ideal.*

"Odrade told me she trusts your loyalty to the Atreides."

"I'm loyal to Atreides honour, Murbella." *And I make my*

own moral decisions—about the Sisterhood, about this child they've thrust into my care, about Sheeana and . . . and about my beloved.

Murbella bent close to him, breast brushing his arm, and whispered in his ear: "Sometimes, I could kill any of them within my reach!"

Does she think they can't hear? He sat upright, dragging her with him. "What's set you off?"

"*She* wants me to work on Scytale."

Work on. Honoured Matre euphemism. *Well, why not? She "worked on" plenty of men before she ran afoul of me.* But he had an antique husband's reaction. Not only that . . . Scytale? A damned Tleilaxu?

"Mother Superior?" He had to be sure.

"The one, the only." Almost light-hearted now that she had unburdened herself.

"What's your reaction?"

"She says it was your idea."

"My . . . No way! I suggested we could try to pry information out of him but . . ."

"She says it's an ordinary thing for Bene Gesserits just as it is with Honoured Matres. Go breed with this one. Seduce that one. All in a day's work."

"I asked for *your* reaction."

"Revolted."

"Why?" *Knowing your background . . .*

"It's you I love, Duncan, and . . . and my body is . . . is to give you pleasure . . . just as you . . ."

"We're an old married couple and the witches are trying to pry us apart."

His words ignited in him a clear vision of Lady Jessica, lover of his long-dead Duke and mother of Muad'Dib. *I loved her. She didn't love me but . . .* The look he saw now in Murbella's eyes, he had seen Jessica look at the Duke that way: blind, unswerving love. The thing the Bene Gesserit distrusted. Jessica had been softer than Murbella. Hard at the core, though. And Odrade . . . she was hard at the beginning. Plasteel all the way.

"Work on" Scytale?

276

Could Odrade be malicious? Only if it served that plasteel core. That belonged to the Bene Gesserit. She would crush anything that failed to serve her Sisterhood's necessities.

Then what of the times when he had suspected her of sharing human emotions? The way she spoke of the Bashar when they learned the old man was dead on Dune.

"He was my father, you know."

In his quarters on that memorable afternoon, he seated and she standing with back to a wall, arms folded across her breast. Resemblance to the Bashar stronger than he had ever seen it.

"Then why did you let him die?"

"Are you accusing me, Duncan?"

"Sorry! I'm not permitted to accuse you."

"You enjoy the occasional quarrel with me, don't you?" Knife edge in her voice.

She was telling him she permitted periodic impertinence. Controlled quarrels. Never lose your temper. Screen out the harsher words.

Murbella dragged him out of reverie. "You may share their dream, whatever that is, but . . ."

"Grow up, humans!"

"What?"

"That's their dream. Start acting like adults and not like angry children in a schoolyard."

"Mama knows best!"

"Yes . . . I believe she does."

"Is that how you really see them? Even when you call them witches?"

"It's a good word. Witches do mysterious things."

"You don't believe it's the long and severe training plus the spice and the Agony?"

"What's belief have to do with it? Unknowns create their own mystique."

"But you don't think they trick people into doing what they want?"

"Sure they do!"

"Words as weapons, Voice, Imprinters . . ."

"None as beautiful as you."

"What's beauty, Duncan?"

277

"There're styles in beauty, sure."

"Exactly what she says. 'Styles based on procreative roots buried so deeply in our racial psyche we dare not remove them.' So they've thought of meddling there, Duncan."

"And they might dare anything?"

"She says, 'We won't distort our progeny into what we judge to be non-human.' They judge, they condemn."

He thought of the alien figures in his vision. Face Dancers. And he asked: "Like the amoral Tleilaxu? Amoral—not human."

"I can almost hear the gears whirling in Odrade's head. She and her sisters—they watch, they listen, they tailor every response, everything calculated."

Is that what you want, my darling? He felt trapped. She was right and she was wrong. Ends justifying means? How could he justify losing Murbella?

"You think them amoral?" he asked.

It was as though she did not hear. "Always asking themselves what to say next to get the desired response."

"What response?" Couldn't she hear his pain?

"You never know until too late!" She turned and looked at him. "Exactly like Honoured Matres. Do you know how Honoured Matres trapped me?"

He could not suppress awareness of how avidly the watchdogs would hang on Murbella's next words.

"I was picked off the streets after an Honoured Matre sweep. I think the whole sweep was because of me. My mother was a great beauty but she was too old for them."

"A sweep?" *The watchdogs would want me to ask.*

"They go through an area and people disappear. No bodies, nothing. Whole families vanish. It's explained as punishment because people plot against them."

"How old were you?"

"Three . . . maybe four. I was playing with friends in an open place under trees. Suddenly, there was a lot of noise and shouting. We hid in a hole behind some rocks."

He was caught in a vision of this drama.

"The ground shook." Her gaze went inward with the memory. "Explosions. After a while it was quiet and we peeked out. The whole corner where my house had been was a hole."

"You were orphaned?"

"I remember my parents. He was a big, robust fellow. I think my mother was a servant somewhere. They wore uniforms for such jobs and I remember her in uniform."

"Didn't you ever ask?"

"They discourage such questions."

"How can you be sure your parents were killed?"

"The sweep is all I know for sure but they're always the same. There was screaming and people running about. We were terrified."

"Why do you think the sweep was because of you?"

"They do that sort of thing."

They. What a victory the watchers would count in that one word.

Murbella was still deep in memory. "I think my father refused to succumb to an Honoured Matre. That was always considered dangerous. Big, handsome man . . . strong."

"So you hate them."

"Why?" Really surprised by his question. "Without that, I would never have been an Honoured Matre."

Her callousness shocked him. "So it was worth anything!"

"Love, do you resent whatever brought me to your side?"

Touché! "But don't you wish it had happened some other way?"

"It happened."

What utter fatalism. He had never suspected this in her. Was it Honoured Matre conditioning or something the Bene Gesserits did?

"You were just a valuable addition to their stables."

"Right. Enticers, they called us. We recruited valuable males."

"And you did."

"I repaid their investment many times over."

"Do you realize how the sisters will interpret this?"

"Don't make a big thing of it."

"So you're ready to *work on* Scytale?"

"I didn't say that. Honoured Matres manipulated me without my consent. The sisters need me and want to use me the same way. My price may be too high."

He was a moment speaking past a dry throat. "Price?"

She glared at him. "You, you're just part of my price. No working on Scytale. And more of their famous candour about why they need me!"

"Careful, love. They might tell you."

She turned an almost Bene Gesserit stare toward him. "How could you restore Teg's memories without pain?"

Damn! And just when he thought they were free of that slip. No escape. He could see in her eyes that she guessed.

Murbella confirmed this. "Since I would not agree, I'm sure you've discussed it with Sheeana."

He could only nod. His Murbella had gone farther into the Sisterhood than he suspected. And she knew how his multiple ghola memories had been restored by her *Imprinting*. He suddenly saw her as a Reverend Mother and wanted to cry out against it.

"How does this make you different from Odrade?" she asked.

"Sheeana was trained as an Imprinter." His words felt empty even as he spoke.

"That's different from my training?" Accusing.

Anger flared in him. "You'd prefer the pain? Like Bell?"

"You'd prefer the defeat of the Bene Gesserit?" Voice milky soft.

He heard the distance in her tone, as though she already had retreated into the cold observational stance of the Sisterhood. They were freezing his lovely Murbella! There was still that vitality in her, though. It tore at him. She gave off an aura of health, especially in pregnancy. Vigour and boundless enjoyment of life. It glowed in her. The sisters would take that and dampen it.

She became quiet under his watchful stare.

Desperate, he wondered what he could do.

"I had hoped we were being more open with each other lately," she said. Another Bene Gesserit probe.

"I disagree with many of their actions but I don't distrust their motives," he said.

"I'll know their motives if I live through the Agony."

He went very still, caught in realization that she might not survive. Life without Murbella? Yawning emptiness deeper than anything he had ever imagined. Nothing in his many lives compared with it. Without conscious volition, he reached out and caressed her back. Skin so soft and yet resilient.

"I love you too much, Murbella. That's my Agony."

She trembled under his touch.

He found himself wallowing in sentimentality, building an image of grief until he recalled a Mentat teacher's words about "emotional binges".

The difference between sentiment and sentimentality is easy to see. When you avoid killing somebody's pet on the glazeway, that's sentiment. If you swerve to avoid the pet and that causes you to kill pedestrians, that is sentimentality.

She took his caressing hand and pressed it against her lips.

"Words plus body, more than either," he whispered.

His words plunged her back into nightmare but now she went with a vengeance, aware of words as tools. She was filled with special relish for the experience, willingness to laugh at herself.

As she exorcized the nightmare, it occurred to her that she had never seen an Honoured Matre laugh at herself.

Holding his hand, she stared down at Duncan. Mentat flickering of his eyelids. Did he realize what she had just experienced? Freedom! It no longer was a question of how she had been confined and driven into inevitable channels by her past. For the first time since accepting the possibility that she could become a Reverend Mother, she glimpsed what it might mean. She felt awe and shock.

Nothing more important than the Sisterhood?

They spoke of an oath, something more mysterious than the Proctor's words at the acolyte initiation.

My oath to Honoured Matres was only words. An oath to the Bene Gesserit can be no more.

She remembered Bellonda growling that diplomats were chosen for ability to lie. *"Would you be another diplomat, Murbella?"*

It was not that oaths were made to be broken. How childish!

Schoolyard threat: *"If you break your word, I'll break mine! Nyaa, nyaa, nyaaaaa!"*

Futile to worry about oaths. Far more important to find that place in herself where freedom lived. It was a place where something always listened.

Cupping Duncan's hand against her lips, she whispered: "They listen. Oh, how they listen."

> *Enter no conflict against fanatics unless you can defuse them. Oppose a religion with another religion only if your proofs (miracles) are irrefutable or if you can mesh in a way that the fanatics accept you as god-inspired. This has long been the barrier to science assuming a mantle of divine revelation. Science is so obviously man-made. Fanatics (and many are fanatic on one subject or another) must know where you stand, but more important, must recognize who whispers in your ear.*
>
> —Missionaria Protectiva,
> Primary Teaching

The flow of time nagged at Odrade as much as did constant awareness of the hunters approaching. Years passed so quickly that days became a blur. Two months of arguments to gain approval of Sheeana as successor to Tam!

Bellonda had taken to standing day watch when Odrade was absent as she had been today, briefing a new Bene Gesserit remnant being sent Scattering. The Council continued this but with reluctance. Idaho's suggestion that it was a futile strategy had sent shock waves through the Sisterhood. Briefings now carried new defensive plans for "what you may encounter".

When Odrade entered the workroom late in the afternoon, Bellonda sat at the table. Her cheeks looked puffy and her eyes had that hard stare they got when she suppressed fatigue. With Bell here, the daily summation would include sharp comments.

"They've approved Sheeana," she said, pushing a small crystal toward Odrade. "Tam's support did it. And Murbella's new one will be born in eight days, so the Suks *claim*."

Bell had little faith in Suk doctors.

New one? She could be so damned impersonal about life! Odrade found her pulses quickening at the prospect.

When Murbella recovers from this birth—the Agony. She is ready.

"Duncan's extremely nervous," Bellonda said, vacating the chair.

Duncan yet! Those two are getting remarkably familiar.

Bell was not finished. "And before you ask, no word from Dortujla."

Odrade took her seat behind the table and balanced the report crystal on her palm. Dortujla's trusted acolyte, now Reverend Mother Fintil, would not risk the no-ship journey or any of the other message devices they had prepared just to stroke a Mother Superior. No news meant the bait was still out there . . . or wasted.

"Have you told Sheeana she's confirmed?" Odrade asked.

"I left that for you. She's late with her daily report again. Not right for someone on the Council."

So Bell still disapproved the appointment.

Sheeana's daily messages had taken on a repetitious note. *"No wormsign. Spice mass intact."*

Everything upon which they pinned their hopes lay in terrible suspension. And nightmare hunters crept closer. Tensions accumulated. Explosive.

"You've seen that exchange between Duncan and Murbella enough times," Bellonda said. "Is that what Sheeana was hiding and, if so, why?"

"Teg was my father."

"Such delicacy! A Reverend Mother has qualms about imprinting the ghola of Mother Superior's father!"

"She was my personal student, Bell. She has concerns for me you could not feel. Besides, this is not just a ghola, this is a child."

"We must be certain of her!"

Odrade saw the name form on Bellonda's lips but it remained unspoken. *"Jessica."*

Another flawed Reverend Mother? Bell was right, they must be sure of Sheeana. *My responsibility.* A vision of Sheeana's black sculpture flickered in Odrade's awareness.

"Idaho's plan has some attraction, but . . ." Bellonda hesitated.

Odrade spoke up: "This is a very young child, growth incomplete. Pain of the usual memory restoration could approach the Agony. It might alienate him. But this . . ."

"Control him with an Imprinter, that part I approve. But what if it doesn't restore his memories?"

"We still have the original plan. And it *did* have that effect on Idaho."

"Different for him but the decision can wait. You're late for your meeting with Scytale."

Odrade hefted the crystal. "Daily summation?"

"Nothing you haven't seen too many times already." From Bell, that was almost a note of concern.

"I'll bring him back here. Have Tam waiting and you come in later on some pretext."

Scytale had become almost accustomed to these walks outside the ship and Odrade observed this in his casual manner when they emerged from her transporter south of Central.

It was more than a stroll and they both knew it but she had made these excursions regular, designing repetition to lull him. *Routine. So useful on occasion.*

"Kind of you to take me for these walks," Scytale said, looking up sideways. "The air is drier than I recall it. Where do we go this evening?"

How tiny his eyes when he squinted against the sun.

"To my workroom." She nodded at outbuildings of Central about half a klick north. It was cold under a cloudless spring sky and warm colours of roofs, lights coming on in her tower, beckoned with promise of relief from a chilling wind that accompanied almost every sunset these days.

With peripheral attention, Odrade watched the Tleilaxu beside her carefully. Such tension! She could feel this also in guardian Reverend Mothers and acolytes close behind them, all charged to special watchfulness by Bellonda.

We need this little monster and he knows it. And we still don't know the extent of Tleilaxu abilities! What talents has he accumulated? Why does he probe with such evident casualness for contact with his fellow prisoners?

Tleilaxu made the Idaho ghola, she reminded herself. Did they hide secret things in him?

Odrade found Scytale vaguely repulsive. *Why did they choose to be so grey? Genetic knowledge could have given them a far more acceptable appearance. It was deliberate. They want to stir up antique fears.*

"I am a beggar come to your door, Mother Superior," he said in that whining elfin voice. "Our planets in ruins, my people slain. Why do we go to your quarters?"

"To bargain in more pleasant surroundings."

"Yes, it is very confining in the ship. But I do not understand why we always leave the car so far away from Central. Why do we walk?"

"I find it refreshing."

Scytale glanced around him at the plantings. "Pleasant, but quite cold, don't you think?"

Odrade glanced to the south. These southern slopes were planted to grapes, crests and colder northern faces reserved for orchards. Improved vinifera, these vineyards. Developed by Bene Gesserit gardeners. Old vines, roots "gone down to hell" where (according to ancient superstition) they stole water from burning souls. The winery was underground, as were storage and ageing caves. Nothing to mar a landscape of tended vines in orderly rows, plantings just far enough apart for pickers and tilling equipment.

Pleasant to him? She doubted Scytale saw anything pleasing here. He was properly nervous as she wanted him to be, asking himself: *Why does she really choose to walk me through these rustic surroundings?*

It galled Odrade that they dared not employ more powerful Bene Gesserit persuasives on this little man. But she agreed with advice that said if those efforts failed, they would not get a second chance. Tleilaxu had demonstrated they would die rather than give up secret (and sacred) knowledge.

"Several things puzzle me," Odrade said, picking her way around a pile of vine trimmings as she spoke. "Why do you insist on having your own Face Dancers *before* acceding to our requests? And what is this interest in Duncan Idaho?"

"Dear lady, I have no companions in my loneliness. That

answers both questions." He rubbed absently at his breast where the nullentropy capsule lay concealed.

Why does he rub himself there so frequently? It was a gesture she and analysts had puzzled over. *No scar, no skin inflammation. Perhaps merely a carryover from childhood. But that was so long ago! A flaw in this reincarnation?* No one could say. And that grey skin carried a metallic pigmentation that resisted probing instruments. He was sure to have been sensitized to heavier rays and would know those were used. No . . . now, it was all diplomacy. *Damn this little monster!*

Scytale wondered: Did this powindah female have no natural sympathies on which he could play? *Typicals* were ambivalent on that question.

"The Wekht of Jandola is no more," he said. "Billions of us slain by those whores. To the farthest reaches of the Yaghist, we are destroyed and only I remain."

Yaghist, she thought. *Land of the unruled.* It was a revealing word in Islamiyat, the Bene Tleilax language.

In that language, she said: "The magic of our God is our only bridge."

Once more she claimed to share his Great Belief, the Sufi-Zensunni ecumenism that had spawned the Bene Tleilax. She spoke the language flawlessly, knew the proper words, but he saw falsehoods. *She calls God's Messenger "Tyrant" and disobeys the most basic precepts!*

Where did these women meet in kehl to feel the presence of God? If they truly spoke the Language of God, they would already know what they sought from him with crude bargaining.

As they climbed the last slope to the paved landing at Central, Scytale called on God for help. *The Bene Tleilax come to this! Why have You put this trial upon us? We are the last legalists of the Shariat and I, the last Master of my people, must seek answers from You, God, when You no longer can speak to me in kehl.*

Once more in flawless Islamiyat, Odrade said: "You were betrayed by your own people, ones you sent into the Scattering. You have no more Malik brothers, only sisters."

Then where is your sagra chamber, powindah deceiver?

Where is a deep and windowless place only brothers may enter?

"This is a new thing for me," he said. "Malik Sisters? Those two words have always been self negating. Sisters cannot be Malik."

"Waff, your late Mahai and Abdl, had trouble with that. And he led your people almost to extinction."

"Almost? You know of survivors?" He could not keep excitement from his voice.

"No Masters . . . but we hear of a few Domel and all in Honoured Matre hands."

She paused where the edge of a building would cut off their view of the setting sun in the next steps and, still in the secret language of the Tleilaxu, said: "The sun is not God."

The dawn and sunset cry of the Mahai!

Scytale felt faith wavering as he followed her into an arched passage between two squat buildings. Her words were proper but only the Mahai and Abdl should utter them. In the shadowy passage, footsteps of their escort close behind, Odrade confounded him by saying: "Why did you not say the proper words? Are you not the last Master? Does that not make you Mahai and Abdl?"

"I was not chosen so by Malik brothers." It sounded weak even to him.

Odrade summoned a liftfield and paused at the tubeslot. In Other Memory detail, she found kehl and its right of ghufran familiar—words whispered in the night by lovers of long-dead women. "And then we . . ." "And so if we speak these sacred words . . ." *Ghufran!* Acceptance and readmission of one who had ventured among powindah, the returned one begging pardon for contact with unimaginable sins of aliens. *The Masheikh have met in kehl and felt the presence of their God!*

The tubeslot opened. Odrade motioned Scytale and two guards ahead. As he passed, she thought: *Something must give soon. We cannot play our little game to the end he desires.*

Tamalane stood at the bow window, her back to the door, when Odrade and Scytale entered the workroom. Sunset light slanted sharply across rooftops. The brilliance vanished then and left behind it a sense of contrast, the night darker because of that last glow along the horizon.

In the milky gloom, Odrade waved the guards away, noting their reluctance. Bellonda had charged them to stay, obviously, but they would not disobey Mother Superior. She indicated a chairdog across from her and waited for him to sit. He looked back suspiciously at Tamalane before sinking into the 'dog but covered it by saying: "Why are there no lights?"

"This is a relaxing interlude," she said. *And I know darkness worries you!*

She stood a moment behind her table, identifying bright patches in the gloom, a lustre of artifacts placed around her to make this her setting: the bust of long-dead Chenoeh in its niche beside the window, and there on the wall at her right, a pastoral landscape from the first human migrations into space, a stack of ridulian crystals on the table and a silvery reflection off her lightscribe concentrating faint illumination from the windows.

He has roasted long enough.

She touched a plate on her console. Glowglobes set strategically around walls and ceiling came to life. Tamalane turned on cue, her robe swishing deliberately. She stood two paces behind Scytale, the very picture of ominous Bene Gesserit mystery.

Scytale twitched slightly at Tamalane's movement but now he sat quietly. The chairdog was somewhat too large for him and he looked almost childlike there.

Odrade said, "Sisters who rescued you say you commanded a no-ship at Junction preparing for the first Foldspace leap when Honoured Matres attacked. You were coming to your ship in a one-man skitter, they said, and veered away just before the explosions. You detected the attackers?"

"Yes." Reluctance in his voice.

"And knew they might locate the no-ship from your trajectory. So you fled, leaving your brothers to be destroyed."

He spoke with the utter bitterness of a tragic witness: "Earlier, when we were outbound from Tleilax, we saw that attack begin. Our explosions to destroy everything of value to attackers and the burners from space created a holocaust. We fled then, too."

"But not directly to Junction."

"Everywhere we searched, they had been before us. They had the ashes but I had our secrets." *Remind her that I still have something of value to trade!* He tapped a finger against his head.

"You sought Guild or CHOAM sanctuary at Junction," she said. "How fortunate our spy ship was there to scoop you up before the enemy could react."

"Sister . . ." How difficult that word! ". . . if you truly are my sister in kehl, why will you not provide me with Face Dancer servants?"

"Still too many secrets between us, Scytale. Why, for instance, were you leaving Bandalong when attackers came?"

Bandalong!

Naming the great Tleilax city constricted his chest and he thought he felt the nullentropy capsule pulse, as though it sought release for its precious contents. *Lost Bandalong. Never again to see the city of carnelian skies, never to feel the presence of brothers, of patient Domel and . . .*

"Are you ill?" Odrade asked.

"I am sick with what I have lost!" He heard fabric slither behind him and sensed Tamalane closer. How oppressive it was in this place! "Why is she behind me?"

"I am the servant of my sisters and she is here to observe us both."

"You've taken some of my cells, haven't you? You're growing a replacement Scytale in your tanks!"

"Of course we are. You don't think Sisters would let the last Master end here, do you?"

"No ghola of me will do anything I would not!" *And it will carry no nullentropy tube!*

"We know." *But what is it we do not know?*

"This is not bargaining," he complained.

"You misjudge me, Scytale. We know when you lie and when you conceal. We employ senses others do not."

It was true! They detected things from odours of his body, from small movements of muscles, expressions he could not suppress.

Sisters? These creatures are powindah! All of them!

"You were on lashkar," Odrade prodded.

Lashkar! How he wished he were *here* on lashkar. Face Dancer warriors, Domel assistants—eliminating this abominable evil! But he dared not lie. The one behind him probably was a Truthsayer. Experience in many lives told him Bene Gesserit Truthsayers were the best.

"I commanded a force of khasadars. We sought a herd of Futars for our defence."

Herd? Did Tleilaxu know something of Futars not revealed to the Sisterhood?

"You went prepared for violence. Did Honoured Matres learn of your mission and cut you off? I think it likely."

"Why do you call them Honoured Matres?" His voice lapsed almost into a screech.

"Because that is what they call themselves." *Very calm now. Let him stew in his own mistakes.*

She is right! We were betrayed. Bitter thought. He held it close, wondering how he should reply. *A small revelation? There is never a small revelation with these women.*

A sigh shook his breast. The nullentropy capsule and its contents. His most important concern. *Anything* to get him access to his own axolotl tanks.

"Descendants of people we sent into the Scattering returned with captive Futars. A mingling of human and cat, as you doubtless know. But they did not reproduce in our tanks. And before we could determine why, the ones brought to us died." *The betrayers brought us only two! We should have suspected.*

"They didn't bring you very many Futars, did they? You should have suspected they were bait."

See? That is what they do with small revelations!

"Why did the Futars not hunt and kill Honoured Matres on Gammu?" It was Duncan's question and deserved an answer.

"We were told no orders were given. They do not kill without orders." *She knows this. She is testing me.*

"Face Dancers also kill on order," she said. "They would even kill you if you ordered it. Not so?"

"That order is reserved for keeping our secrets from the hands of enemies."

"Is that why you want your own Face Dancers? Do you consider us enemies?"

Before he could compose a response, Bellonda's projected figure appeared above the table, lifesize and partly translucent, dancing crystals of Archives behind her. "Urgent from Sheeana!" Bellonda said. "The spice blow has occurred. Sandworms!" The figure turned and looked at Scytale, comeyes perfectly coordinating her movements. "So you have lost a bargaining chip, Master Scytale! We have our spice at last!" The projected figure vanished with an audible *click* and a faint smell of ozone.

"You're trying to trick me!" he blurted.

But the door at Odrade's left opened. Sheeana entered towing a small suspensor pod no more than two metres long. Its transparent sides repeated the glowglobes of the workroom in tiny bursts of yellow light. Something squirmed in the pod!

Sheeana stood aside without speaking, giving them a full view of the contents. So small! The worm was less than half the length of its container but perfect in every detail, stretched out there on a shallow bed of golden sand.

Scytale could not contain a gasp of awe. The Prophet!

Odrade's reaction was pragmatic. She bent close to the pod, peering into the miniature mouth. The scorching huff-huff of a great worm's internal fires reduced to this? What a tiny mimicry!

Crystal teeth flashed as it lifted its front segments.

The worm sent its mouth questing left and right. They all saw behind the teeth the miniature fire of its alien chemistry.

"Thousands of them," Sheeana said. "They came to a spice blow as they always do."

Odrade remained silent. *We have done it!* But this was Sheeana's moment of triumph. Let her make the most of it. Scytale had never looked this defeated.

Sheeana opened the pod and lifted the worm from it, cradling it as though it were an infant. It lay quiescent in her arms.

Odrade took a deep, satisfied breath. *She still controls them.*

"Scytale," Odrade said.

He could not take his gaze from the worm.

"Do you still serve the Prophet?" Odrade asked. "There he is!"

291

He did not know how to respond. Truly a revenant of the Prophet? He wanted to deny his first awed response but his eyes would not permit it.

Odrade spoke softly. "While you were out on your foolish mission, your *selfish* mission! we were serving the Prophet! We rescued his last revenant and brought him here. Chapter House will become another Dune!"

She sat back and steepled her hands in front of her. Bell was watching through the comeyes, of course. A Mentat's observations would be valuable. Odrade wished Idaho were also watching. But he could look at a holo. It was clear to her that Scytale had seen the Bene Gesserit only as tools for restoration of his precious Tleilaxu civilization. Would this development force him to reveal inner secrets of his tanks? What would he offer?

"I must have time to think." A tremor in his voice.

"About what would you think?"

He did not answer but kept his attention on Sheeana who was replacing the tiny worm in its pod. She stroked it once before sealing the lid.

"Tell me, Scytale," Odrade insisted. "How can there be anything for you to reconsider? This is our Prophet! You say you serve the Great Belief. Then serve it!"

She could see his dreams dissolving. *His own Face Dancers to print memories of those they killed, copying each victim's shape and manner.* He had never hoped to gull a Reverend Mother . . . but acolytes and simple workers of Chapter House . . . all the secrets he had hoped to acquire, gone! Lost as certainly as the charred husks of Tleilaxu planets.

Our *Prophet,* she said. He turned a stricken look toward Odrade but did not focus. *What am I to do? These women no longer need me. But I need them!*

"Scytale." How softly she spoke. "The Great Convention is ended. It's a new universe out there."

He tried to swallow in a dry throat. Why did she speak of the Great Convention? He knew the whole concept of violence had taken on a new dimension. In the Old Empire, the Convention had guaranteed retaliation against anyone who dared burn an enemy planet by attacking from space. Political motivations might have tempted foolhardy ones . . . But when that would bring retaliation by massed forces of your peers? No-ships and whores from the Scattering had changed that irretrievably.

"Escalated violence, Scytale." Odrade's voice was almost a whisper. "We *Scatter* pods of rage."

He focused on her. *What is she saying?*

"The hatred being stored up against Honoured Matres," she said. *You are not the only one with losses, Scytale. Once, when problems arose in our civilization, the cry went out: "Bring a Reverend Mother!" Honoured Matres prevent that. And the myths are recomposed. Golden light is cast upon our past. "It was better in the old days when Bene Gesserits could help us. Where do you go for reliable Truthsayers these days? Arbitration? These Honoured Matres have never heard the word! They were always courteous, the Reverend Mothers. You have to say that for them."*

When Scytale did not respond, she said: "Think of what might happen if that rage were loosed in a Jihad!"

When he still did not speak, she said: "You have seen it. Tleilaxu, Bene Gesserit, priests of the Divided God and who knows how many more—all hunted like wild game."

"They cannot kill us all!" An agonized cry.

"Can't they? Your Scattered ones made common cause with Honoured Matres. Is that a sanctuary you would seek in the Scattering?"

And there goes another dream: Little pods of Tleilaxu, persistent as festering sores, awaiting the day of Scytale's Great Revival.

"People grow strong under oppression," he said, but there was no force in his words. "Even the Priests of Rakis are finding holes in which to hide!" Desperate words.

"Who says this? Some of your returned *friends*?"

His silence was all the answer she needed.

"Bene Tleilax have killed Honoured Matres and they know it," she said, hammering at him. "They will be satisfied only with your extermination."

"And yours!"

"We are partners by necessity if not by shared belief." She

said it in purest Islamiyat and saw hope leap into his eyes. *Kehl and Shariat may yet take on their old meanings among people who compose their thoughts in the Language of God.*

"Partners?" Faint and extremely tentative.

She adopted new bluntness. "In some ways, that's a more reliable basis for common action than any other. Each of us knows what the other wants. An intrinsic design: Screen everything through that and something reliable can occur."

"And what is it you want from me?"

"You already know."

"How to make the finest tanks, yes." He shook his head, obviously unsure. The changes implied by her demands!

Odrade wondered if she dared snap at him in open anger. How dense he was! But he was close to panic. Old values had changed. Honoured Matres were not the only source of turmoil. Scytale did not even know the extent of changes that had infected his own Scattered Ones!

"Times are changing," Odrade said.

Change, what a disturbing word, he thought.

"I must have my own Face Dancer attendants! And my own tanks?" Almost begging.

"My Council and I will consider it."

"What is there to consider?" throwing her own words at her.

"You need only your own approval. I require approval of others." She gave him a grim smile. "So you do get time to think." Odrade nodded to Tamalane who summoned guards.

"Back to the no-ship?" He spoke from the doorway, such a diminutive figure amidst burly guards.

"But tonight you ride all the way."

He gave a last lingering stare at the worm as he left.

When Scytale and guards were gone, Sheeana said: "You were right not to press him. He was ready to panic."

Bellonda entered. "Perhaps it would be best just to kill him."

"Bell! Get the holo and go through our meeting again. This time as a Mentat!"

That stopped her.

Tamalane chuckled.

"You take too much joy in your sister's discomfiture, Tam," Sheeana said.

Tamalane shrugged but Odrade was delighted. *No more teasing of Bell?*

"When you spoke of Chapter House becoming another Dune, that was when he began to panic," Bellonda said, her voice Mentat distant.

Odrade had seen the reaction but had not yet made the association. This was a Mentat's value: patterns and systems, building blocks. Bell sensed a pattern to Scytale's behaviour.

"I ask myself: Is it the thing become real once more?" Bellonda said.

Odrade saw it at once. An odd thing about lost places. As long as Dune had been a known and living planet, there existed an historical firmness about its presence in the Galactic Register. You could point to a projection and say: "That is Dune. Once called Arrakis and latterly, Rakis. Dune for its total desert character in Muad'Dib's day."

Destroy the place, though, and a mythological patina inveighed against projected *reality*. In time, such places became totally mythic. *Arthur and his Round Table. Camelot where it only rains at night. Pretty good Weather Control for those days!*

But now, a new Dune had appeared.

"Myth power," Tamalane said.

Ahhhh, yes. Tam, close to her final departure from flesh, would be more sensitive to workings of myths. Mystery and secrecy, tools of the Missionaria, had been used also on Dune by Muad'Dib and the Tyrant. The seeds were planted. Even with priests of the Divided God gone to their own perdition, myths of Dune proliferated.

"Melange," Tamalane said.

The other sisters in the workroom knew immediately what she meant. New hope could be injected into the Bene Gesserit Scattering.

Bellonda said: "Why do they want us dead and not captives? That has always puzzled me."

Honoured Matres might not want *any* Bene Gesserits alive . . . only the spice knowledge perhaps. But they destroyed Dune. They destroyed the Tleilaxu. It was a cautioning thought to take into any confrontation with the Spider Queen—should Dortujla succeed.

"No useful hostages?" Bellonda asked.

Odrade saw the looks on the faces of her sisters. They were following on a single track as though all of them thought with one mind. Object lessons by Honoured Matres, leaving few survivors, only made potential opposition more cautious. It invoked a rule of silence within which bitter memories became bitter myths. Honoured Matres were like barbarians in any age: Blood instead of hostages. Strike with random viciousness.

"The Folk say every brutalized victim creates two more enemies." Bellonda again.

Even silent foes of barbarians would cheer when they could or would be dumb when asked by Honoured Matres to supply information about the hunted. Victims and potential victims would not see things Honoured Matres needed to know. *Respond with massive ignorance when that is your only weapon.* Silence was a sharp sword when forged by brutality.

This was common cant for Reverend Mothers, kept alive by first-hand history.

"Dar's right," Tamalane said. "We've been seeking allies too close to home."

"Futars did not create themselves," Sheeana said.

"The ones who created them hope to control us," Bellonda said. There was the clear sound of Prime Projection in her voice. "That's the hesitation Dortujla heard in the Handlers."

There it was and they faced it with all of its perils. It came down to people (as it always did). People—contemporaries. You learned valuable things from people living in your own time and from knowledge they carried out of their pasts. Other Memory was not the only conveyance of history.

Odrade felt that she had come home after a long absence. There was a familiarity about the way all four of them were thinking now. It was a familiarity that transcended place. The Sisterhood itself was Home. Not where they lodged in transient housing but the association.

Bellonda voiced it for them. "I fear we have been working at cross purposes."

"Fear does that," Sheeana said.

Odrade dared not smile. It could be misinterpreted and she did not want to explain. *Give us Murbella as a sister and a restored Bashar! Then we might have our fighting chance!*

Right there with that good feeling in her, the message signal clicked. She glanced at the projection surface, a pure reflex, and recognized crisis. Such a small thing (relatively) to precipitate crisis. Clairby mortally injured in a 'thopter crash. Mortal unless . . . The unless was spelled out for her and it added up to cyborg. Her companions saw the message in reverse but you got good at reading mirrored information in here. They knew.

Where do we draw the line?

Bellonda with her antique spectacles when she could have had artificial eyes or any of numerous other prosthetics, voted with her body. *This is what it means to be human. Try to hold on to youth and it mocks you while it sprints away. Melange is enough . . . and perhaps too much.*

Odrade recognized what her own emotions were telling her. But what of Bene Gesserit necessity? Bell could lodge her individual vote and everyone recognized it, even respected it. But Mother Superior's vote carried the Sisterhood with her.

First the axolotl tanks and now this.

Necessity said they could not afford to lose specialists of Clairby's calibre. They had few enough as it was. "Spread thin" did not describe it. Gaps were appearing. Cyborg Clairby, though, and that was the opening wedge.

The Suks were prepared. "A precautionary arrangement" should it be required for someone irreplaceable. *Such as Mother Superior?* Odrade knew she had approved that with her usual cautious reservations. Where were those reservations now?

Cyborg was one of those potpourri words, too. Where did mechanical additions to human flesh become dominant? When was the Cyborg no longer human? Temptations intensified—"Just this one little adjustment." And so easy to *adjust* until the potpourri-human became unquestioningly obedient.

But . . . Clairby?

Conditions of extremis said, "Cyborg him!" Was the

Sisterhood that desperate? She was forced to answer in the affirmative.

There it was then—decision not entirely out of her hands, but the ready excuse at hand. *Necessity dictates it.*

The Butlerian Jihad had left its indelible mark on humans. Fought and won . . . for then. And here was another battle in that long-ago conflict.

She thought of the prosthetics that would be brought into service—Ixian, some of them, and others the products of Bene Gesserit Suks. This was not a new battlefield in human affairs. Ix had been offering its opulent prosthetic services for eons. The very rich were always trying to buy "a few more years . . . months . . . days . . . hours . . . minutes . . . seconds . . ."

Just one more orgasmic bang!

But now, survival of the Sisterhood was in the balance. How many technical specialists remained on Chapter House? She knew the answer without looking. Not enough.

Odrade leaned forward and keyed for transmit. "Cyborg him," she said.

Bellonda grunted. *Approval or disapproval?* She would never say. This was Mother Superior's arena and welcome to it!

Who won this battle? Odrade wondered.

> We walk a delicate line, perpetuating Atreides (Siona) genes
> in our population because that hides us from prescience. We
> carry the kwisatz haderach in that bag! Wilfulness created
> Muad'Dib. Prophets make predictions come true! Will we
> ever again dare ignore our Tao sense and cater to a culture
> that hates chance and begs for prophecy?
>
> —Archival Summary (adixto)

It was just after dawn when Odrade arrived at the no-ship but Murbella was up and working with a training mek when Mother Superior strode onto the practice floor.

Odrade had walked the last klick through ring orchards around the spacefield. Night's limited clouds had thinned at the approach of dawn, then dissipated to reveal a sky thick with stars.

She recognized a delicate weather shift to wrench another crop from this region but decreasing rainfall was barely enough to keep orchards and pastures alive.

As she walked, Odrade was overcome by dreariness. Winter just past had been a hard-bought silence between storms. Life was holocaust. Dusting of pollen by eager insects, fruiting and seeding that followed the flower. These orchards were a secret storm whose power lay hidden in torrential flows of life. But ohhh! the destruction. New life carried change. The Changer was coming, always different. Sandworms would bring the desert purity of ancient Dune.

The desolation of that transforming power invaded her imagination. She could picture this landscape reduced to windswept dunes, habitat for Leto II's descendants.

And the arts of Chapter House would undergo mutation—one civilization's myths replaced by another's.

The aura of these thoughts went with Odrade on to the practice floor and coloured her mood as she watched Murbella complete a round of flashing exertion, then step back, panting.

A thin scratch reddened the back of Murbella's left hand where she had missed a move by the big mek. The automated trainer stood there in the centre of the room like a golden pillar, its weapons flicking in and out—probing mandibles of an angry insect.

Murbella wore tight green leotards and her exposed skin glistened with perspiration. Even with the prominent mounding of her pregnancy, she appeared graceful. Her skin glowed with health. It came from within, Odrade decided, partly the pregnancy but something more fundamental as well. This had impressed itself on Odrade at their first encounter, a thing Lucilla had remarked after capturing Murbella and rescuing Idaho from Gammu. Health lived below the surface in her, there like a lens to focus attention on a deep freshet of vitality.

We must have her!

Murbella saw the visitor but refused to be interrupted.

Not yet, Mother Superior. My baby is due soon but this body's needs will continue.

Odrade saw then that the mek was simulating anger, a programmed response brought on by frustration of its circuitry. An extremely dangerous mode!

"Good morning, Mother Superior."

Murbella's voice came out modulated by her exertions as she dodged and twisted with that almost blinding speed she commanded.

The mek slashed and probed for her, its sensors darting and whirring in attempts to follow her movements.

Odrade sniffed. To speak at such a time amplified the peril of the mek. Risk no distractions when you played this dangerous game. *Enough!*

The mek's controls were in a large green wall panel to the right of the doorway. Murbella's changes could be seen in the circuits—dangling wires, beamfields with memory crystals dislocated. Odrade reached up and stilled the mechanism.

Murbella turned to face her.

"Why did you change the circuitry?" Odrade demanded.

"For the anger."

"Is that what Honoured Matres do?"

"As the twig is bent?" Murbella massaged her wounded hand. "But what if the twig knows how it is bent and approves?"

Odrade felt sudden excitement. "Approves? Why?"

"Because there's something . . . grand about it."

"You follow your adrenalin high?"

"You know it's not that!" Murbella's breathing returned to normal. She stood glaring at Odrade.

"Then what is it?"

"It's . . . being challenged to do more than you ever thought possible. You never suspected you could be this . . . this good, this expert and accomplished at anything."

Odrade concealed elation.

Mens sana corpus sanum. We have her at last!

Odrade said: "But what a price you pay!"

"Price?" Murbella sounded astonished. "As long as I have the capacity, I'm delighted to pay."

"Take what you want and pay for it?"

"It's your Bene Gesserit magic cornucopia: As I become

300

. . . .

increasingly accomplished, my ability to pay increases."

"Beware, Murbella. That cornucopia, as you call it, can become Pandora's box."

Murbella knew the allusion. She stood quite still, her attention fixed on Mother Superior. "Oh?" The sound barely escaped.

"Pandora's box releases powerful distractions that waste energies of your life. You speak glibly of being 'in the chute' and becoming a Reverend Mother but you still don't know what that means nor what we want from you."

"Then it was never our sexual abilities you wanted."

Odrade moved eight paces forward, majestically deliberate. Once Murbella got on that subject there would be no stopping her short of the usual resolution—argument cut short by Mother Superior's peremptory command.

"Sheeana easily mastered your abilities," Odrade said.

"So you *will* use her on that child!"

Odrade heard displeasure. It was a cultural residue. When did human sexuality begin? Sheeana, waiting now in the no-ship guard chambers, had been forced to deal with it. *"I hope you recognize the source of my reluctance and why I was so secretive, Mother Superior."*

"I recognize that a Fremen society filled your mind with inhibitions before we took you in hand!"

That had cleared the air between them. But how was this exchange with Murbella to be redirected? *I must let it run while I seek a way out.*

There would be repetition and unresolved issues would emerge. The fact that almost every word Murbella uttered could be anticipated, that would be a trial.

"Why do you evade this tested way of dominating others now that you say you need it with Teg?" Murbella asked.

"Slaves, is that what you want?" Odrade countered.

Eyes almost closed, Murbella considered this. *Did I consider the men our slaves? Perhaps. I produced in them periods of wildly unthinking abandon, a giving up to heights of ecstasy they had never dreamed possible. I was trained to give them that and, thereby, make them subject to our control.*

Until Duncan did the same to me.

301

Odrade saw the hooding of Murbella's eyes and recognized there were things in this woman's psyche twisted in a way difficult to uncover. *Wildness running where we have not followed.* It was as though Murbella's original clarity had been stained indelibly and then that mark covered over and even this cover masked. There was a harshness in her that distorted thoughts and actions. Layer upon layer upon layer . . .

"You're afraid of what I can do," Murbella said.

"There's truth in what you say," Odrade agreed.

Honesty and candour—limited tools now to be used with care.

"Duncan." Murbella's voice came out flat with new Bene Gesserit abilities.

"I fear what you share with him. You find it odd, Mother Superior admitting fear?"

"I know about candour and honesty!" She made candour and honesty sound repellent.

"Reverend Mothers are taught never to abandon self. We are trained not to encumber ourselves that way with concerns of others."

"Is that all of it?"

"It goes deeper and has other threads. Being Bene Gesserit marks you in its own ways."

"I know what you're asking: Choose Duncan or the Sisterhood? I know your tricks."

"I think not."

"There are things I won't do!"

"Each of us is constrained by a past. I make my choices, do what I must because my past is different from yours."

"You'll continue to train me despite what I've just said?"

Odrade heard this in the total receptivity these encounters with Murbella demanded, every sense alerted to things not spoken, messages that hovered on edges of words as though they were cilia wavering there, reaching for contact with a dangerous universe.

The Bene Gesserit must change its ways. And here is one who could guide us into change.

Bellonda would be horrified at the prospect. Many sisters would reject it. But there it was.

302

When Odrade remained silent, Murbella said: "Trained. Is that the proper word?"

"Conditioned. That's probably more familiar to you."

"What you really want is to conjoin our experiences, make me sufficiently like you that we can create trust between us. That's what all education does."

Don't play erudite games with me, girl!

"We would flow in the same stream, eh, Murbella?"

Any third-stage acolyte would have become watchfully cautious hearing that tone from Mother Superior. Murbella appeared unmoved. "Except that I will not give him up."

"That is for you to decide."

"Did you let the Lady Jessica decide?"

The way out of this cul de sac at last.

Duncan had prompted Murbella to study Jessica's life. *Hoping to thwart us!* Holos of his performance had ignited severe analysis of records.

"An interesting person," Odrade said.

"Love! After all of your teaching, your *conditioning!*"

"You did not think her behaviour treasonous?"

"Never!"

Delicately now. "But look at consequences: a kwisatz haderach . . . and that grandchild, the Tyrant!" *Argument dear to Bellonda's heart.*

"Golden Path," Murbella said. "Survival of humankind."

"Famine Times and the Scattering."

Are you watching this, Bell? No matter. You will watch it.

"Honoured Matres!" Murbella said.

"All because of Jessica?" Odrade asked. "But Jessica returned to the fold and lived out her years on Caladan."

"Teacher of acolytes!"

"Example to them, as well. See what happens when you defy us?" *Defy us, Murbella! Do it more adroitly than Jessica.*

"Sometimes you repel me!" Natural honesty forced her to add: "But you know I want what you have."

What we have.

Odrade recalled her own first encounters with Bene Gesserit attractions. Everything of the body done with exquisite precision, senses honed to detect smallest details, muscles trained to perform in marvellous exactitude. These abilities in an Honoured Matre could only add a new dimension amplified by bodily speed.

"You're throwing it back on me," Murbella said. "Trying to force my choice when you already know it."

Odrade remained silent. This was a form of argument ancient Jesuits had almost perfected. Simulflow superimposed disputational patterns: Let Murbella do her own convincing. Supply only the most subtle of nudges. Give her small excuses upon which to enlarge.

But hold fast, Murbella, to love for Duncan!

"You're very clever at parading your Sisterhood's advantages past me," Murbella said.

"We are not a cafeteria line!"

An insouciant grin flicked Murbella's mouth. "I'll take one of those and one of these and I think I'd like one of those creamy things over there."

Odrade enjoyed the metaphor but omnipresent watchers had their own appetites. "A diet that might kill you."

"But I see your offerings displayed so attractively. Voice! What a marvellous thing you've cooked up there. I have this wonderful instrument in my throat and you can teach me to play it in that ultimate way."

"Now, you're a concert master."

"I want your ability to influence those around me!"

"To what end, Murbella? For whose goals?"

"If I eat what you eat, will I grow into your kind of toughness: plasteel on the outside and even harder inside?"

"Is that how you see me?"

"The chef at my banquet! And I must eat whatever you bring—for my good and for yours."

She sounded almost manic. An odd person. Sometimes she appeared to be the most wretched of women, pacing her quarters like a caged beast. That mad look in her eyes, orange flecks in the corneas . . . as there were now.

"Do you still refuse to *work on* Scytale?"

"Let Sheeana do it."

"Will you coach her?"

"And she will use my coaching on the child!"

304

They stared at each other, realizing they shared a similar thought. *This is not confrontation because each of us wants the other.*

They were in a dance, a pavane with formal structure that neither could change. Within the structure, they were forced to improvise steps. It was like a confined reproduction of wildly unrhythmic Rakian dances, the basis for Sheeana's control of the worms. Structure limited the things that could be said and ever the excuse: *"I might like to tell you other things but that is not permitted."*

"Limited communication," Odrade said.

Murbella thought this might be taken out of its limits but then they would be into another kind of bargaining, an excursion in places where the Bene Gesserit excelled. *They always find a way.*

Dirty hands, Odrade thought. *That is what she fears. Our dirt on her conscience.* It was an excellent limb on to which they could graft Bene Gesserit morality

"I am committed to you for what you can give me," Murbella said, her voice low. "But you want to know if I may ever act against that commitment?"

"Could you?"

"No more than you could if circumstances demanded it."

"Do you think you will ever regret your decision?"

"Of course I will!" What kind of damnfool question was that? People always had regrets. Murbella said this.

"Just confirming your self honesty. We like it that you don't fly under false colours."

"You get false ones?"

"Indeed."

"You must have ways of weeding them out."

"The Agony does that for us. Falsehoods don't come through the Spice."

Odrade sensed Murbella's drumbeat flickering faster.

"And you're not going to demand I give up Duncan?" Very spiny.

"That attachment presents difficulties, but they are your difficulties."

"Another way of asking me to give him up?"

"Accept the possibility, that is all."

"I can't."

"You won't?"

"I mean what I say. I'm incapable."

"And if someone showed you how?"

Murbella stared into Odrade's eyes for a long beat, then: "I almost said that would set me free . . . but . . ."

"Yes?"

"I could not be free while he was bound to me."

"Is that renunciation of Honoured Matre ways?"

"Renunciation? Wrong word. I've merely grown beyond my former sisters."

"Former sisters?"

"Still my sisters, but they're sisters of childhood. Some I remember fondly, some I dislike intensely. Playmates in a game that no longer interests me."

"That decision satisfies you?"

"Are you satisfied, Mother Superior?"

Odrade clapped her hands with unrestrained elation. How swiftly Murbella acquired Bene Gesserit riposte!

"Satisfied? What a hellishly deadly word!"

As Odrade spoke, Murbella felt herself move as in a dream to the edge of an abyss, unable to awaken and prevent the plunge. Her stomach ached with secret emptiness and Odrade's next words came from echoing distance.

"The Bene Gesserit is all to a Reverend Mother. You will never be able to forget that."

As quickly as it had come, the dream sensation passed. Mother Superior's next words were cold and immediate.

"Prepare for absences from the ship soon after your baby is born. We will take you out more often for advanced training."

"Under guard, of course."

"For now." *Until you meet the Agony—live or die.*

Odrade lifted her gaze to the ceiling comeyes. "Send Sheeana in here. She begins at once with her new teacher."

"So you're going to do it! You're going to *work on* that child."

"Think of him as Bashar Teg," Odrade said. "That helps." *And we're not giving you time to reconsider.*

"I didn't resist Duncan and I can't argue with you."

"Don't even argue with yourself, Murbella. Pointless. Teg was my father and still I must do this."

Until that moment, Murbella had not realized the force behind Odrade's earlier statement. *The Bene Gesserit is all to a Reverend Mother. Great Dur protect me! Will I be like that?*

> We witness a passing phase of eternity. Important things happen but some people never notice. Accidents intervene. You are not present at episodes. You depend on reports. And people shutter their minds. What good are reports? History in a news account? Preselected at an editorial conference, digested and excreted by prejudice? Accounts you need seldom come from those who make history. Diaries, memoirs and autobiographies are subjective forms of special pleading. Archives are crammed with such suspect stuff.
>
> —Darwi Odrade

Scytale noticed the excitement of guards and others when he reached the barrier at the end of his corridor. Rapid movement of people, especially this early in the day, had attracted him first and sent him to the barrier. There went that Suk doctor, Jalanto. He recognized her from the time Odrade had sent her "because you are looking ill". *Another Reverend Mother to spy on me!*

Ahhhh, Murbella's baby. That was why this rushing around and the Suk.

But who were all those others? Bene Gesserit robes in an abundance he had never before seen here. Not just acolytes. Reverend Mothers outnumbered the others he saw rushing about down there. They reminded him of great carrion birds. There went an acolyte at last, carrying a child on her shoulders. Very mysterious. *If only I had a link to Shipsystems!*

He leaned against a wall and waited but the people vanished into various hatches and doorways. Some destinations he could place with fair certainty, others remained a mystery.

By the Holy Prophet! There went Mother Superior herself! She went through a wider doorway where most of the others had gone.

Useless to ask Odrade when next he saw her. She had him in her trap now.

The Prophet is here and in powindah hands!

He would not accept Bene Gesserit claims to a common devotion. Another of their tricks.

When no more people appeared in the corridor, Scytale returned to his quarters. The Identification monitor at his doorway flickered at his passage but he forced himself not to look at it. *ID is the key.* With his knowledge, this flaw in the Ixian Ship's control system beckoned like a siren.

When I move, they will not give me much time.

It would be an act of desperation with ship and contents hostage. Seconds in which to succeed. Who knew what false panels might have been built, what secret hatches where those awful women could leap out at him. He dared not gamble before exhausting all other avenues. Especially now . . . with the Prophet restored.

Tricky witches. What else did they change in this ship? A disquieting thought. *Does my knowledge still apply?*

The presence of Scytale beyond the barrier had not escaped Odrade's notice but she had other matters to concern her. Murbella's accouchement (she liked the ancient term) had come at an opportune moment. Odrade wanted a distracted Idaho with her for Sheeana's attempt at restoring the Bashar's memories. Idaho was often distracted by thoughts of Murbella. And Murbella obviously could not be with him here, not just now.

Odrade maintained prudent watchfulness in his presence. He was, after all, a Mentat.

She had found him at his console again. As she emerged from the dropchute into the access corridor to his quarters, she heard the clicking of relays and that characteristic buzzing of the comfield and knew immediately where to find him.

He revealed an odd mood when she took him into the observation room where they would monitor Sheeana and the child.

Worry about Murbella? Or about what they would presently see?

The observation room was long and narrow. Three rows of chairs faced the *seewall* common with the secret room where the experiment would occur. The observation area had been left in grey gloom with only two tiny glowglobes at upper corners behind the chairs.

Two Suks were present . . . although Odrade worried that they might be ineffective. Jalanto, the Suk Idaho considered their best, was with Murbella.

Demonstrate our concern. It's real enough.

Slingchairs had been set up along the seewall. An emergency access hatch into the other room was near at hand.

Streggi brought the child down the outer passage where he would not see the watchers and took him into the room. It had been prepared under Murbella's directions: a bedroom, some of his own things brought from his quarters and some things from the rooms shared by Idaho and Murbella.

An animal's cave, Odrade thought. There was a shabbiness about the place that came from the deliberate disarray often found in Idaho's chambers: discarded clothing on a sling chair, sandals in a corner. The sleeping mat was one Idaho and Murbella had used. Inspecting it earlier, Odrade had noted that smell akin to saliva, an intimate sexual odour. That, too, would work unconsciously on Teg.

Here is where the wild things originate, the things we cannot suppress. What daring, to think we can control this. But we must.

As Streggi undressed the boy and left him naked on the mat, Odrade found her pulse quickening. She shifted her chair forward, noticing her Bene Gesserit companions imitate the same hitching motion.

Dear me, she thought. *Are we nothing but voyeurs?*

Such thoughts were necessary at this moment but she felt them demean her. She lost something in that intrusion. Extremely non-Bene Gesserit thinking. But very human!

Duncan had lapsed into a studied air of indifference, an easily recognized pretence. Too much subjectivity in his thoughts for him to function well as a Mentat. And that was precisely how she wanted him now. Participation Mystique. Orgasm as energizer. Bell had recognized it correctly.

To one of three nearby Proctors, all chosen for strength and here ostensibly as observers, Odrade said: "The ghola wants his original memories restored and fears that utterly. That's the major barrier to be sundered."

"Bullcrap!" Idaho said. "You know what we have working for us right now? His mother was one of you and she gave him the deep training. How likely is it she failed to protect him against your Imprinters?"

Odrade turned sharply toward him. *Mentat?* No, he was back in his immediate past, reliving and making comparisons. That reference to Imprinters, though . . . Was that how the first 'sexual collision' with Murbella restored memories of other ghola lifetimes? Deep resistance against Imprinting?

The Proctor Odrade had addressed chose to ignore this impertinent interruption. She had read the Archives material when Bellonda briefed her. All three of them knew they might be called on to kill the ghola child. Did he have powers dangerous to them? The watchers would not know until (or unless) Sheeana succeeded.

To Idaho, Odrade said: "Streggi told him why he is here."

"What did she tell him?" Very peremptory with Mother Superior. The Proctors glared at him.

Odrade held her voice to deliberate mildness. "Streggi told him Sheeana would restore his memories."

"What did he say?"

"Why isn't Duncan Idaho doing it?"

"She answered him honestly?" *Getting some of his own back.*

"Honestly but revealing nothing. Streggi told him Sheeana had a better way. And that you approved."

"Look at him! He isn't even moving. You haven't drugged him, have you?"

Idaho glared back at the Proctors.

"We wouldn't dare. But he is focused inward. You do recall the necessity for that, don't you?"

Idaho sank back into his chair, shoulders slumping.

"Murbella keeps saying: 'He's just a child. He's just a child.' You know we had a fight over it."

"I thought your argument pertinent. The Bashar was not a child. It's the Bashar we're awakening."

He raised crossed fingers. "I hope."

She drew back, looking at the crossed fingers. "I didn't know you were superstitious, Duncan."

"I'd pray to Dur if I thought it would help."

He remembers his own re-awakening pains.

"Don't reveal compassion," he muttered. "Turn it back on him. Keep him focused inward. You want his anger."

Those were words from his own pratique.

Abruptly, he said: "This may be the stupidest thing I ever suggested. I should go and be with Murbella."

"You're in good company, Duncan. And there's nothing you can do for Murbella right now. Look!" As Teg leaped off the mat and stared up at the ceiling comeyes.

"Isn't someone coming to help me?" Teg demanded. More desperation in his voice than predicted for this stage. "Where's Duncan Idaho?"

Odrade put a hand on Idaho's arm as he hitched forward. "Stay where you are, Duncan. You can't help him, either. Not yet."

"Isn't someone going to tell me what to do?" The young voice had a lonely, piping sound. "What're you going to do?"

Sheeana's cue and she entered the room through a hidden hatch behind Teg. "Here I am." She wore only a gossamer robe of pale blue, almost transparent. It clung to her as she strode around to face the boy.

He gawked. This was a Reverend Mother? He had never seen one robed that way. "You're going to give me back my memories?" Doubt and desperation.

"I will help you give them back to yourself." As she spoke, she slipped out of the robe and tossed it aside. It floated to the floor like a great blue butterfly.

Teg stared at her. "What're you doing?"

"What do you think I'm doing?" She sat down beside him and put a hand on his penis.

His head tipped forward as though pushed from behind and he stared at her hand as an erection formed in it.

"Why're you doing that?"

"Don't you know?"

"No!"

"The Bashar would know."

He looked up at her face so close to his. "You know! Why won't you tell me?"

"I'm not your memory!"

"Why're you humming like that?"

She put her lips against his neck. The humming was clear to the watchers. Murbella called it an intensifier, feedback keyed to the sexual response. It grew louder.

"What're you doing?" Almost a shriek as she sat him astraddle of her. She swayed, massaging the small of his back.

"Answer me, damn you!" A definite shriek.

Where did that "damn you!" come from? Odrade wondered.

Sheeana slipped him into her. "Here's your answer!"

His mouth formed a soundless "Ohhhhhhhhhh."

The watchers saw her concentration on Teg's eyes but Sheeana *watched* him with other senses as well.

"Feel the tensing of his thighs, the telltale vagus pulse and especially note the darkening of his nipples. When you have him at that point, sustain it until his pupils dilate."

"Imprinter!" Teg's scream made the watchers jump.

He beat his fists against Sheeana's shoulders. All of them at the seewall observed an inner flickering of his eyes as he twisted back and forth, something new peering out of him.

Odrade was on her feet. "Has something gone wrong?"

Idaho remained in his chair. "What I predicted."

Sheeana thrust Teg away to escape his clawing fingers.

He sprawled to the floor and whirled with a speed that shocked the watchers. Sheeana and Teg confronted each other for several long heartbeats. Slowly, he straightened and only then did he look down at himself. Presently, he lifted his attention to his left arm held in front of him. His gaze went to the ceiling, to each wall in turn. Again, he looked at his body.

"What in the nether hell . . ." Still childish piping but oddly matured.

312

"Welcome, ghola Bashar," Sheeana said.

"You were trying to imprint me!" Angry accusation. "You think my mother didn't teach me how to prevent that?" A distant expression came over his face. "Ghola?"

"Some prefer to think of you as a clone."

"Who're . . . Sheeana!" He whirled, looking all around the room. It had been selected for its concealed access, no visible hatches. "Where are we?"

"In the no-ship you took to Dune just before you were killed there." Still according to the rules.

"Killed . . ." Again, he looked at his hands. Watchers could almost see ghola-imposed filters drop from his memories. "I was killed . . . on Dune?" almost plaintive.

"Heroic to the end," Sheeana said.

"My . . . the men I took from Gammu . . . were they . . ."

"Honoured Matres made an example of Dune. It's a lifeless ball, charred to cinders."

Anger touched his features. He sat and crossed his legs, placing a clenched fist on each knee. "Yes . . . I learned that in the history of the . . . of me." Again, he glanced at Sheeana. She remained seated on the mat quite still. This was such a plunge into memories as only one who had been through the Agony could appreciate. Utter stillness was required now.

Odrade whispered: "Don't interfere, Sheeana. Let it happen. Let him work it out." She made a hand signal to the three Proctors. They went to the access hatch, watching her instead of the secret room.

"I find it odd to consider myself a subject of history," Teg said. The child's voice but that recurring sense of maturity in it. He closed his eyes and breathed deeply.

In the observation room, Odrade sank back into her chair and asked: "What did you see, Duncan?"

"When Sheeana pushed him away from her, he turned with a swiftness I have never seen except in Murbella."

"Faster even than that."

"Perhaps . . . it's because his body is young and we have given him prana-bindu . . ."

"Something else. You alerted us, Duncan. An unknown in

313

Atreides marker cells." She glanced at the watchful Proctors and shook her head. *No. Not yet.* "Damn that mother of his! Hypno-induction to block an Imprinter and she hid it from us."

"But look what she gave us," Idaho said. "A more effective way to restore . . ."

"We should have seen that on our own!" Odrade felt anger at herself. "Scytale claims Tleilaxu used pain and confrontation. I wonder."

"Ask him."

"It's not that simple. Our Truthsayers are not certain of him."

"He is opaque."

"When have you studied him?"

"Dar! I have access to comeye records."

"I know, but . . ."

"Dammit! Will you keep your eyes on Teg? Look at him! What's happening?"

Odrade snapped her attention to the seated child.

Teg looked at the comeyes, an expression of terrible intensity on his face.

It had been for him like awakening from sleep in the stress of conflict, an aide's hand shaking him. Something needed his attention! He recalled sitting in the no-ship's command centre, Dar standing beside him with a hand on his neck. *Scratching him?* Something urgent to do. What? His body felt wrong. Gammu . . . and now they were on Dune and . . . He remembered different things: childhood on Chapter House? Dar as . . . as . . . More memories meshed. *They tried to imprint me!*

Awareness flowed around this thought like a river spreading itself for a rock.

"Dar! Are you there? You're there!"

Odrade sat back and put a hand to her chin. *What now?*

"Mother!" What an accusatory tone!

Odrade touched a transplate beside her chair. "Hello, Miles. Shall we go for a walk in the orchards?"

"No more games, Dar. I know why you need me. I warn you, though: violence projects the wrong kinds of people into power. As if you didn't know!"

"Still loyal to the Sisterhood, Miles, in spite of what we just tried?"

He glanced at the watchful Sheeana. "Still your obedient dog."

Odrade shot an accusatory look at the smiling Idaho. "You and your damned stories!"

"All right, Miles—No more games but I have to know about Gammu. They say you moved faster than the eye could follow."

"True." Flat, what-the-hell tone.

"And just now . . ."

"This body's too small to carry that load."

"But you . . ."

"I used it up in just one burst and I'm starving."

Odrade glanced at Idaho. He nodded. *Truth*.

She motioned the Proctors back from the hatch. They hesitated before obeying. What had Bell told them?

Teg was not through. "Do I have it right, daughter? Since every individual is accountable ultimately to the self, formation of that self demands the utmost care and attention?"

That damned mother of his taught him everything!

"I apologize, Miles. We did not know how your mother prepared you."

"Whose idea was it?" He looked at Sheeana as he spoke.

"My idea, Miles," Idaho said.

"Oh, you're there, too?" More memory trickled back.

"And I recall the pain you caused me when you restored my memories," Idaho said.

That sobered him. "Point taken, Duncan. No apology needed." He looked at the speakers relaying their voices. "How's the air at the top, Dar? Rarefied enough for you?"

Damned silly idea! she thought. *And he knows it. Not rarefied at all*. The air was thick with the breathing of those around her, including ones wanting to share her dramatic presence, ones with ideas (sometimes the idea they would be better at her job), ones with offering hands and demanding hands. Rarefied, indeed! She sensed that Teg was trying to tell her something. What?

"Sometimes I must be the autocrat!"

315

She heard herself saying this to him during one of their orchard walks, explaining autocrat to him and adding: *"I have the power and must use it. That drags on me terribly."*

You have the power, so use it! That was what this Mentat Bashar was telling her. *Kill me or release me, Dar.*

Still, she stalled for time and knew he would sense it. "Miles, Burzmali's dead, but he kept a reserve force here he trained himself. The best of . . ."

"Don't bother me with petty details!" What a voice of command! Thin and reedy but all other essentials there.

Without being told, the Proctors returned to the hatch. Odrade waved them away with an angry gesture. Only then did she realize that she had reached a decision.

"Give him back his clothes and bring him out," she said. "Get Streggi in here."

Teg's first words on emerging alarmed Odrade and made her wonder if she had made a mistake.

"What if I will not do battle the way you want?"

"But you said . . ."

"I've said many things in my . . . lives. Battle doesn't reinforce moral sense, Dar."

She (and Taraza) had heard the Bashar on that subject more than once. *"Warfare leaves a residue of 'eat drink and be merry' that often leads inexorably to moral breakdown."*

Correct but she did not know what he had in mind with his reminder. *"For every veteran who returns with a new sense of destiny ('I survived; that must be God's purpose.') more come home with barely submerged bitterness, ready to take 'the easy way' because they saw so much of it in the stresses of war."*

They were Teg's words but her belief.

Streggi hurried into the room but before she could speak, Odrade motioned her to stand aside and wait silently.

For once, the acolyte had the courage to disobey Mother Superior.

"Duncan should know he has another daughter. Mother and child live and are healthy." She looked at Teg. "Hello, Miles." Only then did Streggi remove herself to the rear wall and stand quietly.

She is better than I hoped, Odrade thought.

Idaho relaxed into his chair, feeling now the tensions of worry that had interfered with his appreciation of what he had observed here.

Teg nodded to Streggi but spoke to Odrade: "Any more words to whisper in God's ear?" It was essential to control their attention and count on Odrade recognizing it. "If not, I'm really famished."

Odrade raised a finger to signal Streggi and heard the acolyte leave. *Very sensitive to Mother Superior's needs . . . and to Teg's.*

She sensed where Teg was directing her attention and, sure enough, he said: "Perhaps you've really created a scar this time."

A barb directed at the Sisterhood's boast that "We don't let scars accumulate on our pasts. Scars often conceal more than they reveal."

"Some scars *reveal* more than they conceal," he said. He looked at Idaho. "Right, Duncan?" *One Mentat to another.*

"I believe I've come in on an old argument," Idaho said.

Teg looked at Odrade. "See, daughter? A Mentat knows old argument when he hears it. You pride yourselves on knowing what's required of *you* at every turn, but the monster at this turning is of your own making!"

"Mother Superior!" That was a Proctor who did not want her addressed thus.

Odrade ignored her. She felt chagrin, harsh and compelling. Taraza Within remembered the dispute: *"We are shaped by Bene Gesserit associations. In peculiar ways, they blunt us. Oh, we cut swift and deep when we must, but that's another kind of blunting."*

"I'll not take part in blunting you," Teg said. So he remembered.

Streggi returned with a bowl of stew, brown broth with meat floating in it. Teg sat on the floor and spooned it into his mouth with urgent motions.

Odrade remained silent, her thoughts moving where Teg had sent them. There was a hard shell Reverend Mothers put around themselves and against which all things from outside (including emotions) played like projections. Murbella was

317

right and the Sisterhood had to relearn emotions. If they were only observers, they were doomed.

She addressed Teg. "You won't be asked to blunt us."

Both Teg and Idaho heard something else in her voice. Teg put aside his empty bowl but Idaho was first to speak. "Cultivated," he said.

Teg agreed. Sisters were seldom impulsive. You got ordered reactions from them even in times of peril. They went beyond what most people thought of as cultivated. They were driven not so much by dreams of power as they were by their own long view, a thing compounded of immediacy and almost unlimited memory. So, Odrade was following a carefully thought out plan. Teg glanced at the watchful Proctors.

"You were prepared to kill me," he said.

No one answered. There was no need. They all recognized Mentat Projection.

Teg turned and looked back into the room where he had regained his memories. Sheeana was gone. More memories whispered at the edge of awareness. They would speak in their own time. This diminutive body. That was difficult. And Streggi . . . He focused on Odrade. "You were more clever than you thought. But my mother . . ."

"I don't think she anticipated this," Odrade said.

"No . . . she was not that much Atreides."

An electrifying word in these circumstances, it charged a special silence in the room. The Proctors moved closer.

That mother of his!

Teg ignored the hovering Proctors. "In answer to the questions you have not asked, I cannot explain what happened to me on Gammu. My physical and mental speed defies explanation. Given the size and energy, in one of your heartbeats I could be clear of this room and well on my way out of the ship. Ohhh . . . ." hand upraised. "I'm still your obedient dog. I'll do what you require but perhaps not in the way you imagine."

Odrade saw consternation in the faces of her sisters. *What have I loosed upon us?*

"We can prevent any living thing from leaving this ship," she said. "You may be fast but I doubt you are faster than the

318

fire that would engulf you should you try to leave without our permission."

"I will leave in my own good time and *with* your permission. How many of Burzmali's special troops do you have?"

"Almost two million." Startled out of her.

"So many!"

"He had more than twice that number with him at Lampadas when Honoured Matres obliterated them."

"We shall have to be more clever than poor Burzmali. Would you leave me to discuss this with Duncan? That is why you keep us around, isn't it? Our speciality?" He aimed a smiling look at the overhead comeyes. "I'm sure you'll review our discussion thoroughly before approving."

Odrade and her sisters exchanged glances. They shared an unspoken question: *What else can we do?*

As she stood, Odrade looked at Idaho. "Here's a real job for a Truthsayer-Mentat!"

When the women were gone, Teg pulled himself up on to one of the chairs and looked into the empty room visible beyond the seewall. It had been close there and he still felt his heart pumping hard from the effort. "Quite a show," he said.

"I've seen better." Extremely dry.

"What I'd like right now is a large glass of Marinete, but I doubt this body could take it."

"Bell will be waiting for Dar when she gets back to Central," Idaho said.

"To the nethermost hell with Bell! We have to defuse those Honoured Matres before they find us."

"And our Bashar has just the plan."

"Damn that title!"

Idaho inhaled a sharp breath restricted by shock.

"Tell you something, Duncan!" Intense. "Once when I was arriving for an important meeting with potential enemies, I heard an aide announce me. 'The Bashar is here.' I damned near stumbled, caught by the abstraction."

"Mentat blur."

"Of course it was. But I knew the title removed me from something I did not dare lose. Bashar? I was more than that! I was Miles Teg, the name given me by my parents."

"You were on the name-chain!"

"Certainly, and I realized my name stood at a distance from something more primal. Miles Teg? No, I was more basic than that. I could hear my mother saying, 'Oh, what a beautiful baby.' So there I was with another name: 'Beautiful Baby'."

"Did you go deeper?" Idaho found himself fascinated.

"I was caught. Name leads to name leads to name leads to nameless. When I walked into that important room, I was nameless. Did you ever risk that?"

"Once." A reluctant admission.

"We all do it at least once. But there I was. I'd been briefed. I had a reference for everyone at that table—face, name, title, plus all the backgrounding."

"But you weren't really there."

"Oh, I could see the expectant faces measuring me, wondering, worrying. But they did not know me!"

"That gave you a feeling of great power?"

"Exactly as we were warned in Mentat school. I asked myself: 'Is this Mind at its beginning?' Don't laugh. It's a tantalizing question."

"So you went deeper?" Caught by Teg's words, Idaho ignored tugs of warning at the edge of his awareness.

"Oh, yes. And I found myself in the famous 'Hall of Mirrors' they described and warned us to flee."

"So you remembered how to get out and . . ."

"Remembered? You've obviously been there. Did memory get you out?"

"It helped."

"Despite the warnings, I lingered, seeing my 'self of selves' and infinite permutations. Reflections of reflections ad infinitum."

"Fascination of the 'ego core'. Damn few ever escape from that depth. You were lucky."

"I'm not sure it should be called luck. I knew there must be a First Awareness, an awakening . . ."

"Which discovers it is not the first."

"But I wanted a self at the root of the self!"

"Didn't the people at this meeting notice anything odd about you?"

"I found out later I sat down with a wooden expression that concealed these mental gymnastics."

"You didn't speak?"

"I was struck dumb. This was interpreted as 'the Bashar's expected reticence'. So much for reputation."

Idaho started to smile and remembered the comeyes. He saw at once how the watchdogs would interpret such revelations. Wild talent in a dangerous descendant of the Atreides! Sisters knew about the mirrors. Anyone who escaped must be suspect. What did the mirrors show him?

As though he heard the dangerous question, Teg said: "I was caught and knew it. I could visualize myself as a bedridden vegetable but I didn't care. The mirrors were everything until, like something floating up out of water, I saw my mother. She looked more or less the way she had just before she died."

Idaho inhaled a trembling breath. Didn't Teg know what he had just said for the comeyes to record?

"The sisters will now imagine I'm at least a potential kwisatz haderach," Teg said. "Another Muad'Dib. Bullcrap! As you're so fond of saying, Duncan. Neither of us would risk that. We know what he created and we're not stupid!"

Idaho could not swallow. Would they accept Teg's words? He spoke the truth but still . . .

"She took my hand," Teg said. "I could feel it! And she led me right out of the Hall. I expected her to be with me when I felt myself seated at the table. My hand still tingled from her touch but she was gone. I knew that. I just brought myself to attention and took over. The Sisterhood had important advantages to gain there and I gained them."

"Something your mother planted in . . ."

"No! I saw her the same way Reverend Mothers see Other Memory. It was her way of saying: 'Why the hell are you wasting time here when there's work to do?' She had never left me, Duncan. The past never leaves any of us."

Idaho abruptly saw the purpose behind Teg's recital. *Honesty and candour, indeed!*

"You have Other Memory!"

"No! Except what anyone has in emergencies. The Hall of

Mirrors was an emergency and it also let me see and feel the source of help. But I'm not going back there!"

Idaho accepted this. Most Mentats risked one dip into Infinity and learned the transient nature of names and titles but Teg's account was much more than a statement about Time as flow and tableau.

"I figured it was time we introduced ourselves fully to the Bene Gesserit," Teg said. "They should know how far they can trust us. There's work to do and we've wasted enough time on stupidities."

Spend energies on those who make you strong. Energy spent on weaklings drags you to doom. (HM rule) Bene Gesserit Commentary: Who judges?

—**The Dortujla Record**

The day of Dortujla's return did not go well for Odrade. A weapons conference with Teg and Idaho ended without decision. *Englobement?* The cost appalled her. *Encrypted spy messages. Drama!* She had sensed the hunter's axe all during the meeting and knew this coloured her reactions.

Then the afternoon session with Murbella—words, words, words. Murbella was tangled in questions of philosophy. A dead-end if Odrade had ever encountered one.

"We've gone through our fair share of philosophies and psychological theories. We've examined systems of ethics and morality, justice, fairness—the lot. We don't think by any means we've exhausted these subjects nor that all are puerile and devoid of use but they have a tendency to inhibit action."

Odrade felt these words to Murbella coming back to haunt her as she stood in the early evening at the westernmost edge of Central's perimeter paving. It was one of her favourite places but Bellonda beside her continued an argument that had been going on for three days now and this deprived Odrade of the anticipated quiet enjoyment.

Sheeana found them there and asked: "Is it true you have given Murbella the freedom of Central?"

322

"There!" This was one of Bellonda's deepest fears.

"Bell," Odrade cut her off and pointed at the ring orchards. "That little rise over there where we've planted no trees. I want you to order a Folly in that place, built to my requirements. A gazebo with lattice framing for the views."

No stopping Bellonda now. Odrade had seldom seen her this incensed. And the more Bellonda ranted, the more adamant Odrade became.

"You want a . . . a Folly? In that orchard? What else will you waste our substance on? Folly! A most appropriate label for another of your . . ."

It was a silly argument. Both of them knew it twenty words into the thing. Mother Superior could not unbend first and Bell seldom unbent for anything. Even when Odrade fell silent, Bellonda charged onward into empty ramparts. At the end, when Bellonda ran out of energy, Odrade said: "You owe me a fine dinner, Bell. See that it's the best you can arrange."

"Owe you . . ." Bellonda started to splutter.

"A peace offering," Odrade said. "I want it served in my gazebo . . . my Fancy Folly."

When Sheeana laughed, Bellonda was forced to join but with an icy edge. She knew when she had been out-faced.

"Everyone will see it and say: 'See how confident Mother Superior is,'" Sheeana said.

"So you want it for morale!" At this point, Bellonda would have accepted almost any justification.

Odrade beamed at Sheeana. *My clever little darling!* Not only had Sheeana ceased teasing Bellonda, she had taken to reinforcing the older woman's self esteem wherever possible. Bell knew it, of course, and there remained an inevitable Bene Gesserit question: *Why?*

Recognizing the suspicion, Sheeana said: "We're really arguing about Miles and Duncan. And I, for one, am sick of it."

"If I just knew what you were really doing, Dar!" Bellonda said.

"Energy has its own patterns, Bell!"

"What do you mean?" Quite startled.

"They are going to find us, Bell. And I know how."

Bellonda actually gaped.

"We are slaves of our habits," Odrade said. "Slaves of energies we create. Can slaves break free? Bell, you know the problem as well as I do."

For once, Bellonda was nonplussed.

Odrade stared at her.

Pride, that was what Odrade saw when she looked at her sisters and their places. Dignity was only a mask. No real humility. Instead, there was this visible conformity, a true Bene Gesserit pattern that, in a society aware of the peril in patterns, sounded a warning klaxon.

The argument Odrade had used on Murbella came full circle.

There is an unconscious component to all human be-haviour. Words try to mask this. It's often better to watch what people do and ignore what they say. Disagreement between behaviour and words is extremely revealing. Action speaks.

Sheeana was confused. "Habits?"

"Your habits always come hunting after you. The self you construct will haunt you. A ghost wandering around in search of your body, eager to possess you. We are addicted to the self we construct. Slaves to what we have done. We are addicted to Honoured Matres and they to us!"

"More of your damned romanticism!" Bellonda said.

"Yes, I'm a romantic . . . in the same way the Tyrant was. He sensitized himself to the fixed shape of his creation. I am sensitive to his prescient trap."

But oh how close the hunter and oh how deep the pit.

Bellonda was not placated. "You said you know how they . . ."

"They have only to recognize their own habits and they . . . Yes?" This was to an acolyte messenger emerging from a covered passage behind Bellonda.

"Mother Superior, it's Reverend Mother Dortujla. Mother Fintil has brought her to the Landing Flat and they will be here within the hour."

"Bring her to my workroom!" Odrade looked at Bellonda with a stare that was almost wild. "Has she . . ."

"Mother Dortujla is ill,' the acolyte said.

324

Ill? What an extraordinary thing to say about a Reverend Mother.

"Reserve judgment." It was Bellonda-Mentat speaking, Bellonda foe of romanticism and wild imagination.

"Get Tam up there as an observer," Odrade said.

Dortujla hobbled in on a cane with Fintil and Streggi helping her. There was a firmness to Dortujla's eyes, though, and a sense of measuring behind every look she focused on her surroundings. She had her hood thrown back revealing hair the dark mottled brown of antique ivory and when she spoke her voice conveyed a sense of fatigue.

"I have done as you ordered, Mother Superior." As Fintil and Streggi left the room. Dortujla sat without being invited, a slingchair beside Bellonda. Brief glances at Sheeana and Tamalane on her left, then a hard stare at Odrade. "They will meet with you on Junction. They think the place is their own idea and your Spider Queen is there!"

"How soon?" Sheeana asked.

"They want one hundred Standard days counting from just about now. I can be more precise if you . . ."

"Why so long?" Odrade asked.

"My opinion? They will use the time to reinforce their defences on Junction."

"What guarantees?" That was Tam, terse as usual.

"Dortujla, what has happened to you?" Odrade was shocked by the trembling weakness apparent in the woman.

"They conducted experiments on me. But that is not important. The arrangements are. For what it's worth, they promise you safe passage in and out of Junction. Don't believe it. You are allowed a *small* entourage of servants, no more than five. Assume they will kill everyone who accompanies you, although . . . I may have taught them the error in that."

"They expect me to bring submission of the Bene Gesserit?" Odrade's voice had never been colder. Dortujla's words raised a spectre of tragedy.

"That was the inducement."

"The sisters who went with you?" Sheeana asked.

Dortujla tapped her forehead, a common Sisterhood

gesture. "I have them. We agree the Honoured Matres should be punished."

"Dead?" Odrade forced the word between tight lips.

"Attempting to force me into their ranks. *'You see? We will kill another one if you don't agree.'* I told them to kill us all and have done with it and to forget about meeting Mother Superior. They did not accept this until they ran out of hostages."

"You Shared them all?" Tamalane asked. Yes, that would be Tam's concern as she neared her own death.

"While pretending to assure myself they were dead. You may as well know the whole thing. These women are grotesque! They possess caged Futars. The bodies of my sisters were thrown into the cages where the Futars ate them. The Spider Queen—an appropriate name—made me watch this."

"Gross!" Bellonda said.

Dortujla sighed. "They did not know, naturally, that I have worse visions in Other Memory."

"They sought to overwhelm your sensibilities," Odrade said. "Foolish. Were they surprised when you didn't react as they wished?"

"Chagrined, I would say. I think they had seen others react as I did. I told them it was as good a way as any to get fertilizer. I believe that angered them."

"Cannibalism," Tamalane muttered.

"Only in appearance," Dortujla said. "Futars definitely are not human. Barely-tamed wild animals."

"No Handlers?" Odrade asked.

"I saw none. The Futars did speak. They said, 'Eat!' before they ate and they jibed at Honoured Matres around them. 'You hungry?' That sort of thing. More important was what happened after they ate."

Dortujla lapsed into a fit of coughing. "They tried poisons," she said. "Stupid women!"

When she regained her breath, Dortujla said, "A Futar came to the bars of its cage after their . . . banquet? It looked at the Spider Queen and it screamed. I have never heard such a sound. Chilling! Every Honoured Matre in that room froze and I swear to you they were terrified."

326

Sheeana touched Dortujla's arm. "A predator immobilizing its prey?"

"Undoubtedly. It had qualities of Voice. The Futars appeared surprised that it did not freeze me."

"The Honoured Matres' reaction?" Bellonda asked. Yes, a Mentat would require that datum.

"A general clamour when they found their voices. Many shouted for Great Honoured Matre to destroy the Futars. She, however, took a calmer view. 'Too valuable alive,' she said."

"A hopeful sign," Tamalane said.

Odrade looked at Bellonda. "I will order Streggi to bring the Bashar here. Objections?"

Bellonda gave a curt nod. They knew the gamble must be taken despite questions about Teg's intentions.

To Dortujla, Odrade said: "I want you in my own guest quarters. We'll bring in Suks. Order what you need and prepare for a full Council meeting. You are a special adviser."

Dortujla spoke while struggling to her feet. "I've not slept in almost fifteen days and I will need a special meal."

"Sheeana, see to that and get the Suks up here. Tam, stay with the Bashar and Streggi. Regular reports. He'll want to go to the cantonment and take personal charge. Get him a Comlink with Duncan. Nothing must impede them."

"You want me here with him?" Tamalane asked.

"You are his leech. Streggi takes him nowhere without your knowledge. He wants Duncan as Weapons Master. Make sure he accepts Duncan's confinement in the ship. Bell, any weapons data Duncan requires—priority. Comments?"

There were no comments. Thoughts about consequences, yes, but the decisiveness of Odrade's behaviour infected them.

Sitting back, Odrade closed her eyes and waited until silence told her she was alone. The comeyes were still watching, of course.

They know I'm tired. Who wouldn't be under these circumstances? Three more sisters killed by those monsters! Bashar! They must feel our lash and know the lesson!

When she heard Streggi arrive with Teg, Odrade opened her eyes. Streggi led him in by the hand but there was something about them saying this was not an adult guiding a child. Teg's movements said he gave Streggi permission to treat him this way. She would have to be warned.

Tam followed and went to a chair near the windows directly beneath the bust of Chenoeh. Significant positioning? Tam did strange things lately.

"Do you wish me to stay, Mother Superior?" Streggi released Teg's hand and stood near the door.

"Sit over there beside Tam. Listen and do not interrupt. You must know what will be required of you."

Teg hitched himself on to the chair recently occupied by Dortujla. "I suppose this is a council of war."

That's an adult behind the childish voice.

"I won't ask your plan yet," Odrade said.

"Good. The unexpected takes more time and I may not be able to tell you what I intend until the moment of action."

"We've been observing you with Duncan. Why are you interested in ships from the Scattering?"

"Long-haul ships have a distinctive appearance. I saw them on the flat at Gammu."

Teg sat back and let this sink in, glad of the briskness he sensed in Odrade's manner. Decisions! No more long deliberations. That suited his needs. *They must not learn the full extent of my abilities. Not yet.*

"You would disguise an attack force?"

Bellonda came through the door as Odrade was speaking and growled an objection while sitting: "Impossible! They'll have recognition codes and secret signals for . . ."

"Let me decide that, Bell, or remove me from command."

"This is the Council!" Bellonda said. "You don't . . ."

"Mentat?" He looked fully at her, the Bashar apparent in his gaze.

When she fell silent, he said: "Don't question my loyalty! If you would weaken me, replace me!"

"Let him have his say." That was Tam from her position beneath the bust of Chenoeh. "This isn't the first Council where the Bashar has appeared as our equal."

Bellonda lowered her chin a fractional millimetre.

To Odrade, Teg said: "Avoiding warfare is a matter of intelligence—the gathered variety and intellectual power."

Throwing our own cant at us! She heard Mentat in his voice and Bellonda obviously heard this as well. Intelligence and intelligence: the doubled view. Without it, warfare often occurred as an accident.

The Bashar sat silently, letting them stew in their own historical observations. The urge to conflict went far deeper than consciousness. The Tyrant had been right. Humankind acted as "one beast". The forces impelling that great collective animal went back to tribal days and beyond, as did so many forces to which humans responded without thinking.

Mix the genes.

Expand lebensraum for your own breeders.

Gather the energies of others: collect slaves, peons, servants, serfs, markets, workers . . . The terms often were interchangeable.

Odrade saw what he was doing. Knowledge absorbed from the Sisterhood helped make him the incomparable Mentat Bashar. He held these things as instincts. Energy-eating drove war's violence. This was described as "greed, fear (that others will take your hoard), power hunger" and on and on into futile analyses. Odrade had heard these even from Bellonda who obviously was not taking it well that a *subordinate* should remind them of what they already knew.

"The Tyrant knew," Teg said. "Duncan quotes him: 'War is behaviour with roots in the single cell of the primeval seas. Eat whatever you touch or it will eat you.'"

"What do you propose?" Bellonda at her most snappish.

"A feint at Gammu then strike their base on Junction. For that we need first-hand observations." He stared steadily at Odrade.

He knows! The thought flared in Odrade's mind.

"You think your studies of Junction when it was a Guild base are still accurate?" Bellonda demanded.

"They haven't had time to change the place much from what I stored here." He tapped his forehead in an odd parody of the Sisterhood's gesture.

"Englobement," Odrade said.

Bellonda looked at her sharply. "The cost!"

"Losing everything is more costly," Teg said.

"Foldspace sensors don't have to be large," Odrade said. "Duncan would set them to create a Holzmann explosion on contact?"

"The explosions would be visible and would give us a trajectory." He sat back and looked at an indefinite area on Odrade's rear wall. Would they accept it? He dared not frighten them with another display of wild talent. If Bell knew he could *see* the no-ships!

"Do it!" Odrade said. "You have the command. Use it."

There was a distinct sense of chuckling from Taraza in Other Memories. *Give him his head! That's how I got such a great reputation!*

"One thing," Bellonda said. She looked at Odrade. "You're going to be his spy?"

"Who else can get in there and transmit observations?"

"They'll be monitoring every means of transmission!"

"Even the one that tells our waiting no-ship we have not been betrayed?" Odrade asked.

"'An encrypted message hidden in the transmission," Teg said. "Duncan has devised an encryption that would take months to break but we doubt they'll detect its presence."

"Madness," Bellonda muttered.

"I met an Honoured Matre military commander on Gammu," Teg said. "Slack when it came to necessary details. I think they're overconfident."

Bellonda stared at him and there was the Bashar staring back at her out of a child's innocent eyes. "Abandon all sanity ye who enter here," he said.

"Get out of here, all of you!" Odrade ordered. "You have work to do. And Miles . . ."

He already had slid off the chair but he stood there looking much as he always had when waiting for *Mother* to tell him something important.

"Did you refer to the lunacy of dramatic events that warfare always amplifies?"

"What else? Surely you didn't think I referred to your Sisterhood!"

"Duncan plays this game sometimes."

330

"I don't want us catching the Honoured Matre madness," Teg said. "It is contagious, you know."

"They've tried to control the sex drive," Odrade said. "That always gets away from you."

"Runaway lunacy," he agreed. He leaned against the table, his chin barely above the surface. "Something drove those women back here. Duncan's right. They're looking for something and running away at the same time."

"You have ninety Standard days to get ready," she said. "Not one day more."

When she was alone, Odrade felt almost crotchety. Her own long overview said wars were always disgustingly similar. Most of them largely unnecessary, as Teg said. The motives were hidden behind masking systems, transferred and translated into rational explanations that concealed deeper forces.

What do I hide from myself?

The Tyrant's thirty-five-hundred-year lesson lay there in her awareness. The young did most of the brutal things—dying or getting maimed into cripples for the remainder of painful lives. Mental pains, too. Subjective wounds, the ones carried silently, those were equally debilitating. How easy it was to think of the many rather ordinary things you could have done otherwise and thus escaped. A mind full of *what-ifs* and *might-have-beens.* "*If only I hadn't stepped on that soft place. If only I hadn't gone to piss just then.*"

Am I one of the old and powerful who create these sorry stupidities?

This (she knew) was precisely the train of thought into which Teg had aimed her. Deliberately! Damn that mother of his! She almost made a sister out of him.

But I am not one of those who stays in a safe place of command where I can issue my orders with minimal danger to myself. I must go to Junction. And who do I dare take with me?

That was another element of the Bashar's silent message. He had risked his own flesh in battle. But even there, Mentat capacities told him when the impact of his gesture was worth the risk.

She felt her most cynical when such thoughts came. It was

331

necessary to remind herself of the enemy, the grim *addiction* the Sisterhood now opposed. *A measured amount of massacre has a salutary effect on survivors!* What an awful parody of the Bene Gesserits. She became almost volatile at this thought.

Should I send someone else to Junction in my place? Everyone would understand. "There but for the grace of my own cowardice, go I."

Oh, to be a survivor!

And how often did humans translate cowardice into wisdom. "*I was too wise to play their stupid game!*" And sometimes it could be true.

But we are committed.

About the only saving grace these periodic stupidities possessed, she thought, was a certain stylish grace demonstrated by some participants. A few military figures had observed this and practised it over the eons. Teg was one. He had style. Once more she turned cynical. The masses who trusted their histories said: "Teg? Gods! There was a man!" But how much of the man remained in that immature body?

Could he still live up to his mythology? But his real strength lay in another realm. *Wise in our ways.*

Warning me about the contagion of sexual power. Honoured Matre madness! No matter their overwhelming numbers, they still were like a child dipping a toy waterwheel into a flood. And what could they say when disaster struck? "Oh, mummy! The nasty dark water took my toy!" They already were desperate, just as Teg said, and hiding something, hiding it even from themselves. What an enormous lever that gave the Bene Gesserit! Honoured Matres grabbed for dominance out there in the Scattering and then ducked the responsibility. That was what got them and they didn't want to face up to their folly.

Teg knew it, too. Always superb at reading the evidence, divining true intentions, getting inside the masks.

He puts his trust in people.

She saw that this also was in his silent message to her.

He knows what I'm going to do. He has seen Murbella and he knows!

332

Ish yara al-ahdab hadbat-u. (A hunchback does not see his own hunch.—Folk Saying.) BG Commentary: The hunch may be seen with the aid of mirrors but mirrors show the whole being.

—The Bashar Teg

It was a weakness in the Bene Gesserit that Odrade knew the entire Sisterhood soon must recognize. She gained no consolation from having seen it first. *Denying our deepest resource when we need it most!* The Scatterings had gone beyond the ability of humans to assemble the experiences in manageable form. *We can only extract essentials, and that is a matter of judgment.* Vital data would remain dormant in great and small events, accumulations called instant. So that was it finally—they must fall back on unspoken knowledge.

In this age, the word "refugees" took on the colour of its pre-space meaning. Small bands of Reverend Mothers sent out by the Sisterhood held something in common with old scenes of displaced stragglers trudging down forgotten roads, pitiful belongings bound in bits of cloth, wheeled on decrepit prams and toy wagons, or piled atop lopsided vehicles, remnant humanity clinging to the outsides and densely packed within, every face blank with despair or heated by desperation.

So we repeat history and repeat it and repeat it.

As she entered a tubeslot shortly before lunch, Odrade's thoughts clung to her Scattered Sisters: political refugees, economic refugees, pre-battle refugees.

Is this your Golden Path, Tyrant?

Visions of her Scattered ones haunted Odrade as she entered Central's Reserved Dining Room, a place only Reverend Mothers might enter. They served themselves here at cafeteria lines.

It had been twenty days since she had released Teg to the cantonment. Rumours were flying in Central, especially among Proctors, although there still was no sign of another vote. New decisions must be announced today and they would have to be more than naming the ones who would accompany her to Junction.

333

She glanced around the dining room, an austere place of yellow walls, low ceiling, small square tables that could be latched in rows for larger groups. Chairs were individual possessions, positioned as marks of standing in a hierarchy.

Even here, Odrade thought. *Place and face*.

Serving staff already were setting out food from the kitchen pass-through. Bouillabaisse and vegetarian fare, today, she noted. The room was beginning to fill with groups of staff— Proctors, specialists from various niches; she recognized four from Weather Control liaison.

Windows along one side revealed a garden court under a translucent cover. Dwarf apricots in green fruit, lawn, benches, small tables. Sisters ate outside when sunlight poured into the enclosed yard. No sunlight today.

She ignored a cafeteria line where a place was being made for her. *Later, sisters*.

At the corner table near the windows reserved for her, she deliberately moved the chairs. Bell's brown chairdog pulsed faintly at this unaccustomed disturbance. Odrade sat with her back to the room, knowing this would be interpreted correctly: *Leave me to my own thoughts*.

While she waited, she stared at at the courtyard. An enclosing hedge of exotic purple-leaved shrubs was in red flower—giant blossoms with delicate stamens of deep yellow.

Bellonda arrived first, dropping into her chairdog with no comment on its new position. Bell frequently appeared untidy, belt loose, robe wrinkled, bits of food on the bosom. Today, she was neat and clean.

Now, why is that?

Reverend Mothers presented a fairly constant persona to sisters and chosen intimates. Only outside the enclosing band was it "witch face and Bene Gesserit masks".

She must see I'm curious about this neatness.

Bellonda said, "Tam and Sheeana will be late."

Odrade accepted this without stopping her study of this different Bellonda. Was she a bit slimmer? There was no way to insulate a Mother Superior completely from what went on within her sensory area of concerns but sometimes pressures of work distracted her from small changes. These were a Reverend Mother's natural habitat, though, and negative evidence was as illuminating as positive. On reflection, Odrade realized that this new Bellonda had been with them for several weeks.

Bellonda was oddly silent after that initial announcement. *Bell, the rebel?* Good ones usually rebelled in one way or another, a thing watchdogs always considered when observing Mother Superior. *Watch me now, Sisters!*

Something had happened to Bellonda. Any Reverend Mother could exercise reasonable control over weight and figure. A matter of internal chemistry—banking fires or letting them burn high. For years now, rebellious Bellonda had flaunted a gross body.

"You've lost weight," Odrade said.

"Fat was beginning to slow me too much."

That had never been sufficient reason for Bell to change her ways. She had always compensated with speed of mind, with projections and faster transport.

"Duncan really got to you, didn't he?"

"I'm not a hypocrite nor criminal!"

"Time to send you to a punishment Keep, I guess."

This recurrent humour thrust usually annoyed Bellonda. Today, it did not arouse her. But under pressure of Odrade's stare, she said: "If you must know, it's Sheeana. She has been after me to improve my appearance and broaden my circle of associates. Annoying! I'm doing it to shut her up."

"Why are Tam and Sheeana late?"

"Reviewing your latest meeting with Duncan. I have severely limited who has access to it. No telling what will happen when it becomes general knowledge."

"As it will."

"Inevitable. I only buy us time to prepare."

"I did not want it suppressed, Bell."

"Dar, what *are* you doing?"

"I will announce that at a Convocation."

No words but Bellonda glared her surprise.

"A Convocation is my right," Odrade said.

Bellonda leaned back and stared at Odrade, assessing,

335

questioning . . . all without words. The last Convocation of the Bene Gesserit had been at the Tyrant's death. And before that, at the Tyrant's seizure of power. A Convocation had not been thought possible since Honoured Matres attacked. Too much time taken from desperate labours.

Presently, Bellonda asked: "Will you risk bringing Sisters from our surviving Keeps?"

"No. Dortujla will represent them. There is precedent, as you know."

"First, you free Murbella; now it's a Convocation."

"Free? Murbella is tied by chains of gold. Where would she go without her Duncan?"

"But Duncan himself is . . ."

"Has he left the ship?"

"He had better not try!"

"Unless you sit in my chair, don't override me."

"You open the ship's armoury to him and now . . ."

"You've seen the record. Review it!" Mother Superior's order. Bell must obey or precipitate a crisis.

Odrade sensed the passage of that encounter through Bellonda's mind. Comeyes had captured every movement.

Early morning in the ship just two days ago. Duncan in his sitting room when Odrade entered. He heard the swish of her robes and turned to face her. How open his expression! Flaunting emotions as a key to his frustrations and anger. She did not try to hide her response.

"Duncan! You disturb us with your anger. It's one thing to call Bell a hypocrite but Mother Superior . . ."

". . . is above such things? Or do you have excuses? After all, you can always grow other gholas."

"I don't offer excuses. You resent how I would use Murbella and you think I send Teg to death."

"Am I mistaken?"

"These are not your concerns, Mentat! This is a time for battle decisions. That's why I free you now to decide your own future."

"What?" Really puzzled.

"I am removing your guards. Only Scytale remains a prisoner."

336

"You mean I . . ." He pointed vaguely to his right indicating the outside.

"Your decision. I do not wash my hands of you; I merely set you free. You will not feel the cruelty of this until you reflect on it."

"Do you mean I can leave the ship?"

"If you choose."

"But if the hunters are using Guild Navigators . . ."

"As they most certainly are."

"Damn you!"

"An Atreides gift to you, Duncan."

"Gift!"

"You see? Complete trust in your conscience."

"Would I betray you by . . . you would put all of the Sisterhood on my conscience!"

"I put nothing on your conscience! That's your own possession to do with as you will."

She watched his silent struggle. *Ahhhh, I have alarmed you deeply.*

"Freedom," he muttered.

You see it, Duncan. Freedom puts you on your own. You no longer can look to exterior forces, to rules laid down by others. Were you ready for this?

He turned his back on her and went to the Van Gogh reproduction he had fixed to the wall where he could see it from his favourite chair.

Odrade held her silence.

Does the Orange Catholic Bible serve you now, Duncan? You never gave it much attention in your pasts. Where do you look for moral guidance? Not outside, Duncan! Within. You know your debts and debtors. What do you call on in extremis? Have you kept an accounting of balances payable? Never a complete accounting, I'm certain. You're not the type. Wipe the slate clean and go on, that's you. Carry your hates and angers as hand luggage. You're a survivor. Or you never would have escaped Gammu when the Harkonnens were torturing and killing your family. You survived Harkonnen slave pits. See if you can survive freedom!

He faced her. "Determinism!"

"Just another noise now, Duncan."

"The Bashar requires innovative weaponry. I need only my freedom of the ship's armoury."

"An admirable interpretation of freedom," she said.

In the Reserved Dining Room, Bellonda repeated Odrade's closing remark to Duncan, then: "You think that's all he'll take?"

"I know it."

"I am reminded of Jessica turning her back on the Mentat who would have killed her."

"The Mentat was immobilized by his own beliefs."

"Sometimes the bull gores the matador, Dar."

"More often the chains cannot be removed."

"Our survival should not depend on statistics!"

"Agreed. That is why I call Convocation."

"Acolytes included?"

"Everyone."

"Even Murbella? Does she get an acolyte's vote?"

"I think she may be a Reverend Mother by then."

Bellonda gasped, then: "You move too fast, Dar!"

"These times require it."

Bellonda glanced toward the dining room door. "Here's Tam. Later than I expected. I wonder if they took time to consult Murbella?"

Tamalane arrived, breathing hard from hurrying. She dropped into her blue chairdog, noted the new positions and said: "Sheeana will be along presently. She is showing records to Murbella."

"Murbella won't work against Duncan," Odrade said.

"But what a revelation to watch her!" Tamalane said.

Odrade could only agree. Watching Murbella revealed much but Tam's words reflected fear, a distraction. Fears that even the Litany would not dispel weakened them all. Weakness brought the axe that much closer.

Bellonda addressed Tamalane. "She's going to put Murbella through the Agony and call a Convocation."

"I'm not surprised." Tamalane spoke with her old precision. "The position of that Honoured Matre must be resolved as soon as possible."

Sheeana joined them then and took the slingchair at Odrade's left, speaking as she sat. "Have you watched Murbella walk?"

Odrade was caught by the way this abrupt question, uttered without preamble, fixed the attention. *Murbella walking across the quad*. Observed from a high window just that morning. Beauty in Murbella and the eye could not avoid it. To other Bene Gesserits, Reverend Mothers and acolytes alike, she was something of an exotic. She had arrived full grown from the dangerous Outside. *One of them*. It was her movements, though, that compelled the eye. Homeostasis in her that went beyond the norms.

Sheeana's question redirected the observer's mind. Something about Murbella's quite acceptable passage across the quad required new examination. What was it?

Murbella's motions were always carefully chosen. She excluded anything not required to go from here to there. *Path of least resistance?* It was a view of Murbella that sent a pang through Odrade. Sheeana had seen it, of course. Was Murbella one of those who would choose an easy way every time? Odrade could see that question on the faces of her companions.

"The Agony will sort it out," Tamalane said.

Odrade looked squarely at Sheeana. "Well?" She had asked the question, after all.

"Perhaps it's only that she does not waste energy. But I agree with Tam: the Agony."

"Are we making a terrible mistake?" Bellonda asked.

Something in the way this question was asked told Odrade that Bell had made a Mentat summation. *She has seen what I intend!*

"If you know a better course reveal it now," Odrade said. *Or hold your peace.*

Silence gripped them. Odrade looked at her companions in succession, lingering on Bell.

Help us, whatever gods there may be! And I, being Bene Gesserit, am too much agnostic to make that plea with anything more than a hope of covering all possibilities. Don't reveal it,

339

Bell. If you know what I will do, you know it must be seen in its own time.

"No mistake, Bell," Odrade said. "Remember Murbella's joke."

A smile twitched Sheeana's mouth but Bellonda heard another plea from Odrade. *Murbella is our key?*

The joke in question had gone all through Chapter House, having a similar effect to many of Sheeana's pranks.

"The Agnostic's Prayer", it had been labelled when it appeared on the wall of the Acolyte dining room inscribed on common reusable they employed for temporary notes. Purest doggerel.

> *Hey, God! I hope you're there.*
> *I want You to hear my prayer.*
> *That graven image on my shelf:*
> *Is it really You or just myself?*
> *Well, anyway, here it goes.*
> *Please keep me on my toes.*
> *Help me past my worst mistakes,*
> *Doing that for both our sakes,*
> *For an example of perfection*
> *To the Proctors in my section;*
> *Like bread, for the leaven of it,*
> *Or merely for the Heaven of it.*
> *For whatever reason may incline,*
> *Please act for Yours and Mine.*

In the crush of arriving diners, the perpetrator had not been seen by comeyes but everyone assumed it was written by an advanced acolyte for the amusement of her fellows. It was a joke, though, and there was a pervasive awareness that it must be rooted out by Proctors and the offender punished.

Odrade had chuckled over the doggerel and posted it to the Managing Sisters of the Missionaria. Tamalane and those other serious-minded women who guided creation of religions to guard the Sisterhood needed an occasional fire built under them. Get them up and chomping around. Odrade had known they would worry about why Mother Superior sent them this thing. Mother Superior was, after all, *technically* supreme commander. They must do nothing overt out there in the human universe without consulting her, especially in these times.

Mother Superior (with advice of Council and watchdog monitoring) pulled the major strings. *Technically*. Actuality was something different but sending along that doggerel created a stir and speeded finding the culprit.

Thank you, anonymous acolyte, Odrade had thought and two mornings later sent for the offender, considering enough time had passed for watchdogs to identify her.

The identity of the doggerel writer astonished Odrade. Streggi ushered the guilty one into the workroom and left precipitately.

"Murbella? You?"

"I'm afraid so."

"You're *afraid* so?" No contrition in her at all. It could be seen in the way she stood there.

"Only a figure of speech." Defensive.

"Never *only* a figure of speech."

Murbella accepted this, recognizing a tiny flexing of fear in her choice of words. Fear. Like an infant just gaining strength to lift its head. "Proctors teach me that humour often is a response to fear," she admitted.

"And you joke about the Missionaria? Oh, don't protest! That was your intent. Why, Murbella?"

"They're so damned pretentious!"

"Damned and pretentious. Quite possibly. I agree."

"You do?" It was Murbella's turn to be astonished.

"You and I should get to know each other better."

And Odrade thought: *Look for rebellion. It's a symptom. What ferments until we are forced to notice?*

Murbella stood in thoughtful silence. Her original fear, source of her jest, had been replaced by a new one. *The Bene Gesserit will dare anything!* The Missionaria was a form of ultimate daring, a probe into mystical unknowns. But wasn't that a definition of the Scattering, as well?

Observing Murbella, Odrade felt a sense of kinship. Similarities of thought. Resentments shared.

I fought in just that way against the teachings and everlasting

341

disciplines "*which will make you strong, child*". What was Murbella like as a child? *Not like me. But she has become like me because of pressures.*

Odrade saw unasked questions on Murbella's face, recognizable because Odrade had asked similar questions.

"*Is this living? What good is a life devoted to such constant pressures?*"

Ahhhhh, younger sister, life is always reaction to pressures. Some give in to easy distractions and are shaped by them. Pores bloated and reddened by excesses with a narcotic or some other source of illusion. Bacchus leering at them. Lust fixing its shape on their features. Reverend Mothers know this through millennial observation. We give in to pressures and are shaped by them. Or we react against pressures and are shaped by that. Pressures and shapings, that is life.

Bellonda brought Odrade out of reverie with a cough. "Are we going to eat or talk? People are staring."

"Should we have another go at Scytale?" Sheeana asked.

Was that an attempt to divert my attention?

Bellonda said: "Give him nothing! He's in reserve. Let him sweat."

Odrade looked carefully at Bellonda. She was fuming over the silence imposed on her by Odrade's secret decision. Avoiding a meeting of eyes with Sheeana. *Jealous! Bell is jealous of Sheeana!*

Tamalane said, "I am only an adviser now but . . ."

"Stop that, Tam!" Odrade snapped.

"Tam and I have been discussing that ghola," Bellonda said. (Idaho was "that ghola" when Bellonda had something disparaging to say.) "Why did he think he needed to talk secretly to Sheeana?" A hard stare at Sheeana.

Odrade saw shared suspicion. *She does not accept the explanation. Does she reject Duncan's emotional bias?*

Sheeana spoke quickly. "Mother Superior explained that!"

"Emotion," Bellonda sneered.

Odrade raised her voice and was surprised at this reaction. "Suppressing emotions is a weakness!"

Tamalane's shaggy eyebrows lifted.

Sheeana intruded: "If we won't bend, we can break."

Before Bellonda could respond, Odrade said: "Ice can be chipped apart or melted. Ice maidens are vulnerable to a single form of attack."

"I'm hungry," Sheeana said.

Peace-making? Not a role expected of The Mouse.

Tamalane stood. "Bouillabaisse. We must eat the fish before our sea is gone. Not enough nullentropy storage."

In the softest of simulflows, Odrade noted the departure of her companions to the cafeteria line. Tamalane's accusatory words recalled that second day with Sheeana after the decision to phase out the Great Sea. Standing at Sheeana's window in the early morning, Odrade had watched a seabird move against the desert background. It winged its way northward, a creature completely out of place in that setting but beautiful in a profoundly nostalgic way because of it.

White wings glistened in early sunlight. A touch of black beneath and in front of its eyes. Abruptly, it hovered, wings motionless. Then, lifting on an air current, it tucked its wings like a hawk and plummeted out of view behind the farther buildings. Reappearing, it carried something in its beak, a morsel it swallowed on the wing.

A seabird alone and adapting.

We adapt. We do indeed adapt.

It was not a quiet thought. Nothing to induce repose. Shocking rather. Odrade had felt jarred out of a dangerously drifting course. Not only her beloved Chapter House but their entire human universe was breaking out of its old shapes and taking on new forms. Perhaps it was right in this new universe that Sheeana continued to conceal things from Mother Superior. *And she is concealing something.*

Once more, Bellonda's acidic tones brought Odrade to full awareness of her surroundings. "If you won't serve yourself, I suppose we must take care of you." Bellonda placed a bowl of aromatic fish stew in front of Odrade, a great chunk of garlic bread beside it.

When each had sampled the bouillabaisse, Bellonda put down her spoon and stared hard at Odrade. "You're not going to suggest we 'love one another' or some such debilitating nonsense?"

"Thank you for bringing my food," Odrade said.

Sheeana swallowed and a wide grin came over her features. "It's delicious."

Bellonda returned to eating. "It's all right." But she had heard the unspoken comment.

Tamalane ate steadily, shifting attention from Sheeana to Bellonda and then to Odrade. Tam appeared to agree with a proposed softening of emotional strictures. At least, she voiced no objections and older sisters were most likely to object.

The love the Bene Gesserit tried to deny was everywhere, Odrade thought. In small things and big. How many ways there were to prepare delectable, life-sustaining foods, recipes that really were embodiments of loves old and new. This bouillabaisse so smoothly restorative on her tongue; it's origins were planted deeply in love: the wife at home using that part of the day's catch her husband could not sell.

Odrade pictured it in Other Memory immediacy. Tired fisherman bringing home the leavings. Keep it uncooked and it will spoil. Wife use her educated palate to prepare a tempting dish for her weary man. His fatigue so obvious, elbows on table, head bent close to his bowl. Man and woman are renewed. Frustrations, angers, the depletions of living are held at bay for another interval.

How important such bits of time. Intervals between meals, between breaths, between heartbeats . . . Then banquets, deep breaths, the best of life itself. The very essence of the Bene Gesserit was concealed in loves. Why else minister to those unspoken needs humanity always carried? Why else work for the perfectibility of humankind?

Bowl empty, Bellonda put down her spoon and wiped up the dregs with the last of her bread. She swallowed, looking pensive. "Love weakens us," she said. No force in her voice.

An acolyte could have said it no differently. Right out of the Coda. Odrade concealed amusement and countered with another Coda stepping stone. "Beware jargon. It usually hides ignorance and carries little knowledge."

Respectful wariness entered Bellonda's eyes.

Sheeana pushed herself back from the table and wiped her

mouth with her napkin. Tamalane did the same. Her chairdog adjusted as she leaned back, eyes bright and amused.

Tam knows! The wily old witch is still wise in my ways. But Sheeana . . . what game is Sheeana playing? I would almost say she hopes to distract me, to keep my attention away from her. She is very good at it, learned it at my knee. Well . . . two can play that game. I press Bellonda, but watch my little Dune waif.

"What price respectability, Bell?" Odrade asked.

Bellonda accepted this thrust in silence. Hidden in Bene Gesserit jargon was a definition of respectability and they all knew it.

What keeps the respect of my sisters?

There was something antique about it. They had preserved this thing from their most ancient past, taking it out regularly to polish and make necessary repairs that time required of human creations. And here it was today, not brought up to date (all the powers that be forbid!) but held in unspoken reverence.

Thus you are a Reverend Mother and by no other judgment shall that be true.

How workable was this antique contraption?

"Should we honour the memory of the Lady Jessica for her humanity?" Odrade asked. *Sheeana is surprised!*

"Jessica put the Sisterhood in jeopardy!" *Bellonda accuses.*

"To thine own sisters be true," Tamalane murmured.

"Our antique definition of respectability helps keep us human," Odrade said. *Hear me well, Sheeana.*

Her voice little more than a whisper, Sheeana said, "If we lose that we lose it all."

Odrade suppressed a sigh. *So that's it!*

Sheeana met her gaze. "You are instructing us, of course."

"Twilight thoughts," Bellonda muttered. "Best we avoid them."

"Taraza called us 'Latter day Bene Gesserits'," Sheeana said.

Odrade's mood went self accusatory.

The bane of our present existence. Sinister imaginings can destroy us.

How easy it was to conjure a future that looked at them from

345

blazing orange eyes of berserk Honoured Matres. Fears out of many pasts crouched within Odrade, breathless moments focused on fangs that went with such eyes.

Looking squarely at Odrade, Bellonda said, "Idaho has been domesticated. Domestication . . . a form of love?"

Tamalane shook her head from side to side. *An old cow who has borne many a choice bull questions her motives at last.*

Sheeana looked at Odrade the way a trapped bird might look at a snake.

You know I must force it, Sheeana!

"Domesticate the Honoured Matres?" Bellonda insisted.

Bell does not recognize what is happening here. How odd for a Mentat. Doesn't she see that our future could hold things we do not imagine? Madness beyond whatever our fears might create. Domestication? Everything ordered into Bene Gesserit service? Animals of the field given us by our personally-created gods? Measured rows of grain and heaped-up bushes heavy with fruit? Every growing thing trained only to perform for our benefit?

"Bell would have us fall into Honoured Matre madness," Tamalane said.

The Bashar's warning.

Odrade raised a hand to forestall comment but kept her attention on Sheeana. "Who will accompany me to Junction?"

They knew Dortujla's harrowing experience and word of it had spread throughout Chapter House.

"Whoever goes with Mother Superior could well be fed to Futars."

"Tam," Odrade said. "You and Dortujla." *And that may be a death sentence. The next step is obvious.* "Sheeana," Odrade said, "you will Share with Tam. Dortujla and I will share with Bell. And I also will share with *you* before I go."

Bellonda was aghast. "Mother Superior! I am not suited to take your place."

Odrade held her attention on Sheeana. "That is not being suggested. I will merely make you the repository of my lives." Definite fear on Sheeana's face but she dared not refuse a direct order. Odrade nodded to Tamalane. "I will Share later. You and Sheeana will do it now."

346

Tamalane leaned toward Sheeana. The strictures of great age and imminent death made this a welcome thing for her but Sheeana involuntarily pulled away.

"Now!" Odrade said. *Let Tam judge whatever it is you hide.*

There was no escape. Sheeana bent her head to Tamalane's until they touched. The flash of the exchange was electric and the entire dining room felt it. Conversation stopped, every gaze turned toward the table by the window.

There were tears in Sheeana's eyes when she withdrew.

Tamalane smiled and made a gentle caressing motion with both hands along Sheeana's cheeks. "It's all right, dear. We all have these fears and sometimes do foolish things because of them. But I am pleased to call you Sister."

Tell us, Tam! Now!

Tamalane did not choose to do that. She faced Odrade and said, "We must cling to our humanity at any cost. Your lesson is well received and you have taught Sheeana well."

"When Sheeana Shares with you, Dar," Bellonda began, "could you not reduce the influence she has on . . ."

"I will not weaken a possible Mother Superior," Odrade said. "Thank you, Tam. I think we will make our venture to Junction without excess baggage. Now! I want a report by tonight on Teg's progress. His leech has been too long away from him."

"Will he learn that he has two leeches now?" Sheeana asked. *Such joy in her!*

Odrade stood.

If Tam accepts her then I must. Tam would never betray our Sisterhood. And Sheeana—of us all, Sheeana most reveals the natural traits from our human roots. Still . . . I wish she had never created that statue she calls 'The Void'.

A thick cloud cover had moved over Central this morning and Odrade's workroom took on a grey silence to which she felt herself responding with inner stillness, as though she dared not move because that disturbed dangerous forces.

Murbella's day of Agony, she thought. *I must not think of omens.*

Weather had issued a peremptory warning about clouds. They were an *accidental displacement*. Corrective measures were being taken but would require time. Meanwhile, expect high winds and there could be precipitation.

Sheeana and Tamalane stood at the window looking at this poorly controlled weather. Their shoulders touched.

Odrade watched them from her chair behind the table. Those two had become like a single person since yesterday's Sharing, not an unexpected occurrence. Precedents were known, although not many of them. Exchanges, occurring in the presence of poisonous spice essence or at an actual moment of death, did not often allow further living contact between participants. It was interesting to observe. The two backs were oddly alike in their rigidity.

The force of extremis that made Sharing possible dictated powerful changes in personality and Odrade knew this with an intimacy that compelled tolerance. Whatever it was Sheeana concealed, Tam also concealed. *Something tied to Sheeana's basic humanity.* And Tam could be trusted. Until another sister Shared with one of them, Tam's judgment must be accepted. Not that watchdogs would cease probing and observing minutiae but they needed no new crises just now.

Bellonda sat hunched forward in her chairdog across from Odrade, almost sulking after a repulse by Tamalane. Bell often considered herself chief watchdog. *Did not most comeyes funnel through Archives?* Bell sensed the presence of a secret. She would gnaw at it like a beaver at a tree until the secret came tumbling down.

"Our history tells us that secrets can be dangerous." Anger openly displayed.

Tamalane had waved a clawed hand as though chasing insects from her face. "Be more cautious with your angers, Bell!"

Sheeana, for once, had not spared Bellonda. "Anger weakens!"

Sitting there with that glowering expression, Bellonda obviously was composing a new attack. She had never taken frustration easily but Odrade knew this must be diverted. Narrowing the focus, as they called it, was a cardinal sin among the sisters. First cousin to ignorance. Those who aspired to making history dared not view the universe through a restricting lens.

"This is Murbella's day," Odrade said. "Other things should not muddy our powers of observation."

"The odds are long she won't survive," Bellonda said. "What happens to our precious plan then?"

Our plan!

"Extremis," Odrade said.

In that context, it was a word with several meanings. Bellonda interpreted it as a possibility of acquiring Murbella's persona/memories at the moment of her death. "Then we must not permit Idaho to observe!"

"My order stands," Odrade said. "It's Murbella's wish and I have given my word."

"Mistake . . . mistake . . ." Bellonda muttered.

Odrade knew the source of Bellonda's doubts. Visible to all of them: Somewhere in Murbella lay something extremely painful. It caused her to shy away from certain questions like an animal confronted by a predator. Whatever it was, the thing went deep. Hypnotrance induction might not explain it.

"All right!" Odrade spoke loudly to emphasize it was for all of her listeners. "It's not the way we've ever done it before. But we cannot take Duncan from the ship so we must go to him. He will be present."

Bellonda was still well and truly shocked. No man, *barring the damned kwisatz haderach himself and his Tyrant son*, had ever known the particulars of this Bene Gesserit secret. Both of *those monsters* had felt the Agony. Two disasters! No matter that the Tyrant's Agony had worked its way inward a cell at a time to transform him into a sandworm symbiote (no more original worm, no more original human). And Muad'Dib! He dared the Agony and look what came of that!

349

Sheeana turned from the window and took one step toward the table, giving Odrade the curious feeling that the two women standing there had become a Janus figure: back to back but only one persona.

"Bell is *confused* by your promise," Sheeana said. How soft her voice.

"He could be the catalyst to pull Murbella through," Odrade said. "You tend to underestimate the power of love."

"No!" Tamalane spoke to the window in front of her. "We fear its power."

"Could be!" Bell still was scornful but that came naturally to her. The expression on her face said she remained implacably stubborn.

"Hubris," Sheeana murmured.

"What?" Bellonda whirled in her chairdog causing it to squeak with indignation.

"We share a common failing with Scytale," Sheeana said.

"Oh?" Bellonda was back gnawing at the secret.

"We think we make history," Sheeana said. She returned to her position beside Tamalane, both of them staring out the window.

Bellonda returned her attention to Odrade. "Do you understand that?"

Odrade ignored her. Let the Mentat work it out for herself. The projector on the worktable clicked and a message was displayed. Odrade reported it. "Still not ready at the ship." She looked at those two rigid backs in front of the window.

History?

On Chapter House, there had been little of what Odrade liked to think of as history-making before the Honoured Matres. Only the steady graduation of Reverend Mothers passing through the Agony.

Like a river.

It flowed and it went somewhere. You could stand on the bank (as Odrade sometimes thought they did here) and you could observe the flow. A map might tell you where the river went but no map could reveal more essential things. A map could never show intimate movements of the river's cargo.

Where did they go? Maps had limited value in this age. A printout or projection from Archives; that was not the map they required. There had to be a better one somewhere, one attached to all of those lives. You could carry *that* map in your memory and have it out occasionally for a closer look.

What ever happened to the Reverend Mother Perinte we sent out last year?

The *map-in-the-mind* would take over and create a "Perinte Scenario". It was really yourself on the river, of course, but this made little difference. It still was the map they needed.

We don't like it that we're caught in someone else's currents, that we don't know what may be revealed at the river's next bend. We always prefer overflight even though any commanding position must remain part of other currents. Every flow contains unpredictable things.

Odrade looked up to see her three companions watching her. Tamalane and Sheeana had turned their backs to the window.

"Honoured Matres have forgotten that clinging to any form of conservatism can be dangerous," Odrade said. "Have we forgotten it as well?"

They continued to stare at her but they had heard. Become too conservative and you were unprepared for surprises. That was what Muad'Dib had taught them, and his Tyrant son had made the lesson forever unforgettable.

Bellonda's glum expression did not change.

In the deep recesses of Odrade's consciousness, Taraza whispered: *"Careful, Dar. I was lucky. Quick to grab advantage. Just as you are. But you cannot depend on luck and that is what bothers them. Don't even expect luck. Much better to trust your water images. Let Bell have her say."*

"Bell," Odrade said, "I thought you accepted Duncan."

"Within limits." Definitely accusatory.

"I think we should go out to the ship." Sheeana spoke with demanding emphasis. "This is not the place to wait. Do we fear what she may become?"

Tam and Sheeana turned toward the door simultaneously as though the same puppet master controlled their strings.

Odrade found the interruption welcome. Sheeana's question alarmed them. *What could Murbella become? A catalyst, my sisters. A catalyst.*

The wind shook them when they emerged from Central and for once Odrade was thankful for tube transport. Walking could await warmer temperatures without this blustering minitempest tugging at their robes.

When they were seated in a private car, Bellonda once more took up her accusatory refrain. "Everything he does could be camouflage."

Once more, Odrade voiced the oft-repeated Bene Gesserit warning to limit their reliance on Mentats. "Logic is blind and often knows only its own past."

Tamalane chimed in with unexpected support. "You are getting paranoid, Bell!"

Sheeana spoke more softly. "I've heard you say, Bell, that logic is good for playing pyramid chess but often too slow for needs of survival."

Bellonda sat in glowering silence, only a faint hissing rumble of their tube passage intruding on the quiet.

Wounds must not be taken into the ship.

Odrade matched her tone to Sheeana's: "Bell, dear Bell. We do not have time to consider all ramifications of our plight. We no longer can say, 'If this happens, then that must surely follow, and in such a case, our moves must be so and so and so . . .'"

Bellonda actually chuckled. "Oh, my! The ordinary mind is such a clutter. And I must not demand what we all need and cannot have—sufficient time for every plan."

It was Bellonda-Mentat speaking, telling them she knew she was flawed by pride in her ordinary mind. What a badly organized, untidy place that was. *Imagine what the non-Mentat puts up with, imposing so little order.* She reached across the aisle and patted Odrade's shoulder.

"It's all right, Dar. I'll behave."

What would an outsider think, seeing that exchange? Odrade wondered. All four of them acting in concert for the needs of one sister.

For the needs of Murbella's Agony, as well.

352

People saw only the outside of this Reverend Mother mask they wore.

When we must (which is most of the time these days) we function at astonishing levels of competence. No pride in that; a simple fact. But let us relax and we hear gibberish at the edges as ordinary folk do. Ours merely has more volume. We live our lives in little congeries like anyone else. Rooms of the mind, rooms of the body.

Bellonda had composed herself, hands clasped in her lap. She knew what Odrade planned and kept it to herself. It was a trust that went beyond Mentat Projection into something more basically human. Projection was a marvellously adaptable tool but a tool nonetheless. Ultimately, all tools depended on the ones who used them. Odrade was at a loss how to show her thanks without reducing trust.

I must walk my tightrope in silence.

She sensed the chasm beneath her, the nightmare image conjured by these reflections. The unseen hunter with an axe was closer. Odrade wanted to turn and identify the stalker but resisted. *I will not make Muad'Dib's mistake!* The prescient warning she had first sensed on Dune in the ruins of Sietch Tabr would not be exorcized until she ended or the Sisterhood ended. *Did I create this terrible threat by my fears? Surely not!* Still, she felt she had stared at Time in that ancient Fremen stronghold as though all past and all future were frozen into a tableau that could not be changed. *I must break free of you utterly, Muad'Dib!*

Their arrival at the Landing Flat pulled her from these fearful musings.

Murbella waited in rooms Proctors had prepared. At the centre was a small amphitheatre about seven metres along its enclosing back wall. Padded benches were stepped upward in a steep arc, seating for no more than twenty observers. Proctors had left her without explanation on the lowest bench staring at a suspensor-buoyed table. Straps hung over the sides to confine whoever lay on it.

Me.

An astonishing series of rooms, she thought. She had never before been permitted into this part of the ship. She felt

353

exposed here even more so than she had under the open sky en route from Central. The smaller rooms through which they had brought her to this amphitheatre were clearly designed for medical emergencies: resuscitation equipment, sanitary odours, antiseptics.

Her removal to the ship had been peremptory, none of her questions answered. Proctors had taken her from an advanced acolyte class in prana bindu exercises. They said only: "Mother Superior's orders."

The quality of her guardian Proctors told her much. *Gentle but firm.* They were here to prevent flight and to make sure she went where ordered. *I won't try to escape!*

Where was Duncan?

Odrade had promised he could be with her for the Agony. Did his absence mean this was not to be her ultimate trial? Or had they concealed him behind some secret wall through which he could see and not be seen?

I want him at my side!

Didn't they know how to rule her? Certainly they did!

Threaten to deprive me of this man. That's all it takes to hold me and satisfy me. Satisfy! What a useless word. Complete me. That's better. I am less when we're apart. He knows it, too, damn him.

Murbella smiled. *How does he know it? Because he is completed in the same way.*

How could this be love? She felt no weakening from the tugs of desire. Bene Gesserit and Honoured Matres alike said love weakened. She felt strengthened by Duncan. Even his small attentions were strengthening. When he brought her a steaming cup of stimtea in the morning, it was better coming from his hands. *Perhaps we have something more than love.*

Odrade and companions entered the amphitheatre at the uppermost tier and stood a moment looking down at the figure seated below them. Murbella wore the white-trimmed long robe of a senior acolyte. She sat with elbow on knee, chin resting on fist, her attention concentrated on the table.

She knows.

"Where is Duncan?" Odrade asked.

At her words, Murbella stood and turned. The question confirmed what she had suspected.

"I'll find out," Sheeana said and left them.

Murbella waited in silence, matching Odrade stare for stare.

We must have her, Odrade thought. Never had the Bene Gesserit need been greater. What an insignificant figure Murbella was down there to carry so much in her person. The almost oval face with its widening at the brows revealed new Bene Gesserit composure. Widely set green eyes, arched brows—no squinting—no more orange. Small mouth—no more pouting.

She is ready.

Sheeana returned with Duncan at her side.

Odrade spared him a brief glance. *Nervous.* So Sheeana had told him. *Good.* That was an act of friendship. He might need friends here.

"You will sit up here and remain here unless I call you," Odrade said. "Stay with him, Sheeana."

Without being told, Tamalane flanked Duncan, one of them on each side. At a gentle gesture from Sheeana, they sat.

Bellonda beside her, Odrade descended to Murbella's level and went to the table. Oral syringes on the far side were ready to lift into position but remained empty. Odrade gestured at the syringes and nodded to Bellonda who went out of a side door in search of the Suk Reverend Mother in charge of spice essence.

Moving the table away from the back wall, Odrade began laying out straps and adjusting pads. She moved methodically, checking that everything had been provided on the small ledge beneath the table. Mouth pad to keep the Agonized One from biting her tongue. Odrade felt it to be sure it was strong. Murbella had a muscular jaw.

Murbella watched Odrade work, keeping silent, trying to make no disturbing noises.

Mother Superior at work was a fascinating study even in ordinary times. Murbella had seen early in their association that Odrade was a virtuoso performer, decisions made almost before attendants finished stating problems. Imaginative questions.

"Why have we not captured another Honoured Matre and

355

brought her into contact with Murbella here?" Slight nod of head toward Murbella who, hearing her name, only blinked. As they taught me to do. Odrade so quick with sharp responses to useless questions! "Canned data! Must we parade the same old suggestions every time we confront our difficulties?"

Murbella suddenly saw Odrade as an ally. The two of them were alike in many ways.

Bellonda returned with spice essence and proceeded to fill the syringes. The poisonous essence had a pungent odour—bitter cinnamon.

Catching Odrade's attention, Murbella said, "I'm grateful that you're supervising this yourself."

"She's grateful!" Bellonda sneered, not looking up from her work.

"Leave this to me, Bell." Odrade kept her attention on Murbella.

Bellonda did not pause but something withdrawn took over her movements. Bellonda effacing herself? It never ceased to astonish Murbella how acolytes effaced themselves when they entered Mother Superior's presence. There but not there. Murbella had never quite achieved this even when she left probation and entered advanced status. *Bellonda, too?*

Staring hard at Murbella, Odrade said: "I know what reservations you hold in your breast, limits you place on your commitment to us. Well and good. I make no argument about that because, by and large, your reservations are very little different from those held by any of us."

Candour.

"The difference, if you would know it, is in the sense of responsibility. I am responsible for my sisterhood . . . as much of it as still survives. They are a deep responsibility and one I sometimes look at with a jaundiced eye."

Bellonda sniffed.

Odrade appeared not to notice this as she continued. "The Bene Gesserit Sisterhood has gone somewhat sour since the Tyrant. Our contact with your Honoured Matres has not improved matters. Honoured Matres have the stench of death and decadence about them, going down hill into the great silence."

356

"Why do you tell me these things now?" Fear in Murbella's voice.

"Because, somehow, the worst of Honoured Matre decadence did not touch you. Your spontaneous nature, perhaps. Although that has been dampened somewhat since Gammu."

"Your doing!"

"We've just taken a little wildness out of you, given you a better balance. You can live longer and healthier because of it."

"If I survive this!" Jerk of her head toward the table behind her.

"Balance is what I want you to remember, Murbella. Homeostasis. Any group choosing suicide when it has other options does so out of insanity. Homeostasis gone haywire."

When Murbella looked at the floor, Bellonda snapped: "Listen to her, fool! She's doing her best to help you."

"All right, Bell. This is between us."

When Murbella continued to stare at the floor, Odrade said: "This is Mother Superior giving you an order. Look at me!"

Murbella's head snapped up and she stared into Odrade's eyes.

It was a tactic Odrade had used infrequently but with excellent results. Acolytes could be reduced to hysteria by it and then taught how to deal with their excessive response to emotions. Murbella appeared to be more angered than fearful. Excellent! But now was a time for caution.

"You have complained about the slow pacing of your education," Odrade said. "It was done with your needs foremost in our minds. Your key teachers all were chosen for steadiness, none of them impulsive. My instructions were explicit: 'Don't give her too many abilities too rapidly. Don't open a floodgate of power that might be more than she can handle.'"

"How do you know what I can handle?" Still angry.

Odrade only smiled.

When Odrade continued silent, Murbella appeared flustered. Had she made a fool of herself before Mother Superior, before Duncan and these others? How humiliating.

Odrade reminded herself it was not good to make Murbella too conscious of her vulnerability. A bad tactic just now. No need to provoke her. She had a sharp sense of the germane, fitting herself into needs of the moment. That was the thing they feared might have its source in a motivation always to choose the path of least resistance. *Let it not be that.* Complete honesty now! The ultimate tool of Bene Gesserit education. The classical technique that bound acolyte to teacher.

"I will be at your side throughout your Agony. If you fail, I will grieve."

"Duncan?" Tears in her eyes.

"Any help he can give, he will be permitted to give."

Murbella looked up the rows of seats and, for a brief moment, her gaze locked with Idaho's. He lifted slightly but Tamalane's hand on his shoulder restrained him.

They may kill my beloved! Idaho thought. *Must I sit here and just watch it happen?* But Odrade had said he would be permitted to help. *There is no stopping this now. I must trust Dar. But, gods below! She does not know the depth of my grief if . . . if . . ."* He closed his eyes.

"Bell." Odrade's voice carried a sense of casting off, a knife edge in its brittleness.

Bellonda took Murbella's arm and helped her on to the table. It bounced slightly adjusting to the weight.

This is the real chute, Murbella thought.

She had only the remotest sense of straps being fastened around her, of purposeful movement beside her.

"This is the usual routine," Odrade said.

Routine? Murbella had hated the routines of becoming Bene Gesserit, all of that study, listening and reacting to Proctors. She had particularly loathed the necessity to refine reactions she had believed adequate but there could be no sloughing off under those watchful eyes.

Adequate! What a dangerous word.

This recognition had been precisely what they sought. Precisely the leverage their acolyte required.

If you loathe it, do it better. Use your loathing guidance; home in on exactly what you need.

The fact that her teachers saw so directly into her behaviour, what a marvellous thing! She wanted that ability. Oh, how she wanted it!

I must excel in this.

It was a thing any Honoured Matre might envy. She saw herself abruptly with a form of doubled vision: both Bene Gesserit and Honoured Matre. A daunting perception.

Murbella sensed then what Odrade had been doing with words and tone.

A hand touched her cheek, moved her head and went away.

Responsibility. I am about to learn what they mean by "a new sense of history".

The Bene Gesserit view of history fascinated her. How did they look at multiple pasts? Was it something immersed in a grander scheme? The temptation to become one of them had been overwhelming.

This is the moment when I learn.

She saw an oral syringe swing into position above her mouth. Bellonda's hand moved it.

"*We carry our grail in our heads.*" Odrade had said. "*Carry this grail gently if it comes into your possession.*"

The syringe touched her lips. Murbella closed her eyes but felt fingers open her mouth. Cold metal touched her teeth. Odrade's remembered voice was with her.

"*Avoid excesses. Overcorrect and you always have a fine mess on your hands, the necessity to make larger and larger corrections. Oscillation. Fanatics are marvellous creators of oscillation.*

"*Our grail. It has linearity because each Reverend Mother carries the same determination. We will perpetuate this together.*"

Bitter liquid gushed into her mouth. Murbella swallowed convulsively. She felt fire flow down her throat into her stomach. No pain except the burning. She wondered if this could be the extent of it. Her stomach felt merely warm now.

Slowly, so slowly she was several heartbeats recognizing it, the warmth flowed outward. When it reached the tips of her fingers she felt her body convulse. Her back arched off the padded table. Something soft but firm replaced the syringe in her mouth.

Voices. She heard them and knew people were speaking but could not distinguish words.

As she concentrated on the voices she became aware she had lost touch with her body. Somewhere, flesh writhed and there was pain but she was removed from it.

A hand touched a hand and clasped it firmly. She recognized Duncan's touch and abruptly, there was her body and agony. Her lungs pained when she exhaled. Not when she inhaled. Then they felt flat and never full enough. Her sense of presence in living flesh became a thin thread that wound through many presences. She sensed others all around her, far too many people for the tiny amphitheatre.

Another human being floated into view. Murbella felt herself to be in a factory shuttle . . . in space. The shuttle was primitive. Too many manual controls. Too many blinking lights. A woman at the controls, small and untidy with the sweat of her labours. She had long brown hair and it had been bound up in a chignon from which paler strands escaped to hang around her narrow cheeks. She wore a single garment, a short dress of brilliant reds, blues and greens.

Machinery.

There was awareness of monstrous machinery just beyond this immediate space. The woman's dress contrasted severely with the drab and dragging sense of machinery. She spoke but her lips did not move. "Listen, you! When it comes time for you to take over these controls, don't become a destroyer. I'm here to help you avoid the destroyers. Do you know that?"

Murbella tried to speak but had no voice.

"Don't try so hard, girl!" the woman said. "I hear you."

Murbella tried to shift her attention away from the woman. *Where is this place?*

One operator, a giant warehouse . . . factory . . . everything automated . . . webs of feedback lines centred into this tiny space with its complex controls.

Thinking to whisper, Murbella asked: *"Who are you?"* and heard her own voice roar. Agony in her ears!

"Not so loud! I'm your guide of the mohalata, the one who steers you clear of the destroyers."

Dur protect me! Murbella thought. *This is no place; it's me!*

On that thought, the control room vanished. She was a migrant in the void, condemned never to be quiet, never to find a moment of sanctuary. Everything but her own fleeting thoughts became immaterial. She had no substance, only a wispy adherence that she recognized as consciousness.

I have constructed myself out of fog.

Other Memory came, bits and pieces of experiences she knew were not her own. Faces leered at her and demanded her attention but the woman at the shuttle controls pulled her away. Murbella recognized necessities but could not put them into coherent form.

"These are lives in your past." It was the woman at the shuttle controls but her voice had a disembodied quality and came from no discernible place.

"We are descendants of people who did nasty things," the woman said. "We don't like to admit there were barbarians in our ancestry. A Reverend Mother must admit it. We have no choice."

Murbella had the knack of only thinking her questions now. *Why must I . . .*

"The victors bred. We are their descendants. Victory often was gained at great moral price. Barbarism is not even an adequate word for some of the things our ancestors did."

Murbella felt a familiar hand on her cheek. *Duncan!* The touch restored agony. *Oh, Duncan! You're hurting me.*

Through the pain, she sensed gaps in the lives being revealed to her. Things withheld.

"Only what you're capable of accepting now," the disembodied voice said. "Others come later when you're stronger . . . if you survive."

Selective filter. Odrade's words. *Necessity opens doors.*

Persistent wailing came from the other presences. Laments: *"See? See what happens when you ignore common sense?"*

Agony increased. She could not escape it. Every nerve was touched with flame. She wanted to cry, to scream threats, to implore for help. Tumbling emotions accompanied the agony but she ignored them. Everything happened along a thin thread of existence. The thread could snap!

I'm dying.

The thread was stretching. It was going to break! Hopeless to resist. Muscles would not obey. There probably were no muscles remaining to her. She did not want them anyway. They were pain. It was hell and would never end . . . not even if the thread snapped. Flames burned along the thread, licking at her awareness.

Hands shook her shoulders. *Duncan . . . don't.* Each movement was pain beyond anything she had imagined possible. This deserved to be called The Agony.

The thread no longer was stretching. It was pulling back, compressing. It became one small thing, a sausage of such exquisite pain that nothing else existed. The sense of *being* became vague, translucent . . . transparent.

"Do you see?" the voice of her mohalata guide came from far away.

I see things.

Not exactly seeing. A distant awareness of others. Other sausages. Other Memory encased in the skins of lost lives. They extended behind her in a train whose length she could not determine. Translucent fog. It ripped apart occasionally and she glimpsed events. No . . . not events themselves. Memory.

"Share witness," her guide said. "You see what our ancestors have done. They debase the worst curse you can invent. Don't make excuses about necessities of the times! Just remember: There are no innocents!"

Ugly! Ugly!

She could hold onto none of it. Everything became reflections and ripping fog. Somewhere there was a glory that she knew she might attain.

Absence of this Agony.

That was it. How glorious that would be!

Where is that glorious condition?

Lips touched her forehead, her mouth. *Duncan!* She reached up. *My hands are free.* Her fingers slipped into remembered hair. *This is real!*

Agony receded. Only then did she realize that she had come through pain more terrible than words could describe. Agony?

362

It seared the psyche and remoulded her. One person entered and another emerged.

Duncan! She opened her eyes and there was his face directly above her. *Do I still love him? He is here. He is an anchor to which I clung in the worst moments. But do I love him? Am I still balanced?*

No answer.

Odrade spoke from somewhere out of view. "Strip those clothes off her. Towels. She's drenched. And bring her a proper robe!"

There were scurrying sounds, then Odrade once more: "Murbella, you did that the hard way I'm glad to say."

Such elation in her voice. Why was she glad?

Where is the sense of responsibility? Where is the grail I'm supposed to feel in my head. Answer me someone!

But the woman at the shuttle controls was gone.

Only I remain. And I remember atrocities that might make an Honoured Matre quail. She glimpsed the grail then and it was not a *thing* but a question: How to set those balances aright?

> *Our household god is this thing we carry forward generation*
> *after generation: our message for humankind if it matures.*
> *The closest thing we have to a household goddess is a failed*
> *Reverend Mother—Chenoeh there in her niche.*
>
> **—Darwi Odrade**

Idaho thought of his Mentat abilities as a retreat now. Murbella stayed with him in the ship as frequently as their duties allowed—he with his weapons development and she recovering strength while she adjusted to her new status.

She did not lie to him. She did not try to tell him she felt no difference between them. But he sensed the pulling away, elastic being stretched to its limits.

"My sisters have been taught not to divulge secrets of the heart. There's the danger they perceive in love. Perilous intimacies. The deepest sensitivities blunted. Do not give someone a stick with which to beat you."

She thought her words reassuring to him but he heard the inner argument. *Be free! Break entangling bonds!*

He saw her often these days in the throes of Other Memory. Words escaped her in the night.

"Dependencies . . . group soul . . . intersection of living awareness . . . Fish Speakers . . ."

She had no hesitations about sharing some of this. "The intersection? Anyone can sense nexus points in the natural interruptions of life. Deaths, diversions, incidental pauses between powerful events, births . . ."

"Birth an interruption?"

They were in his bed, even the chrono darkened . . . but that did not hide them from comeyes, of course. Other energies fed the Sisterhood's curiosity.

"You never thought of birth as an interruption? A Reverend Mother finds that amusing."

Amusing! Pulling away . . . pulling away . . .

Fish Speakers, that was the revelation the Bene Gesserit absorbed with fascination. They had suspected, but Murbella gave them confirmation. Fish Speaker democracy became Honoured Matre autocracy. No more doubts.

"The tyranny of the minority cloaked in the mask of the majority," Odrade called it, her voice exultant. "Downfall of democracy. Either overthrown by its own excesses or eaten away by bureaucracy."

Idaho could hear the Tyrant in that judgment. If history had any repetitive patterns, here was one. A drumbeat of repetition. First, a Civil Service law masked in the lie that it was the only way to correct demagogic excesses and spoils systems. Then the accumulation of power in places voters could not touch. And finally, aristocracy.

"Bene Gesserits may be the only ones ever to create the all-powerful jury," Murbella said. "Juries are not popular with legalists. Juries oppose the law. They can ignore judges."

She laughed in the darkness. "Evidence! What is evidence except those things you are allowed to perceive? That's what Law tries to control: carefully managed reality."

Words to divert him, words to demonstrate her new Bene Gesserit powers. Her words of love fell flat.

364

She speaks them out of memory.

He saw this bothered Odrade almost as much as it dismayed him. Murbella did not notice either reaction.

Odrade had tried to reassure him. "Every new Reverend Mother goes through an adjustment period. Manic at times. Think of the new ground under her, Duncan!"

How can I not think of it?

"First law of bureaucracy," Murbella told the darkness.

You do not divert me, love.

"Grow to the limits of available energy!" Her voice was indeed manic. "Use the lie that taxes solve all problems." She turned toward him in the bed but not for love. "Honoured Matres played the whole routine! Even a social security system to quiet the masses, but everything went into their own energy bank."

"Murbella!"

"What?" Surprised at the sharpness of his tone. *Didn't he know he was talking to a Reverend Mother?*

"I know all of this, Murbella. Any Mentat does."

"Are you trying to shut me up?" Angry.

"Our job is to think like our enemy," he said. "We do have a common enemy?

"You're sneering at me, Duncan."

"Are your eyes orange?"

"Melange doesn't allow that and you know . . . Oh."

"The Bene Gesserit need your knowledge but you must *cultivate* it!" He turned on a glowglobe and found her glaring at him. Not unexpected and not really Bene Gesserit.

Hybrid.

The word leaped into his mind. Was it hybrid vigour? Did the Sisterhood expect this in Murbella? They surprised you sometimes. You found them facing you in odd corridors, eyes unwavering, faces masked in that way of theirs and, behind the masks, unusual responses brewing. That was where Teg learned to do the unexpected. But this? Idaho thought he could grow to dislike this new Murbella.

She saw this in him, naturally. He remained open to her as to no other person.

"Don't hate me, Duncan." No pleading but something deeply hurt behind the words.

"I'll never hate you." But he turned off the light.

She nestled against him almost the way she had before the Agony. *Almost.* The difference tore at him.

"They've had me talking about Honoured Matre terrorism all day," she said.

He already had seen most of this record, hoping for a clue to new weapons. Terror was an exceedingly unstable commodity. You had to keep raising the stakes. *What do the masses want, Spider Queen? They want out of your prison.*

"Then make the bars more painful!"

You did that last time.

"And we'll do it again!"

Forever?

"As long as necessary!"

That's another euphemism for Infinity.

And it was another way of denying Infinity, of not admitting there were limits other than your own. Forever not only was longer than humans cared to imagine, it was longer than most *could* imagine. It contained a freedom that blinded and deafened consciousness. Demagogues and religious leaders counted on this.

The blind and deaf are more easily led.

"Honoured Matres see the Bene Gesserit as competitors for power," Murbella said. "It's not so much that men who follow my former sisters are fanatics, but they're made incapable of self determination by their addiction."

"Is that the way *we* are?"

"Now, Duncan."

"You mean I could get this commodity at another store?"

She chose to assume he was talking about Honoured Matre fears. "Many would abandon them if they could." Turning toward him fiercely, she demanded a sexual response. Her abandon shocked him. As though this might be the last time she could experience such ecstasy.

Afterward, he lay exhausted.

"I hope I'm pregnant again," she whispered. "We still need our babies."

We need. The Bene Gesserit need. No longer "they need".

He fell asleep to dream he was in the ship's armoury. It was a dream touched by realities. The ship remained a weapons factory as it actually had become. Odrade was talking to him in the dream armoury. "I make decisions of necessity, Duncan. Little likelihood you'll break out and run amok."

"I am too much the Mentat for that!" How self important his dream voice! *I'm dreaming and I know I dream. Why am I in the armoury with Odrade?*

A list of weapons scrolled before his eyes.

Atomics. (He saw big blasters and deadly dusts.)

Lasguns. (No counting the various models.)

Bacteriologicals.

The scroll was interrupted by Odrade's voice. "We can assume smugglers concentrate as usual on small things that bring a big price."

"Soostones, of course." Still self important. *I'm not that way!*

"Assassination weapons," she said. "Plans and specifications for new devices."

"Theft of trade secrets is a big item with smugglers." *I'm insufferable!*

"There are always medicines and the diseases that require them," she said.

Where is she? I can hear her but I can't see her. "Do Honoured Matres know our universe harbours blackguards not above sowing the problem before providing the solution?" *Blackguards? I never use that word.*

"All things relative, Duncan. They burned Lampadas and butchered four million of our finest."

He awoke and sat upright. *Specifications for new devices!* There it was in delicate detail, a way to miniaturize Holzmann generators. Two centimetres, no more. And much cheaper! *How was that smuggled into my mind?*

He slipped out of bed, not awakening Murbella and groped his way to a robe. He heard her snuffle as he let himself out into the workroom.

Seating himself at his console, he copied the design from his mind and studied it. Perfect! Englobement for sure. He transmitted to Archives with a flag for Odrade and Bellonda.

With a sigh, he sat back and examined his design once more. It vanished in a return to his dream scroll. *Am I still dreaming? No!* He could feel the chair, touch the console, hear the field buzzing. *Dreams do that.*

The scroll produced cutting and stabbing weapons, including some designed to introduce poisons or bacteria into enemy flesh.

Projectiles.

He wondered how to stop the scroll and study details.

"It's all in your head!"

Humans and other animals bred for attack scrolled past his eyes, hiding the console and its projection. *Futars? How did Futars get in there? What do I know about Futars?*

Disruptors replaced the animals. Weapons to cloud mental activity or interfere with life itself. *Disruptors? I've never heard that name before?*

Disruptors were succeeded by null-G "seekers" designed to hunt specific targets. *Those, I know.*

Explosives next, including ones to spread poisons and bacteriologicals.

Deceptives, to project false targets. Teg had used those.

Energizers appeared next. He had a private arsenal of those: ways of increasing capacities of your troops.

Abruptly, the shimmering net from his vision replaced scrolling weapons and he saw the elderly couple in their garden setting. They glared at him. The man's voice became audible. "Stop spying on us!"

Idaho gripped the arms of his chair and jerked himself forward but the vision disappeared before he could study details.

Spying?

He sensed a residue of the scroll in his mind, no longer visible but a musing voice . . . masculine.

"Defences often must take on characteristics of the attack weapons. Sometimes, however, simple systems can divert the most devastating weapons.

Simple systems! He laughed aloud. "Miles! Where the hell are you, Teg? I have your disguised attack vessels! Inflated decoys! Empty except for a miniature Holzmann generator and lasgun." He added this to his Archives transmissions.

When he was finished, he asked himself once more about the visions. *Influencing my dreams? What have I tapped?*

In every spare minute since becoming Teg's Weapons Master, he had been calling up Archival records. There had to be some clue in all of that massive accumulation!

Resonances and tachyon theory held his attention for a time. Tachyon theory figured in Holzmann's original design. "Techys", Holzmann had called his energy source.

A *wave system* that ignored light speed's limits. Light speed obviously did not limit foldspace ships. Techys?

"It works because it works," Idaho muttered. "Faith. Like any other religion."

Mentats squirrelled away much seemingly inconsequential data. He had a storehouse marked "Techys" and proceeded to unreel it without satisfaction.

Not even Guild Navigators professed knowledge of how they guided foldspace ships. Ixian scientists made machines to duplicate Navigator abilities but still could not define what they did.

"Holzmann's formulae can be trusted."

No one claimed to understand Holzmann. They merely used his formulae because these worked. It was the "ether" of space travel. You *folded* space. One instant you were here and the next instant you were countless parsecs distant.

Someone "out there" has found another way to use Holzmann's theories! It was a full Mentat Projection. He knew its accuracy from the new questions it produced.

Murbella's Other Memory ramblings haunted him now even though he recognized basic Bene Gesserit teachings in them.

Power attracts the corruptible. Absolute power attracts the absolutely corruptible. This is the danger of entrenched bureaucracy to its subject population. Even spoils systems are preferable because levels of tolerance are lower and the corrupt can be thrown out periodically. Entrenched bureaucracy seldom can be touched short of violence. Beware when Civil Service and Military join hands!

The Honoured Matre achievement.

Power for the sake of power . . . an aristocracy bred from unbalanced stock.

Who were those people he saw? Strong enough to drive out Honoured Matres. He knew it for a Projection datum.

Idaho found this realization profoundly dislocating. Honoured Matres fugitives. Barbaric but ignorant in the way of all such raiders even from before the Vandals. Moved by impulsive greed as much as by any other force. *"Take Roman gold!"* They filtered all distractions out of awareness. It was a stupefying ignorance that faltered only when the more sophisticated culture insinuated itself into the . . .

Abruptly, he saw what Odrade was doing.

Gods below! What a fragile plan!

He pressed his palms against his eyes and forced himself not to cry out in anguish. *Let them think I'm tired.* But seeing Odrade's plan told him also he would lose Murbella . . . one way or another.

> When are the witches to be trusted? Never! The dark side of the magic universe belongs to the Bene Gesserit and we must reject them.
>
> —Tylwyth Waff
> Master of Masters

The great Common Room of Central with its tiered seating and raised platform at one end was packed with Bene Gesserit sisters, more than had ever before been assembled here. Chapter House was almost at a standstill this afternoon because few wanted to send proxies and important decisions could not be delegated to the service cadre. Black-robed Reverend Mothers dominated the assemblage in their aloof clusterings close to the stage but the room swirled with acolytes in white-trimmed robes and there were even the newly enrolled. Groups of white robes marking the youngest acolytes were sprinkled around in tight little groups, flocking for mutual support. All others had been excluded by Convocation Proctors.

The air was heavy with melange-perfumed breaths and it

370

had that dank, overused quality it got when conditioning machinery was overloaded. Odours of the recent lunch, strong with garlic, rode on this atmosphere like an uninvited intruder. This and stories being spread throughout the room heightened tensions.

Most kept their attention on the raised platform and the side door where Mother Superior must enter. Even while talking to companions or moving about, they focused on that place where they knew someone soon would enter and create profound changes in their lives. Mother Superior did not herd them all into the great Common Room with a promise of important announcements unless something to shake the Bene Gesserit foundations was at hand.

The room had used ancient sports stadiums as prototype and seating reserved by long usage separated sisters to some degree. Closer to the stage, more important. Acolytes quipped that this demonstrated how you sank into the Sisterhood, moving downward as you progressed in abilities.

Acolytes far from the Agony suspected they were being manoeuvred. After all, the Bene Gesserit had raised crowd control to a fine art. There were tiny pheromone emitters, for example. Get a whole mass of people twitchy and uncertain. Reverend Mothers in mufti moving in such a throng pitched their voices to just the proper level, saying just the right things.

"I don't care about you, friend, but I'm getting out of here. This is no place for someone who values his skin." "I think the important ones went down that street. I saw some activity there a few minutes ago." "The whole thing's been settled. I heard it from you-know-who back there at the corner."

"You-know-who" was a marvellous label. It said: "We both know the name and it's too important to speak out here among peasants." A wise nod, a covert wink. Body messages to go with carefully pitched voices. Reverend Mothers had been known to bring a mob under control in only a few minutes and not a single person aware they had been manoeuvred.

Younger acolytes sniffed the air for pheromones and looked for strange devices or odd movements among Reverend Mothers. Proctors were busy, employing candour to its utmost in the effort to reduce tensions.

Mother Superior was never subjected to the mass scrimmage attendant on appearance for assemblies. She never had elbows jammed into her ribs or felt the trodding of a neighbour's foot. She was never forced to move as others moved in a kind of inchworm flow composed of bodies pressed together in unwanted proximity.

Bellonda preceded Odrade into the room, mounting to the platform with that belligerent waddle which made her easily recognizable even at a distance. Odrade followed at five paces. Then came senior councillors and aides, black-robed Murbella (still looking somewhat dazed from her Agony only two weeks past) among them. Dortujla limped close behind Murbella with Tam and Sheeana at her side. At the end of this procession came Streggi carrying Teg on her shoulders. There were excited murmurs when he appeared. Males seldom shared assemblies but everyone on Chapter House knew this was the ghola of their Mentat Bashar, living now at the cantonment with all that remained of a Bene Gesserit military.

Seeing the massed ranks of the Sisterhood this way, Odrade experienced an empty feeling. Some ancient had said it all, she thought. "Any damned fool knows one horse can run faster than another." Often at the minor assemblages here in this copy of a sports stadium she had been tempted to quote that bit of advice but she knew the ritual had its better purposes as well. Assembly showed you to one another.

Here we are together. Our kind.

Mother Superior and attendants moved like a peculiar bundle of energy through the throng to the platform, her position of eminence at the edge of the arena.

Thus did Caesar arrive. Thumbs down on the whole damned thing! To Bellonda, she said: "Let it begin."

Afterward, she knew she would wonder why she had not delegated someone to make this ritual appearance and utter portentous words. Bellonda would love the pre-eminent position and, for that reason, must never have it. But perhaps there was some lower-echelon sister who would be embarrassed by elevation and would obey only out of loyalty, out of that underlying need to do what Mother Superior commanded.

372

Gods! If there are any of you around, why do you permit us to be such sheep?

There they were, Bellonda preparing them for her. *The battalions of the Bene Gesserit*. They were not really battalions, but Odrade often imagined ranked sisters, cataloguing them by function. *That one is a squad leader. That one is a Captain General. This one is a lowly sergeant and here is a messenger.*

The sisters would be outraged if they knew this quirk in her. She kept it well concealed behind an 'ordinary assignment' attitude. You could assign lieutenants without calling them lieutenants. Taraza had done the same thing.

Questioned once by Bellonda, Odrade had said: "We are professionals of wide expertise and that is a curious thing in itself, Bell. Specialists tend to gravitate to the place where they can be employed. Think about it."

Odrade contemplated her own thoughts glumly. This was not the kind of analysis she preferred. It led into an either-or cul de sac. *No way out unless we choose one of two options: Grasp the reins and become tyrants in our own right or vanish into a history written by others.*

Bell was telling them now that the Sisterhood might have to make a new accommodation with their captive Tleilaxu. Bitter words for Bell: "We have gone through the crucible, Tleilaxu and Bene Gesserit alike, and we have come out changed. In a way, we have changed each other."

Yes, we are like rocks rubbed against each other for so long that each takes on some of the conforming shape required by the other. But the original rock is still there at the core!

The audience was becoming restive. They knew this was preliminary, no matter the hidden message within these hints about Tleilaxu. Preliminary and relative in importance. Odrade stepped to Bellonda's side, signalling her to cut it short.

"Here is Mother Superior."

How hard the old patterns die. Does Bell think they don't recognize me?

Odrade spoke in compelling tones, just short of Voice.

"Actions have been taken that require me to meet on

373

Junction with Honoured Matre leadership, a meeting from which I may not emerge alive. I *probably* will not survive. That meeting will be partly distraction. We are about to punish them."

Odrade waited for murmurs to subside, hearing both agreement and disagreement in the sounds. Interesting. The ones who agreed were closer to the stage and farther back among new acolytes. Disagreement from advanced acolytes? Yes. They knew the warning: *We dare not feed that fire*.

She pitched her voice lower, letting remotes carry it to those in the high tiers. "Before leaving, I will Share with more than one sister. These times require such caution."

"Your plan?" "What will you do?" Questions were shouted at her from many places.

"We will feint at Gammu. That should drive Honoured Matre allies to Junction. We then will take Junction and, I hope, capture the Spider Queen."

"The attack will occur while you are on Junction?" This question came from Garimi, a sober-faced Proctor directly below Odrade.

"That is the plan. I will be transmitting my observations to the attackers." Odrade gestured to Teg seated on Streggi's shoulders. "The Bashar will lead the attack in person."

"Who goes with you?" "Yes. Who are you taking?" No mistaking the worry in those cries. So the word had not yet spread through Chapter House.

"Tam and Dortujla," Odrade said.

"Who will Share with you?" Garimi again. *Indeed! That is the political question of most interest. Who may succeed Mother Superior?* Odrade heard nervous stirring behind her. *Bellonda excited? Not you, Bell. You already know that.*

"Murbella and Sheeana," Odrade said. "And one other if Proctors care to name a candidate."

Proctors formed little consulting groups, shouting suggestions from group to group, but no names were submitted. Someone had a question though: "Why Murbella?"

"Who knows Honoured Matres better?" Odrade asked.

That silenced them.

Garimi moved closer to the stage and looked up at Odrade

with a penetrating stare. *Don't try to mislead a Reverend Mother, Darwi Odrade!* "After our feint at Gammu, they will be even more alert and reinforced on Junction. What makes you think we can take them?"

Odrade stepped aside and motioned Streggi forward with Teg.

Teg had been watching Odrade's performance with fascination. He looked down now at Garimi. She was currently Chief Assignment Proctor and no doubt had been chosen to speak for a bloc of sisters. It occurred to Teg then that this ludicrous position on the shoulders of an acolyte had been planned by Odrade with reasons other than those she voiced.

To put my eyes closer to a level with adults around me . . . but also to remind them of my lesser stature, to reassure them that a Bene Gesserit (if only an acolyte) still controls my movements.

"I will not go into all of the weaponry details at the moment," he said. *Damn this piping voice!* He had their attention, though. "But we are going for mobility, for decoys that will destroy a great deal of the area around them if a lasgun beam hits them . . . and we are going to englobe Junction with devices to reveal the movements of their no-ships."

When they continued to stare at him, he said: "If Mother Superior confirms my previous knowledge of Junction, we will know our enemy's positions intimately. There should not be significant changes. Not enough time has passed . . ."

Surprise and the unexpected. What else did they expect from their Mentat Bashar? He stared back at Garimi, daring her to voice more doubts of his military ability.

She had another question. "Are we to presume that Duncan Idaho advises you on weapons?"

"When you have the best, you would be a fool not to use it," he said.

"But will he accompany you as Weapons Master?"

"He chooses not to leave the ship and you all know why. What is the meaning of that question?"

He had deflected her and silenced her and she did not like it. A man should not be able to manoeuvre a Reverend Mother that way!

Odrade stepped forward and put a hand on Teg's arm.

"Have you all forgotten that this ghola is our loyal friend, Miles Teg?" She stared at particular faces in the throng, choosing ones she was certain watchdogged the comeyes and knew Teg was her father, moving her gaze from face to face with a deliberate slowness that could not be misinterpreted.

Is there one among you who dares cry "nepotism"? Then look once more at his record in our service!

Sounds of the Convocation became once more those in keeping with other graces they expected in assemblies. No more vulgar clash of demanding voices vying for attention. Now, they fitted their speech into a pattern much like plainsong and yet not quite a chant. Voices moved and flowed together. Odrade always found this remarkable. No one directed the harmony. It happened because they were Bene Gesserit. Naturally. This was the only explanation they needed. It happened because they were practised in adjusting to each other. The dance of their everyday movements continued in their voices. Partners no matter transitory disagreements.

"It is never enough to make accurate predictions of distressful events," she said. "Who knows this better than we? Is there one among us who has not learned the lesson of the kwisatz haderach?"

No need to elaborate. Evil prediction should not alter their course. That kept Bellonda silent. The Bene Gesserit were enlightened. Not dullards who attacked the bearer of bad tidings. Discount the messenger? *(Who could expect anything useful from the likes of that one?)* That was a pattern to be avoided at all costs. *Will we silence disagreeable messengers, thinking the deep silence of death obliterates the message?* The Bene Gesserit knew better than that! *Death makes a prophet's voice louder. Martyrs are truly dangerous.*

Odrade watched reflective awareness spread through the room, even up to the highest tiers.

We are entering hard times, sisters, and must accept that. Even Murbella knows it. And she knows now why I was so anxious to make a sister of her. We all know it one way or another.

Odrade turned and glanced at Bellonda. No disappointment

376

there. Bell knew why she was not among the chosen. *It's our best course, Bell. Infiltrate. Take them before they even suspect what we're doing.*

Shifting her gaze to Murbella, Odrade saw respectful awareness. Murbella was beginning to get her first batches of good advice from Other Memory. The manic stage had passed and she was even regaining a *fondness* for Duncan. In time perhaps . . . Bene Gesserit training assured that she would judge Other Memory on her own. Nothing in Murbella's stance said: "Keep your lousy advice to yourself!" She had historical comparisons and could not evade their obvious message.

Don't march in the streets with others who share your prejudices. Loud shouts are often the easiest to ignore. "I mean, look at them out there shouting their fool heads off! You want to make common cause with them?"

I told you, Murbella: now judge for yourself. "To create change you find leverage points and move them. Beware blind alleys. Offers of high positions are a common distraction paraded before marchers. Leverage points are not all in high office. They are often at economic or communications centres and unless you know this, high office is useless. Even lieutenants can alter our course. Not by changing reports but by burying unwanted orders. Bell sits on orders until she believes them ineffective. I give her orders sometimes for this purpose: so she can play her delaying game. She knows it and yet she plays her game anyway. Know this, Murbella! And after we Share, study my performance with great care."

Harmony had been achieved but at a cost. Odrade signalled that Convocation was ended, knowing well that all questions had not been answered nor even asked. But the unasked questions would come filtering through Bell where they would get the most appropriate treatment.

Alert ones among the sisters would not ask. They already saw her plan.

As she left the great Common Room, Odrade felt herself accept full commitment for choices she had made, recognizing previous hesitancy for the first time. There were regrets, but only Murbella and Sheeana might know them.

Walking behind Bellonda, Odrade thought about *the places*

377

I will never go, the things I will never see except as a reflection in the life of another.

It was a form of nostalgia that centred on the Scatterings and this eased her pain. There was just too much for one person to see out there. Even the Bene Gesserit with its accumulated memories could never hope to catch up with all of it, not with every last interesting detail. It was back to grand designs. The Big Picture, the Mainstream. *The specialities of my Sisterhood.* Here were essentials Mentats employed: patterns, movements of currents and what those currents carried, where they were going. Consequences. Not maps but the flowings.

At least, I have preserved key elements of our jury-monitored democracy in original form. They may thank me for that one day.

> *Seek freedom and become captive of your desires. Seek discipline and find your liberty.*
>
> —**The Coda**

"Who expected the air machinery to break down?"

The Rabbi asked his question of no one in particular. He sat on a low bench, a scroll clutched to his breast. The scroll had been reinforced by modern artifice but it still was old and fragile. He was not sure of the time. Midmorning probably. They had eaten not long ago food that could be described as breakfast.

"*I* expected it."

He appeared to be addressing the scroll. "Passover has come and gone and our door was locked."

Rebecca came to stand over him. "Please, Rabbi. How does this help Joshua at his labours?"

"We have not been abandoned," the Rabbi told his scroll. "It is we who have hidden ourselves away. When we cannot be found by strangers, where would anyone look who might help us?"

He peered up abruptly at Rebecca, owlish behind his glasses. "Have you brought evil to us, Rebecca?"

378

She knew his meaning. "Outsiders always think there's something nefarious about the Bene Gesserit," she said.

"So now I, your Rabbi, am Outsider!"

"You estrange yourself, Rabbi. I speak from the viewpoint of the Sisterhood you made me help. What they do is often boring. Repetitious but not evil."

"I *made* you help? Yes, I did that. Forgive me, Rebecca. If evil joins us, I have done it."

He tried to inhale a deep breath. Fears and the fetid, overheated air made this difficult.

"Rabbi, the sisters have seen so much they are perhaps more sensitive to the presence of evil than anyone who has not shared their Agony."

"Agony? You speak of agony to one whose ancestors knew every suppression monsters could imagine?"

"I speak of the Spice Agony, Rabbi. And Other Memory that presses upon one when there is urgent demand for data. The Others show you the evil patterns and they say: 'Oh, no! Not again!' But off the fools go to repeat some idiocy."

"Other Memory! You say it presses. Evil presses you, Rebecca. The vileness of those who . . ."

"Rabbi! Stop this. They are an extended clan. And still, they keep a touchy individualism. Does an extended clan mean nothing to you? Does my dignity offend you?"

"I tell you, Rebecca, what offends me. By my hand you have learned to follow different books than . . ." He raised the scroll as though it were a bludgeon.

"No books at all, Rabbi. Oh, they have a Coda but it's just a collection of reminders, sometimes useful, sometimes to be discarded. They always adjust their Coda to current requirements."

"There are books that cannot be *adjusted*, Rebecca!"

She stared down at him with ill-concealed dismay. Was this how he saw the Sisterhood? Or was it fear talking?

"They have harnessed a creative imagination, Rabbi. And they use it for all of us."

"Imagination!" He waved the scroll in front of her. "Is this imagination?"

Rebecca reached out and touched the scroll. The Rabbi jerked it back as though she contaminated it.

"Imagination was an ill-chosen word on my part, perhaps," she said. "But imagination projects possibilities from which we pick and choose. That works until it gets too romantic."

"Chaos," he said, clutching the scroll to his breast.

"True. When things get too romantic they are self-limiting. They loose chaos among us."

"And that is what you bring!"

A soft smile touched her mouth. "You fear I will urge us to abandon homely reality, things we can touch with our hands? Still, romantic imagination is where most great ideas originate."

Joshua came to stand beside her, hands greasy, black smears on forehead and cheeks. "Your suggestion was the right one. It's working again. How long I don't know. The problem is . . ."

"You do not know the problem," the Rabbi interrupted.

"The mechanical problem, Rabbi," Rebecca said. "This no-chamber's field distorts machinery."

"We could not bring in frictionless machinery," Joshua said. "Too revealing, not to mention the cost."

"Your machinery is not all that has been distorted."

Joshua looked at Rebecca with raised eyebrows. *What's wrong with him?* So Joshua trusted Bene Gesserit insights, too. That offended the Rabbi. His flock sought guidance elsewhere.

The Rabbi surprised her then. "You think I'm jealous, Rebecca?"

She shook her head from side to side.

"You display talents," the Rabbi said, "that others are quick to use. Your suggestion fixed the machinery? These . . . these Others told you how?"

Rebecca shrugged. This was the Rabbi of old, not to be challenged in his own house.

"I should praise you?" the Rabbi asked. "You have power? Now, you will govern us?"

"No one, least of all I, ever suggested that, Rabbi." She was offended and did not mind showing it.

"Forgive me, daughter. That is what you call 'flip'."

"I don't need your praise, Rabbi. And of course I forgive."

"Your Others have something to say about this?"

"The Bene Gesserits say fear of praise goes back to an ancient prohibition against praising your child because that brings down the wrath of the gods."

He bowed his head. "Sometimes a bit of wisdom."

Joshua appeared embarrassed. "I'm going to try sleeping. I should be rested." He aimed a meaningful glance at the machinery area where a laboured rasping could be heard.

He left them for the darkened end of the chamber, stumbling on a child's toy as he went.

The Rabbi patted the bench beside him. "Sit, Rebecca."

She sat.

"I am fearful for you, for us, for all of the things we represent." He caressed the scroll. "We have been true for so many generations." His gaze swept the room. "And we don't even have a minyan here."

Rebecca wiped tears from her eyes. "Rabbi, you misjudge the Sisterhood. They wish only to perfect humans and their governments."

"So they say."

"So *I* say. Government, to them, is an art form. You find that amusing?"

"You arouse my curiosity. Are these women self-deluded by dreams of their own importance?"

"They think of themselves as watchdogs."

"Dogs?"

"*Watch*dogs, alert to when a lesson may be taught. That is what they seek. Never try to teach someone a lesson he cannot absorb."

"Always these bits of wisdom." He sounded sad. "And they govern themselves *artistically*?"

"They think of themselves as a jury with absolute powers that no law can veto."

He waved the scroll in front of her nose. "I thought so!"

"No *human* law, Rabbi."

"You tell me these women who make religions to suit

381

themselves believe in a . . . in a power greater than themselves."

"Their belief would not accord with ours, Rabbi, but I do not think it evil."

"What is this . . . this belief?"

"They call it the 'levelling drift'. They see it genetically and as instinct. Brilliant parents are likely to have children closer to the average, for example."

"A drift? *This* is a belief?"

"That is why they avoid prominence. They are advisers, even king-makers on occasion, but they do not want to be in the target foreground."

"This drift . . . do they believe there is a Drift-Maker?"

"They don't assume there is. Only that there is this observable movement."

"So what do they do in this drift?"

"They take precautions."

"In the presence of Satan, I should think so!"

"They don't oppose the current but seem only to move across it, making it work for them, using the back eddies."

"Oyyy!"

"Ancient sailing masters understood this quite well, Rabbi. The Sisterhood has what amounts to current charts telling them places to avoid and where to make their greatest efforts."

Again, he waved the scroll. "This is no current chart."

"You misinterpret, Rabbi. They know the fallacies about overwhelming machines." She glanced at the labouring machinery. "They see us in currents machinery cannot breast."

"These little wisdoms. I do not know, daughter. Meddling in politics, I accept. But in holy matters . . ."

"A levelling drift, Rabbi. Mass influence on brilliant innovators who move out of the pack and produce new things. Even when the new helps us, the drift catches the innovator."

"Who is to say what helps, Rebecca?"

"I merely tell what they believe. They see taxation as evidence of the drift, taking away free energy that might create more new things. A sensitized person detects it, they say."

"And these . . . these Honoured Matres?"

"They fit the pattern. Power-closed government intent on making all potential challengers ineffectual. Screen out the bright ones. Blunt intelligence."

A tiny beeping sound came from the machinery area. Joshua was past them before they could stand. He bent over the screen that revealed events on the surface.

"They are back," he said. "See! They dig in the ashes directly above us."

"Have they found us?" The Rabbi sounded almost relieved. Joshua watched the screen.

Rebecca placed her head beside his, studying the diggers—ten men with that dreaming look in their eyes of those who had been bonded to Honoured Matres.

"They only dig at random," Rebecca said, straightening.

"You're sure?" Joshua stood and looked into her face, seeking secret confirmation.

Any Bene Gesserit could see it.

"Look for yourself." She gestured at the screen. "They are leaving. They go the sligsty now."

"Where they belong," the Rabbi muttered.

> *Making workable choices occurs in a crucible of informative*
> *mistakes. Thus Intelligence accepts fallibility. And when*
> *absolute (infallible) choices are not known, Intelligence*
> *takes chances with limited data in an arena where mistakes*
> *not only are possible but necessary.*
>
> **—Darwi Odrade**

Mother Superior did not just board an outgoing lighter and transfer to any convenient no-ship. There were plans, arrangements, strategies—contingencies on contingencies.

It took eight hectic days. Timing with Teg had to be precise. Consultations with Murbella ate up hours. Murbella had to know what she faced.

Grab the core, Murbella, their Achilles' heel, and you have it all. Stay on the observation ship when Teg attacks but watch carefully.

383

Odrade took detailed advice from all who could help. Then came the vital-signs implant with encrypting to transmit her secret observations. A no-ship and long-range lighter had to be refitted, crew chosen by Teg.

Bellonda muttered and growled until Odrade intervened.

"You are distracting me! Is that your intent? Weaken me?" It was late morning four days before departure and they were temporarily alone in the workroom. Weather clear but unseasonably cold and air an ochre tinge from a dust storm that had blown across Central in the night.

"Convocation was a mistake!" Bellonda needed her parting shot.

Odrade found herself snapping back at Bellonda who had become a bit too caustic. "Necessary!"

"To you, maybe! Saying goodbye to your *family*. Now, you leave us here taking in each other's laundry."

"You don't think we perform real services?" *Softly, softly*.

"And how does Mother Superior determine what's real?" Unmistakably sneering. Bell was much too nervy and showing it. Upsetting to others.

"I'm surprised you should ask. Real services are always known because they sustain life. They carry us along like the paddle strokes of the canoist."

"Aren't we poetic!"

"Did you just come up here to complain about the Convocation?"

"I don't like your latest comments on Honoured Matres! You should have consulted us before spreading . . ."

"They're parasites, Bell! It's time we made that clear: a known weakness."

"You ignore their strengths and that could . . ."

"What does a body do when afflicted by parasites?" Odrade delivered this with a broad grin.

"Dar, when you assume this . . . this pseudo-humorous pose I would like to throttle you!"

"Would you smile as you did it, Bell?"

"Damn you, Dar! One of these days . . ."

"We don't have many more days together, Bell, and that's what's eating you. Answer my question."

384

"Answer it yourself!"

"The body welcomes periodic delousing. Even addicts dream of freedom."

"Ahhhhh " A Mentat peered from Bellonda's eyes. "You think addiction to Honoured Matres could be made painful?"

"In spite of your dreadful inability at humour, you still can function."

A cruel smile flexed Bellonda's mouth.

"I've managed to amuse you," Odrade said.

"Let me discuss this with Tam. She has a better head for strategy. Although . . . Sharing softened her."

When Bellonda had gone, Odrade leaned back and laughed quietly. *Softened! "Don't go soft tomorrow, Dar, when you Share." The Mentat stumbles on logic and misses the heart. She sees the process and worries about failure. What do we do if . . . We open windows, Bell, and let in common sense. Even hilarity. Puts more serious matters in perspective. Poor Bell, my flawed sister. Always something to occupy your nervousness.*

Odrade left Central on departure morning much entangled in her thinking—an introspective mood worried by what she had learned Sharing with Murbella and Sheeana.

I'm being self-indulgent.

That offered no relief. Her thoughts were framed by Other Memory and almost cynical fatalism.

Queen bees swarming?

That had been suggested of Honoured Matres.

But Sheeana? And Tam approves?

This carried more in it than a Scattering.

I cannot follow into your wild place, Sheeana. My task is to produce order. I cannot risk what you have dared. There are different kinds of artistry. Yours repels me.

Absorbing lifetimes of Murbella's Other Memory helped. Murbella's knowledge was a powerful leverage on Honoured Matres but full of disturbing nuances.

Not hypnotrance. They use cellular induction, a byproduct of their damned T-probes! Unconscious compulsion! How tempting to use it for ourselves. But this is where Honoured Matres are most vulnerable—enormous unconsciousness content locked in by their own decisions. Murbella's key only emphasizes its danger to us.

They arrived at the Landing Flat in the midst of a windstorm that buffeted them when they emerged from their car. Odrade had vetoed a walk through what remained of orchards and vineyards.

Leaving for the last time? The question in Bellonda's eyes as she said goodbye. In Sheeana's worried frown.

Does Mother Superior accept my decision?

Provisionally, Sheeana. Provisionally. But I have not warned Murbella. So . . . perhaps I do share Tam's judgment.

Dortujla in the van of Odrade's party was withdrawn.

Understandable. She has been there . . . and watched her sisters eaten. Courage, sister! We are not yet defeated.

Only Murbella appeared to take this in stride but she was thinking ahead to Odrade's encounter with the Spider Queen.

Have I armed Mother Superior sufficiently? Does she know in her guts how very dangerous this will be?

Odrade pushed such thoughts aside. There were things to do on the crossing. None of them more important than gathering her energies. Honoured Matres could be analysed almost out of reality, but the actual confrontation would be played as it came—a jazz performance. She liked the *idea* of jazz although the music distracted her with its antique flavours and the dips into wildness. Jazz spoke about life, though. No two performances ever identical. Players reacted to what was received from the others: Jazz.

Feed us with jazz.

Air and space travel did not often concern itself with weather. Bludgeon your way through transitory interferences. Depend on Weather Control to provide launch windows through storms and cloud cover. Desert planets were an exception and that would have to be entered into Chapter House equations before long. Many changes, including return to Fremen mortuary practices. Bodies rendered for water and potash.

Odrade spoke of this as they waited for transport up to the ship. That wide cummerbund of hot, dry land expanding around the planet's equator would begin generating

386

dangerous winds before long. One day, there would be coreolis storms: a blast-furnace from the desert interior with speeds in hundreds of kilometres an hour. Dune had seen winds of more than seven hundred kmh. Even space lighters took notice of such force. Air travel would be subject to the constant whims of surface conditions. And frail human flesh must find whatever shelter it could.

As we always have.

The lounge at the Flat was old. Stone inside and out, their first major building material here. Spartan slingchairs and low tables of moulded plaz were more recent. Economy could not be ignored even for Mother Superior.

The lighter arrived in a dusty maelstrom. No nonsense about suspensor cushioning. This would be a quick lift with uncomfortable Gees but not high enough to damage flesh.

Odrade felt almost disembodied as she said her final farewells and turned Chapter House over to a triumvirate of Sheeana, Murbella and Bellonda. One last word: "Don't interfere with Teg. And I don't want anything nasty happening to Duncan. Hear me, Bell?"

All of the wonderful technological things they could accomplish and they still could not keep a thick sandstorm from almost blinding them as they lifted. Odrade closed her eyes and accepted the fact that she was not to get a last low-level overview of her beloved planet. She awoke to the thump of docking. Buzzcar waiting in a corridor just beyond the lock. A humming traverse to their quarters. Tamalane, Dortujla and the acolyte servant maintained silence, respecting Mother Superior's desire to be with her own thoughts.

The quarters, at least, were familiar, standard on BG ships: a small sitting-dining room in elemental plaz of uniform light green; smaller sleeping chamber with walls in the same colour and a single hard cot. They knew Mother Superior's preferences. Odrade glanced into a usiform bath and toilet. Standard facilities. Adjoining quarters for Tam and Dortujla were similar. Time later to look at the ship's refittings.

All essentials had been provided. Including unobtrusive elements of psychological support: subdued colours, familiar furnishings, a setting to disturb none of her mental processes.

She gave orders for departure before returning to her sitting-dining room.

Food was waiting on a low table—blue fruit, sweet and plummy, a savoury yellow spread on bread tailored to her energy needs. Very good. She watched the assigned acolyte at her self-effacing work arranging Mother Superior's effects. The name evaded Odrade for a second, then: *Suipol*. A dark little thing with a round, calm face and manners to match. *Not one of our brightest but guaranteed efficient.*

It struck Odrade suddenly that these assignments had an element of callousness in them. *A small entourage, not to offend Honoured Matres. And keep our losses to a minimum.*

"Have you unpacked all of my things, Suipol?"

"Yes, Mother Superior." Very proud of having been chosen for this important assignment. It showed in her walk as she left.

There are some things you cannot unpack for me, Suipol. I carry those in my head.

No Bene Gesserit from Chapter House ever left the planet without taking along a certain amount of chauvinism. Other places were never quite as beautiful, never quite as serene, never as pleasant a habitat.

But that is the Chapter House that was.

It was an aspect of the desert transformation she had never before viewed in quite that way. Chapter House was removing itself. Going away, never to return, at least not in the lifetimes of those who knew it now. It was like being abandoned by a beloved parent—disdainfully and with malice.

You are no longer important to me, child.

On the way to becoming a Reverend Mother, they were taught early that travel could provide a peaceful byway for rest. Odrade fully intended to take advantage of this and told her companions immediately after eating, "Spare me details."

Suipol was sent to summon Tamalane. Odrade spoke in Tam's own terse metre. "Inspect the refitting and tell me what I should see. Take Dortujla."

"Good head, that one." High praise from Tam.

"When we're through, isolate me as much as possible."

During part of the crossing, Odrade strapped herself into

the webbing of her cot and occupied herself composing what she thought of as a last will and testament.

Who would be executor?

Murbella was her personal choice, especially after the Sharing with Sheeana. Still . . . the Dune waif remained a potent candidate if this venture to Junction failed.

Some assumed any Reverend Mother could serve if responsibility fell on her. But not in these times. Not with this trap set. Honoured Matres were unlikely to avoid the pitfall.

If we've judged them correctly. And Murbella's data says we've done our best. The opening is there for Honoured Matres to enter, and oh, how inviting it will appear. They won't see the dead end until they're well into it. Too late!

But what if we fail?

Survivors (if any) would hold Odrade in contempt.

I have often felt diminished but never an object of contempt. Yet, the decisions I made may never be accepted by my sisters. At least, I make no excuses . . . not even to the ones with whom I Shared. They know my response comes from the darkness before a human dawn. Any of us may do a futile thing, even a stupid thing. But my plan can give us victory. We will not "just survive". Our grail requires us to persist together. Humans need us! Sometimes, they need religions. Sometimes, they need merely to know their beliefs are as empty as their hopes for nobility. We are their source. After the masks are removed, that remains: Our Niche.

She felt then that this ship was taking her into the pit. Closer and closer to awful threat.

I go to the axe; it does not come to me.

No thoughts of exterminating this foe. Not since the Scattering magnified human population had that been possible. A flaw in Honoured Matre schemes.

The high-pitched beep and flashing orange light that signalled arrival brought her out of repose. She struggled from her sling straps and, with Tam, Dortujla and Suipol close behind, followed a guide to the transport lock where a long-range lighter clung to its shiptit. Odrade looked at the lighter visible in bulkhead scanners. Incredibly small!

"It'll only be nineteen hours," Duncan had said. "But that's as close as we dare bring the no-ship. They're sure to have foldspace sensors close around Junction."

Bell, for once, had agreed. *Don't risk the ship. It's there to plot outer defences and receive your transmissions, not just to deliver Mother Superior.* The lighter was the no-ship's forward sensor, signalling what it encountered.

And I am the foremost sensor, a fragile body with delicate instruments.

There were guide arrows at the lock. Odrade led the way. They went through a small tube in free-fall. She found herself in a surprisingly rich cabin. Suipol, tumbling behind, recognized it and went up a notch in Odrade's estimation.

"This was a smuggler ship."

One person awaited them. Male by his smell but an opaque pilot's hood bristling with connectors concealed his face.

"Everyone strap in."

Male voice within that instrumentation.

Teg chose him. He'll be the best.

Odrade slipped into a seat behind a landing port and found the lumpy protrusions that unreeled into web harness. She heard the others obeying the pilot's command.

"All secure? Stay strapped in unless I say otherwise." His voice came from a floating speaker behind his seat at the drive console.

The umbilicus went "Bap!" Odrade felt gentle motions but the view in the relay beside her showed the no-ship receding at a remarkable rate. It winked out of existence.

Going about its business before anyone can come out to investigate.

The lighter had surprising speed. Scanners reported planetary stations and transition barriers at eighteen-plus hours but winking dots identifying them were visible only because they had been enhanced. A window in the scanner said the stations would be naked-eye visible in a little more than twelve of those hours.

The sense of motion ceased abruptly and Odrade no longer felt the acceleration her eyes reported. *Suspensor cabin. Ixian technology for a nullfield this small.* Where had Teg acquired it?

Not necessary for one to know. Why tell Mother Superior where every oak plantation is located?

She watched sensor contacts begin within the hour and gave silent thanks for Idaho's astuteness.

We're beginning to know these Honoured Matres.

Junction's defensive pattern was apparent even without scanner analysis. Overlapping planes! Just as Teg predicted. With knowledge of how barriers were spaced, Teg's people could weave another globe around the planet.

Surely it's not that simple.

Were Honoured Matres so confident of overwhelming power that they ignored elementary precautions?

Planetary Station Four began calling when they were just under three hours out. "Identify yourself!"

Odrade heard an "or else" in that command.

The pilot's response obviously surprised the watchers. "You come in a little smuggler ship?"

So they recognize it. Teg is right once more.

"I'm about to burn the sensor equipment in the drive," the pilot announced. "It will add to our thrust. Make sure you're all securely harnessed."

Station Four noticed. "Why are you increasing velocity?"

Odrade leaned forward. "Repeat the countersign and say our party is fatigued from too long in cramped quarters. Add that I have equipped myself with a precautionary vital-signs transmitter to alert my people should I die."

They won't find the encryption! Clever Duncan. And wasn't Bell surprised to discover what he hid in Shipsystems. "More romantics!"

The pilot relayed her words. Back came the order: "Reduce velocity and lock on to these coordinates for landing. We are taking over your ship control at this point."

The pilot touched a yellow field on his board. "Just the way the Bashar said they would." A gloating sound in his voice. He lifted the hood off his head and turned.

Odrade was shocked.

Cyborg!

The face was a metal mask with two glittering silver balls for eyes.

391

We enter dangerous ground.

"They didn't tell you?" he asked. "Waste no pity. I was dead and this gave me life. It's Clairby, Mother Superior. And when I die this time, that will buy me life as a ghola."

Damn! We're trading in coin that may be denied us. Too late to change. And that was Teg's plan. But . . . Clairby?

The lighter landed with a smoothness that spoke of superb control by Station Four. Odrade knew the moment because a manicured landscape visible in her scanner no longer moved. The nullfield was turned off and she felt gravity. The hatch directly in front of her opened. Temperature pleasantly warm. Noise out there. Children playing some competitive game?

Luggage floating behind, she stepped on to a short flight of steps and saw that the noise did indeed come from a large group of children in a nearby field. In their high 'teens and female. They were butting a suspensor float-ball back and forth, shouting and screaming as they played.

Staged for our benefit?

Odrade thought it likely. There probably were two thousand young women on that field.

Look how many recruits we have coming along!

No one to greet her but Odrade saw a familiar structure down a paved lane to her left. Obvious Spacing Guild artifact with a recent tower added. She spoke of the tower as she glanced around her, giving the implanted transmitter data on a change from Teg's groundplan. Nobody who had ever seen a Guild building could mislabel this place, though.

So this was like other Junction planets. Somewhere in Guild records there doubtless was a serial number and code for it. So long under Guild control before Honoured Matres that, in these first moments of debarking, getting their "ground legs", everything around them could be seen to have that special Guild flavour. Even the playing field—designed for outdoor meetings of Navigators in their giant containers of melange gas.

The Guild flavour: it was compounded of Ixian technology and Navigator design—buildings wrapped around space in the most energy-conserving way, paths direct; few slide-walks. They were wasteful and only the gravity-bound needed them.

No flowery plantings near the Landing Flat. They were susceptible to accidental destruction. And that permanent greyness to all construction—not silver but as dull as Tleilaxu skin.

The structure on her left was a great bulging shape with extrusions, some rounded and some angular. This had been no lavish hostelry. Opulent little nooks, of course, but those were rare, built for VVIPs, mostly inspectors from the Guild.

Once more, Teg is right. Honoured Matres kept existing structures, remodelling minimally. A tower!

Odrade reminded herself then: *This not only is another world but another society with its own social glue.* She had a handle on that from Sharing with Murbella but did not think she had plumbed what held Honoured Matres together. Surely not just a lusting after power.

"We'll walk," she said and led the way down the paved lane toward the giant structure.

Goodbye, Clairby. Blow your ship as soon as you can. Let it be our first great surprise for Honoured Matres.

The Guild structure loomed higher as they approached.

The most astonishing thing to Odrade whenever she saw one of these functional constructions was that someone had taken a great deal of care in planning it. Intentional detail in everything although you sometimes had to dig for it. Budget dictated reduced quality in many choices, endurance preferred over luxury or eye appeal. Compromise and, like most compromise, satisfying no one. Guild comptrollers undoubtedly had complained at the price, and present occupants still could feel irritated at shortcomings. No matter. The thing was tangible substance. It was here to be used now. Another compromise.

The lobby was smaller than she had expected. Some interior changes. Only about six metres long and perhaps four metres wide. Reception slot was on their right as they entered. Odrade motioned Suipol to register their party and indicated that the rest of them should wait in the open area well within striking distance of each other. Treachery had not been ruled out.

Dortujla obviously expected it. She looked resigned.

Odrade made a careful inspection and commented on their

surroundings. Plenty of comeyes but the rest of it . . .

Each time she entered one of these places, she had the sensation of being in a museum. Other Memory said hostelries of this sort had not changed significantly in eons. Even in early times she found prototypes. A glimpse of the past in the chandeliers—gigantic glittering things imitative of electric devices but furnished with glowglobes. Two of them dominated the ceiling like imaginary space ships descending in splendour from the void.

There were more glimpses of the past that few transients in this age would notice. The arrangement of reception area behind grilled slots, space for waiting with its mixture of seats and inconvenient lighting, signs directing them to services—restaurants, narcoparlours, assignation bars, swimming and other exercise facilities, automassage rooms and the like. Only language and script had changed from ancient times. Given an understanding of the language, the signs would be recognizable to pre-space primitives. This was a temporary stopping place.

Plenty of security installations. Some had the look of artifacts from the Scattering. Ix and Guild had never wasted gold on comeyes and sensors.

A frenetic dance of roboservants in the reception area—darting here and there, cleaning, picking up litter, guiding newcomers. A party of four Ixians had preceded Odrade's group. She gave them close attention. How self important yet fearful.

To her Bene Gesserit eye, the people of Ix were always recognizable no matter the disguises. Basic structure of their society coloured its individuals. Ixians displayed a Hogben-esque attitude toward their science: that political and economic requirements determined permissible research. That said the innocent naivete of Ixian social dreams had become the reality of bureaucratic centralism—a new aristocracy. So they were headed into a decline that would not be stopped by whatever accommodation this Ixian party made with Honoured Matres.

No matter the outcome of our contest, Ix is dying. Witness: no great Ixian innovations in centuries.

Suipol returned. "They ask us to wait for an escort."

Odrade decided to start negotiations immediately with a chat for the benefit of Suipol, the comeyes and listeners on her no-ship.

"Suipol, did you notice those Ixians ahead of us?"

"Yes, Mother Superior."

"Mark them well. They are products of a dying society. It is naive to expect any bureaucracy to take brilliant innovations and put them to good use. Bureaucracies ask different questions. Do you know what those are?"

"No, Mother Superior." Spoken after a searching look at their surroundings.

She knows! But she sees what I'm doing. What have we here? I've misjudged her.

"These are typical questions, Suipol—Who gets the credit? Who will be blamed if it causes problems? Will it shift the power structure, costing us jobs? Or will it make some subsidiary department more important?"

Suipol nodded on cue but her glance at the comeyes might have been a little obvious. No matter.

"These are political questions," Odrade said. "They demonstrate how motives of bureaucracy are directly opposed to the need for adapting to change. Adaptability is a prime requirement for life to survive."

Time to talk directly to our hosts.

Odrade turned her attention upward, picking a prominent comeye in a chandelier. "Note those Ixians. Their 'mind in a deterministic universe' has given way to 'mind in an unlimited universe' where *anything* may happen. Creative anarchy is the path to survival in this universe."

"Thank you for this lesson, Mother Superior."

Bless you, Suipol.

"After all of their experiences with us," Suipol said, "surely they no longer question our loyalty to each other."

Fates preserve her! This one is ready for the Agony and may never see it.

Odrade could only agree with the acolyte's summation. Compliance with Bene Gesserit *ways* came from within, from those constantly monitored details that kept their own house in order. It was not philosophical but a pragmatic view of free will. Any claim the Sisterhood might have to making its own way in a hostile universe lay in scrupulous adherence to mutual loyalty, an agreement forged in the Agony. Chapter House and its few remaining subsidiaries were nurseries of an order founded in sharing and Sharing. Not based on innocence. That had been lost long ago. It was set firmly in political consciousness and a view of history independent of other laws and customs.

"We are not machines," Odrade said, glancing at the automata around them. "We always rely on personal relationships, never knowing where those my lead us."

Tamalane stepped to Odrade's side. "Don't you think they should be sending us a message at the very least?"

"They're already sent us a message, Tam, putting us up in a second-class hostelry. And I have responded."

Ultimately, all things are known because you want to believe you know.

—Zensunni koan

Teg took a deep breath. Gammu lay directly ahead, precisely where his navigators had said it would be when they emerged from foldspace. He stood beside a watchful Streggi seeing this in displays of his flagship's command bay.

Streggi did not like it that he stood on his own feet instead of riding her shoulders. She felt superfluous amidst military hardware. Her gaze kept going to the multi-projection fields at command bay centre. Aides moving efficiently in and out of pods and fields, bodies draped with esoteric hardware, knew what they were doing. She had only the vaguest idea of these functions.

The comboard to relay Teg's orders lay under his palms, riding there on suspensors. Its command field formed a faint blue glow around his hands. The silvery horseshoe linking him to the attack force rested lightly on his shoulders, feeling familiar there in spite of being much larger relative to his small body than comlinks of his previous lifetime.

None of those around him any longer questioned that this was their famous Bashar in a child's body. They took his orders with brisk acceptance.

The target system looked ordinary from this distance: a sun and its captive planets. But Gammu in centre focus was not ordinary. Idaho had been born there, his ghola trained there, his original memories restored there.

And I was changed there.

Teg had no explanation for what he had found in himself under the stresses of survival on Gammu. Physical speed that drained his flesh and an ability to *see* no-ships, to locate them in an image field like a block of space reproduced in his mind.

He suspected a wild outcropping in Atreides genes. Marker cells had been identified in him but not their purpose. It was the heritage Bene Gesserit breeding mistresses had meddled with for eons. There was little doubt they would view this ability as something potentially dangerous to them. They might use it but he would certainly lose his freedom.

He put these reflections out of his mind.

"Send in the decoys."

Action!

Teg felt himself assume a familiar stance. There was a sense of climbing on to a refreshing eminence when planning ended. Theories had been articulated, alternatives carefully worked out and subordinates deployed, all thoroughly briefed. His key squad leaders had committed Gammu to memory—where partisan help might be available, every bolt hole, every known strongpoint and which access routes were most vulnerable. He had warned them especially about Futars. The possibility that humanoid beasts might be allies could not be overlooked. Rebels who had helped ghola Idaho escape from Gammu had insisted Futars were created to hunt and kill Honoured Matres. Knowing the accounts of Dortujla and others, you could almost pity Honoured Matres if this were true except that no pity could be spared for those who never showed it to others.

The attack was taking its designed shape—scout ships laying down a decoy barrage and heavy carriers moving into strike position. Teg became now what he thought of as "the instrument of my instruments". It was difficult to determine which commanded and which responded.

Now, the delicate part.

Unknowns were to be feared. A good commander kept that firmly in mind. There were always unknowns.

Decoys were nearing the defensive perimeter. He *saw* enemy no-ships and foldspace sensors—bright dots arrayed through his awareness. Teg superimposed this on to the positions of his force. Every order he gave must appear to originate from a battle-plot they all shared.

He felt thankful Murbella had not joined him. Any Reverend Mother might see through his deception. But no one had questioned Odrade's order that she wait with her party at a safe distance.

"Potential Mother Superior. Guard this one well."

Explosive demolition of decoys began with a random display of brilliant flashes around the planet. He leaned forward, staring at projections.

"There's the pattern!"

There was no such pattern but his words created belief and pulses quickened. No one questioned that the Bashar had seen vulnerability in the defences. His hands flashed over the comboard, sending his ships forward in a blazing display that littered space behind them with enemy fragments.

"All right! Let's go!"

He fed the flagship's course directly into Navigation, then turned full attention to Fire Control. Silent explosions dotted space around them as the flagship mopped up surviving elements of Gammu's perimeter guardians.

"More decoys!" he ordered.

Globes of white light blinked in the projection fields.

Attention in the command bay concentrated on the fields, not on their Bashar. *The unexpected!* Teg, justly famous for that, was confirming his reputation.

"I find this oddly romantic," Streggi said.

Romantic? No romance in this! The time for romance was past and yet to come. A certain aura might surround *plans* for violence. He accepted that. Historians created their own brand of drama-cum-romance. But now? This was adrenalin time! Romance distracted you from necessities. You had to be cold inside, a clear and unimpaired line between mind and body.

As his hands moved in the comboard's field, Teg realized what had driven Streggi to speak. Something primitive about the death and destruction being created here. This was a moment cut out of normal order. A disturbing return to ancient tribal patterns.

She sensed a tom-tom in her breast and voices chanting: "Kill! Kill! Kill!"

His vision of guardian no-ships showed survivors fleeing in panic.

Good! Panic has a way of spreading and weakening your enemies.

"There's Barony."

Idaho had converted him to the old Harkonnen name for the sprawling city with its giant black centrepiece of plasteel.

"We'll land on the Flat to the north."

He spoke the words but his hands gave the orders.

Quickly now!

For brief moments when they disgorged troops, no-ships were visible and vulnerable. He held elements of the entire force responsive to his comboard and responsibility was heavy.

"This is only a feint. We go in and out after inflicting serious damage. Junction is our real target."

Odrade's parting admonition lay there in memory. "Honoured Matres must be taught a lesson such as never before. Attack us and you get hurt badly. Press us and the pain can be enormous. They've heard about Bene Gesserit punishments. We're notorious. No doubt Spider Queen sniggered a bit. You must shove that snigger down her throat!"

"Quit ship!"

This was the vulnerable moment. Space above them remained empty of threat but fire lances arced inward from the east. His gunners could handle those. He concentrated on the possibility that enemy no-ships might return for a suicide attack. Command bay projections showed his hammerships and troop carriers pouring from the holds. The shock force, an

399

armoured elite on suspensors, already had the perimeter secured.

There went the portable comeyes to spread his field of observation and relay the intimate details of violence. Communication, the key to responsive command, but it also displayed bloody destruction.

"All clear!"

The signal rang through the bay.

He lifted off the Flat and repositioned in full invisibility. Now, only the comlinks gave defenders a clue to his position and that was masked by decoy relays.

Projection displayed the monstrous rectangle of the ancient Harkonnen centre. It had been built as a block of light-absorbing metal to confine slaves. The elite had lived in garden mansions on top. Honoured Matres had returned it to its former oppression.

Three of his giant hammerships came into view.

"Clear the top of that thing!" he ordered. "Wipe it clean but do as little damage as possible to the structure."

He knew his words were superfluous but spoke for the release. Everyone in the attack force knew what he wanted.

"Relay reports!" he ordered.

Information began flowing from the horseshoe on his shoulders. He brought it up on secondary. Comeyes showed his troops clearing the perimeter. Battle overhead and on the ground was well in hand for at least fifty klicks out. Going far better than he had expected. So Honoured Matres kept their heavy stuff off-planet, not anticipating bold attack. A familiar attitude and he had Idaho to thank for predicting it.

"They're power-blind. They think heavy armour is for space and only light stuff for the ground. Heavy weapons are brought down as needed. No sense keeping them on planet. Takes too much energy. Besides, awareness of all that heavy stuff up there has a quieting effect on captive populations."

Idaho's concepts of weaponry were devastating.

"We tend to fix our minds on what we believe we know. A projectile is a projectile even when miniaturized to contain poisons or biologicals."

Innovations in protective equipment improved mobility.

Built into uniforms where possible. And Idaho had brought back the shield with its awesome destruction when struck by a lasgun beam. Shields on suspensors hidden in what appeared to be soldiers (but were actually inflated uniforms) spread out ahead of troops. Lasgun fire at them produced clean atomics to clear large areas.

Will Junction be this easy?

Teg doubted it. Necessity enforced quick adaptation to new methods.

They could have shields on Junction in two days.

And no inhibitions about how to employ them.

Shields had dominated the Old Empire, he knew, because of that oddly important set of words called 'Great Convention". Honourable people did not misuse weapons of their feudal society. If you dishonoured The Convention, your peers turned against you with united violence. More than that, there had been the intangible, "Face", that some called "Pride".

Face! My position in the pack.

More important to some than life itself.

"This is costing us very little," Streggi said.

She was becoming quite the battle analyst and much too banal for Teg's liking. Streggi meant they were losing few lives but perhaps she spoke truer than she knew.

"It's difficult to think of cheap devices doing the job," Idaho had said. *"But that's a powerful economic weapon."*

If your weapons cost only a small fraction of the energy your enemy spent, you had a potent lever that could prevail against seemingly overwhelming odds. Prolong the conflict and you wasted enemy substance. Your foe toppled because control of production and workers was lost.

"We can begin to pull out," he said turning away from the projections as his hands repeated the order. "I want casualty reports as soon as . . ." He broke off and turned at a sudden stir.

Murbella?

Her projection was repeated in all of the bay's fields. Her voice blared from the images: "Why are you disregarding reports from your perimeter?" She overrode his board and the projections displayed a field commander caught in mid-sentence: ". . . orders, I will have to deny their request."

"Repeat," Murbella said.

The field commander's sweaty features turned toward his mobile comeye. The comsystem compensated and he appeared to look directly into Teg's eyes.

"Repeating: I have self-styled refugees here asking for asylum. Their leader says he has an agreement requiring the Sisterhood tò honour his request but without orders . . ."

"Who is he?" Teg demanded.

"He calls himself Rabbi and he has the Suk . . ."

Teg moved to resume control of his comboard. "I don't know of any . . ."

"Wait!" Murbella overrode his board.

How does she do that?

Again her voice filled the bay. "Bring him and his party to the flagship. Make it quick." She silenced the perimeter relay.

Teg was outraged but at a disadvantage. He chose one of the multiple images and glared at it. "How dare you interfere with . . ."

"Because you don't have the proper data. The Rabbi is within his rights. Prepare to recéive him with honours."

"Explain."

"No! There's no need for you to know. But it was proper for me to make this decision when I saw you were not responding to . . ."

"That commander was in a diversionary area! Not important to . . ."

"But the Rabbi's request has priority."

"You're as bad as Mother Superior!"

"Perhaps worse. Now hear me! Get those refugees into your flagship. And prepare to receive me."

"Absolutely not! You are to stay where . . ."

"Bashar! There's something about this request that demands a Reverend Mother's attention. He says they are in peril because they gave temporary sanctuary to the Reverend Mother Lucilla. Accept this or step down."

"Then let me get my people aboard and pull back first. We'll rendezvous when we're clear."

"Agreed. But treat those refugees with courtesy."

"Now, get off my projections. You've blinded me and that was foolish!"

"You have everything well in hand, Bashar. During this hiatus another of our ships accepted four Futars. They came asking that we take them to Handlers but I ordered them confined. Treat them with extreme caution."

The bay's projections resumed battle status. Teg once more called in his force. He was seething and it was minutes before he restored a sense of command. Did Murbella know how she undermined his authority? Or should he take this as a measure of the importance she attached to the refugees?

When the situation was secure, he turned the bay over to an aide and, riding on Streggi's shoulders, went to see these *important* refugees. What was so vital about them that Murbella risked interference?

They were in a troop-carrier hold, a congealed party held apart by a cautious commander.

Who knows what may be concealed among these unknowns?

The Rabbi, identifiable because he was being deferred to by the field commander, stood with a brown-robed woman at the near side of his people. He was a small, bearded man wearing a white skullcap. Cold light made him appear ancient. The woman shielded her eyes with a hand. The Rabbi was speaking and his words became audible as Teg approached.

The woman was under verbal attack!

"The prideful one will be brought low!"

Without removing her hand from its defensive position, the woman said: "I am not proud of what I carry."

"Nor of the powers this knowledge may bring you?"

With knee pressure, Teg ordered Streggi to stop them about ten paces away. His commander glanced at Teg but stayed in position, ready to act defensively if this should prove to be a diversion.

Good man.

The woman bent her head even lower and pressed her hand against her eyes when she spoke. "Are we not offered knowledge that we might use it in holy service?"

"Daughter!" The Rabbi held himself stiffly erect. "Whatever we may learn that we may better serve, it never can be a great thing. All we call knowledge, were it to encompass everything a humble heart could hold, all of that would be no more than one seed in the furrows."

Teg felt reluctant to interfere. *What an archaic way of speaking.* This pair fascinated him. The other refugees listened to the exchange with rapt attention. Only Teg's field commander appeared aloof, keeping his attention on the strangers and giving an occasional hand signal to aides.

The woman kept her head respectfully lowered and the shielding hand in place but she still defended herself. "Even a seed lost in the furrows may bring forth life."

The Rabbi's lips tightened into a grim line, then: "Without water and care, which is to say, without the blessing and the word, there is no life."

A great sigh shook the woman's shoulders but she held herself in that oddly submissive position when she responded: "Rabbi, I hear and obey. Still, I must honour this knowledge that has been thrust upon me because it contains the very admonition you have just voiced."

The Rabbi placed a hand on her shoulder. 'Then convey it to those who want it and may no evil enter where you go."

Silence told Teg the argument had ended. He urged Streggi forward. Before she could move, Murbella strode past and nodded to the Rabbi while keeping her gaze on the woman.

"In the name of the Bene Gesserit and our debt to you, I welcome you and give you sanctuary," Murbella said.

The brown-robed woman lowered her hand and Teg saw contact lenses glittering in the palm. She lifted her head then and there were gasps all around. The woman's eyes were the total blue of spice addiction but they also held that inner force marking one who had survived the Agony.

Murbella made instant identification. *A wild Reverend Mother!* Not since Dune's Fremen days had one of these been known.

The woman curtsied to Murbella. "I am called Rebecca. And I am filled with joy to be with you. The Rabbi thinks I am a silly goose but I have a golden egg for I carry Lampadas:

seven million six hundred and twenty-two thousand and fourteen Reverend Mothers and they are rightfully yours."

Answers are a perilous grip on the universe. They can appear sensible yet explain nothing.

—The Zensunni Whip

As the wait for their promised escort lengthened, Odrade became first angry and then amused. Finally, she began following lobby robos, interfering with their movements. Most were small and none appeared humanoid.

Functional. Hallmark of Ixian servos. Busy, busy, busy little accompaniments to a sojourn at Junction or its equivalent anywhere.

They were so commonplace that few people noticed them. Since they were not capable of dealing with deliberate interference, they subsided into motionless humming.

"Honoured Matres have little or no sense of humour." I know, Murbella. I know. But, do they get my message?

Dortujla obviously did. She came out of her funk and watched these antics with a wide grin. Tam looked disapproving but tolerant. Suipol was delighted. Odrade had to restrain her from helping to immobilize the devices.

Let me do the antagonizing, child. I know what is in store for me.

When she was sure she had made her point, Odrade took a position under one of the chandeliers.

"Attend me, Tam," she said.

Tamalane obediently placed herself in front of Odrade with an attentive expression.

"Have you noticed, Tam, that modern lobbies tend to be quite small?"

Tamalane spared a glance for her surroundings.

"Lobbies once were large," Odrade said. "To provide a prestigious feeling of space for the powerful, and impressing others with your importance, of course."

Tamalane caught the spirit of Odrade's playlet and said: "These days you're important if you travel at all."

Odrade looked at the immobilized robos scattered across the lobby floor. Some hummed and jittered. Others waited quietly for someone or some thing to restore order.

The autoreceptionist, a phallic tube of black plaz with a single glittering comeye, came out from behind its cage and picked its way through the stalled robos to confront Odrade.

"Much too humid today." It had a soupy feminine voice. "Don't know what Weather is thinking of."

Odrade spoke past it to Tamalane. "Why do they have to programme these mechanicals to simulate friendly humans?"

"It's obscene," Tamalane agreed. She forcibly shouldered the autoreceptionist aside and it swivelled to study the source of this intrusion but made no other move.

Odrade was suddenly aware she had touched on the force that had powered the Butlerian Jihad—mob motivation.

My own prejudice!

She studied the mechanical confronting them. Was it waiting for instructions or must she address the thing directly?

Four more robos entered the lobby and Odrade recognized her party's luggage piled on them.

All of our things carefully inspected, I'm sure. Search where you will. We carry no hint of our legions.

The four scurried along the edge of the room and found their passage blocked by the ones rendered motionless. The luggage robos stopped and waited for this unique state of affairs to be sorted out. Odrade smiled at them. "There go the signs of the transient concealing our secret selves."

Concealing and secret.

Words to annoy the watchers.

Come on, Tam! You know the ploy. Confuse that enormous content of unconsciousness, arouse feelings of guilt they will be incapable of recognizing. Give them the jitters the way I did with the robos. Make them wary. What are the real powers of these Bene Gesserit witches?

Tamalane took her cue. *Transients and secret selves.* She explained for the comeyes in tones one used with children. "What do you carry when you leave your nest? Are you one who tries to pack it all? Or do you prune to necessities?"

What would the watchers classify as necessities? Tools of

hygiene and washable or replaceable clothing? Weapons? They sought those in our luggage. But Reverend Mothers tend not to carry visible weapons.

"What an ugly place this is," Dortujla said, joining Tamalane in front of Odrade and picking up on the drama. "You would almost think it deliberate."

Ahhh, you nasty watchers. Observe Dortujla. Remember her? Why has she returned when she must know what you might do to her? Food for Futars? See how little that concerns her?

"A transition point, Dortujla," Odrade said. "Most people would never want this as their destination. And inconvenience and the small discomforts serve only to remind you of that."

"A wayside stop and it will never be much more unless they completely rebuild," Dortujla said.

Would they hear? Odrade aimed a look of utter composure at the selected comeye.

This is ugliness that betrays intent. It says to us: "We will provide something for the stomach, a bed, a place to evacuate bladder and bowels, a place to conduct the little maintenance rituals flesh requires, but you will be gone quickly because all we really want is the energy you leave behind."

The autoreceptionist backed around Tamalane and Dortujla, once more trying to make contact with Odrade.

"You will send us to our quarters immediately!" Odrade said, glaring into the cyclopean eye.

"Dear me! We've been inconsiderate."

Where had they found that syrupy voice? Repulsive. But Odrade was on her way out of the lobby in less than a minute, luggage on its robos ahead of them, Suipol close behind, Tamalane and Dortujla following.

The goading little drama they had staged for Honoured Matres had set Odrade's mind on an old track.

Hidden messages. Ancient patterns. Except for those damned chandeliers, no baroque or rococo flourishes. Everything stamped out of moulds no doubt kept somewhere for the day when replacements may be required. Ultimate conservatism!

The place was functionally related to Ixian beliefs. Decorators had achieved a standard form, one so proper it forced itself on the senses of transients. It was possible to think of this place as acceptable even to travellers from ancient times. Bits and pieces of modern technology might bother some of those imagined ancients but not for long. Functionalism—a self-serving answer.

"Oh, I see. That thing cleans floors. And that over there answers questions? Clever."

Security installations were visible even to the casual eye. Glitterings at cornices and along upper edges of halls. Monitors and worse. Ixian, some of them. Probably not up to equipment from the Scattering but telling in the fact that it still was in use. Some of these installations she recognized as vicious.

Zap you dead.

But the Guild had been notoriously cautious. Like the Bene Gesserit. Make as few enemies as possible. Not an injunction against making *any* enemies. The right enemies gave you lustre. An underdog position had its attractions as various religious groups had demonstrated over the eons.

There was an air of neglect to one wing clearly visible as they passed it. Did that mean Junction's traffic had declined? Interesting. Shutters had been sealed along an entire corridor. Hiding something? In the resulting gloom she detected dust on floor and ledges with only a few tracks of maintenance mechs. Concealment of what lay outside those windows? Unlikely. This had been closed off for some time.

She detected a pattern in what was being maintained. Very little traffic. Honoured Matre effect. Who dared move around much when it felt safer to dig in and pray you would not be noticed by dangerous prowlers? Access lanes to elite private quarters were being kept up. Only the best was being maintained at its best.

When Gammu's refugees arrive, there will be room.

In the lobby, they had handed Suipol a guide pulser. "To find your way later." Round blue ball with a yellow arrow floating in it to point your chosen way. "Rings a tiny bell when you arrive."

How charming.

Over all else at Junction was this odd patina of hospitality, like a ghost at the feast, completely out of place. This was not (whatever else it might be) a hospitable structure and never had been. Functionalism triumphed over comfort and was displayed as though designers did you a favour.

The pulser's tiny bell rang.

And where have we arrived?

Another place where their hosts had provided "every luxury" while keeping it repellent. Rooms with soft yellow floors, pale mauve walls, white ceilings. No chairdogs. Be thankful for that even though the absence spoke of economics rather than care for a guest's preferences. Chairdogs required sustenance and expensive staff. She saw furnishings with permaflox fabrics. And behind the fabrics she felt plastic resilience. Everything done in the other colours of the rooms.

"See! We matched it all."

The bed was a small shock. Someone had taken the request for a hard mat too literally. Flat surface of black plaz without cushion. No bedding.

Suipol, seeing this, started to object but Odrade silenced her. Despite Bene Gesserit resources, comfort sometimes fell by the wayside. Get the job done! That was their first order. If Mother Superior had to sleep occasionally on a hard surface without covers, this could be passed off in the name of duty. Besides, Bene Gesserits had ways of adjusting to such inconsequentials. Odrade steeled herself to discomfort, aware that if she objected she might find another deliberate insult.·

Let them add this to all of that unconscious content and worry about it.

Her summons came while she was inspecting the rest of their quarters, displaying minimal concerns and open amusement. A voice piped through ceiling vents intruded as Odrade and her companions emerged into the common sitting room: "Return to the lobby where you will meet your escort to Great Honoured Matre."

"I will go alone," Odrade said, silencing objections.

A green-robed Honoured Matre waited on a fragile chair where the corridor entered the lobby. She had a face built up like a castle wall—stone laid on stone. Mouth a watergate through which she inhaled some liquid via a transparent straw. Flow of purple up the straw. Sugar odour in the liquid. The eyes were weapons peeking over ramparts. Nose: a slope down which eyes dispatched their hatred. Chin: weak. Not necessary, that chin. An afterthought. Something left over from earlier construction. You could see the infant in it. And hair: artificially darkened to muddy brown. Unimportant. Eyes, nose and mouth, those were important.

The woman stood slowly, insolently, emphasizing what a favour she did merely by noticing Odrade.

"Great Honoured Matre agrees to see you."

Heavy, almost masculine voice. Pride walled up so high she exposed it whatever she did. Packed solid with immovable prejudice. She *knew* so many things she was a walking display of ignorance and fears. Odrade saw her as a perfect demonstration of Honoured Matre vulnerability.

At the end of many turnings and corridors, all of them bright and clean, they came to a long room—sun pouring in a line of windows, sophisticated military console at one end; space maps and terrain maps projected there. Centre of Spider Queen's web? Odrade entertained doubts. Console too obvious. Something of different design from the Scattering but no mistaking its purpose. Fields that humans could manipulate had physical limits and a hood for mental interface could be nothing else even though it was a towering oval shape and a peculiar dirty yellow.

She swept her gaze over the room. Sparsely furnished. A few sling chairs and small tables, a large open area where (presumably) people could await orders. No clutter. This was supposed to be an action centre.

Impress that upon the witch!

Windows on one long wall revealed flagstones and gardens beyond. This whole thing was a set piece!

Where is Spider Queen? Where does she sleep? What is the appearance of her lair?

Two women came in through an arched doorway from the flagstones. Both wore red robes with glittering arabesques and dragon shapes on them. Soostones shattered for decorations.

Odrade held her silence, exercising caution until after introductions by the escort, who uttered as few words as possible and left hurriedly.

410

Without Murbella's hints, the tall one standing beside Spider Queen was the one Odrade would have taken for commander. But it was the smaller one. Fascinating.

This one did not just climb to power. She sneaked between the cracks. One day, her sisters awoke to accomplished fact. There she was, firmly seated at the centre. And who could object? Ten minutes after leaving her you would have difficulty remembering the target of your objections.

The two women examined Odrade with equal intensity.

Well and good. That is needed at this moment.

Spider Queen's appearance was more than a surprise. Until this moment, no physical description of her had been achieved by the Bene Gesserit. Only temporary projections, imaginative constructs based on scattered bits of evidence. Here she was, finally. A small woman. Expected stringy muscles visible under red leotards beneath her robe. Face a forgettable oval with bland brown eyes, orange flecks dancing in them.

Fearful and angered by it but cannot place the precise reasons for her fear. All she has is a target—me. What does she think to gain from me?

The aide was something else: in appearance, far more dangerous. Golden hair so carefully coifed, slight hook to the nose, thin lips, skin stretched tightly over high cheekbones. And that venomous glare.

Odrade passed her gaze once more over Spider Queen's features: a nose that some would have trouble describing a minute after leaving her.

Straight? Well, somewhat.

Eyebrows a match to straw-coloured hair. The mouth opened to become pinkly visible and almost vanished when closed. It was a face where you had difficulty finding a central focus and thus the entire thing became blurred.

"So you lead the Bene Gesserit."

Voice equally low key. Oddly inflected Galach and no jargon yet you sensed it just behind her tongue. Linguistic tricks were there. Murbella's knowledge emphasized that.

"They have something close to Voice. Not the equal of what you gave me but there are other things they do, word tricks of a sort."

411

Word tricks.

"How should I address you?" Odrade asked.

"I hear you call me the Spider Queen." Orange flecks dancing viciously in her eyes.

"Here at the centre of your web and considering your vast powers, I'm afraid I must confess to it."

"So that is what you notice—my powers." Vain!

The first thing Odrade actually had marked was the woman's smell. She was bathed in some outrageous perfume.

Covering up pheromones?

Warned about Bene Gesserit ability to judge on the basis of minuscule sense data? Perhaps. Just as probable she preferred this perfume. The odious concoction had about it an underlying hint of exotic flowers. Something from her homeland?

The Spider Queen put a hand to her forgettable chin. "You may call me Dama."

The companion objected. "This is the last enemy in the Million Planets!"

So that's how they think of the Old Empire.

Dama held up a hand for silence. How casual and how revealing. Odrade saw a lustre reminiscent of Bellonda in the aide's eyes. Viciousness watchful in there and looking for places to attack.

"Most are required to address me as Great Honoured Matre," Dama said. "I have conferred an honour upon you." She gestured toward the arched doorway behind her. "We will walk outside, just the two of us, while we talk."

No invitation; it was a command.

Odrade paused beside the door to look at a map displayed there. Black on white, little lines of paths and irregular outlines with labels in Galach. It was the gardens beyond the flagstones, identification of plantings. Odrade bent close to study it while Dama waited with amused tolerance. Yes, esoteric trees and bushes, very few bearing edible fruits. Pride of possession and this map was here to emphasize it.

"Useless beauty and all of it mine!"

On the patio, Odrade said: "I noticed your perfume."

Dama was thrown back into memories and her voice carried subtle undertones when she responded.

412

Floral identity marker for her own flamebush. Imagine that! But she is both sad and angry when she thinks of this. And she wonders why I bring it to attention.

"Otherwise, the bush would not have accepted me," Dama said.

Interesting choice of verb tense.

The accented Galach was not hard to understand. She obviously adjusted unconsciously for the listener.

Good ear. Spends a few seconds, watching, listening and adjusts to make herself understood. Very old art form that most humans adopt quickly.

Odrade saw the origins as protective colouration.

Don't want to be taken for an alien.

An adjustable characteristic built into the genes. Honoured Matres had not lost it but this was a vulnerability. Unconscious tonalities were not completely covered and they revealed much.

Despite her blatant vanity, Dama was intelligent and self-disciplined. It was a pleasure to come to that opinion. Certain circumlocutions were not necessary.

Odrade stopped where Dama stopped at the edge of the patio. They stood almost shoulder to shoulder and Odrade, gazing outward at the garden, was struck by the almost Bene Gesserit appearance.

"Speak your piece," Dama said.

"What value do I have as a hostage?" Odrade asked.

Orange glare!

"You've obviously asked the question," Odrade said.

"Do continue." Orange subsiding.

"The Sisterhood has three replacements for me." Odrade produced her most penetrating stare. "It is possible for us to weaken each other in ways that would destroy us both."

"We could crush you as we would swat an insect!"

Beware the orange!

Odrade was not deflected by warnings from within. "But the hand that *swatted* us would fester, and eventually sickness would consume you."

It could not be stated plainer without specific details.

"Impossible!" An orange glare.

413

"Do you think us unaware of how you were driven back here by your enemies?"

My most dangerous gambit.

Odrade watched it take effect. A dark scowl was not Dama's only visible response. Orange vanished, leaving her eyes an oddly bland discrepancy on the glowering face.

Odrade nodded as though Dama had answered. "We could leave you vulnerable to those who assail you, those who drove you into this cul de sac."

"You think we . . ."

"We know."

At least, now I know.

The knowledge produced both elation and fear.

What is out there to subdue these women?

"We merely gather our forces before . . ."

"Before returning to an arena where you are sure to be crushed . . . where you cannot count on overwhelming numbers."

Dama's voice relapsed into soft Galach that Odrade had difficulty understanding. "So they have been to you . . . and made their offer. What fools you are to trust the . . ."

"I have not said we trust."

"If Logno back there . . ." Nod of head indicating the aide in the room. ". . . heard you talking to me this way you would be dead in less time than I take to warn you of it."

"I am fortunate there are only the two of us."

"Don't count on that to carry you much farther."

Odrade glanced over her shoulder at the building. Alterations in Guild design were visible: a long facade of windows, much exotic wood and jewelled stones.

Wealth.

She was dealing with wealth in an extreme it would be hard for some to imagine. Nothing Dama wanted, nothing that could be provided by the society subservient to her, would be denied. Nothing except freedom to go back into the Scattering.

How firmly did Dama cling to the fantasy that her exile might end? And what was the force that had driven such power back to the Old Empire? Why here? Odrade dared not ask.

"We will continue this in my quarters," Dama said.

Into the Spider Queen's lair at last!

Dama's quarters were a bit of a puzzle. Richly carpeted floors. She kicked off sandals and went barefoot on entering. Odrade followed this lead.

Look at the calloused condition along the outsides of her feet! Dangerous weapons kept well-conditioned.

Not the soft floor but the room itself puzzled Odrade. One small window looking over the carefully manicured botanical garden. No hangings or pictures on the walls. No decorations. An air vent grill drew shadowy stripes above the door they had entered. One other door in the right. Another air vent. Two soft grey couches. Two small side tables in glistening black. Another larger table in tones of gold with a green shimmer above it to indicate a control field. Odrade identified the fine rectangular outline of a projector inset into the golden table.

Ahhhh, this is her workroom. Are we here to work?

A refined concentration about this place. Care had been taken to eliminate distractions. What distractions would Dama accept?

Where are the decorated rooms? She has to live in particular ways with her surroundings. You cannot always be forming mental barriers to reject things around you that sit disagreeably in your psyche. If you want real comfort, your home cannot be set up in a way that attacks you, especially no attacks on the unconscious side. She is aware of unconscious vulnerabilities! This one is truly dangerous but she has the power to say "Yes".

It was an ancient Bene Gesserit insight. You looked for the ones who could say "Yes". Never bother with underlings who can only say "No". You sought the one who could make an agreement, sign a contract, pay off on a promise. Spider Queen did not often say "Yes" but she had that power and knew it.

I should have realized when she took me aside. She sent me the first signal when she permitted me to call her Dama. Have I been too precipitate, setting up Teg's attack in a way I cannot stop? Too late for second thoughts. I knew it when I unleashed him.

415

But what other forces may we attract?

Odrade had Dama's dominance pattern registered. Words and gestures were likely to make Spider Queen recoil, crouching back to intense awareness of her own heartbeats.

The drama must go forward.

Dama was doing something with her hands in the green field atop the golden table. She concentrated on it, ignoring Odrade in a way that was both insult and compliment.

You will not interfere, witch, because that is not in your best interest and you know it. Besides, you are not important enough to distract me.

Dama appeared agitated.

Has the attack on Gammu been successful? Are refugees beginning to arrive?

An orange glare focused on Odrade. "Your pilot has just destroyed himself and your ship rather than submit to our inspection. What did you bring?"

"Ourselves."

"There is a signal coming from you!"

"Telling my companions whether I am alive or dead. You already knew that."

"Some of our ancestors burned their ships before an attack. No retreat possible."

Odrade spoke with exquisite care, tone and timing adjusted to Dama's responses. "If I am successful, you will provide my transport. My pilot was a cyborg and shere could not protect him from your probes. His orders were to kill himself rather than fall into your hands."

"Providing us with coordinates to your planet." The orange subsided from Dama's eyes, but she still was disturbed. "I did not think your people obeyed you to that extent."

How do you hold them without sexual bonding, witch? Is the answer not obvious? We have secret powers.

Careful now, Odrade cautioned herself. *A methodical approach, alert for new demands. Let her think we choose one method of response and stick to it. How much does she know about us? She does not know that even Mother Superior may be only a morsel of bait, a lure to gain vital information. Does that*

416

make us superior? If so, can superior training surmount superior speed and numbers?

Odrade had no answer.

Dama seated herself behind the golden table, leaving Odrade standing. There was a nesting sense about the movement. She did not leave this place often. This was the true centre of her web. All things she thought she needed were here. She had brought Odrade to this room because it was an inconvenience to be elsewhere. She was uncomfortable in other settings, perhaps even felt threatened. Dama did not court danger. She had done so once but that was long ago, shut off behind her somewhere. Now, she wanted only to sit here in a safe and well-organized cocoon where she could manipulate others.

Odrade found these observations a welcome affirmation of Bene Gesserit deductions. The Sisterhood knew how to exploit this leverage. Bureaucracies were based on cowardice, fear that something might impede career advancement or retirement comforts.

Cover your ass!

It was an age-old rule.

"Compassion is not in my job description."

"Have you nothing more to say?" Dama asked.

Stall for time.

Odrade ventured a question. "I am extremely curious why you agreed to this meeting."

"Why are you curious?"

"It seems so . . . so out of character for you."

"We determine what is in character for us!" Quite testy there.

"But what is it about us interests you?"

"You think we find you interesting?"

"Perhaps you even find us remarkable because that is certainly how we look at you."

A pleased expression made its fleeting appearance on Dama's face. "I knew you would be fascinated by us."

"The exotic interests the exotic," Odrade said.

This brought a knowing smile to Dama's lips, the smile of someone whose pet has been clever. She stood and went to the

417

one window. Summoning Odrade to her side, Dama gestured to a stand of trees beyond the first flowering bushes and spoke in that soft accent so difficult to follow.

Odrade listened with concentration. Dama called those trees cedars? That said something about her interest in things arboreal. The technical label accepted by those who dealt in such things was "junipers". Dama did not indulge in technical frivolities nor did she care that her labels revealed dependence on a common idiom.

Something ticked off an inner alarm. Odrade fell into simulflow, seeking the source. Something in the room or in Spider Queen? There was a lack of spontaneity about the setting matched by much that Dama did. So all of this was designed to create an effect. Carefully schemed.

Is this one really my Spider Queen? Or is there a more powerful one watching us?

Odrade explored this thought, sorting swiftly. It was a process that provided more questions than answers, a mental shorthand akin to that of Mentats. Sort for relevance and bring up the latent (but orderly) backgrounds. Order generally was a product of human activity. Chaos existed as raw material from which to create order. That was the Mentat approach, giving no unalterable truths but a remarkable lever for decision making: orderly assemblage of data in a non-discrete system.

She arrived at a Projective.

They revel in chaos! Prefer it! Adrenalin addicts!

So Dama was Dama, Great Honoured Matre. Forever the patroness, forever the superior.

There is no greater one watching us. But Dama believes this is bargaining. One would think she had never done it before. Precisely!

Dama touched an unmarked place below the window and the wall folded back, revealing that the window was but an artful projection. The way was opened on to a high balcony paved with dark green tiles. It overlooked plantations much different from those in the window projection. Here was chaos preserved, wilderness left to its own devices and made more remarkable by ordered gardens in the distance. Brambles, fallen trees, thick bushes. And beyond: evenly spaced rows of what appeared to be vegetables with automated harvesters passing back and forth, leaving bare ground behind them.

Love of chaos, indeed!

Spider Queen smiled and led the way on to the balcony.

As she emerged, Odrade once more was stopped by what she saw. A decoration on the parapet to her left. A life-size figure shaped from an almost ethereal substance, all feathery planes and curved surfaces.

When she squinted at the figure, Odrade saw it was intended to represent a human. Male or female? In some positions male, and in some female. Planes and curves responded to vagrant breezes. Thin, almost invisible wires (looked to be shigawire) suspended it from a delicately curving tube anchored in a translucent mound. The lower extremities of the figure almost touched the pebbled surface of the supporting base.

Odrade stared, captivated.

Why does it remind me of Sheeana's "The Void"?

When the wind moved it, the whole creation appeared to dance, relapsing sometimes into a graceful walk, then a slow pirouette and sweeping turns with outstretched leg.

"It is called 'Ballet Master'," Dama said. "In some winds it will kick its feet high. I have seen it running as gracefully as a marathoner. Sometimes it is just ugly little motions, arms jerking as though they held weapons. Beautiful and ugly—it is all the same. I think the artist misnamed it. 'Being Unknown' would have been better."

Beautiful and ugly—all the same. Being Unknown.

That was a terrible thing about Sheeana's creation. Odrade felt a cold wash of fear. "Who was the artist?"

"I've no idea. One of my predecessors took it from a planet we were destroying. Why does it interest you?"

It's the wild thing no one can govern. But she said: "I presume we're both seeking a basis for understanding, trying to find similarities between us."

This brought the orange glare. "You may try to understand us but we have no need to understand you."

"Both of us come from societies of women."

"It is dangerous to think of us as your offshoots!"

419

But Murbella's evidence says you are. Formed in the Scattering by Fish Speakers and Reverend Mothers in extremis.

All ingenuous and fooling nobody, Odrade asked: "Why is that dangerous?"

Dama's laugh conveyed no amusement. Vindictive.

Odrade experienced an abrupt new assessment of danger. More than a Bene Gesserit probe-and-review was demanded here. These women were accustomed to killing when angered. A reflex. Dama had said as much when speaking of her aide, and Dama had just signalled there were limits to her tolerance.

Yet, in her own way, she is trying to bargain. She displays her mechanical marvels, her powers, her wealth. No offer of alliance. Be willing servants, witches, our slaves, and we will forgive much. To gain the last of the Million Planets? More than that, certainly, but an interesting number.

With a new caution, Odrade reformed her approach. Reverend Mothers too easily fell into an adaptive pattern. *I am, of course, quite different from you but I will unbend for the sake of accord.* That would not do with Honoured Matres. They would accept nothing to suggest they were not in absolute control. It was a statement of Dama's superiority over her sisters that she allowed Odrade so much latitude.

Once more, Dama spoke in her imperious manner.

Odrade listened. How odd that Spider Queen thought one of the most attractive things the Bene Gesserit could provide was immunity from new diseases.

Was that the form of attack that drove them here?

Her sincerity was naive. None of this tiresome periodic checking to see if you had acquired secret inhabitants in your flesh. Sometimes not so secret. Sometimes disgustingly perilous. But the Bene Gesserit could end all that and would be suitably rewarded.

How pleasant.

Still that vindictive tone in every word. Odrade caught herself in this thought: Vindictive? That did not catch the proper flavour. Something carried at a deeper level.

Unconsciously jealous of what you lost when you broke away from us!

This was another pattern and it had been stylized!

420

Honoured Matres fell back on repetitious mannerisms.

Mannerisms we abandoned long ago.

This was more than refusal to recognize Bene Gesserit origins. This was garbage disposal.

Drop your discards wherever they lose your interest. Underlings take out the garbage. She is more concerned with the next thing she wants to consume than she is with fouling her own nest.

The Honoured Matre flaw was larger than suspected. Much more deadly to themselves and all they controlled. And they could not face it because, to them, it was not there.

Never existed.

Dama remained an untouchable paradox. No question of alliance entered her mind. She would seem to dance up to it but only to test her enemy.

I was right after all to unleash Teg.

Logno came out of the workroom with a tray on which stood two spindly glasses almost filled with golden liquid. Dama took one, sniffed it and sipped with a pleased expression.

What is that vicious glitter in Logno's eyes?

"Try some of this wine," Dama said, gesturing to Odrade. "It's from a planet I'm sure you've never heard of but where we have concentrated the required elements to produce the perfect golden grape for the perfect golden wine."

Odrade was caught by this long association of humans with their precious ancient drink. The god Bacchus. Berries fermented on the bush or in tribal containers.

"It is not poisoned," Dama said as Odrade hesitated. "I assure you. We kill where it suits our needs but we are not crass. We reserve our more blatant deadliness for the masses. I do not mistake you for one of the masses."

Dama chuckled at her own witticism. The laboured friendliness was almost gross.

Odrade took the proffered glass and sipped.

"It's a thing someone devised to please us," Dama said, her attention fixed on Odrade.

The one sip was enough. Odrade's senses detected a foreign substance and she was several heartbeats identifying its purpose.

To nullify the shere protecting me from their probes.

She adjusted her metabolism to render the substance harmless, then announced what she had done.

Dama glared at Logno. "So that is why none of these things work with the witches! And you never suspected!" The rage was an almost physical force directed at the hapless aide.

"It is one of the immune systems with which we combat disease," Odrade said.

Dama hurled her glass to the tiles. She was some time regaining composure. Logno retreated slowly, holding the tray almost as a shield.

So Dama did more than sneak into power. Her sisters consider her deadly. And so must I consider her.

"Someone will pay for this wasted effort," Dama said. Her smile was not pleasant.

Someone.

Someone made the wine. Someone made the dancing figure. Someone will pay, the identity was never important, only the pleasure or the need for retribution. Subservience.

Did she not suspect the consequences? The hope of all she conquered that someday she might safely be forgotten. Even Logno shared this hope, although it was coloured by her own desire to succeed Dama. Very limited in their concepts, these Honoured Matres.

The perfect golden wine!

Did she not know its fate? All of those famous wines and dishes concocted to please famous conquerors—none survived unchanged. Something in humans (genetic memory?) responded to past subservience by adjusting flavours until they no longer were those the conqueror had enjoyed.

"Do not interrupt my thoughts," Dama said. She went to the parapet and gazed at her Being Unknown, obviously recomposing her *bargaining* stance.

Odrade turned her attention to Logno. What was that continued watchfulness, rapt attention fixed on Dama. No longer simple fear. Logno suddenly appeared supremely dangerous.

Poison!

422

Odrade knew it as certainly as though the aide had shouted the word.

I am not Logno's target. Not yet. She has taken this opportunity to make her bid for power.

There was no need to look at Dama. The moment of Spider Queen's death was visible on Logno's face. Turning, Odrade confirmed it. Dama lay in a heap under Being Unknown.

"You will call *me* Great Honoured Matre," Logno said. "And you will learn to thank me for it. She (pointing at the red heap in the balcony corner) intended to betray you and exterminate your people. I have other plans. I am not one to destroy a useful weapon at the moment of our greatest need."

> *Battle? There's always a desire for breathing space motivating it somewhere.*
>
> —**The Bashar Teg**

Murbella watched the struggle for Junction with a detachment that did not reflect her feelings. She stood with a coterie of Proctors in her no-ship's command centre, attention fixed on relay projections from groundside comeyes.

There were battles all around Junction—bursts of light on darkside, grey eruptions dayside. A major engagement directed by Teg centred on "The Citadel"—a giant mound of Guild design with a new tower near its rim. Although Odrade's vital-signs transmissions had stopped abruptly, her early reports confirmed that Great Honoured Matre was in there.

The need to observe from a distance helped Murbella's sense of detachment but she felt the excitement.

Interesting times!

This ship contained precious cargo. The millions from Lampadas were being Shared and prepared for Scattering in a suite ordinarily reserved for Mother Superior. The wild Sister with her cargo of Memory dominated their priorities here.

Golden Egg for sure!

Murbella thought of the lives being risked in that suite. Preparing for the worst. No lack of volunteers and the threat in the Junction conflict minimized need for spice poison to ignite Sharings, reducing danger. Anyone on this ship could sense all-or-nothing in Odrade's gamble. Imminent threat of death was recognized. Sharing necessary!

Transformation of a Reverend Mother into sets of memories passed around at perilous cost among the sisters no longer carried a mysterious aura for her, but Murbella still was awed by the responsibility. The courage of Rebecca . . . and Lucilla! demanded admiration.

Millions of Memory Lives! All concentrated in what the Sisterhood called Extremis Progressiva, two by two then four by four and sixteen by sixteen, until each held all of them and any survivor could preserve the precious accumulation.

What they were doing in Mother Superior's suite had some of that flavour. The concept no longer terrified Murbella but it was not yet ordinary. Odrade's words comforted.

"Once you have fully accommodated to the bundles of Other Memory, all else falls into a perspective that is utterly familiar, as though you had known it always."

Murbella recognized that Teg was prepared to die in defence of this multiple-awareness that was the Sisterhood of the Bene Gesserit.

Can I do less?

Teg, no longer completely an enigma, remained an object of respect. Odrade Within amplified this with reminders of his exploits, then: *"I wonder how I'm doing down there? Ask."*

Comcommand said, "No word. But her transmissions may have been blocked by energy shielding."

They knew who really asked the question. It was on their faces.

She has Odrade!

Murbella again focused on the battle at The Citadel.

Her own reactions surprised Murbella. Everything coloured by historical disgust at repetition of war's nonsense, but still this exuberant spirit revelling in newly acquired Bene Gesserit abilities.

Honoured Matre forces had good weapons down there, she noted, and Teg's heat-absorption pads were taking punishment but even as she watched, the defensive perimeter collapsed. She could hear howling as a large Idaho-designed disruptor went bouncing down a passage between tall trees, knocking out defenders right and left.

Other Memory gave her a peculiar comparison. It was like a circus. Ships landing, disgorging their human cargoes.

"In the centre ring! The Spider Queen! Acts never before seen by the human eye!"

Odrade's persona produced a sense of amusement. *How's this for closeness of sisterhood?*

Are you dead down there, Dar? You must be. Spider Queen will blame you and be enraged.

Trees placed long afternoon shadows across Teg's lane of attack, she saw. Inviting cover. He ordered his people to go around. Ignore inviting avenues. Look for hard ways to approach and use them.

The Citadel lay in a gigantic botanical garden, strange trees and even stranger bushes mingled with prosaic plantings, all scattered around as though thrown there by a dancing child.

Murbella found the circus metaphor attractive. It gave perspective to what she witnessed.

Announcements in her mind.

Over there, dancing animals, defenders of Spider Queen, all bound to obey! And in the first ring, the main event supervised by our Ringmaster, Miles Teg! His people do mysterious things. Here is the talent!

It had aspects of a staged battle in the Roman Circus. Murbella appreciated the allusion. It made observation richer.

Battle towers filled with armoured soldiers approach. They engage. Flames cut the sky. Bodies fall.

But these were real bodies, real pains, real deaths. Bene Gesserit sensitivities forced her to regret the waste.

Is this how it was for my parents caught in the sweep?

Metaphors from Other Memory vanished. She saw Junction then as she knew Teg must see it. Bloody violence, familiar in memory and yet new. She saw attackers advancing, heard them.

Woman's voice, distinct with shock: "That bush screamed at me!"

Another voice, male: "No telling where some of this originated. That sticky stuff burns your skin."

Murbella heard action on the far side of The Citadel but it grew eerily quiet around Teg's position. She saw his troops flitting through shadows, closing in on the tower. There was Teg on Streggi's shoulders. He took a moment to stare up at the facade confronting them about half a klick away. She chose a projection that looked where he looked. Motion behind windows there.

Where were the mysterious last-ditch weapons Honoured Matres were supposed to possess?

What will he do now?

Teg had lost his Command Pod to a laser hit outside the main engagement area. The pod lay on its side behind him and he sat astride Streggi's shoulders in a patch of screening bushes, some still smouldering. He had lost his comboard with the pod but retained the silvery horseshoe of his comlink, although it was crippled without the pod's amplifiers. Communications specialists crouched nearby, jittering because they had lost close contact with the action.

The battle beyond the buildings grew louder. He heard hoarse shouts, the high hissing of burners and the lower buzz of large lasguns mingled with tinny zip-zips of hand weapons. Somewhere off there to his left was a thrum-thrum he recognized as heavy armour in trouble. A scraping sound with it, metal agony. Energy system damaged in that one. It was dragging itself over the ground, probably making a mess of the gardens.

Haker, Teg's personal aide, came dodging down the lane behind the Bashar.

"Good man in a pinch," Idaho described him, but it had taken weeks for him to adjust to the fact that the famed Bashar Teg occupied a child's body on an acolyte's shoulders.

Streggi noticed him first and turned without warning, forcing Teg to look at the man. Haker, dark and muscular, with heavy eyebrows (sweat-dampened now), stopped directly in front of Teg and spoke before fully regaining his breath.

"We have the last pockets bottled up, Bashar."

Haker raised his voice to override the battle sounds and a

buzzing squawker over his left shoulder producing low conversations, battle urgency in clipped tones.

"The far perimeter?" Teg demanded.

"Mop up in a half hour, no more. You should get out of here, Bashar. Mother Superior warned us to keep you out of needless danger."

Teg gestured at his useless pod. "Why don't I have a Communications backup?"

"A big laze got both backups in the same burn as they were coming in."

"They were together?"

Haker heard the anger. "Sir, they were . . ."

"No important equipment is sent in together. I'll want to know who disobeyed orders." The quiet voice from immature vocal chords carried more menace than a shout.

"Yes, Bashar." Strictly obedient and no sign from Haker that the mistake was his own.

Damn! "How soon will replacements arrive?"

"Five minutes."

"Get my reserve pod in here as fast as you can." Teg touched Streggi's neck with a knee.

Haker spoke before she could turn. "Bashar, they got the reserve, too. I've ordered another."

Teg repressed a sigh. These things happened in battle but he didn't like depending on primitive coms. "We'll set up here. Get more squawkers." They, at least, had the range.

Haker glanced at the greenery around them. "Here?"

"I don't like the look of those buildings up ahead. That tower commands this area. And they must have underground access. I would."

"There's nothing on the . . ."

"My memory layout doesn't include that tower. Get sonics in here to check the ground. I want our plan brought up to the minute with secure information."

Haker's squawker came alive with an override voice: "Bashar! Is the Bashar available?"

Streggi moved him next to Haker without being told. Teg took the squawker, whistling his code as he grabbed it.

427

"Bashar, it's a mess at the Flat. About a hundred of them tried to lift and ran into our screen. No survivors."

"Any sign of Mother Superior or her Spider Queen?"

"Negative. We can't tell. I mean it's a real mess. Shall I screen a view?"

"Get me dispatch. And keep looking for Odrade!"

"I tell you nothing survived here, Bashar." There was a click and a low hum, then another voice: "Dispatch."

Teg brought his voice-print coder from beneath his chin and barked quick orders. "Scramble a hammership over The Citadel. Put the scene at the Landing Flat and their other disasters on open relay. All bands. Make sure they can see it. Announce no survivors at the Flat."

The double click of *received/confirmed* broke the link. Haker said: "Do you really think you can terrify them?"

"Educate them." He repeated Odrade's parting words: "Their education has been sadly neglected."

What had happened to Odrade? He felt sure she must be dead, perhaps the first casualty here. She had expected that. Dead but not lost if Murbella could restrain her impetuosity.

Odrade, at that moment, had Teg in direct sight from the tower. Logno had silenced her vital-signs transmissions with a counter-signal shield and had brought her to the tower after the arrival of the first refugees from Gammu. No one questioned Logno's supremacy. A dead Great Honoured Matre and a live one could only be something familiar.

Expecting to be killed at any moment, Odrade still gathered data as she went up in a nulltube with guards. The tube was an artifact from the Scattering, a transparent piston in a transparent cylinder. Few obstructing walls at the floors they passed. Mostly views of living areas and esoteric hardware Odrade surmised had military purposes. Lush evidence of comfort and quiet increased the higher they went.

Power climbs physically as well as psychologically.

Here they were at the top. A section of the tube cylinder swung outward and a guard pushed her roughly on to a thickly carpeted floor.

The workroom Dama showed me down there was another set piece.

428

Odrade recognized secrecy. Equipment and furnishings here would have been almost unrecognizable were it not for Murbella's knowledge. So other action centres were for show. Potemkin villages built for Reverend Mother.

Logno lied about Dama's intentions. I was expected to leave unharmed . . . carrying no useful information.

What other lies had they paraded in front of her?

Logno and all but one guard went to a console on Odrade's right. Pivoting on one foot, Odrade looked around. This was the real centre. She studied it with care. Odd place. An aura of the sanitary. Treated with chemicals to make it clean. No bacterial or viral contaminants. No strangers in the blood. Everything *debugged* like a showcase for rare viands. And Dama showed interest in Bene Gesserit immunity to diseases. There was bacterial warfare in the Scattering.

They want one thing from us!

And just one surviving Reverend Mother would satisfy them if they could wrest information from her.

A full Bene Gesserit cadre would have to examine the strands of this web and see where they led.

If we win.

The operations console where Logno concentrated her attention was smaller than the showcase ones. Fingerfield manipulation. The hood on a low table beside Logno was smaller and transparent revealing the medusa tangle of probes.

Shigawire for sure.

The hood showed a close affinity to T-probes from the Scattering Teg and others had described. Did these women possess more technological marvels? They must.

A glittering wall behind Logno, windows on her left opening on to a balcony, a far vista of Junction visible out there with movement of troops and armour. She recognized Teg in the distance, a figure on the shoulders of an adult, but gave no sign she saw anything extraordinary. She continued her slow study. Door to a passage with another nulltube partly visible in a separate area to her immediate left. More green tile on the floor there. Different functions in that space.

A sudden burst of noises erupted beyond the wall. Odrade

identified some of them. Boots of soldiers made a distinctive sound on tiles. Swish of exotic fabrics. Voices. She distinguished accents of Honoured Matres responding to each other in tones of shock.

We're winning!

Shock was to be expected when the invincible were brought low. She studied Logno. Would it be a plunge into despair?

If so, I may survive.

Murbella's role might be changed. Well, that could wait. Sisters had been briefed on what to do in the event of victory. Neither they nor anyone else in the attack force would lay rough hands on an Honoured Matre—erotic or otherwise. Duncan had prepared the men, making the perils of sexual entrapment thoroughly known.

Risk no bondage. Raise no new antagonisms.

The new Spider Queen was revealed now as someone even stranger than Odrade had suspected. Logno left her console and came to within a pace of Odrade. "You have won this battle. We are your prisoners."

No orange in her eyes. Odrade swept her gaze around at the women who had been her guards. Blank expressions, clear eyes. Was this how they showed despair? It did not feel right. Logno and the others revealed no expected emotional responses.

Everything under wraps?

Events of the past hours should create emotional crisis. Logno gave no sign of it. Not a twitch of revealing nerve or muscle. Perhaps a casual concern and that was all.

A Bene Gesserit mask!

It had to be unconscious, something automatic ignited by defeat. So they did not really accept defeat.

We are still in there with them. Latent . . . but there! No wonder Murbella almost died. She was confronting her own genetic past as a supreme prohibition.

"My companions," Odrade said. "The three women who came with me. Where are they?"

"Dead." Logno's voice was as dead as the word.

Odrade suppressed a pang for Suipol.

Another good one lost. And isn't that a bitter lesson!

"I will identify the ones responsible if you desire revenge," Logno said.

Lesson two.

"Revenge is for children and the emotionally retarded."

A small return of orange in Logno's eyes.

Human self delusions took many forms, Odrade reminded herself. Aware that the Scattering would produce the unexpected, she had armed herself accordingly with a protective remoteness that would allow her a space to assess new places, new things and new people. She had known she would be forced to put many things in different categories to serve her or deflect threats. She took Logno's attitude as a threat.

"You do not seem disturbed, Great Honoured Matre."

"Others will avenge me." Flat, very self-composed.

The words were even stranger than her composure. She held everything under that close cover, bits and pieces revealed now in flickering movements aroused by Odrade's observation. Deep and intense things, but buried. It was all inside there, masked the way a Reverend Mother would mask it. Logno appeared to have no power at all and yet she spoke as though nothing essential had changed.

"I am your captive but that makes no difference."

Was she truly powerless? *No!* But that was the impression she wished to convey and all of the other Honoured Matres around her mirrored this response.

"See us? Powerless except for the loyalty of our sisters and the followers they have bonded to us."

Were Honoured Matres that confident of their vengeful legions? Possible only if they had never before suffered a defeat of this kind. Yet, someone had driven them back into the Old Empire. Into the Million Planets.

Teg found Odrade and her *captives* while seeking a place to assess victory. Battle always required its analytical aftermath, especially from a Mentat commander. It was a comparison test this battle demanded of him more than any other in his experience. This conflict would not be lodged in memory until assessed and shared as far as possible among those who depended on him. It was his invariable pattern and he did not

431

care what it revealed about him. Break that link of interlocking interests and you prepared yourself for defeat.

I need a quiet place to assemble the threads of this battle and make a preliminary summary.

In his estimation, a most difficult problem of battle was to conduct it in a way that did not release human wildness. A Bene Gesserit dictum. Battle must be conducted to bring out the best in those who survived. Most difficult and sometimes all but impossible. The more remote the soldier from carnage, the more difficult. It was one reason Teg always tried to move to the battle scene and examine it personally. If you did not see the pain, you could easily cause greater pain without second thoughts. That was the Honoured Matre pattern. But their pains had been brought home. What would they make of this?

That question was in his mind as he and aides emerged from the tube to see Odrade confronting a party of Honoured Matres.

"Here is our commander, the Bashar Miles Teg," Odrade said, gesturing.

Honoured Matres stared at Teg.

A child riding on the shoulders of an adult? This is their commander?

"Ghola," Logno muttered.

Odrade spoke to Haker. "Take these prisoners somewhere nearby where they can be comfortable."

Haker did not move until Teg nodded, then politely indicated that captives should precede him into the tiled area on their left. Teg's dominance was not lost on Honoured Matres. They glowered at him as they obeyed Haker's invitation.

Men ordering women about!

With Odrade beside him, Teg touched a knee to Streggi's neck and they went on to the balcony. There was an oddity to the scene that he was a moment identifying. He had viewed many battle scenes from high vantages, most often from a scout 'thopter. This balcony was fixed in space, giving him a sense of immediacy. They stood about one hundred metres above the botanical gardens where much of the fiercest conflict had taken place. Many bodies lay sprawled in final dislodgment—dolls thrown aside by departing children. He recognized uniforms of some of his troops and felt a pang.

Could I have done something to prevent this?

He had known this feeling many times and called it "Command Guilt". But this scene was different, not just in that uniqueness found in any battle but in a way that nagged at him. He decided it was partly the landscaped setting, a place better suited to garden parties, now torn by an ancient pattern of violence.

Small animals and birds were returning, nervously furtive after the upset of all that noisy human intrusion. Little furry creatures with long tails sniffed at casualties and scampered up neighbouring trees for no apparent reason. Colourful birds peered from screening foliage or flitted across the scene—lines of blurred pigmentation that became camouflage when they ducked abruptly under leaves. Feathered accents to the scene, trying to restore that non-tranquillity human observers mistook for peace in such settings. Teg knew better. In his pre-ghola life, he had grown up surrounded by wilderness: farm life close by but wild animals just beyond cultivation. It was not really tranquil out there.

With that observation he recognized what had tugged at his awareness. Considering the fact they had stormed a well-manned defensive emplacement occupied by heavily armed defenders, the number of casualties down there was extremely small. He had seen nothing to explain this since entering The Citadel. Were they caught off balance? Their losses in space were one thing—his ability to *see* defender ships produced a devastating advantage. But this complex held prepared positions where defenders could have fallen back and made the assault more costly. Collapse of Honoured Matre resistance had been abrupt and now it remained unexplained.

I was wrong to assume they responded to display of their disasters.

He glanced at Odrade. "That Great Honoured Matre in there, did she give the command for defence to stop?"

"That's my assumption."

Cautious and a typical Bene Gesserit answer. She, too, was subjecting the scene to careful observation.

Was her assumption a reasonable explanation for the abruptness with which defenders threw down their arms?

Why would they do it? To prevent more bloodshed?

Given the callousness Honoured Matres usually demonstrated, that was unlikely. The decision had been made for reasons that plagued him.

A trap?

Now that he thought about it, there were other strange things about the battle scene. None of the usual calls from wounded, no scurrying about with cries for stretchers and medics. He could see Suks moving among the bodies. That, at least, was familiar, but every figure they examined was left where it had fallen.

All dead? No wounded?

He experienced griping fear. Not an unusual fear in battle but he had learned to read it. Something profoundly wrong. Noises, things within his view, the smells took on a new intensity. He felt himself acutely atuned, a predatory animal in the jungle, knowing his terrain but aware of something intrusive that must be identified lest he become hunted instead of hunter. He registered his surroundings at a different level of consciousness, reading himself as well, searching out arousal patterns that had achieved this response. Streggi trembled beneath him. So she felt his distress.

"Something's very wrong here," Odrade said.

He pushed a hand at her, demanding silence. Even in this tower surrounded by victorious troops, he felt exposed to a threat his clamouring senses failed to reveal.

Danger!

He was sure of it. The unknown frustrated him. It required every bit of his training to keep from falling into a nervous fugue.

Nudging Streggi to turn, Teg barked an order to an aide standing in the balcony doorway. The aide listened quietly and ran to obey. They must get casualty figures. How many wounded compared to deaths? Reports on captured weapons. Urgent!

When he returned to his examination of the scene, he saw another disturbing thing, a basic oddity his eyes had tried to

434

report. Very little blood on those fallen figures in Bene Gesserit uniforms. You expected battle casualties to show that ultimate evidence of common humanity—flowing red that darkened on exposure but always left its indelible mark in the memories of those who saw it. Lack of bloody carnage was an unknown and, in warfare, unknowns had a history of bringing extreme peril.

He spoke softly to Odrade. "They have a weapon we have not discovered."

Do not be quick to reveal judgment. Hidden judgment often is more potent. It can guide reactions whose effects are felt only when too late to divert them.

—BG Advice to Postulants

Sheeana smelled worms at a distance: cinnamon undertones of melange mingled with bitter flint and brimstone, the crystal-banked inferno of the great Rakian sand-eaters. But she sensed these tiny descendants only because they existed out there in such numbers.

They are so small.

It had been hot here at Desert Watch today and now in late afternoon she welcomed the artificially cooled interior. There was a tolerable temperature adjustment in her old quarters although the windows on the west had been left open. Sheeana went to that window and stared out at glaring sand.

Memory told her what this vantage would be tonight: starlight bright in dry air, thin illumination on sand waves that reached to a darkly curved horizon. She remembered Rakian moons and missed them. Stars alone did not satisfy her Fremen heritage.

She had thought of this as retreat, a place and time to think about what was happening to her Sisterhood.

Axolotl tanks, cyborgs and now this.

Odrade's plan held no mysteries since their Sharing. A gamble? And if it succeeded?

435

We will know perhaps tomorrow and then what will we become?

She admitted to a magnet in Desert Watch, more than a place to consider consequences. She had walked in sun-scorched heat today, proving to herself she could still call worms with her dance, emotion expressed as action.

Dance of Propitiation. My language of the worms.

She had gone dervish-whirling on a dune until hunger shattered her memory-trance. And little worms were spread all around in gaping watchfulness, remembered flames within the frames of crystal teeth.

But why so small?

The words of investigators explained but did not satisfy. *"It is the dampness."*

Sheeana recalled giant shai-hulud of Dune, "the Old Man of the Desert", large enough to swallow spice factories, ring surfaces hard as plastrete. Masters in their own domain. God and devil in the sands. She sensed the potential from her window vantage.

Why did the Tyrant choose symbiotic existence in a worm?

Did those tiny worms carry his endless dream?

Sandtrout inhabited this desert. Accept them as a new skin and she might follow the Tyrant's path.

Metamorphosis. The Divided God.

She knew the lure.

Do I dare?

Memories of her last moments of ignorance came over her—barely eight then, the month of Igat on Dune.

Not Rakis. Dune, as my ancestors named it.

Not difficult to recall herself as she had been: a slender, dark-skinned child, streaked brown hair. Melange hunter (because that was a task for children) running into open desert with childhood companions. How dear it felt in memory.

But memory had its darker side. Focusing attention into the nostrils, a girl detected intense odours—a pre-spice mass!

The Blow!

Melange explosion brought Shaitan. No sandworm could resist a spice blow in its territory.

You ate it all, Tyrant, that miserable collection of shacks and hovels we called "home" and all of my friends and family. Why did you spare me?

What a rage had shaken that slender child. Everything she loved taken by a giant worm that refused her attempts to sacrifice herself in its flames and carried her into the hands of Rakian priests, thence to the Bene Gesserit.

"She talks to the worms and they spare her."

"They who spared me are not spared by me." That was what she had told Odrade.

And now Odrade knows what I must do. You cannot suppress the wild thing, Dar. I dare call you Dar now that you are within me.

No response.

Was there a pearl of Leto II's awareness in each of the new sandworms? Her Fremen ancestors insisted on it.

Someone handed her a sandwich. Walli, the senior acolyte assistant who had assumed command of Desert Watch.

At my insistence when Odrade elevated me to the Council. But not just because Walli learned my immunity to Honoured Matre sexual bonding. And not because she is sensitive to my needs. We speak a secret language, Walli and I.

Walli's large eyes no longer were entrances to her soul. They were filmed barriers giving evidence she already knew how to block probing stares; a light blue pigmentation that soon would be all blue if she survived the Agony. Almost albino and a questionable genetic line for breeding. Walli's skin reinforced this judgment: pale and freckled. A skin you saw as a surface transparency. You did not focus on the skin itself but on what lay beneath: pink, blood-suffused flesh unprotected from a desert sun. Only here in the shade could Walli expose that sensitive surface to questioning eyes.

Why this one in command over us?

Because I trust her best to do what must be done.

Sheeana ate the sandwich absently while she returned her attention to the sandscape. The whole planet thus one day. Another Dune? No . . . similar but different. How many such places are we creating in an infinite universe? Senseless question.

Desert vagary placed a small black dot in the distance.

Sheeana squinted. Ornithopter. It grew slowly larger and then smaller. Quartering the sand. Inspecting.

What are we really creating here?

When she looked at encroaching dunes, she sensed arrogant hubris.

Look upon my works, tiny human, and despair.

But we did this, my sisters and I.

Did you?

"I can feel a new dryness in the heat," Walli said.

Sheeana agreed. No need to speak. She went to the large worktable while she still had daylight to study the topomap spread out there: little flags sticking in it, green thread on pushpins just as she had designed it.

Odrade had asked once: "Is this really preferable to a projection?"

"I need to touch it."

Odrade accepted that.

Projections palled. Too far removed from dirt. You could not draw a finger down a projection and say, "We will go down here." A finger in a projection was a finger in empty air.

Eyes are never enough. The body must feel its world.

Sheeana detected pungency of male perspiration, a musty smell of exertion. She lifted her head and saw a dark young man standing in the doorway, arrogant pose, arrogant look.

"Oh," he said. "I thought you would be alone, Walli. I'll come back later."

One piercing stare at Sheeana and he was gone.

There are many things the body must feel to know them.

"Sheeana, why are you here?" Walli asked.

You who are so busy on the Council, what do you seek? Don't you trust me?

"I came to consider what the Missionaria still thinks I may do. They see a weapon—the myths of Dune. Billions pray to me: 'The Holy One who spoke to the Divided God'."

"Billions is not an adequate number," Walli said.

"But it measures the force my sisters see in me. Those worshippers believe I died with Dune. I've become 'a powerful spirit in the pantheon of the oppressed'."

"More than a missionary?"

438

"What might happen, Walli, if I appeared in that waiting universe, a sandworm beside me? The potential of such a thing fills some of my sisters with hope and misgivings."

"Misgivings I understand."

Indeed. The very kind of religious implant Muad'Dib and his Tyrant son let loose on an unsuspecting humankind.

"Why do they even consider it?" Walli insisted.

"With me as fulcrum, what a lever they would have to move the universe!"

"But how could they control such a force?"

"That is the problem. Something so inherently unstable. Religions are never really controllable. But some sisters think they could *aim* a religion built around me."

"And if their aim is poor?"

"They say the religions of women always flow deeper."

"True?" Questioning a superior source.

Sheeana could only nod. Other Memory confirmed it.

"Why?"

"Because within us, life renews itself."

"That's all of it?" Openly doubting.

"Women often bear the aura of underdog. Humans reserve a special sympathy for ones at the bottom. I am a woman and if Honoured Matres want me dead then I must be blessed."

"You sound as though you agree with the Missionaria."

"When you're one of the hunted, you consider any path of escape. I am revered. I cannot ignore the potential."

Nor the danger. So my name has become a shining light in the darkness of Honoured Matre oppression. How easy for that light to become a consuming flame!

No . . . the plan she and Duncan had worked out was better. Escape from Chapter House. It was a death trap not only for its inhabitants but for Bene Gesserit dreams.

"I still don't understand why you're here. We may no longer be hunted."

"May?"

"But why just now?"

I cannot speak it openly because then the watchdogs would know.

"I have this fascination with the worms. It's partly because one of my ancestors led the original migration to Dune."

You remember this, Walli. We spoke of it once out there on the sand with only the two of us to hear. And now you know why I have come visiting.

"I remember you saying she was a proper Fremen."

"And a Zensunni Master."

I will lead my own migration, Walli. But I will need worms only you can provide. And it must be done quickly. The reports from Junction urge speed. And the first ships will return soon. Tonight . . . tomorrow. I fear what they bring.

"Are you still interested in taking a few worms back to Central where you can study them closely?"

Oh, yes, Walli! You do remember.

"It might be interesting. I don't have much time for such things but any knowledge we gain may help us."

"It will be too wet for them back there."

"The Great Hold of the no-ship on the Flat could be reconverted into a desert lab. Sand, controlled atmosphere. The essentials are there from when we brought the first worm."

"Bellonda may think you're wasting time."

Don't overdo it, Walli.

"Bellonda has become almost human. She even jokes occasionally."

"Really? I remember her telling me, 'Levity is dangerous!'"

"Now, she only says humour should sadden us a bit."

"Humans are ridiculous."

"There are strange energies in you, Walli."

That should mislead the watchdogs.

"It's that new young man I'm polishing for Duncan. He's very good, arrogant as Shaitan and thinks I cannot do without him."

My Walli does not like that.

"I've already signed the order sending him on his way," Walli said. "He doesn't know it yet but he leaves tomorrow."

"And you have regrets?"

"Nothing I won't shake off in a day or so."

Ahhh, you will make a proper Reverend Mother, Walli. And that is what the watchdogs are saying right now.

440

Sheeana glanced at the western window. "Sunset. I would like to go down again and walk on the sand."

Will the first ships return tonight?

"Of course, Reverend Mother." Walli stood aside, opening the way to the door.

Sheeana spoke as she was leaving. "Desert Watch will have to be moved before long."

"We are prepared."

The sun was dipping below the horizon when Sheeana emerged from the arched street at the edge of the community. She strode into starlit desert, exploring with her senses as she had done as a child. Ahhh, there was the cinnamon essence. Worms near.

She paused and, turning northeast away from the last sunglow, placed her palms flat above and below her eyes in the old Fremen way, confining view and light. She stared out of a horizontal frame. Whatever fell from heaven must pass this narrow slit.

Tonight? They will come just after dark to delay the moment of explanation. A full night for reflection.

She waited with Bene Gesserit patience.

An arc of fire drew a thin line above the northern horizon. Another. Another. They were positioned right for the Landing Flat.

Sheeana felt her heart beating fast.

They have come!

And what would be their message for the Sisterhood? *Returning warriors triumphant or refugees?* There could be little difference, given the evolution of Odrade's plan.

She would know by morning.

Sheeana lowered her hands and found she was trembling. Deep breath. The Litany.

Presently, she walked the desert, sandwalking in the remembered stride of Dune. She had almost forgotten how the feet dragged. As though they carried extra weight. Seldom-used muscles were called into play but the random walk, once learned, was never forgotten.

Once, I never dreamed I would ever again walk this way.

If watchdogs detected that thought they might wonder about their Sheeana.

It was a failure in herself, she thought. She had grown into the rhythms of Chapter House. This planet talked to her at a subterranean level. She felt earth, trees and flowers, every growing thing as though all were part of her. And now, here was disturbing movement, something in a language from a different planet. She sensed the desert changing and that, too, was an alien tongue. Desert. Not lifeless but living in a way profoundly different from once-verdant Chapter House.

Less life but more intense.

She heard the desert: small slitherings, creaking chirps of insects, a dark rustle of hunting wings overhead and the quickest of *ploppings* on the sand—kangaroo mice brought here in anticipation of this day when worms would once more begin their rule.

Walli will remember to send flora and fauna from Dune.

She stopped atop a tall barracan. In front of her, darkness blurring its edges, was an ocean caught in stop motion, a shadow surf beating on a shadow beach of this changing land. It was a limitless desert-sea. It had originated far away and it would go to stranger places than this.

I will take you there if I am able.

A night breeze from drylands to moister places behind her deposited a film of dust on her cheeks and nose, lifting the edges of her hair as it passed. She felt saddened.

What might have been.

That no longer was important.

The things that are—they matter.

She took a deep breath. Cinnamon stronger. Melange. Spice and worms near. Worms aware of her presence. How soon would this air be dry enough for sandworms to grow great and work their crop as they had on Dune?

The planet and the desert.

She saw them as two halves of the same saga. Just as the Bene Gesserit and the humankind they served. Matched halves. Either without the other was diminished, an emptiness with lost purpose. Not better dead, perhaps, but moving aimlessly. There lay the threat of Honoured Matre victory. Aimed by blind violence!

Blind in a hostile universe.

And *there* was why the Tyrant had preserved the Sisterhood.

He knew he only gave us the path without direction. A paper chase laid down by a jokester and left empty at the end.

A poet in his own right, though.

She recalled his "Memory Poem" from Dar-es-Balat, a bit of jetsam the Bene Gesserit preserved.

And for what reason do we preserve it? So I can fill my mind with it now? Forgetting for the moment what I may confront tomorrow?

> *The fair night of the poet,*
> *Fill it with innocent stars.*
> *A pace apart Orion stands.*
> *His glare sees everything,*
> *Marking our genes forever.*
> *Welcome darkness and stare,*
> *Blinded in the afterglow.*
> *There's barren eternity!*

Sheeana felt abruptly that she had won a chance to become the ultimate artist, filled to overflowing and presented with a blank surface where she might create as she wished.

An unrestricted universe!

Odrade's words from those first childhood exposures to Bene Gesserit purpose came back to her. "Why did we fasten on to you, Sheeana? It's really simple. We recognized in you a thing we had long awaited. You arrived and we saw it happen."

"It?" *How naive I was!*

"Something new lifting over the horizon."

My migration will seek the new. But . . . I must find a planet with moons.

Looked at one way, the universe is Brownian movement, nothing predictable at the elemental level. Muad'Dib and his Tyrant son closed the cloud chamber where movement occurred.

—Stories from Gammu

Murbella entered a time of incongruent experiences. It bothered her at first, seeing her own life with multiple vision. Chaotic events at Junction had ignited this, creating a jumble of immediate necessities that would not leave her, not even when she returned to Chapter House.

I warned you, Dar. You can't deny it. I said they could turn victory into defeat. And look at the mess you dumped in my lap! I was lucky to save as many as I did.

This inner protest always immersed her in the events that had elevated her to this awful prominence.

What else could I have done?

Memory displayed Streggi slumping to the floor in bloodless death. The scene had played on the no-ship's relays like a fictional drama. The projection framework in the ship's command bay added to the illusion that this was not really happening. The actors would arise and take their bows. Teg's comeyes, humming away automatically, missed none of it until someone silenced them.

She was left with images, an eerie afterglow: Teg sprawled on the floor of that Honoured Matre eyrie. Odrade staring in shock.

Loud protests greeted Murbella's declaration that she must rush groundside. The Proctors were adamant until she laid out the details of Odrade's gamble and demanded: "Do you want total disaster?"

Odrade Within won that argument. But you were prepared for it from the first, weren't you Dar? Your plan!

The Proctors said: "There's still Sheeana." They gave Murbella a one-man lighter and sent her to Junction alone.

Even though she transmitted her Honoured Matre identity ahead of her, there were touchy moments at the Landing Flat. A squad of armed Honoured Matres confronted her as she emerged from the lighter beside a smoking pit. The smoke smelled of exotic explosives.

Where Mother Superior's lighter was destroyed.

An ancient Honoured Matre led the squad, her red robe stained, some of its decorations gone and a rip down the left shoulder. She was like some dried-up lizard, still poisonous, still with a bite but running on well-used angers, most of her energy gone. Disarrayed hair like the outer skin of a fresh-dug ginger root. There was a demon in her. Murbella saw it peering from orange-flecked eyes.

For all the fact that a full squad backed up the old one, the two of them faced each other as though isolated at the foot of the lighter's drop, wild animals cautiously sniffing, trying to judge the extent of danger.

Murbella watched the old one carefully. This lizard would dart her tongue a bit, testing the air, giving vent to her emotions, but she was sufficiently shocked to listen.

"Murbella is my name. I was taken captive by the Bene Gesserit on Gammu. I am an adept of the Hormu."

"Why are you wearing a witch's robes?" The old one and her squad stood ready to kill.

"I have learned everything they had to teach and have brought that treasure to my sisters."

The old one studied her a moment. "Yes, I recognize your type. You're a Roc, one we chose for the Gammu project."

The squad behind her relaxed slightly.

"You did not come all the way in that lighter," the old one accused.

"I escaped from one of their no-ships."

"Do you know where their nest is?"

"I do."

A wide smile spread the old one's lips. "Well! You are a prize! How did you escape?"

"Do you have to ask?"

The old one considered this. Murbella could read the thoughts on her face as though they were spoken: *These ones we brought from Roc—deadly, all of them. They can kill with hands, feet or any other movable part of their bodies. They all should carry a sign: "Dangerous in any position."*

Murbella moved away from the lighter, displaying the sinewy grace that was a mark of her identity.

Speed and muscle, sisters. Beware.

Some of the squad pressed forward, curious. Their words were full of Honoured Matre comparisons, eager questions Murbella was forced to parry.

"Did you kill many of them? Where is their planet? Is it rich? Have you bonded many males there? You were trained on Gammu?"

"I was on Gammu for the third stage. Under Hakka."

"Hakka! I've met her. Did she have that injured left foot when you knew her?"

Still testing.

"It was the right foot and I was with her when she took the injury!"

"Oh, yes, the right foot. I remember now. How was she injured?"

"Kicking a lout in the rear. He had a sharp knife in his hip pocket. Hakka was so angry she killed him."

Laughter swept through the squad.

"We will go to Great Honoured Matre," the old one said.

So I've passed first inspection.

Murbella sensed reservations, though.

Why is this Hormu adept wearing those enemy robes? And she has a strange look to her.

Best face that one at once.

"I took their training and they accepted me."

"The fools! Did they really?"

"You question my word?" How easy it was to revert, adopting touchy Honoured Matre ways.

The old one bristled. She did not lose hauteur but she sent a warning look to her squad. All of them took a moment to digest what Murbella had said.

"You became one of them?" someone behind her asked.

"How else could I steal their knowledge? Know this! I was the personal student of their Mother Superior."

"Did she teach you well?" That same challenging voice from behind.

446

Murbella identified the questioner: middle echelon and ambitious. Anxious for notice and advancement.

This is the end of you, anxious one. And little loss to the universe.

A Bene Gesserit feint drifted the feather that was her foe into range. One Hormu-style kick for them to recognize. The questioner lay dead on the ground.

Marriage of Bene Gesserit and Honoured Matre abilities creates a danger you should all recognize and envy.

"She taught me admirably," Murbella said. "Any other questions?"

"Ehhhhh!" the old one said.

"How are you called?" Murbella demanded.

"I am a Senior Dame, Honoured Matre of the Hormu. I am called Elpek."

"Thank you, Elpek. You may call me Murbella."

"I am honoured, Murbella. It is indeed a treasure you have brought us."

Murbella studied her a moment with Bene Gesserit watchfulness before smiling without humour.

The exchange of names! You in your red robe that marks you as one of the powerful surrounding Great Honoured Matre, do you know what you have just accepted into your circle?

The squad remained shocked and looked at Murbella with wariness. She saw this with her new sensitivity. The Old Girl network had never gained a foothold in the Bene Gesserit but it performed for Honoured Matres. Simulflow amused her with a parade of confirmation. How subtle the power transfers: right school, right friends, graduation and transfer on to the first rungs of the ladder—all guided by relatives and their connections, mutual back-scratching that managed alliances, including marriages. Simulflow told her it led into the pit but ones on the ladder, the ones in controlling niches, never let that worry them.

Today is sufficient unto today, and that is how Elpek sees me. But she does not see what I have become, only that I am dangerous but potentially useful.

Turning slowly on one foot, Murbella studied Elpek's

447

squad. No bonded males here. This was too sensitive a duty for any but trusted women. Good.

"Now, you will listen to me, all of you. If you have any loyalty to our sisterhood, which I will judge on future performance, you will honour what I have brought. I intend it as a gift for those who deserve it."

"Great Honoured Matre will be pleased," Elpek said.

But Great Honoured Matre did not appear pleased when Murbella was presented.

Murbella recognized the tower setting. Almost sunset now but Streggi's body still lay where it had fallen. Some of Teg's specialists had been killed, mostly the comeye crew who doubled as his guard.

No, we Honoured Matres do not like others spying on us.

Teg still lived, she saw, but he was swathed in shigawire and shoved disdainfully into a corner. Most surprising of all: Odrade stood unfettered near Great Honoured Matre. It was a gesture of contempt.

Looking at Murbella, Great Honoured Matre said, "So this is the bag of insolence you say you trained in your ways."

Odrade almost smiled at the description.

Bag of insolence?

A Bene Gesserit would accept it without rancour. This rheumy-eyed Great Honoured Matre faced a quandary and could not call on her weapon that killed without blood. Very delicate balance of power. Agitated conversations among Honoured Matres had revealed their problem.

"We have weakened ourselves! We could have waited, saved some of them!"

All of their secret weapons had been exhausted and could not be reloaded, something they had lost when driven back here.

"Our weapon of last resort and we wasted it!"

Logno, who thought herself supreme, stood in a different arena now. And she had just learned of the fearful ease with which Murbella could kill one of the elect.

Murbella cast a measuring gaze over Great Honoured Matre's entourage, gauging their potentials. They recognized this situation, of course. Familiar. How did they vote?

Neutral?

Some were wary and all were waiting.

Anticipating a diversion. No concern over who triumphed as long as power continued to flow in their direction.

Murbella let her muscles flow into the waiting stance of combat she had learned from Duncan and the Proctors. She felt as cool as though standing on the practice floor, running through responses. Even as she reacted, she knew she moved in ways for which Odrade had prepared her—mentally, physically and emotionally.

Voice first. Give them a taste of inner chill.

"I see you have assessed the Bene Gesserit quite poorly. The arguments of which you are so proud, these women have heard them so many times your words go beyond boredom."

This was delivered with scathing vocal control, a tone that brought orange to Logno's eyes but held her motionless.

Murbella was not through with her. "You consider yourself powerful and clever. One begets the other, eh? What idiocy! You're a consummate liar and you lie to yourself."

As Logno remained motionless in the face of this attack, those around her began moving away, opening space that said, *"She is all yours."*

"Your fluency in these lies does not hide them," Murbella said. She swept a scornful gaze across the ones behind Logno. "Like the ones I know in Other Memory, you are headed for extinction. The problem is that you take so infernally long dying. Inevitable but oh, the boredom meanwhile. You dare call yourself Great Honoured Matre!" Returning her attention to Logno. "Everything about you is a cesspool. You have no style."

It was too much. Logno attacked, left foot slashing outward with blinding speed. Murbella grasped the foot as she would catch a wind-blown leaf and, continuing the flow of it, levered Logno into a threshing club that ended with her head pulped on the floor. Without pausing, Murbella pirouetted, left foot almost decapitating the Honoured Matre who had stood at Logno's right, the right hand crushing the throat of the one who had stood at Logno's left. It was over in two heartbeats.

Examining the scene without breathing hard (*to show how*

easy it was, sisters), Murbella experienced a sense of shock and recognition of the inevitable. Odrade lay on the floor in front of Elpek, who obviously had chosen sides without hesitation. The twisted position of Odrade's neck and flaccid appearance of her body said she was dead.

"She tried to interfere," Elpek said.

Having killed a Reverend Mother, Elpek expected Murbella (a sister, after all!) to applaud. But Murbella did not react as expected. She knelt beside Odrade and put her head against that of the corpse, staying there an interminable time.

The surviving Honoured Matres exchanged questioning looks but dared not move.

What is this?

But they were immobilized by Murbella's terrifying abilities.

When she had Odrade's recent past, all of the new added to previous sharing, Murbella stood.

Elpek saw death in Murbella's eyes and took one backward step before trying to defend herself. Elpek was dangerous but no match for this demon in the black robe. It was over with the same shocking abruptness that had taken Logno and her aides: a kick to the larynx. Elpek sprawled across Odrade.

Once more, Murbella studied the survivors, then stood a moment looking down at Odrade's body.

In a way, that was my doing, Dar. And yours!

She shook her head slowly from side to side, absorbing consequences.

Odrade is dead. Long live Mother Superior! Long live Great Honoured Matre! And may the heavens protect us all.

She gave her attention then to what must be done. These deaths had created an enormous debt. Murbella took a deep breath. This was another Gordian knot.

"Release Teg," she said. "Clean up in here as quickly as possible. And somebody get me a proper robe!"

It was Great Honoured Matre giving orders but those who leaped to obey sensed the Other in her.

The one who brought her a red robe elaborate with soostone dragons, held it deferentially from a distance. Large woman with heavy bones and square face. Cruel eyes.

450

"Hold it for me," Murbella said and when the woman tried to take advantage of proximity to attack her, Murbella dumped the woman hard. "Try again?"

This time there were no tricks.

"You are the first member of my Council," Murbella said. "Name?"

"Angelika, Great Honoured Matre." *See! I was first to call you by your proper title. Reward me.*

"Your reward is that I promote you and let you live."

Proper Honoured Matre response. Accepted as such.

When Teg came to her rubbing his arms where the shigawire had bitten deep, some Honoured Matres tried to caution Murbella. "Do you know what this one can . . ."

"He serves me now," Murbella interrupted. Then in Odrade's mocking tones: "Isn't that right, Miles?"

He gave her a rueful smile, an old man on a child's face. "Interesting times, Murbella."

"Dar liked apples," Murbella said. "See to that."

He nodded. Return her to a cemetery orchard. Not that prized Bene Gesserit orchards would endure long in a desert. Still, some traditions were worth perpetuating while you could.

Well within Teg's original timetable, Murbella had her picked Honoured Matre entourage and returned to Chapter House. She expected certain problems and the messages she sent ahead paved the way for solutions.

"I bring Futars to attract Handlers. Honoured Matres fear a biological weapon from the Scattering that made vegetables of them. Handlers may be the source."

"Prepare to keep Rabbi and party in no-ship. Honour their secrecy. And remove the protective mines from the ship!" (That went in keeping of a Proctor messenger.)

She was tempted to ask after her children but that was non-Bene Gesserit. Someday . . . maybe.

Immediately on returning, she had Duncan to accommodate and this confused Honoured Matres. They were as bad as the Bene Gesserit. "What's so special about one man?"

No longer a reason for him to remain in the ship but he refused to leave. "I've a mental mosaic to assemble: a piece that cannot be moved, extraordinary behaviour, and willing participation in their dream. I must find limits to test. That's missing. I know how to find it. Get in tune. Don't think; do it."

It made no sense. She humoured him although he was changed. A stability to this new Duncan that she accepted as a challenge. By what right did he assume a self-satisfied air? No . . . not self satisfied. It was more being at peace with a decision. He refused to share it!

"I've accepted things. You must do the same."

She had to admit this described what she was doing.

On her first morning back, she arose at dawn and entered the workroom. Wearing the red robe, she sat in Mother Superior's chair and summoned Bellonda.

Bell stood at one end of the worktable. She knew. The design became clear in execution. Odrade had imposed a debt on her as well. Thus, the silence: assessing how she must pay.

Service to this Mother Superior, Bell! That is how you pay. No Archival declension of these events will put them into proper perspective. Action is required.

Bellonda spoke finally. "The only crisis I'd care to compare with this one is the advent of the Tyrant."

Murbella reacted sharply. "Hold your tongue, Bell, unless you've something useful to say!"

Bellonda took the reprimand calmly (uncharacteristic response). "Dar had changes in mind. This what she expected?"

Murbella softened her tone. "We'll rehash ancient history later. This is only an opening chapter."

"Bad news." That was the old Bellonda.

Murbella said: "Admit the first group. Be cautious. They are Great Honoured Matre's High Council."

Bell left to obey.

She knows I have every right to this position. They all know it. No need for a vote. No room for a vote!

Now was the time for the historical art of politics she had learned from Odrade.

"In all things you must appear important. No minor decisions pass through your hands unless they are quiet acts called 'favours' done for people whose loyalty can be earned."

Every reward came from on high. Not a good policy with the

452

Bene Gesserit but this group entering the workroom, they were familiar with a Patroness Great Honoured Matre; they would accept "new political necessities". Temporarily. It was always temporary, especially with Honoured Matres.

Bell and watchdogs knew she would be a long time sorting this out. *Even with amplified Bene Gesserit abilities.*

It would require extremely demanding attention from all of them. And the first thing was the sharply discerning gaze of innocence.

That is what Honoured Matres lost and we must restore it before they can fade into the background where 'we' belong.

Bellonda ushered in the Council and retired silently.

Murbella waited until they were seated. A mixed lot: some aspirants to supreme power. Angelika there smiling so prettily. Some waiting (not even daring to hope yet) but gathering what they could.

"Our Sisterhood was acting with stupidity," Murbella accused. She noted the ones who took this angrily. "You would have killed the goose!"

They did not understand. She dredged up the parable. They listened with proper attention, even when she added: "Don't you realize how desperately we need every one of these witches? We outnumber them so greatly that each of them will carry an enormous teaching burden!"

They considered this and, bitter though it was, they were forced to a qualified acceptance because she said it.

Murbella hammered it home. "Not only am I your Great Honoured Matre . . . Does anyone question that?"

No one questioned.

". . . but I am Bene Gesserit Mother Superior. They can do little else but confirm me in office."

Two of them started to protest but Murbella cut them short. "No! You would be powerless to enforce your will on them. You would have to kill them all. But they will obey me."

The two continued to babble and she shouted them down: "Compared to me with what I acquired from them, the lot of you are miserable weaklings! Do any of you challenge that?"

No one challenged but orange flecks were there.

"You are children with no knowledge of what you might

become," she said. "Would you return defenceless to face the ones of many faces? Would you become vegetables?"

That caught their interest. They were accustomed to this tone from older commanders. The content held them now. It was difficult to accept from one so young . . . still . . . the things she had done. And to Logno and her aides!

Murbella saw them admire the bait.

Fertilization. This group will carry it away with them. Hybrid vigour. We are fertilized to grow stronger. And flower. And go to seed? Best not dwell on that. Honoured Matres will not see it until they are almost Reverend Mothers. Then they will look back angrily as I did. How could we have been that stupid?

She saw submission take shape in councillors' eyes. There would be a honeymoon. Honoured Matres would be children in a candy store. Only gradually would the inevitable grow plain to them. Then they would be trapped.

As I was trapped. Don't ask the oracle what you can gain. That's the trap. Beware the real fortune teller! Would you like thirty-five hundred years of boredom?

Odrade objected.

Give the Tyrant some credit. It couldn't all have been boredom. More like a Guild Navigator picking his passage through foldspace. Golden Path. An Atreides paid for your survival, Murbella.

Murbella felt burdened. The Tyrant's payment dumped on her shoulders. *I didn't ask him to do it for me.*

Odrade could not let that pass. *He did it nonetheless.*

Sorry, Dar. He paid. Now, I must pay.

So you are a Reverend Mother at last!

The councillors had grown restive under her stare.

Angelika elected to speak for them. *After all, I am first chosen.*

Watch that one! A blaze of ambition in her eyes.

"What response are you asking us to take with these witches?" Alarmed by her own boldness. Was not Great Honoured Matre also a witch now?

Murbella spoke softly. "You will tolerate them and offer them no violence whatsoever."

454

Angelika was emboldened by Murbella's mild tone. "Is that Great Honoured Matre's decision or the . . ."

"Enough! I could bloody the floor of this room with the lot of you! Do you wish to test it?"

They did not wish to test it.

"And what if I say to you it is Mother Superior speaking? You will ask do I have a policy to meet our problem? I will say: Policy? Ahh, yes. I have a policy for unimportant things such as insect infestations. Unimportant things call for policies. For such of you as do not see the wisdom in my decision, I need no policy. Your kind I dispose of quickly. Dead before you know you've been injured! That is my response to the presence of filth. Is there any filth in this room?"

It was language they recognized: The lash of Great Honoured Matre backed by ability to kill.

"You are my Council," Murbella said. "I expect wisdom from you. The least you can do is pretend you are wise."

Humorous sympathy from Odrade: *If that's the way Honoured Matres give and take orders, it won't require much deep analysis by Bell.*

Murbella's thoughts went elsewhere. *I am no longer Honoured Matre.*

The step from one to another was so recent she found her Honoured Matre performance uncomfortable. Her adjustments were a metaphor of what would happen to her former sisters. A new role and she did not wear it well. Other Memory simulated long association with herself as this new person. This was no mystical transubstantiation, merely new abilities.

Merely?

The change was profound. Did Duncan realize this? It pained her that he might never see through to this new person.

Is that the residue of my love for him?

Murbella drew back from her questions, not wanting *an* answer. She felt repelled by something that went deeper than she cared to burrow.

There will be decisions I must make that love would prevent. Decisions for the Sisterhood and not for myself. That is where my fear is pointing.

Immediate necessities restored her. She sent her councillors away, promising pain and death if they failed to learn this new restraint.

Next, Reverend Mothers must be taught a new diplomacy: getting along with Honoured Matres who were accustomed to getting along with no one—not even with each other. It would grow easier in time. Honoured Matres slipping into Bene Gesserit ways. One day, there would be no Honoured Matres; only Reverend Mothers with improved reflexes and augmented knowledge of sexuality.

Murbella felt haunted by words she had heard but not accepted until this moment. "The things we will do for Bene Gesserit survival have no limits."

Duncan will see this. I cannot keep it from him. The Mentat will not hold to a fixed idea of what I was before the Agony. He opens his mind as I open a door. He will examine his net. "What have I caught this time?"

Was this what happened to Lady Jessica? Other Memory carried Jessica threaded into the warp and woof of Sharings. Murbella unravelled a bit and paraded elder knowledge.

Heretic Lady Jessica? Malfeasance in office?

Jessica had plunged into love as Odrade had plunged into the sea and the resultant waves had all but engulfed the Sisterhood.

Murbella sensed this taking her where she did not want to go. Pain clutched her chest.

Duncan! Ohhh, Duncan! She dropped her face into her hands. *Dar, help me. What am I to do?*

Never ask why you're a Reverend Mother.

I must! The progression is clear in my memory and . . .

That's a sequence. Thinking of it as cause-and-effect beguiles you away from totality.

Tao?

Simpler: You are here.

But Other Memory goes back and back and . . .

Imagine it's pyramids—interlocked.

Those are just words!

Is your body still functioning?

I hurt, Dar. You don't have a body any more and it's useless to . . .

456

We occupy different niches. The pains I felt are not your pains. My joys are not yours.

I don't want your sympathy! Ohh, Dar! Why was I born?

Were you born to lose Duncan?

Dar, please!

So you were born and now you know that's never enough. So you became an Honoured Matre. What else could you do? Still not enough? Now you're a Reverend Mother. You think that's enough? It's never enough as long as you're alive.

You're telling me I must always reach beyond myself.

Pah! You don't make decisions on that basis. Didn't you hear him? Don't think; do it! Will you choose the easy way? Why should you feel sad because you've encountered the inevitable? If that's all you can see, confine yourself to improving the breed!

Damn you! Why did you do this to me?

Do what?

Make me see myself and my former sisters this way!

What way?

Damn you! You know what I mean!

Former sisters, you say?

Oh, you are insidious.

All Reverend Mothers are insidious.

You never stop teaching!

Is that what I do?

How innocent I was! Asking you what you really do.

You know that now as well as I do. We wait for humankind to mature. The Tyrant only provided them time to grow but now they need care.

What's the Tyrant have to do with my pain?

You foolish woman! Did you fail the Agony?

You know I didn't!

Stop stumbling over the obvious.

Oh, you bitch!

I prefer witch. Either is preferable to whore.

The only difference between Bene Gesserit and Honoured Matre is the marketplace. You married our Sisterhood.

Our Sisterhood?

You bred for power! How is that different from . . .

Don't twist it, Murbella! Keep your eyes on survival.

457

Don't tell me you had no power!

Temporary authority over people intent on survival.

Survival again!

In a Sisterhood that promotes the survival of others. Like the married woman who bears children.

So it comes down to procreation.

That's a decision you make for yourself: Family and what binds it. What tickles life and happiness?

Murbella began to laugh. She dropped her hands and opened her eyes to find Bellonda standing there watching.

"That's always a temptation for a new Reverend Mother," Bellonda said. "Chat a bit with Other Memory. Who was it this time? Dar?"

Murbella nodded.

"Don't trust anything they give you. It's lore and you judge it for yourself."

Odrade's words exactly. Look through the eyes of the dead at scenes long gone. What a peep show!

"You can get lost in there for hours," Bellonda said. "Exercise restraint. Be sure of your ground. One hand for yourself and one for the ship."

There it was again! The past applied to the present. How rich Other Memory made everyday life.

"It'll pass," Bellonda said. "It gets to be old hat after a time." She laid a report in front of Murbella.

Old hat! One hand for yourself and one for the ship. So much just in idioms.

Murbella leaned back in the slingchair to scan Bellonda's report, fancying herself suddenly in Odrade's idiom: *Queen Spider in the centre of my web*. The web might be a bit frayed just now but it was still there catching things to be digested. Twitch a trigger strand and Bell came running, mandibles flexing in anticipation. The twitch-words were "Archives" and "Analysis".

Seeing Bellonda in this light, Murbella saw the wisdom in the ways Odrade had employed her, flaws as valuable as the strengths. When Murbella finished the report, Bellonda still stood there in a characteristic attitude.

Murbella recognized that Bellonda looked on all who

458

summoned her as ones who had not measured up, people who called on Archives for frivolous reasons and had to be set straight. Frivolity: Bellonda's bête noire. Murbella found this amusing.

Murbella kept amusement masked while enjoying Bellonda. The way to deal with her was to be scrupulous. Nothing to subtract from strengths. This report was a model of concise and pertinent argument. She made her points with few embellishments, just enough to reveal her own conclusions.

"Does it amuse you to summon me?" Bellonda asked.

She's sharper than she was! Did I summon her? Not in so many words but she knows when she's needed. She says here our sisters must be models of meekness. Mother Superior may be anything she needs to be but not so the rest of the Sisterhood.

Murbella touched the report. "A starting point."

"Then we should start before your friends find the comeye centre." Bellonda sank into her chairdog with familiar confidence. "Tam's gone but I could send for Sheeana."

"Where is she?"

"At the ship. Studying a collection of worms in the Great Hold, says any of us can be taught to control them."

"Valuable if true. Leave her. What of Scytale?"

"Still in the ship. Your friends haven't found him yet. We're keeping him under wraps."

"Let's continue that. He's a good reserve bargaining chip. And they're not my friends, Bell. How are the Rabbi and his party?"

"Comfortable but worried. They know Honoured Matres are here."

"Keep them under wraps."

"It's uncanny. A different voice but I hear Dar."

"An echo in your head."

Bellonda actually laughed.

"Now here's what you must spread among the sisters. We act with extreme delicacy while showing ourselves as people to admire and emulate. 'You Honoured Matres may not choose to live as we live but you can learn our strengths.'"

"Ahhhhhh."

"It comes down to ownership. Honoured Matres are owned

by things. 'I want that place, that bauble, that person.' Take what you want. Use it until you tire of it."

"While we go along our path admiring what we see."

"And there's our flaw. We don't give ourselves easily. Fear of love and affection! To be self possessed has its own greed. 'See what I have? You can't have it unless you follow my ways!' Never take that attitude with Honoured Matres."

"Are you telling me we have to love them?"

"How else can we make them admire us? That was Jessica's victory. When she gave, she gave it all. So much bottled up by our ways and then that overwhelming wash: everything given. It's irresistible."

"We don't compromise that easily."

"No more do Honoured Matres."

"That's the way of their bureaucratic origins!"

"Yet, theirs is a training ground for following the path of least resistance."

"You're confusing me, Da . . . Murbella."

"Have I said we should compromise? Compromise not only weakens us but we know there are problems compromise cannot solve, decisions we must make no matter how bitter."

"*Pretend* to love them?"

"That's a beginning.

"It'll be a bloody union, this joining of Bene Gesserit and Honoured Matre."

"I suggest we Share as widely as possible. We may lose people while Honoured Matres are learning."

"A marriage made on the battlefield."

Murbella stood, thinking of Duncan in the no-ship, remembering the ship as she had seen it last. There it was finally, not hidden to any sense. A lump of strange machinery, oddly grotesque. A wild conglomeration of protrusions and juttings with no apparent purpose. Hard to imagine the thing lifting on its own power, enormous as that was, and vanishing into space.

Vanishing into space!

She saw the shape of Duncan's mental mosaic.

A piece that cannot be moved! Get in tune . . . don't think; do it!

With an abruptness that chilled her, she knew his decision.

When you think to take determination of your fate into your own hands, that is the moment you can be crushed. Be cautious. Allow for surprises. When we create, there are always other forces at work.

—Darwi Odrade

"Move with extreme care," Sheeana had warned him.

Idaho did not think he needed warning but appreciated it nonetheless.

Presence of Honoured Matres on Chapter House eased his task. They made the ship's Proctors and other guards nervous. Murbella's orders kept her former sisters out of the ship but everyone knew the enemy was here. Scanner relays showed a seemingly endless stream of lighters disgorging Honoured Matres on the Flat. Most of the new arrivals appeared curious about that monstrous no-ship sitting there but no one disobeyed Great Honoured Matre.

"Not while she's alive," Idaho muttered where Proctors could hear him. "They have a tradition of assassinating their leaders to replace them. How long can Murbella hold out?"

Comeyes did his work for him. He knew his muttering would spread through the ship.

Sheeana came to him in his workroom shortly afterward and made a show of disapproval. "What are you trying to do, Duncan? You're upsetting people."

"Go back to your worms!"

"Duncan!"

"Murbella's playing a dangerous game! She's all that stands between us and disaster."

He already had voiced this worry to Murbella. It was not new to the watchers but reinforcement made everyone who heard him edgy—comeye monitors in Archives, ship guards, everyone.

Except Honoured Matres. Murbella was keeping them out of Bellonda's Archives.

"Time for that later," she said.

Sheeana had her cue. "Duncan, either stop feeding our worries or tell us what we should do. You're a Mentat. Function for us."

Ahhh, the great Mentat performs for all to see.

"What you should do is obvious but it's not up to me. I can't leave Murbella."

But I can be taken away.

Now, it was up to Sheeana. She left him and went to spread her own brand of change.

"We have the Scattering for our example."

By evening, she had the Reverend Mothers in the ship neutralized and gave him a hand signal that they could take the next step.

"They will follow my lead."

Without intending it, the Missionaria had set the stage for Sheeana's ascendancy. Most sisters knew the power latent in her. Dangerous. But it was *there*.

Unused power was like a marionette with visible strings, nobody holding them. A compelling attraction: *I could make it dance.*

Feeding the deception, he called Murbella.

"When will I see you?"

"Duncan, please." Even in projection, she looked harried. "I'm busy. You know the pressures. I'll be out in a few days."

Projection showed Honoured Matres in the background scowling at this odd behaviour in their leader. Any Reverend Mother could read their faces.

"Has Great Honoured Matre gone soft? That's nothing but a man out there!"

When he broke off, Idaho emphasized what every monitor on the ship had seen. "She's in danger! Doesn't she know it?"

And now, Sheeana, it's up to you.

Sheeana had the key to reinstate the ship's flight controls. The mines were gone. No one could destroy the ship at the last instant with a signal to hidden explosives. There was only the human cargo to consider, Teg especially.

462

Teg will see my choices. The others—the Rabbi's party and Scytale will have to take their chances with us.

The Futars in their security cells did not worry him. Interesting animals but not significant at the moment. For that matter, he gave only a passing thought to Scytale. The little Tleilaxu remained under the eyes of guards who were not relaxing their watch on him no matter their other worries.

He went to bed with a nervousness that had ready explanation for any watchdog in archives.

His precious Murbella is in peril.

And she was in peril but he could not protect her.

My very presence is a danger to her now.

He was up at dawn, back to the armoury dismantling a weapons factory. Sheeana found him there and asked him to join her in the guard section.

A handful of Proctors greeted them. The leader they had chosen did not surprise him. Garimi. He had heard about her performance at the Convocation. Suspicious. Worried. Ready to make her own gamble. She was a sober-faced woman. Some said she seldom smiled.

"We have diverted the comeyes in this room," Garimi said. "They show us having a snack and questioning you about weapons."

Idaho felt a knot in his stomach. Bell's people would spot a simulation quickly. Especially a projected mock-up of himself.

Garimi responded to his frown. "We have allies in Archives."

Sheeana said: "We are here to ask if you wish to leave before we escape in this ship."

His surprise was genuine.

Stay behind?

He had not considered it. Murbella was no longer his. The bond had been broken in her. She did not accept it. Not yet. But she would the first time she was asked to make a decision putting him in danger for Bene Gesserit purposes. Now, she merely stayed away from him more than was necessary.

"You're going to Scatter?" he asked, looking at Garimi.

"We'll save what we can. Voting with our feet, it was called once. Murbella is subverting the Bene Gesserit."

There was the unspoken argument he had trusted to win them. Disagreement over Odrade's gamble.

Idaho took a deep breath. "I will go with you."

"No regrets!" Garimi warned.

"That's stupid!" he said, venting his repressed grief.

Garimi would not have been surprised by that response from a sister. Idaho shocked her and she was several seconds recovering. Honesty compelled her.

"Of course it's stupid. I'm sorry. You're sure you won't stay? We owe you the chance to make your own decision."

Bene Gesserit fastidiousness with those who served them loyally!

"I'll join you."

The grief they saw on his face was not simulated. He wore it openly when he returned to his console.

My assigned position.

He did not try to hide his actions when he coded for the ship's ID circuits.

Allies in Archives.

The circuits came flashing up on his projections—coloured ribbons with a broken link into flight systems. The way around that breakage was visible after only a few moments' study. Mentat observations had been prepared for it.

Multiples through the core!

Idaho sat back and waited.

Lift-off was a skull-rattling moment of blankness that stopped abruptly when they were far enough clear of the surface to engage nullfields and enter foldspace.

Idaho watched his projection. There they were: the old couple in their garden setting! He saw the net shimmering in front of them, the man gesturing at it, smiling in round-faced satisfaction. They moved in a transparent overlay that revealed ship circuits behind them. The net grew larger—not lines but ribbons thicker than the projected circuits.

The man's lips shaped words but there was no sound. *"We expected you."*

Idaho's hands went to his console, fingers splayed in the

comfield to grasp required elements of the circuit control. No time for niceties. Gross disruption. He was into the core within a second. From there, it was a simple matter to dump entire segments. Navigation went first. He saw the net begin to thin, the look of surprise on the man's face. Nullfields were next. Idaho felt the ship lurching in foldspace. The net tipped, becoming elongated with the two watchers foreshortened and thinned. Idaho wiped out star-memory circuits, taking his own data dump with him.

Net and watchers vanished.

How did I know they would be there?

He had no answer except a certainty rooted in the repeated visions.

Sheeana did not look up when he found her at the temporary flight-control board in the guard quarters. She was bent over the board, staring at it in consternation. The projection above her showed they had emerged from foldspace. Idaho recognized none of the visible star patterns but he had expected that.

Sheeana swivelled and looked at Garimi standing over her. "We've lost all data storage!"

Idaho tapped his temple with a forefinger. "No we haven't."

"But it'll take years to recover even the most basic essentials!" Sheeana protested. "What happened?"

"We're an unidentifiable ship in an unidentifiable universe," Idaho said. "Isn't that what we wanted?"

There's no secret to balance. You just have to feel the waves.

—**Darwi Odrade**

Murbella felt that an age had passed since recognizing Duncan's decision.

Vanish into space! Leave me!

The unvarying time sense of the Agony told her only seconds had elapsed since awareness of his intentions but she felt she had known this from the first.

He must be stopped!

She was reaching for her comboard when Central began to shudder. The quaking continued for an interminable time and subsided slowly.

Bellonda was on her feet. "What . . ."

"The no-ship at the Flat has just lifted," Murbella said.

Bellonda reached for the comboard but Murbella stopped her.

"It's gone."

She must not see my pain.

"But who . . ." Bellonda fell silent. She had her own assessments of consequences and saw then what Murbella saw.

Murbella sighed. She had all of the curses of history at her disposal and wanted none of them.

"At lunch time, I will eat in my private dining room with councillors and I want you present," Murbella said. "Tell Duana oyster stew again."

Bellonda started to protest but all that came out was: "Again?"

"You will recall I ate alone downstairs last night?" Murbella resumed her seat.

Mother Superior has duties!

There were maps to change and rivers to follow and Honoured Matres to domesticate.

Some waves throw you, Murbella. But you get back up and go on with it. Seven times down, eight times up. You can balance on strange surfaces.

I know, Dar. Willing participation in your dream.

Bellonda stared at her until Murbella said, "I made my councillors sit at a distance from me at dinner last night. It was strange—only the two tables in the whole dining room."

Why do I continue this inane chatter? What excuses do I have for my extraordinary behaviour?

"We wondered why none of us were permitted in our own dining room," Bellonda said.

"To save your lives! But you should have seen their interest. I read their lips. Angelika said: 'She's eating some kind of stew. I heard her discussing it with the chef. Isn't this a marvellous world we've acquired? We must sample that stew she ordered.'"

466

"Samples," Bellonda said. "I see." Then: "You know, don't you, Sheeana took the Van Gogh painting from . . . your sleeping chamber?"

Why does that hurt?

"I noticed it was missing."

"Said she was borrowing it for her room in the ship."

Murbella's lips went thin.

Damn them! Duncan and Sheeana! Teg, Scytale . . . all of them gone and no way to follow. But we still have axolotl tanks and Idaho cells from our children. Not the same . . . but close. He thinks he's escaped!

"Are you all right, Murbella?" Concern in Bell's voice.

You warned me about wild things, Dar, and I didn't listen.

"After we've eaten, I will take my councillors on an inspection tour of Central. Tell my acolyte I'll want cider before retiring."

Bellonda left, muttering. That was more like her.

How do you guide me now, Dar?

You want guidance? A guided tour of your life? Is that why I died?

But they took the Van Gogh, too!

Is that what you'll miss?

Why did they take it, Dar?

Caustic laughter greeted this and Murbella was glad no one else heard.

Can't you see what she intends?

The Missionaria scheme!

Oh, more than that. It's the next phase: Muad'Dib to Tyrant to Honoured Matres to us to Sheeana . . . to what? Can't you see it? The thing is right there at the lip of your thoughts. Accept it as you would swallow a bitter drink.

Murbella shuddered.

See it? The bitter medicine of a Sheeana future? We once thought all medicines had to be bitter or they were not effective. No healing power in the sweet.

Must it happen, Dar?

Some will choke on that medicine. But the survivors may create interesting patterns.

467

"You deliberately let them get away, Daniel!"

The old woman rubbed her hands down the stained front of
her garden apron. It was a summer morning around her,
flowers blooming, birds calling from nearby trees. There was a
misty look to the sky, a yellow radiance near the horizon.

"Now, Marty, it was not deliberate," Daniel said. He took
off his porkpie hat and rubbed the bushy stubble of grey hair
before replacing the hat. "He surprised me. I knew he saw us
but I didn't suspect he saw the net."

"And I had such a nice planet picked out for them," Marty
said. "One of the best. A real test of their abilities."

"No use moaning about it," Daniel said. "They're where we
can't touch them now. He was spread so thin, though, I
expected to catch him easy."

"They had a Tleilaxu Master, too," Marty said. "I saw him
when they went under the net. I would have so liked to study
another Master."

"Don't see why. Always whistling at us, always making it
necessary to stomp them down. I don't like treating Masters
that way and you know it! If it weren't for them . . ."

"They're not gods, Daniel."

"Neither are we."

"I still think you let them escape. You're so anxious to prune
your roses!"

"What would you have said to the Master, anyway?" Daniel
asked.

"I was going to joke when he asked who we were. They
always ask that. I was going to say: 'What did you expect, God
Himself with a flowing beard?'"

Daniel chuckled. "That would've been funny. They have
such a hard time accepting that Face Dancers can be independent of them."

"I don't see why. It's a natural consequence. They gave us

468

the power to absorb the memories and experiences of other people. Gather enough of those and . . ."

"It's personas we take, Marty."

"Whatever. The Masters should've known we would gather enough of them one day to make our own decisions about our own future."

"And theirs?"

"Oh, I'd have apologized to him after putting him in his place. You can just do so much managing of others, isn't that right, Daniel?"

"When you get that look on your face, Marty, I go prune my roses." He went back to a line of bushes with verdant leaves and black blooms as large as his head.

Marty called after him: "Gather up enough people and you get a big ball of knowledge, Daniel! That's what I'd have told him. And those Bene Gesserits in that ship! I'd have told them how many of them I have. Ever notice how alienated they feel when we peek at them?"

Daniel bent to his black roses.

She stared after him, hands on her hips.

"Not to mention Mentats," he said. "There were two of them on that ship—both gholas. You want to play with them?"

"The Masters always try to control them, too," she said.

"That Master is going to have trouble if he tries to mess with that big one," Daniel said, snipping off a ground shoot from the root stock of his roses. "My, this is a pretty one."

"Mentats, too!" Marty called. "I'd have told them. Dime a dozen, they are."

"Dimes? I don't think they'd have understood that, Marty. The Reverend Mothers, yes, but not that big Mentat. He didn't thin out that far back."

"You know what you let get away, Daniel?" she demanded, coming up beside him. "That Master had a nullentropy tube in his chest. Full of ghola cells, too!"

"I saw it."

"That's why you let them get away!"

"Didn't let them." His pruning shears went snick-snick. "Gholas. He's welcome to them."

469

AFTERWORD

Here is another book dedicated to Bev, friend, wife, dependable helper and the person who gave this one its title. The dedication is posthumous and the words below, written the morning after she died, should tell you something of her inspiration.

One of the best things I can say about Bev is there was nothing in our life together I need forget, not even the graceful moment of her death. She gave me then the ultimate gift of her love, a peaceful passing she had spoken of without fear or tears, allaying thereby my own fears. What greater gift is there than to demonstrate you need not fear death?

The formal obituary would read: Beverly Ann Stuart Forbes Herbert, born October 20, 1926, Seattle Washington; died 5:05 p.m. February 7, 1984, at Kawaloa, Maui. I know that is as much formality as she would tolerate. She made me promise there would be no conventional funeral "with a preacher's sermon and my body on display". As she said: "I will not be in that body then but it deserves more dignity than such a display provides."

She insisted I go no further than to have her cremated and scatter her ashes at her beloved Kawaloa "where I have felt so much peace and love". The only ceremony—friends and loved ones to watch the scattering of her ashes during the singing of "Bridge Over Troubled Water".

She knew there would be tears then as there are tears while I write these words but in her last days she often spoke of tears as futile. She recognized tears as part of our animal origins. The dog howls at the loss of its master.

Another part of human awareness dominated her life: Spirit. Not in any mawkish religious sense nor in anything most Spiritualists would associate with the word. To Bev, it was the light shining from living awareness on to everything she encountered. Because of this, I can say despite my grief and even within grief that joy fills my spirit because of the love she gave and continues to give me. Nothing in the sadness at her death is too high a price to pay for the love we shared.

Her choice of a song to sing at the scattering of her ashes went to what we often said to each other—that she was my bridge and I was hers. That epitomizes our married life.

We began that sharing with a ceremony before a minister in Seattle on June 20, 1946. Our honeymoon was spent on a fire-watch lookout atop Kelley Butte in Snoqualmie National Forest. Our quarters were twelve feet square with a cupola above only six feet square and most of that filled by the firefinder with which we located any smoke we saw.

In cramped quarters with a spring-powered Victrola and two portable typewriters taking up considerable space on the one table, we pretty well set the pattern of our life together: work to support music, writing and the other joys living provides.

None of this is to say we experienced constant euphoria. Far from it. We had moments of boredom, fears and pains. But there was always time for laughter. Even at the end, Bev still could smile to tell me I had positioned her correctly on her pillows, that I had eased the aching of her back with a gentle massage and the other things necessary because she no longer could do them for herself.

In her final days, she did not want anyone but me to touch her. But our married life had created such a bond of love and trust she often said the things I did for her were as though she did them. Though I had to provide the most intimate care, the care you would give an infant, she did not feel offended nor that her dignity had been assaulted. When I picked her up in my arms to make her more comfortable or bathe her, Bev's arms always went around my shoulders and her face nestled as it often had in the hollow of my neck.

It is difficult to convey the joy of those moments but I assure you it was there. Joy of the spirit. Joy of life even at death. Her hand was in mine when she died and the attending doctor, tears in his eyes, said the thing I and many others had said of her.

"She had grace."

Many of those who saw that grace did not understand. I remember when we entered the hospital in the pre-dawn hours for the birth of our first son. We were laughing. Attendants looked at us with disapproval. Birth is painful and dangerous. Women die giving birth. Why are these people laughing?

We are laughing because the prospect of new life that was part of both of us filled us with such happiness. We were laughing because the birth was about to occur in a hospital built on the site of the hospital where Bev was born. What a marvellous continuity!

Our laughter was infectious and soon others we met on the way to the delivery room were smiling. Disapproval became approval. Laughter was her grace note in moments of stress.

Hers was also the laughter of the constantly new. Everything she encountered had something new in it to excite her senses. There was an ongoing naivety about Bev that was, in its own way, a form of sophistication. She wanted to find what was good in everything and everyone. As a result, she brought out that response in others.

"Revenge is for children," she said. "Only people who are basically immature want it."

She was known to call people who had offended her and plead with them to put away destructive feelings. "Let us be friends." The source of none of the condolences that poured in after her death surprised me.

It was typical of her that she wanted me to call the radiologist whose treatment in 1974 was the proximate cause of her death and thank him "for giving me these ten beautiful years. Make sure he understands I know he did his best for me when I was dying of cancer. He took the state of the art to its limits and I want him to know my appreciation."

Is it any wonder that I look back on our years together with a happiness transcending anything words can describe? Is it any wonder I do not want or need to forget one moment of it? Most others merely touched her life at the periphery. I shared it in the most intimate ways and everything she did strengthened me. It would not have been possible for me to do what necessity demanded of me during the final ten years of her life, strengthening her in return, had she not given of herself in the preceding years, holding back nothing. I consider that to be my great good fortune and most miraculous privilege.

Frank Herbert,
Port Townsend, WA
April 6, 1984